C000005413

QUOTE THE
ENDLING

A TWIST OF POE MYSTERY

Also By

VELDA BROTHERTON

TWIST OF POE MYSTERIES
The Purloined Skull
The Tell-Tale Stone
The Pit and the Penance
Masque of the Rising Moon
The Fall of Hermitage House
Quote the Endling

THE VICTORIANS
Wilda's Outlaw • Rowena's Hellion
Tyra's Gambler

THE MONTANA SERIES
Montana Promises • Montana Treasures
Montana Dreams • Montana Fire
Montana Destiny • Montana Legacy

OTHER TITLES
Beyond The Moon • A Savage Grace
Once There Were Sad Songs • Stoneheart's Woman
Remembrance

WITH DUSTY RICHARDS
Blue Roan Colt • The Texas Badge

QUOTE THE
ENDLING

A TWIST OF POE MYSTERY

VELDA
BROTHERTON

LAGAN
PRESS

an imprint of
THE OGHMA PRESS

OGHMA

CREATIVE MEDIA

Bentonville, Arkansas • Los Angeles, California
www.oghmacreative.com

Copyright © 2021 by Velda Brotherton

We are a strong supporter of copyright. Copyright represents creativity, diversity, and free speech, and provides the very foundation from which culture is built. We appreciate you buying the authorized edition of this book and for complying with applicable copyright laws by not reproducing, scanning, or distributing any part of it in any form without permission. Thank you for supporting our writers and allowing us to continue publishing their books.

Library of Congress Cataloging-in-Publication Data

Names: Brotherton, Velda, author.
Title: Quote the Endling/Velda Brotherton. | Twist of Poe #6
Description: First Edition. | Bentonville: Lagan, 2021.
Identifiers: LCCN: 2021934702 | ISBN: 978-1-63373-708-2 (hardcover) |
ISBN: 978-1-63373-709-9 (trade paperback) | ISBN: 978-1-63373-710-5 (eBook)
Subjects: BISAC: FICTION/Romance/Police & Law Enforcement |
FICTION/Romance/Action & Adventure | FICTION/Romance/Suspense
LC record available at: https://lccn.loc.gov/2021934702

First Lagan Press hardcover edition April, 2021

Jacket & Interior Design by Casey W. Cowan
Editing by Chelsea Cambeis & Amy Cowan

This book is a work of fiction. Any references to historical events, real people, or real places are used fictitiously. Other names, characters, places, and events are products of the author's imagination, and any resemblance to actual events or places or person, living or dead, is entirely coincidental.

Published by Lagan Press, an imprint of The Oghma Press, a subsidiary of The Oghma Book Group.

To my daughter Jeri,
who makes my writing life possible.

As always, I'm grateful to Casey Cowan og Oghma Creative Media for publishing my stories, creating my gorgeous covers, and asking me for more books. Thanks also go to my wonderful, talented, and helpful editors Chelsea Cambeis and Sarah Dorsey, as well as to the rest of the Oghma crew—Amy Cowan, George "Clay" Mitchell, Dennis Doty, Chrissy Willis, Bob Giel, Vivian Cummings, Dylan and Derek Hale, and Gordon Bonnet, among many others. Last but definitely not least, I'd like to thank the girls of the Sisterhood of the Traveling Pen for their unwavering love and support—Linda Apple, Patty Stith, Pamela Foster, Jan Marler Vanek, and Ruth Weeks.

CHAPTER 1

It wasn't like Dal knew the woman. At any rate, she was gone before he could shake himself clear of the shock of her unsettling view. Resembled his wife, yet a bit off. He didn't need such nonsense after all this time. Leanne was dead, that's all. He'd put it behind him, built a new life here in Cedarton. So what the hell was going on?

Grandfather hadn't been around in a while. This brief vision was probably the old fart nudging him to be more alert. In that case, he opened his eyes to take another look, and she was gone. An empty space where she'd been, while crowds on the square moved around like everything was normal.

Sure enough, this was Grandfather's work.

Why have you returned to haunt me, old man? I thought I was finally free of the damnable curse. The past few months he'd hoped he was the last of the family curse, the endling, as Grandfather had once described with a sad finality. Let the dead lie peacefully. Yet Grandfather refused. He wafted through the meandering clusters of people as if he belonged there and not in another world. Lifting one hand, like he always did to get Dal's attention, his words vibrated as if from a phone.

"The woman searches for you, but you must beware. Her spirit is torn. She will bring you nothing but harm."

"Leave me, Grandfather. I no longer want your world."

He must've spoken aloud because the man next to him glanced his way. "What did you say?"

Dal shook his head. "Sorry." And turned away.

He was just tired. Been up all night out on Highway 23 searching for a fleeing felon in an orange Volkswagen painted with turquoise balloons. It never showed up. And it would'a been hard to miss. One of the deputies on the new highway got the son of a bitch. He needed to write his report and go home to grab some sleep. Maybe he'd feel better.

Inside the door, practically staggering, he fell onto the couch. Sure be good if he had enough energy to get something out of the fridge, but on the other hand there probably wasn't anything in there fit to eat. So there he lay peering into the empty room.

He closed his eyes. A faint glow to his right, while to his left, walls painted with shaded words, gigantic, in bright reds and greens and blacks. Names, figures, one overlapping another. On and on and on. What the hell? Someone kept calling his name in a singing voice. Beautiful notes that echoed up and down and all around. It was the one he'd been looking for.

Leanne, where are you?

He dragged one hand along the wall. It came away wet and red. *Red.* Like blood.

Around the corner and into a room brightly lit by sunshine splashing through the windows. She was sprawled as if hanging from a black and red cross. Not a real cross—that was too much like a TV show—but more of a symbolic blur of lines. Clothing ripped from her body.

"I've been waiting for you for so long. Where have you been?"

He reached out as if to touch her, see if the words came from her. But there was nothing there. His hand slipped right through her, up to his wrist, then his elbow. Shivering, he attempted to embrace her cold body.

"Don't do this to me, please don't. I tried to save you, but you took that poison. Why did you do that? How could you do that? You knew it was poison, I did everything I could to save you. This was not my fault."

He had loved her. He had. Didn't she believe it? Why didn't she listen? Why didn't she try to save herself? Let him save her? The world tilted, turned over, flinging him into outer space. Hands and feet scrambled, paddled, felt for something, anything to stop his flight. But there was nothing there. He cried, tears flying from his cheeks as he rolled over and over through masses of stars that shredded his skin in bloody red streaks. Some stuck to him, leaving strands of light out behind this tumbling, screaming, bleeding man he watched from a distance. A human comet.

God, he needed to wake up. This had to be a dream. No matter how he tried to move, to scream, to bring himself awake, the old guilt would not let go. He carried it buried deep in his soul, from where it returned when he least expected it.

Haunting, accusing, blaming him... until he also blamed himself.

Something hit him. Something hard. Crushing him. Smashing so he couldn't breathe or make a sound. He tumbled head over feet, landed with a thud on a vast empty plain where he was alone. He rose and walked and walked and walked. His world cracked open, and he no longer cared if he was caught up in one of the deep crevices, sent there for the remainder of his life. Punishment was what he deserved.

The phone dragged him awake panting in the black of night. He sat up drenched with sweat, thankful for lawbreakers to tear him away from his latest nightmare. Out back of the Bed & Breakfast, where he rented an apartment, it was pitch dark. The Bakers turned off all lights at ten o'clock saying it was better for those staying there and trying to sleep. He agreed, except when the phone woke him middle of the night. He finally pawed around and found the thing and answered. It had to be important this late. Sure enough, trouble at the animal farm. Would be a great improvement from that dream. First he's seeing his dead wife, now he's dreaming about her. Hell, seeing her is probably why he dreamed about her. Whatever was going on, he'd have to deal with it.

The clock told him he'd had only about three hours sleep, but hey, that ought to be enough to catch a few wild animals. He grinned. Better to let Colby do the catching. He did a better job anyway. Still he had to show up. It was preferable to going back to sleep.

The sky flashed eerily with blue lights. Looked like everyone was there. Including Jessie. He slid in and parked fender to fender with her Jeep, shot the breeze with her for a while, then went to join Mac while she started taking photos that both would share.

Mac walked toward him, waving a hand.

"How's it going?" With one glance Dal took in the scene.

"Colby and Bell, that new deputy who's so good at tracking, are on the job. Looks like a truck of some kind, not real big, and they only took one cat. Our favorite, Maizie."

Dal grunted. "Looks like she prefers adventure. How's July taking it?"

"Upset, of course. Says there are some people selling tiger skins on the Internet. Is afraid she won't see Maizie again."

"Want me to scour the scene, see what I can come up with?"

Mac nodded. "That'd be good. Hate to see something happen to that big purty cat."

Jessie got the news about Maizie while climbing out of the shower. She listened to the phone message, not eager to be interrupted after midnight with a story to cover. But it was Parker, editor of *The Observer* and her boss, and he wouldn't call this late unless it was something newsworthy. Odd, though, for usually he went out to cover events that happened in the night. Said since the new highway went through so close by he didn't like her running around after dark. She pooh-poohed him, but what could she do? He was the boss.

Last year after she got shot in the head by that crazy pervert, she'd applied for and gotten a permit to carry. Kept a .38 revolver with her when she was alone. She'd written one too many stories about the man's wild escapades, so he'd come after her in her own home. He was still in jail.

Wrapping her hair in a towel, she went to the living room, picked up the cordless, and returned Parker's call.

"Sorry to bother you, Jess. This one's a doozy, and I know you'd be furious if I didn't call you. Your choice, but Mac will be there on site when you arrive. If you're interested, that is."

She flopped onto the couch, and Brad leaped into her lap recognizing the excitement. The small pit bull preferred to ride shotgun when allowed to go along on a story, so he always sensed the possibility.

"So, what is it?"

"It's July, out at the animal farm? Seems like someone broke into the compound and stole Maizie. Went so far as to take a shot at July. He's gone

now, and so is the big cat, but it's a hell of a story. I'll get it if you don't want to, but I know how much you love those tigers. And it will be a super follow-up to last year's animal farm opening story. Besides you're the only one July really trusts to treat her right. She won't hardly talk to anyone else. Worries about her cats' reputation."

Even as he gave her information, she went to her bedroom, pulled out a clean pair of jeans and t-shirt, and wiggled into them with the phone propped on her shoulder. Once he stopped and took a breath, she replied. "Of course, I'll go. I take it she's not hurt."

"Nope, you know her. She lunged at the guy with a four-foot steel pole, knocked the gun out of his hand. Our thief already passed the tiger on to a helper with a trailer, and that guy was gone."

"Oh, hey, they've got the one guy?"

"Nope, he slipped away into the woods on foot. Real familiar with the place. Go talk to July, get a feel for the story and some pictures. Then wait till morning and do a side bar on the cats if you don't mind. Readers love your unusual cat facts."

"Hey boss, whatever you want. You know that."

He chuckled. *"Sure, when pigs fly. See you later."*

"Boss? That reminds me of the time we did a story on that blind calf that was led around by its pal, a pig. That pig didn't fly, but still... rememember that?"

He chuckled. *"Not sure it connects. Get going."*

Hanging up, she had the gist of the sidebar in her brain. After a lot of hours with those big cats soaking up July Jones's amazing stories from her years in Africa and India, it was easy to come up with some new facts to entertain her readers.

She finished dressing, told Brad no this time. He had no business prancing about trying to herd those wild animals around. He shot her a look of disappointment and curled up inside the door, peering at her from the tops of his eyes.

"Don't be such a grouch. We'll go for ice cream when I get home."

He knew ice cream and jumped up to wag his stub of a tail.

Lugging her backpack to the Jeep, she stopped to stare at the glitter of stars filling the dark moonless night. Marveled at their beauty, then hopped in, started the WW II Jeep Parker had given her last summer. Said if she was going to flit around in the wilderness, she needed something built for the journeys. Shifting the gears, she headed for the animal farm ten miles into that very wilderness southwest of Cedarton. It wasn't long before the blue strobe lights of the patrol cars illuminated the velvety sky ahead, looking much like aliens were landing.

Question number one, what could be a reason for stealing Maizie? True Bengal tigers, especially white ones, were getting pretty rare, and they could've been looking specifically for one. Neither could be sold without it being reported. So how did the morons hope to get away with such a thing? And if they truly wanted one of real value, they would've taken a white tiger, of which there were four in the compound at last count, with another pregnancy promising at least one, maybe two more.

Getting most of her questions answered by July would be important. Dal would be at the scene because he couldn't stay away from anything, even if his presence wasn't always necessary. But usually he wouldn't talk to her about the crime.

Actually, having him around at a crime scene was fun, cause he got so intense over a reporter's presence, having come from Dallas and hating reporters with a passion cause they so often added untrue stuff to their stories. One had done that when his wife died, so that was understandable. But, geez, it was time he lightened up a bit. It'd been around six years. Besides, hadn't she finally gotten over shooting her ex-lover after he hunted her down and tried to kill her? Looked like Dal could get on with it, too.

Exciting times in the wilderness of the Ozarks. She topped a hill to a panoramic view of the valley where three patrol cars sat, lights flashing. The animal compound was well lit and upset by the excitement. Residents growled, screamed, and raced about whinnying. The animals, not the people. All the while the clownish burro kicked up his heels and loose-lipped that strange hee-haw sound that echoed back off the hills. None could escape, thanks to July's efficient fencing. This truly was an alien site if ever there was one.

Jessie zigzagged the Jeep through some trees and skidded to a stop touching the crime scene tape. Dal's SUV slid expertly to one side, leaving him just enough room to climb out. He nodded and touched the brim of his Stetson. She'd beat him again. Dragging her backpack from the passenger seat, she hunched one shoulder under the strap and ducked below the tape.

"Excuse me, ma'am. This is a crime scene."

She shrugged and stuck out her tongue. "Are you really going to make me call Mac for permission?"

He chuckled. "Just watch where you're stepping. Colby, have you found any tracks?"

"Yep, marking them as we speak. Bell's doing a good job."

"The press would like to take some photos. She says she'll share them."

She waved at the deputies and mouthed Dal's words.

"Just take it easy, Jess." The voice belonged to that of her adopted grandfather, the sheriff of Grace County, Mac Richards.

"Always do." Moving carefully around some tire and boot tracks, she made her way to July, sitting on the tailgate of her own pickup near the enclosure entrance. Stopping, she hollered at Colby. "The little prints are mine."

"Jesus," Dal muttered.

She stopped and studied him for a moment, then went on. Listening to voices and emotions from another world often led him to the criminal element. Even Dal admitted he didn't know how that happened. As a matter of fact, the voices and strange visions had been absent since he'd gone off for a year. Grace was one unusual county in which to work, considering the lack of up-to-date equipment, but somehow the job always got done, the crimes solved. It helped that there weren't a whole lot of them in the first place.

Jess plopped her heavy pack into the bed of the truck and lifted her butt up to sit beside her friend and owner of the animal farm, July Jones.

"How are things going?"

"Pretty scary, knowing someone has my Maizie. Sure hope they know how to handle her. She's liable to take a few bites out of one of them."

"Might teach them not to kidnap a seven-hundred-pound tiger."

July chuckled gruffly. "There is that, but I'd sure hate to have to kill her for biting someone."

Jess rustled around in her pack, came out with a digital recorder and a pad and paper. "So, start from the beginning. I am taping."

July waited till the recorder was on then said, "You can tape this."

One of the silliest damned things she'd ever heard of, but Jessie obeyed the new restrictions since someone had sued and won when an interview was taped without vocal permission.

After getting her name, recording the date and time, Jessie began the interview. July launched into her story, being familiar with the process from the previous year.

"I'd just hand fed all the cubs, checked every food and water provider and was behind the big cat house. That must be why they didn't hesitate. They couldn't see me out here and must've figured I was already inside for the night. I was running a bit late on my schedule or they'd've—"

"Wait, are you thinking someone had been watching and knew your schedule?"

July shrugged. "They knew how to unlock the enclosure, went right to the cage where the cats stay during the night when not loose in the compound. They had to have been watching, thought I'd finished, and they came right in. I can't believe it's someone who knows me and the compound. I won't. Anyway, normally by that time I'm inside watching *National Geographic.*"

"How'd they get her out? She's not friendly to stRangers."

"That's another thing. You know Maizie, she likes you she'll follow you around, especially if you offer her something to eat. She particularly likes deer meat, and I found a partial carcass where they'd tossed it down after getting her loaded. Looked like she'd tore a chunk off it to take along. Still yet, she'd have been too shy to go near a stranger. Makes me wonder if she knew them, though I would hate to blame one of my workers. They're so honest."

That would be worth checking. She'd mentioned the possibility twice. July was too soft-hearted to blame anyone she knew. "Did you see the vehicle or anyone doing the loading?"

July hadn't. While Jessie continued the interview, Dal walked the scene, bending down to touch the tracks of the big animal and the men who'd taken her. Hard to tell if he was getting anything. Colby poured the tracks for castings, and the new guy watched closely. She would share her tape with one of the deputies before they did their own interview of July. Dal would add what he'd picked up, and the investigation would begin then in earnest. It wasn't a typical criminal investigation, the theft of a tiger, but for the type of crimes and the deputies handling it, everything worked out. Long before DNA could come back from Little Rock, they usually had someone in custody with plenty of evidence to take to court.

Usually, that is. There were times when it didn't work out that way, but everyone was flexible.

Duggan came running from parking, his unit just the other side of the tape. "I followed their truck tracks off down the mountain to where the road Ys. Right there, something must've happened cause the tracks skidded way off towards the ditch. There's a stain of what looks like blood, but it's so dry along there it pretty well soaked in. I'd say Maizie got a bite or two and got away. I found a lot of tore up ground and big cat tracks headed off into the woods. Part of the Wildlife Management area. She's found herself a safe place to be."

"Could you tell if they tried to track her?"

"For a ways." He gestured as if indicating the direction they went. "But then they come back, and it looks like they got in the truck and took off."

"Oh, thank goodness." July patted her chest.

"Well, not really. They must've been three of them took off into the woods, but only two come back, and I lost the other'ns tracks up on Red Rock Mountain. The cat's too. Sorry Miss July. We'll put our new tracker on it come daylight where he's got more than this pitiful flashlight. He might be able to pick 'em up again."

Bellamy was one of the best and youngest trackers Mac had ever hired, and he sure came in handy. Mac swore he could track fleas in a patch of Johnson grass. Made up for his lack of good sense. Mac said since he was just a kid his brain hadn't fully developed, and they ought to have a little patience.

"I've been in touch with the Fish and Wildlife, and as soon as it's daylight, they'll be over here to help." Mac scratched under the edge of his Stetson and looked askance at Bell, who didn't appreciate help.

"They'll be hunting armed with dart guns." July slanted a look his way. "Won't they?"

"You know we won't shoot your Maizie unless there's absolutely no choice." Mac patted her shoulder. "And we'll put out a bulletin that no one is to shoot her, but they should notify us if she's spotted. Long as she stays in the management area, things should be okay."

"But there's people live in there, ain't they?" July knew that to be true, she was just talking. "I don't want my cat shot, but I sure don't want her to hurt or kill someone. Little kids appear much like prey to a big predator, even though she is tame."

Mac put an arm around the woman's shoulder. "Don't you worry none. We'll get Maizie home safe to you. I wouldn't be surprised to see her stroll up to her enclosure fore the day is over. You know that big ole cat."

Jessie gathered up her equipment and stuffed it inside the pack. Time to get on over to the paper and get this written before the place filled up with the curious and downright nosy that made so much noise she couldn't concentrate. Last year, she'd begun writing in the wee hours of the morning or late at night when no one was around. Fire Chief Goodscrew stormed in one day and demanded he watch her write every word of a story about a house burning to the ground. The fire department had gotten the address wrong. Parker and Goodscrew almost came to blows over that incident. The man probably had a temper because of being saddled with a name like that. If it had been hers, she'd have changed it a long time ago. It was easy. She'd changed her name before coming home from California... but for a much different reason.

Careful not to step on any of the tracks, even though Colby seemed to have finished casting, she waved goodbye to everyone, climbed in her Jeep, and took off for *The Observer*.

Two hours later, she had her story deposited on Parker's computer and was sitting at the Redbird eating an early breakfast.

And that's where she heard something that just might stir up one heck of a ruckus in the small town of Cedarton. She crossed her fingers and hoped it was only gossip. "Who is building a what?" She waited for one of them to reply.

Bertie Long and her brother Alvin announced the name simultaneously. "Marvin Captree." The brother and sister sat next to her at the Red Bird. Sometimes it was impossible to keep from eavesdropping in the crowded café, so she heard the news that the new couple who'd moved in a few months ago from England, of all places, were planning on opening a pub.

"Can you believe it?" Bertie swirled a straw through her Coke. "Naming it the Purple Bird. Why, they'll go broke before the year's out. Cedarton is no place for a pub. Don't they know this is a dry county? Why would anyone from England come over here anyways?" She shook her head and frowned.

Alvin, who owned the ice cream shop in the same building as Bertie's thrift shop, laughed too loud, the sound of a man covering up fear. "Maybe you heard wrong and it's a tea shop. The English do love their tea. I give them three months, whichever it is. Bertie and I do well to break even."

"Well you don't have to advertise our problems, Alvin. Things will get better soon." A chunky woman, Bertie carried a frozen grimace on her flushed face.

Jessie often wondered if she ever smiled. Better if she stopped listening to them, but she couldn't help dragging her gaze across Alvin's ugly expression as well. Must run in the family. He looked madder than a wet hen. But he said nothing, just ate his hamburger and glared from one to the other of his companions.

Jessie rose from her table, picked up her bill, and went up front to pay Wanda. It was time she went somewhere that she could rely on what she heard.

While walking around the square that morning, Dal caught sight of the same woman again. That was more than enough, and he was getting a tad bothered. Everyone on the square appeared normal, yet he kept seeing ghosts. You'd think a man who talked to his dead grandfather's spirit could deal with something like this, but what the hell? There she was again. Walking around the square enjoying the fall weather and saying good morning to more early risers in town. There was Alvin Long who only recently refurbished the closed ladies wear store and opened an ice cream shop. It was over thirty miles to the nearest Dairy Queen, and so far, he appeared to be doing well, even though he continued to poor mouth.

The blamed woman came rushing around the southwest corner, head down and plowed right into Alvin's sister, Bertie Long, who ran the thrift store. A few people stopped to watch the strange woman stoop to gather her spilled purse without even a murmured sorry. So he wasn't imagining her. When she rose, her gaze caught his. Her eyes were hazel with green flecks predominant exactly like Leanne's. What was going on, anyway? Asleep and awake. His mind was on his dead wife.

The proper mannerly thing to do was tip his hat and try to help her gather the scattering of the kind of junk most women carry in their handbags, but he just stood there like an idiot. Embarrassed, he finally knelt to help her, his fingers dropping more than he picked up.

"Please, it's all right. Don't bother." Her voice rolled over him like a familiar piece of music, and they stared at each other.

It was like being hit with a hammer. "Hello. What are you doing here?" A stupid goddamned thing to say.

She quirked an eyebrow. "Sorry. You're mistaken. We don't know each other." An equally stupid thing to say.

She scooped the last of the spillage into her purse and hurried off before he could apologize, though he wasn't sure for what. In quite a hurry for someone who didn't recognize him. Who wasn't running from him. He watched her till she turned the corner onto Spring Avenue.

"Huh, I could've sworn I seen her before." His dreams were getting to him.

"Small town, hmm, Sheriff? I never saw her before." Bertie watched the woman scurry out of sight.

"Deputy, ma'am." How many times a day did he correct folks who called him sheriff? All the cars said sheriff's deputy except for Mac's, who was the sheriff.

Bertie laughed. "Well, if I was you, I'd look into her background, the way she took off from you. She might've been up to no good. Ordinary folk don't normally run from the law."

While that was true, he had no intention of pursuing the woman who had to be a vision or hallucination or whatever stuff like that was called. Seemed Grandfather had returned from his long absence to bother the hell out of him. And he would not pay any mind to the old man's games. Trouble was gossip being what it was in a small town, Bertie would mention his reaction to the beautiful woman to just about everyone she saw till it'd be around town that he had a new lover. Wonder what Jessie would say. Much as he liked this town and most of the people in it, he did not like the way gossip exploded. On the other hand, when anyone needed anything, someone stepped up to help out.

He finished his walk and started to the sheriff's office when his cell burred in his hip pocket. He fished it out and peered at the screen splashed with bright sunlight so he couldn't see who the call was from. What the hell? "Yep, this is Dal."

"You want the tiger back, bring ten thousand dollars out to the old Sumner schoolhouse." A voice, definitely disguised.

"Is that right?"

"And come alone."

Chuckling, he shoved open the glass door and went into the break room. Someone watching too much television. No one was around, so he wandered into the small kitchen where deputies often grabbed a cup of coffee or Coke while things were quiet. Tinker sat in one of the several chairs scattered about.

"Hey, Tink. What do you think our tiger ought to be worth?"

"Hiya, handsome. The asking price is ten thousand. I think those morons have called every lawman in town trying to sell Maizie back to us. Reckon they don't know that we know she got loose not twenty minutes after they took her." The phone in the office rang. "I'll get that." She strolled out and came back in a few minutes. "Maizie just came home."

"No kidding. Well, that was exciting."

"I'll let everyone know. That was July, and she's one happy camper."

Dal finished his coffee and sat there a minute before getting up and meandering into his desk. There was paperwork to be done, and he might as well do it while things were quiet.

Tinker turned from her desk with a perplexed look. "Everyone's replied to the radio call but Bell."

"Ah, he's probably out of reach. When was the last time you heard from him?"

"This morning at daylight he took off for Red Rock Mountain to track Maizie. Nothing from him since."

"You talk to Fish and Wildlife today?"

"Just now. They haven't seen him. I've touched base with everyone."

Dal rose from his desk. Anything to avoid paperwork. "I'm going out to Sumner School, see if maybe he heard that call and headed out that way. There's no signal out there. Goddamn, I wish they'd get us better communications. You'd think…." He let the gripe fade away. It was an old one that law enforcement in Grace County received less funding than anyplace else. The argument was that they didn't need it. No use in hoping for more crimes just to solve that problem.

Could be they were on the brink of just such an occurrence. A missing deputy was nothing to laugh at. Sumner School was a long-empty building left over from the one-room schools of the olden days and a favorite hang-out for less than savory characters. Considering that Gene Bellamy would wade into anything without hesitation, Dal just might have his hands full. But he didn't wait for backup cause all the deputies were still far out in the county on their way in from looking for a tiger after they got word that the cat came back.

Though a talented tracker, Bell worried Jessie. He was just a kid with little common sense. Not as bad as Mac made out but just about. She left the Red Bird and went out to the Jeep where she tried his cell but only got a voicemail. Tink hadn't heard from the young deputy either. Dal came on and said he was going out to Sumner School to take a look around.

Slipping her phone in a hip pocket, she jumped in the Jeep. Following Dal when he had a hunch usually resulted in a good story. Two in one week would be downright unusual when placed on the front page alongside the city council and school board meetings. Exciting troubles were a-brewing. All coming up in time to make this week's issue of the paper. She was scheduled for the school board while Parker would cover what might be a highly charged city council meeting, considering the news about the Purple Bird or parrot or whatever.

A good idea to warn Parker so he could have Burke and Phil, the current salesmen, get to work selling ads to print enough pages. Hard to convince some people that it took forty percent of each page in ads to pay for the publication.

She left the police radio on for updates on Bell and Dal and the morons who'd stolen Maizie and headed into the remote area around Sumner School. Dal hadn't responded to her messages that she was on her way too. Signals bounced around out here, and sometimes it appeared they were lost in some black hole never to be heard from again. Another tower was a piece of progress she would more than welcome.

October weather touched the trees with magic fingers, turning the mountains into flaming splashes of gold, red, and orange. Black walnuts shed their leaves in a steady flow like huge green snowflakes. A good frost and the lime-green-hulled nuts would carpet the ground. Fall brought a strange sadness to her, always reminding her that all things died, many going out in a blaze of glory.

The road narrowed, tree branches forming a canopy that shut out the crisp blue morning sky. It was like driving into a dark tunnel. The Ozarks offered varieties of beauty and mystery that continuously amazed her. Around every curve or over every rise another surprise appeared.

She topped out to see a low water bridge awash from recent rains. Driving too fast as usual, she slammed on her brakes, but not in time to keep a rooster tail from soaking her in the open Jeep. The cold water brought a squeal, then laughter for the day was warm enough to enjoy the shower. But the old Jeep didn't react as well. The engine sputtered and died.

"Well, now you've done it." Scolding herself, she crawled out, opened the hood, and shook her head. Water soaked everything under there, sending steam from the hot engine block.

Must've thought she was still driving her new baby. Sometimes she regretted falling in love with the old Jeep when she wrecked her car and was left on foot. Parker had rebuilt it but never could give up his shiny black Range Rover, so he loaned her the Jeep. It was still on loan, and as long as he didn't mention it, she kept the relic. Later wrote an article about the World War Two vehicle that fascinated her even with its drawbacks. Plenty of older readers had comments about the article.

How far was it to Sumner School? Left to walk, she shrugged into her backpack, took the keys from the ignition, and headed off down the road. It was a beautiful day for a walk, the silent woods reflecting only the call of songbirds. It couldn't be more than a mile or two, "just around the bend and over the next hill," her father used to say when she asked, "How far is it now, Daddy?"

Last year's leaves papered the rarely-driven-over-ruts, and she playfully kicked them into the gentle breeze sending them fluttering in all directions. Off to her right, deep in the shadows, a squirrel chattered, telling her to move on and not bother him.

Then she rounded the bend, half running and still playing in the leaves, kind of like that child she remembered. Not paying attention, till… a man appeared in the center of the road, wearing a long black coat like cowboys in the movies. He held a black hat down at his side, and a splatter of sunlight gleamed on a crop of golden curls.

Good grief, she'd driven square into one of Dal's visions.

2
CHAPTER

Blinking and shaking her head at the man in black didn't help much. Jessie was either dreaming or she'd wandered into the wild west. She all but ran square into him. Let's see now, last she recalled she drove her Jeep into a water hole and drowned it, then started walking.

"Whoa." He lifted the empty hand. "Where'd you come from, young lady?"

Startled and speechless, not sure how to answer his question, she pointed behind her. Where did he think? "Could ask the same of you. Sort of remote out here."

"True, but we both have a destination, I expect."

She tilted her head. "Yet that's not where we came from. That's where we're going."

A chuckle rolled from his chest. "Indeed that would be correct, ma'am." He nodded his head once more, as if it could be taken for a gentlemanly bow. "It would appear that no matter what locale we left behind, we are both afoot. Name's James Jameson, often mistaken for one of those well-known James boys who once ran rampant over these peaceful hills."

"Looks like you might think you were, but the name is sort of bass-ackward, isn't it?"

He grimaced. "Everyone has some kind of remark."

She sort of wished he were kin to the James boys. Think what a story that would make, the return of the two most famous outlaws in Arkansas, Missouri, and Oklahoma, all put together. And standing right in front of the most famous historical writer in… well, in Cedarton anyway.

She made to move around him. "I'd better get on. Nice meeting you, Mr. Jameson. Y'all take care now."

He reached out a hand, maybe to take her arm, but she jerked away. He pulled back. "Just wantin' to get your name before we move on. Hate to tell this story without all the facts. Sorry I scared you."

The look in his eyes was no longer quite as friendly as she would like, or perhaps it was a bit too much so, and she slid a hand into the outer pocket of the pack where the .38 was snugged.

"I'll be on my way. The sheriff's waiting just a ways yonder." She gestured along the road. Lord, why did she say that that way?

His fingers tightened painfully around her wrist. "That's a good try, but why would that be?"

Without telegraphing her intent, she kicked him soundly in the shin and using the forward movement, shoved him out of reach and pulled the revolver.

His eyes hardened, but he remained crouched, both hands fluttering at shoulder height.

"Not such a hot shit cowboy now, are you? Just keep hunching like you are."

"Man, lady, you are one touchy deputy. Just lower that barrel a tad so when it goes off it'll maybe hit me in the toe while I reach in my pocket. No, now, hang in there. See my fingers only pulling out this." Sure enough he produced a shiny Texas Ranger badge. Silver glittering with star points. She knew it well. No lawmen had as cool a badge.

With a sigh she lifted her shoulders and stuffed the gun away. Not about to shoot a Texas Ranger even if he did annoy her. "Now, see, if I'd a shot you I'd be hip-deep in trouble. What was all that goofiness anyway? I thought Rangers had to pass a few tests, like common sense for one. Hell, I should've shot you in the big toe just to teach you a lesson. So what are you doing out here in the wilds of Arkansas on foot instead of sitting in Austin with your boot propped on a bar rail? You have no jurisdiction out of Texas."

He raised an eyebrow. "I'll just ignore that. I'm purely a tourist roaming these lovely hills and valleys. Would you believe I hit a rock, had a flat, and my spare was flat too? And what's your reason? Better than mine I'd hope."

"Not sure which one of us wins this contest. I drowned out my engine just back there on a low water bridge, and since I don't have far to go decided to walk."

He screwed the white Stetson firmly over his thatch of blond hair. "So, where are we off to?"

His dimpled smile was so friendly she couldn't help grinning. But not forgetting he hadn't answered her questions about his being here and not on his home turf. Other than that vague story about being a tourist.

"That's way better, ma'am. You're the first armed female deputy I've met, and I'm impressed. I'd a been plumb embarrassed to have ended up toe-shot by one so pretty."

"I'm not a deputy, I'm a reporter. And where did you learn that lingo?"

He stopped dead in his tracks. "Now see there, I'd a stayed impressed if you'd let it go at my first guess. A blasted reporter."

"And I'd have much rather you were one of the James boys, so I guess we're even."

She walked away without another word. It wouldn't take much more to get under her skin. It only took kicking him to decide this was no dream. One minute joking, the next throwing innuendos. He must've figured out on his own that she'd had it, so he put his legs in gear and walked beside her, whistling a tune she vaguely recognized.

What was a Texas Ranger doing deep in the Ozarks with a flat tire right where Bell, Dal, and Mac were searching for a tiger thief? It didn't make sense. After a few minutes she couldn't take it any longer, and so she asked him precisely that.

"Just enjoyin' the scenery, ma'am. Look around you and tell me this ain't about as purty as anything you've ever seen."

"Bullshit."

He stopped, took a few steps backward as if she'd struck him. "You tell me, what have you ever seen that's prettier? Except maybe you, ma'am." He tilted the hat back with one thumb. "In Texas our women don't talk like that."

She glared at him, and he did that shrug thing again. "Jest thought I'd say."

He must've gone to some kind of Texas charm school but hard to believe Rangers were trained to be so godawful western. He had some reason for being here that he didn't want her to guess, thus the put-ons. And she would nose around and learn his business. It could be one hell of a story.

He turned his back and started down the road. She skipped to keep up with his long legs. No longer wary of him, but darned curious, she continued the game. "You know if you head south and hang a right at Texarkana you'll be back in Texas before you know it, right where you belong. Unless of course you're working undercover."

Again, that grin, and he lifted the hem of the long coat to reveal tight jeans. Damn, he was one hell of a put-together man. "You don't like my cover?"

She almost told him how much she did like it, till he opened the coat. "I could take it off."

An invitation or a warning?

"Please spare me." The rest of him wasn't bad. Tempted, she rolled her eyes toward the sky. "You've been watching too many western movies. And practicing that Clint Eastwood look."

"Who?"

"Aw, come on. You know, that lip thing and the squint. Let alone the drawl."

A shot followed quickly by a second broke the spell, and he jumped nearly as high as she did.

"What the hell?"

"Run for cover."

Their words tumbled over each other and both pulled their weapons.

"Hunters?" He swiveled toward the silence that followed the gunshots, a Sig Sauer 1911 .45 auto filling his hand. She'd researched for an article but never seen one in person.

"I don't think so." She dragged her gaze away from the weapon and moved to stand beside him, the less impressive .38 ready.

What the hell was going on?

Dal aimed from around a pile of rocks and squeezed the trigger. When the first shot came from behind the old schoolhouse, he'd slid on his belly like going into home plate. The bullet cut dust too close for comfort.

"Bell, where you at?"

No reply. No sign of the shooter. Could be another tiger thief since they had three escaped, and that was the extent of known fugitives for the week. But where was his deputy? The newly hired Bell.

"Dammit, you hit?"

"Nope." Barely loud enough for him to hear. Might be on the other side of the dilapidated building or inside. Bellamy was new in the field, coming from a long stint in Afghanistan. Like Colby, he came out of the Marines. He was one hell of a tracker but tended to stay hid other than that. Mac might figure he wasn't worth it in the long run unless he turned out to be teachable.

Another gunshot from back of the far corner, and Dal leaned out and sent three there, one after the other. Just as the echoes died away, a flurry of firing from behind him chopped splints of wood out of the far siding followed by a shout of pain. Dal whirled, not sure if he was the target. Whoever shot had come danged close to him.

"Dal, it's me. I mean us."

Definitely Jessie. "Where'd you come from, and where'd you pick up an auto?

A large man in a black coat and white hat stepped from the shadows into the sunlight. "Mine. Ranger Jameson. Is everyone okay?"

"Ranger? Where'd you come from?" For an instant the words Lone Ranger flew through his mind, and he almost let go a guffaw.

"Texas, sir?"

"Well, is it Texas or not? I mean what are you doing here?"

"Oh, that. Saving some deputy's ass, sir."

Weary of the exchange, he tackled another problem. "Jessie? Where you at?"

She appeared from the shadows next to the Lone Ranger. "Right here, Dal. And in case you want to know, he ain't kin to the famous brothers of near that name."

"Probably for the best. And tell me what in hell are you doing here?"

"I don't know for sure, myself. Maybe we could talk it over." Jessie's voice trembled.

Dal holstered his weapon and stepped out of hiding. Enough was definitely enough.

One by one they ventured into the clearing next to the schoolhouse. The tiger thief being the last, hugging his arm close.

"Y'all shot me." He sounded a bit like a little kid who'd lost his yo-yo.

"Next time don't come to a gunfight." This from the man in the long coat.

"And don't steal no tiger, either." Jessie put in her two cents worth.

Dal shot the intruder a harsh look. "I'll handle this, whoever you are. You could'a got yourself shot comin' in on us like that. By my count there's still one missing." He gestured toward the injured tiger thief.

"The way things were going I'm surprised everyone didn't get hit." Again, her anger showed in her voice.

"Well, someone damn well shot me. And all I done was drive the damn truck."

"Stop your whining, Tiger Thief. You didn't do a very good job of it. Where's your pal? And does anyone know where Bellamy is? You started this." Dal waited a second. "Okay, let's see if he's around here someplace, maybe shot. That is, if no one has any objections."

Tiger Thief sank to his butt. "I need me a doctor or I'm gonna sue ever one of you. And there ain't but jest me."

Bell sneaked out a window, knocking loose a long plank that hit Tiger Thief across the head. He howled, and Bell said, "I'm here. I'm okay."

Jessie laughed under her breath, then let her merriment loose. Dal wiped his forehead and joined her. Before long the entire bunch howled with hilarity. It'd been quite a day. Dal was the first to admit it.

"I haven't had so much fun in ages." He held up a hand when everyone began to chatter about the excitement, each pointing out their favorite happening. Poor Tiger Thief. He didn't think anything was funny, and he continued to whine and complain about his experience and his tiny old flesh wound.

"After all, I'm going to jail, and the whole thing wasn't my idea at all."

Dal scratched his chin. "Maybe if you told us whose idea it was, we might be generous with you."

"You remember last year when Miz Jones began her animal farm?" He gazed all around the group, now seated in the shade from the old building. They nodded, all but the Lone Ranger who hadn't been present. He looked eager to hear the story, though.

"Well, this… this fella I know said he'd read where tiger skins were worth a lot of money, and Miz July wouldn't miss one of them gold ones, she has so many."

What he was really saying must've hit Jessie first, cause before he could reveal the perp's name, she pinched her mouth and went all white. "But taking a hide, that would kill the tiger. Oh, I mean, that's disgusting. You stupid, ugly, mean man." She scrambled to her feet and lit into Tiger Man, beating him around the head with both fists.

He covered his head with his arms and whimpered. At first everyone cheered her on, but she soon collapsed into the grass and cried into bloody hands. Tiger Man lay on his side as if he'd been hit with a big rock.

Dal reached her first and put an arm around her shoulder. Inspecting her hands revealed it was not her blood. "It's okay, Jess. Maizie is back home, and we caught one of them, anyway."

She peered through her fingers over his shoulder, rage not cooling one bit. "I'll bet there isn't one single law that will see them put in jail, is there? Still, only a fine, if that. They ought to be shot." Somehow she'd lost her backpack in all the ruckus, and she tore loose from Dal to look around for it.

Tiger Thief hollered some more, begged them to protect him from her.

The Lone Ranger, who had spent most of the time after the gun battle ended watching the goins-on with inquisitive humor, rose to the occasion. "I know we just met, Jessie, but I'd be glad to shoot this son of a bitch for you before I'm on my way. If you'd like." He tipped his hat to her and grinned.

She pointed a finger at him. "Don't you dare make fun of me that way. And don't call me Jessie. We haven't been introduced."

He spread both hands palms up, an expression of dismay on his face. "Oh, yes, we were. Don't you remember?" He poked her chest. "Reporter." Then poked his own. "Texas Ranger. We most certainly were introduced. Anyway, what did I do?"

"You know what I think?" Dal had located her backpack and taken it in hand so she couldn't get hold of it and the .38 inside. At this point she might shoot more than just Tiger Thief. You couldn't always tell which way Jess would go once provoked. Though in truth he'd never known her to actually go that far. Well, yeah there was that time with Steve, but he deserved it, and she didn't kill him. And she regretted it for a long time. Dal forgot what he was going to say or what he thought and looked around at the motley crew.

Jessie, in her wet clothes, Tiger Thief with a bloody arm and a snotty nose from bawling like a baby, Bell sitting against a tree as if he wasn't sure where he was, himself playing keep away with her backpack as if it were a game, and the tall Ranger who looked as if he had escaped from a Wild West show.

"No, what do you think?" Tired of waiting for Dal to finish, the Lone Ranger prompted him.

Good God, I'm the only sane one in the bunch, and there could be some disagreement about that. Dal had absolutely no idea what to do with this group. Maybe he could just arrest all of them, take them to the sheriff, and let him sort it out. Charges could probably be brought against everyone save himself and Bell, and the kid might be fired on the spot hiding from the action like he had.

He'd never seen a day like this one in all the years he'd lived in Cedarton. Maybe everyone was right when they said that danged highway with an exit so close would be the ruin of the town. Walmart was supposed to do that, but it had been here a few years, so he didn't think anyone could blame this day on it. That, however, was debatable.

All that had to happen now was if that rumor about an English Pub turned out to be true. He'd have to check it out. They'd have to hire more deputies to watch over all the drunks staggering around the square. He himself had sworn off liquor of any kind years ago considering the terrible reputation Cherokees had for being unable to leave whiskey alone.

Back to his current problem. What to do with Jessie, Tiger Thief, Bell, and The Lone Ranger. Somehow he had to haul them back to town in his unit since they all seemed to be afoot. It resembled the old story of the frog, the fly, and the turtle trying to cross the creek.

"Jessie, how did you and your long, tall stranger arrive here?"

"My Jeep is drowned back there on the low-water bridge. I don't know about him. I think he hiked over from Texas just to annoy us." Her glare told him what she thought of the Ranger.

The fool tried to help out. "I've got a flat tire on up the road a ways. No idea how I got out here, either. Did you know your roads half of them don't have numbers? Last I knew, I was on something called The Pig Trail, capitalized like it was important. I must'a turned off it somewhere. And here I am."

"Okay, here's what we're going to do." Dal took Jessie's arm very gently so she wouldn't smack him. "Her and me are going back to her Jeep. It's no doubt dried out by now. She'll come on back here and pick up Bell, and they'll head back to town. He's probably the only one she's not in the mood to kill at the moment. I'll haul Tiger Thief there and the Lone Ranger in, and he can hire someone to bring him back out here to fix his tire. Asshole here, once known as Tiger Thief, is going to jail, and we'll go from there. I wish you all a nice evening."

Jameson, who had been silent during the rigid instructions, strode to the patrol unit, climbed in front, stretched out his long legs, leaned back with his hat tilted forward, and folded both arms over his chest. That left the back for Tiger Thief and Jessie.

She wasn't very happy. He felt sorry for her. She looked like a drowned pussy cat, and she always called shotgun. It showed how weary she was that she simply sighed, shot Ranger another glare, and crawled in behind the screen that separated law breakers from lawmen.

Dal picked up the still-moaning prisoner by the front of his shirt and dragged him to the car, pushing him into the back seat and slamming the door.

"Good work, Grandson. You must watch the one with the black coat. He is not what he says he is. Listen to the woman."

"Which one?" Dal murmured the words so the Lone Ranger wouldn't think he was talking to himself. Why the hell he cared about that was a good question. He keyed the ignition, hooked the mic, and called in. Tink answered, her voice telling him she wasn't happy to be on desk duty. She was a tough little gal who had conquered her fear of the dark so she could be on call for the field.

Weary from the day's events, all Dal wanted was to go home to his comfortable apartment and crash. He was on-call 24/7, but in Cedarton that could give him some long hours off if he was reachable. It was a damned good job compared to the days and nights undercover in Dallas. Sometimes he almost was grateful for whoever pulled the trigger that put him on disability and finally retired him from that job. When this one came up a few years back, he met with Sheriff Mac, and they hit it off immediately. As was also the case with him and Jessie. He grinned at the thought, cause they fought like badgers at crime scenes, then had sex like bunnies afterward.

Still thinking about sex with Jessie, he backed around in the clearing and headed toward where the Lone Ranger said he'd left his car. Maybe he ought to give Jessie some time to recuperate. She looked like she badly needed some rest.

He spoke without looking at the man. "I'll drop you there and send a truck out to handle your little problem." Best if he separated this one from all the rest.

"Appreciate it. Can't figure how they'll ever find me, but I reckon folks around here are familiar with unmarked roads with no bridges. You have an interesting job. How long you been doing this?"

"Long enough to know the back roads. Takes a while to get used to this place, but the people are decent, for the most part. The rest we manage to take care of quick. Especially when they come in from outside and pull their stunts."

Ranger laughed. Who had a name like James Jameson? It was easier to think of him as the Lone Ranger, though that was pretty dumb when you considered it. However, the guy looked like he'd stepped out of the nineteenth century, maybe working for old Judge Parker out of the US Marshal service in Fort Smith. Dal grinned to himself.

All in all, it'd been more than an interesting day. What about that woman he kept seeing? Who the heck was she, and why was she here? Could she be the woman Grandfather warned him about? Brought her up twice now. What was he supposed to think? Or was she just one of his bad jokes?

Where had the old man been, and why was he now back? His presence usually meant big trouble was brewing. That was okay, it'd been a slow, boring summer. And the mysterious woman stirred something in him. Whether questions or threats, he was anxious to find out more.

He rounded a curve to see a big, black SUV with windows so dark you couldn't see through sitting slaunchwise in the road on a flat. How the hell did you drive a vehicle like that and not have a spare? He didn't bother to ask, just let Ranger out.

"Take her easy and try not to start anymore gun battles in my territory." He laughed, and so did Ranger.

Dal did a three-point turnaround, hoping that was the last he saw of the mysterious Lone Ranger. There was still Jessie's drowned Jeep, and there it sat up to its hubs blocking the low water bridge. He stopped nose to nose with it. Turned to say something to her, and she was sound asleep, her head snugged between the edge of the seat and the door. Rather than waken her before he needed to, he got out of the unit, opened the hatch, and dug out a rag.

"What are we doing?" His prisoner suddenly came alive and began his whining. If he could, he'd stuff the dirty rag in the noisome kid's mouth, but he ignored the moaning, shut the door softly, and used that dirty rag to see that everything under the gaping hood was dried out. Humming under his breath, he sat in the Jeep, turned the key she'd left hanging in the ignition, and after a few taps on the accelerator, the engine turned over. He left it running and eased the door open where Jessie was slumped.

She squinted her eyes, saw him, and smiled. Sweet as a little kid wakening from a nap. He kissed her on the end of her chin, then on each cheek. "Come on, she's running. You good to go on home? Don't forget to pick up Bell. I'll see you later?"

"Okay." She leaned into him for a brief moment, then let him take her hand and lead her from the unit to her vehicle.

"I'll back out of your way so you can turn around." He watched her drive out of sight, thinking thoughts of holding her in his arms that left him feeling better.

"Hey, why are we just sitting here?" His backseat passenger was quite a nuisance, and he'd be more than happy to deliver him to a cell. Charges would be assaulting an officer on top of tiger stealing. The asshole would be in jail for a while.

Crossing the bridge, he veered to the right off the woods road and headed for Cedarton. It was nearing supper time. After checking in his prisoner, he'd have a meal at the Red Bird, then go home and shut out the world for a few hours, then maybe call Jessie. That would finish off the night to perfection.

At the Red Bird he met two people he hoped were only a figment of local gossip's imagination. Turned out they weren't. When Wanda waited on him, she pointed them out.

"Back there in the booth, them two dressed to the nines like they want to impress someone. That's Marvin and Shilo Captree, late of Devonshire in jolly old England. Not the one in Missouri, the one across the waters. They have bought the boutique that Holly used to own? On the square? Next to Marvin's Ice Cream Shoppe? Two Marvin's in one small town. Have to give Captree another name. Cappy would work. Turning it into The—are you ready for this?—Purple Raven. Not Bird. It is what we feared. A pub."

Her lips popped out the title, and she grinned and nodded, then walked away twisting her hips.

For a brief moment, stars danced through his vision. This had to be one of grandfather's creations to warn him of something disastrous on the way.

What he needed was a good dose of Jessie's arms around him, perhaps in her bed or shower or even out in the woods. Anywhere would do. Parts of the day had to be made forgettable, like his memories of Leanne or the appearance of Grandfather, which often warned of trouble to come.

So he ordered double of everything, all to go, and headed for her place. They could eat, lay outside under the stars and make love, talk about stuff. Anything but this day, then make love again. Lord, he loved her. Just having these thoughts made him hard as a fencepost. He could easily forget that woman who came hopping into his dreams. At least when he was with Jessie… who opened the door wrapped in a towel, hair dripping down her back.

Her eyes popped. "Well, imagine that. Just as I was having all sorts of erotic ideas."

"Wow. Dressed for me or having company?"

She let go of the towel and grabbed his upper arm to keep him from dumping the food. "Mmm, you must've read my mind. From the look of the fridge, I thought it was going to be dill pickles and cheese. And, well, a vibrator. Come right on in. Smells wonderful."

By then she was standing before him naked. He must've sent some sort of expression from his bodily desires. She took the sacks from him. "I'll heat it up later."

He hadn't said a word, didn't have to, just unbuttoned his shirt, and while she pulled it off for him, he toed out of his boots, unbuckled his belt, and made short work of skinning out of the uniform trousers.

He couldn't wait for the bed, just went to his knees there in front of her and began tasting, touching, and sniffing her loveliness. That accomplished, and her shuddering and making sweet little sounds down in her throat, he lowered her so they touched from shoulders all the way down to their thighs. He drove his fencepost deep and slow. Piercing her soft, wet, cool flesh, he wanted her so badly he could hardly wait till she found a position that allowed him full entrance. He slipped easily into heaven and almost died of the rapture having her brought. It was like entering the Eden true believers imagined, where everything was sweet and colors shimmered and lips softly enclosed aching parts of the body to satisfy every single need.

He remained in her for a very long time, unwilling to leave her exquisite hold on him. When he slowly withdrew, she clamped him with arms and legs, an orgasm rocking through her, gripping him till he held on and moaned with newfound delight.

She kept whispering, "Oh God," and squirming. He relaxed into that. It felt so damned good on his wilted penis that he didn't want her to stop though he was pretty much done. Or not. Something raised its head, possibly from curiosity, and she captured him with her thighs.

Holy shit. If she went on much longer, he'd need a crane to get him up off the floor. And then it was over, everything sort of melted into a great heap, stars shot across the sky and faded, arms and legs entwined.

A tongue licked his face, and he opened his eyes to see Brad, panting and dancing.

Without budging, he laughed, and she joined him when Brad moved to lick her.

"I think he's hungry." Dal chuckled under his breath.

"Me, too. I'm starving, but I don't know how to get untangled."

"We'll work it out."

What a wild and crazy day it'd been. Finally, they managed to work the knots loose and prepared the burgers and fries without bothering to dress. More was sure to come once they satisfied their appetite for food.

He didn't even think of the British pub or its ridiculous name.

His phone rang while they were cleaning up. Mac wanted him back at the office soonest, so he kissed her and kissed goodbye his hopes for a long night in bed with her.

3
CHAPTER

A dying light darkened the room, wakening Jessie to a puzzling world. Maybe a woodpecker drilling a hole in her head. Or was it someone banging on the door? She raised off the bed. Crap. She lay naked on top of the spread. Had gone right from the shower to sleep when Dal left. But what had she done before that? Lying in his arms came to mind, and she hugged her pillows, experiencing his last embrace.

The knocking increased, and she lowered her feet to a pile of dirty clothes from earlier.

"All right, I'm coming. Shut the hell up." The noise only got more intense. "Stop that hammering. I've got a gun."

"Jessie. Now."

Who is that? Not a familiar voice. "It can wait till I put some clothes on, unless the world is ending, and in that case forget it."

While she shouted at her would-be intruder, she dragged out a sleep shirt, the easiest to slip on over her head and made her way to the door, the cool cotton drifting around her nude body. Releasing the lock she'd only begun using after the shooting last year had left her lying in her own blood, she swung open the door to see Parker, leaned against the jamb, face pale, eyes wide, and mouth moving but saying nothing.

"My God. What's happened?" She slipped an arm around his waist and coaxed him inside, seated him on the couch, fetched a glass of water, and a dampened cloth.

This man was normally the most put together person she'd ever known. He laughed in the face of adversity. His words, not hers. Yet he drank the water, holding the glass with a shaking hand, and closed his eyes while she applied the wet cloth to his forehead. Not a word, not one single word.

She lowered herself next to him, took his hand, and kissed it. "Whatever it is, we'll handle it. Just breathe deep and slow and tell me when you can."

He did as she asked, his head on her shoulder. His soft dark hair tickling her skin reminded her that they had once been lovers, for a very brief time, and though he was her boss, they were as close as brother and sister. Once he loved, he never stopped caring deeply. And he'd done a lot of that.

Words finally came, pitiful and weak. "Loren, she… she…. Dear God, I think she's dead."

"Loren?" Oh, the latest short-lived love affair. He never settled, as if he were trying out every woman he ever met. Younger he married each and every one he loved, to number five. She never knew what happened there. She'd been in California. All she knew was he stopped talking about her then. As if to do so hexed their success somehow. Maybe he searched for something that didn't exist. Perhaps he hoped he'd find someone who would return the intense love he offered. Now this.

Oh, God. What if he only *thinks* she's dead? She gripped his upper arm, spoke slowly and deliberately. "Where is she? Can you tell me that?"

He shook his head vehemently. "No, no, no, no. Awful."

Cupping his cheeks in both hands, she forced him to meet her gaze. "You have to tell me where she is. She might be alive."

"No she isn't. I know dead when I see dead." Each word like individual shots. He squeezed her hand so hard the bones made a cracking sound, lowered his head but kept shaking it.

She pawed on the table till her fingers located the phone. Her thumb hit number one. Dal's number.

He answered. Mac was speaking in the background.

Thank God she'd reached him. She dragged in a shudder.

"Jess, what is it?"

"Need. I need—" Parker knocked the phone away, shouted his no again and again.

Dal would come. She hated he would be frightened by the call but could do nothing about it but wait. He might bring an army with him in the form of first responders, deputies, and the like, but it had to be.

While she waited, Jessie tried a few times to get an explanation out of her boss, but he was nearly comatose except when she asked a question, then he went into the head shaking and muttering no. Over and over. It was driving her crazy, but waiting was the only choice. They arrived, one after the other, vehicles shooting dust into the early morning air. Almost as dramatic as the cavalry arriving to save the day.

Dal burst through the door, stopping short barely in time to keep from running over the two of them huddled on the couch. The cabin wasn't very big, and the door opened into the largest room. Living, dining, and kitchen, then double glass doors on the opposite wall into the back yard. He'd a kept going he would've ended on the large deck or in the vast twenty acres of wilderness beyond.

But he hauled up, mouth agape, stared at her and Parker huddled together in a ball. "Whoa, so this is the emergency? I expected to find a gunshot wound or a hostage situation. What's going on with you two?"

"He thinks Loren is dead, but he won't say any more than that. He's literally speechless."

"Sort of your problem when you called me. Speechless. Loren?"

"Yes, I'm really sorry about that. He was out of hand then. She's his... well, you know. Now he's—well, he's like this."

Two first responders burst through the door carrying the necessary equipment. Jerry put down his heavy bag and stood wide-legged in the center of the room. "What's up? Sick? Hurt? Heart?"

Before another word, four more crowded inside till it would be impossible to make room for any more. Late arrivals peered through the screen, milled about on the front porch, visiting in low voices. Parker appeared unaware of anything that was going on.

"He says his girlfriend is dead, but that's all I can get out of him."

"I think we're all here." Dal tried a little gentle prodding. Each time he went into question mode, Parker started shaking his head and repeating no.

Dal finally turned to Jerry. "Someone needs to check around his farm, see if... hell, I don't know. See if you can find a body. Or if there's anything amiss there. I'll try to find out where he's been. You guys on the porch, go into town. The Red Bird, some of the other places he hangs out. Someone has to know something. Go."

Everyone scattered. Well, almost everyone. Jerry and Hank, the EMTs remained.

Jessie continued to be trapped by Parker's grip on her hand. "If they did, wouldn't they have called it in by now? Does he have his phone?"

"Hey, yeah. Get his phone, see if he has her number."

Everyone stared at Dal. She patted his pockets, shook her head.

"What?" Dal held out his arms.

On his knees, Jerry checked blood pressure, oxygen, and heart again. "Pulse still a bit high, so he's excited about something, but he seems okay."

"He doesn't act or look okay." Words repeated by Dal and Jessie.

Jerry shrugged. "We can take him in, but chances are we might get more out of him here once he gets over whatever's scared him."

"It's like a three-ring circus. I can't find his phone." Jessie remarked if anyone was listening.

Dal shook his head. "Won't do much good. She lives off the grid, hiding? She'd have gotten rid of it."

"Does anyone know where Loren lives?"

Everyone shook their head. "Which one is she? Never even knew about a Loren. Last name, anyone?"

No one seemed to know. His personal life was a well-kept secret.

"I think the tall, well-built blonde. Not the skinny type."

"Sounds like any of the last three. He has a type, you know. Sort of like Jessie there."

Heat crawled up her throat. Everyone giving their opinion so fast she couldn't keep up. She and Parker had been very discreet, but even so, in a small town, everybody knows or guesses everything. It was short and sweet though, and she'd be damned if she were ashamed.

Last year while she and Parker played their short, sweet game, Dal was off searching for himself, so he knew nothing about their brief affair unless someone had told him. She doubted that. He would've reacted.

"So no one here has seen him with this Loren? Out riding or hunting or at the horse races? Come on, think. I'd hate to find out we could've saved this woman had we known where she was."

Parker looked up at Dal. "Loren is dead, and it's my fault."

Dal knelt beside him. "Where is she Parker? We need to find her."

He clasped Jessie's hand, placing it between her breasts. "She's with... MoPac."

"MoPac. Isn't that a railroad company?"

"No, well, yes it is. But he bred one of his mares to a line known as MoPac. She had a foal this spring." Jessie watched Parker's reaction. Absolutely none.

Dal was fast losing his patience. "So the foal would still be out at his farm, you think?"

"Probably. He wouldn't have sold it yet."

Dal headed for the door. "I could use a deputy with me. Say, does anyone know where Mac is? He had to hear this go out over the radio."

"Don't tell me we've got two people missing." Colby stood to volunteer to go with Dal.

"It sure looks like it."

The conversations bounced around among the men gathered near Parker and Jessie. She heard but didn't always identify who spoke.

What she did know was that she wanted to go with Dal, be with him when he found Loren. It was part of an important story, but obviously Parker wanted her here with him. So she would stay.

Once Dal and Colby left, everything sort of calmed. Though Parker didn't speak, the two who remained started small conversations while keeping an eye on the newspaper publisher.

The phone rang, and everyone jumped, looking at Jessie.

She picked it up with her free hand. Listened, nodded, and hung up.

"That was Colby. They found her, in a stall with the foal. MoPac." She glanced at Parker, shook her head. "He wants an ambulance to go out to the farm and said someone needs to call Kathy and Dave for forensics." That meant someone was truly dead, just like Parker said.

After Dal and Colby left she leaned back and closed her eyes. Jerry kept an eye on Parker, who said something else she didn't repeat to the others. He must be confused, for he whispered, "I didn't mean to kill her. I didn't mean to."

Hank knelt close enough to hear and slid a squinty-eyed look her way. She shook her head. No way would this man kill anyone. Never.

Parker had never gone over the edge like this, and if he didn't come out of it, she was taking him to the hospital.

Once everything quieted down, he relaxed and let go of her hand, but he continued to stare out the window as if seeing something she couldn't. Maybe he cared more for Loren than he had some of the others. It could be death itself frightened him since he'd come so close with cancer a few years back. No sense in trying to analyze his behavior. She was a reporter not a psychologist.

Time to make a pot of coffee. Leaving him sitting there as if in a trance, she went to the small kitchen and bustled around finding a filter, measuring grounds, and running water. Anything to stay busy until she heard more about the circumstances.

The farm appeared deathly quiet when Dal skidded the unit to a stop near the large horse barn, Colby hanging to the dash for his life.

Horses grazed in the nearby pasture, birds serenaded chattering squirrels. A typical peaceful fall day for a murder scene.

Dal reached for the door handle. "We don't know what we're coming up on." He slipped from the car, one palm firmly resting on his holstered sidearm. A glance at Colby assured him the deputy would follow his example. Together they crouched behind the patrol unit staring at the barn.

Best if Colby went round to one side where there was a good-sized window while Dal trotted toward the small door next to the open walkway between the rows of stalls. Both had dealt with murder scenes, knew to avoid tracks, human or vehicle. For all he knew someone could be hiding in those shadows where horses hung their heads over the truncheons, soft brown eyes studying the interlopers. He signaled the deputy who nodded and moved out.

Keeping to one side, Dal made his way with caution. He sensed no danger, and with Grandfather keeping watch, all would remain safe. Yet whatever evil had been here left a trail of invisible mist, filthy in its connotation. In it hid an intent he couldn't quite read, but he was approaching its strength. The trouble lay ahead. He signaled Colby to get down and be quiet. One more step and he was wrapped in the left-over action. Just like that. Voices, none of them Parker's.

Expecting to see their fading images, he whirled and glanced over the waist-high truncheon. Inside was the mare and her colt, crowded into the back corner as if something else was in there with them. Something dangerous and invisible. Her protecting the little one. As far as he could tell, they were alone, but his senses whipped about, a fist clutched at his insides, and he slid along the wall to make his way to the two animals. Whatever had been here had left a stink like death behind in the darkest corner of the stall. His foot touched something soft, and he stopped, squatted down.

The body lay in thick hay opposite where the mare guarded her newborn foal, a shaft of sunlight showing gleaming wet spots on its coat. He slipped a flashlight out of his utility belt and clicked it on, the bright cone revealing a woman's head crammed in the corner, features frozen in death, clumps of hay stuffed in her mouth. The squabble of violence around her moved into the distance. His mind reached desperately for their words, but they drifted away.

He called out to Colby, who appeared fast. "We're too late. I guess we've found Loren. I'll call it in. If you prefer to wait outside, I'll stay here with her." Perhaps he could get more information alone at the crime scene while waiting for Kathy and Dave Spacey. If Grandfather had to come back, at least Dal could hope to use him to catch this killer. One thing he was sure of. Parker did not do this. It was way too violent. Yet if he didn't find who did, the gentle man could easily be blamed for it.

They'd have to count on the Spaceys for forensics, but that was only half a case like this. Too often by the time those results came back, the case was solved, and they simply tied a blue ribbon on it. The rest would be up to him and the other deputies... and a lot of old-fashioned foot-and-headwork.

The iridescence descended again, slamming him against the stall divider. Earlier silence vibrated with furious conversation. *"Not the brightest damn thing you ever did."* *"What else could I do?"* *"Walk away, idjit."* *"And then what? She was primed to tell him everything. We couldn't chance it."* *"Jacked as she was no one would believe her."* *"Someone would. Someone always does."* *"You put the latigo around her neck?"* *"It was hanging in the tack room."*

Two men, neither of whose voices he recognized. Talking about Loren, surely. Jacked? New term for high? Coked? Deadly meth? Or just pissed?

He knelt carefully next to her, fingered the leather strap fastened tightly around her throat.

Something soft moved across the back of his neck, nudged him from the trance. He smiled and reached slowly to touch the muzzle of the mare, who whickered and nodded toward the foal, standing under her stomach, four tiny stick legs propping it up.

He rubbed her neck. "Yeah, you done good mommy, real good."

Colby's footsteps caught his attention, and he held up a hand. "Wait outside till they get here, then ask them to wait till I come out. I don't want anyone in here till I've finished."

Colby halted and glanced over the mare and foal and the humped-up body, then left without a word. He had never been around when Grandfather and Dal carried out an investigation, but you could bet your bottom dollar he knew all about how it worked. How crazy the others thought the Cherokee must be, though his solving of cases impressed them all.

The mare's eyes locked on Dal like he didn't know the half of what she'd been through. Or maybe, like she knew what he went through. They'd need her cooperation since she'd been present at the murder and her being a new mother meant that could be difficult. Still she seemed to feel something soothing about him or she'd have bared her teeth and kicked up a fuss instead of showing off her baby. He'd do his best to gather whatever evidence they needed and find who committed this dreadful killing, all the while keeping her calm and preserving the scene. That was his job.

The prospect drove away his dread of this case and dealing with Grandfather, and he began a careful search in the hay strewn floor.

He spent the time till the others arrived sifting through the area around the body. Fingertips can be very sensitive, touching what had been touched by the killers. Especially when they read clues like his did. Three of the killers took part, though only two spoke. He heard bits and pieces of their filthy discussion, never spoken above a whisper, or sounds like growling, their evil bragging, the snickering of only those who had no conscience. The third, well, something odd there. Like shame.

By the time the other deputies arrived, he had picked up a few things from the floor. Not much though. It all belonged to Parker. A gum wrapper, cellophane from crackers. All older. He would go where the murder was committed when they found it. That would tell him more. Once he caught the fragrance of powder, a perfumed sort. Perhaps from Loren. Or had the third who didn't speak been a woman?

When Colby sent Kathy and Dave into the barn, Dal rose to allow them to slip into the stall next to the body.

"Okay if we take this little lady into the next stall?" Dave approached, speaking in his calm voice. The mare regarded him with trusting eyes.

"She will go where the foal goes, just gentle the little one along and mommy will follow. Be careful, she might be protective."

Dal wanted to remain, but it was best if he let these people do what they did the best. He had all he needed till he found where she'd been killed. Kathy was a superb forensics scientist, and Dave knew precisely how to assist her. Colby stepped in to handle the mare and foal, doing his usual good job. He was always that way with animals, not just horses. He and Maizie got along famously. Dal left to see if Parker was ready to talk. If Jessie helped out, maybe he would be.

Hank caught up with Dal at his patrol unit. "Say, Chief, a lady came by the station asking for you last night. Asked me to have you call her first chance." He handed Dal a folded piece of paper with a number on it.

"She give you her name?"

"Nope. She also asked to make sure only you got that number or mention of her coming by." Hank grinned. "Reckon I'm supposed to stay mute, too."

"Huh. Don't ask me." Dal took the note and stuck it in his shirt pocket. Didn't sound like an emergency, and he needed to talk to Parker while this nasty business was fresh on his mind. Didn't have many killings in these parts, but he recalled the best way to conduct the investigation from his time with the Dallas PD. Besides there was always his Cherokee curse. He held up. "Say, Hank, you didn't see Mac today did you?"

The deputy scratched his head. "Come to think of it, no. Reckon where he got off to? Odd for him to just take off without leaving word with someone."

"Well, I'm sure he'll turn up. See you later."

Pretty sure Parker would still be with Jessie, Dal swung by her place first. Sure enough, his vehicle remained angled slaunchwise in her yard where he'd left it when he raced over there earlier. Dal tapped on the door, then went on in. The two sat on the deck in lounge chairs, sweaty glasses of iced tea between them on a small table.

"Jess, it's me." He slid the glass door open.

Turning toward him, she asked if he wanted tea, told him it was in the fridge. "It's sweet," she added. She lay a hand on Parker's arm. "How'd it go over there?"

Without waiting for him to reply, Parker spoke in the softest of voices. "I told you she was dead. Suppose you believe me now." He gritted his teeth. "Christ, who would do a thing like that? She was a nice lady."

Well, at least he no longer claimed to have killed her. That was a relief. "We'll find out, rest assured. You ready to answer some questions so we can get to the bottom of this? You know it's best to get right to it."

"I do. I'm ready. Sorry about earlier. Don't know what got into me. She was a fine, fine woman."

"Sorry I didn't know her then. Fine women are good to know."

Parker patted Jessie's knee. "Indeed they are."

Dal sat in one of the straight chairs, pulling it up close to Parker.

"If you don't mind, Jess."

She nodded at Dal, touched Parker's shoulder, got up, and went inside. None of her business what went on in the interview. Being a member of the press was a double reason she shouldn't sit in on this, even though she was nosy enough to wish she could.

Inside, she opened her computer and began the story that would run in tomorrow's paper. Being a weekly meant they couldn't stay ahead of the dailies, but she'd get a jump on them with the first issue, the breaking story, anyway, even though there wouldn't be much she could write about the murder itself. But people who read her pieces liked the special touch she gave them, and she could do that this very minute including about the nice fine lady.

Parker had talked about her while they sat on the deck, and Jessie made notes. It was the people she wrote about, not the hideous things that happened to them. And that included those who pulled off the crime, whatever it might be. She knew the people involved, which meant a good, internal study of each and every one. Parker and his love of sarcasm in his editorials. Dal and his mysterious way of hunting down criminals. And Mac, everyone loved the sheriff, and most thought he could do no wrong. A quote from him would be worth entire paragraphs. And of course, Loren Jasper, the last woman Parker loved. His words.

"I'm done, Jessie. Gonna become one of those bachelors who collects stuff. Maybe books. That'd be good, wouldn't it?"

She'd brushed away tears. He too was a good man who deserved someone to love him.

So while Dal and Parker talked, Jessie blocked out her story for the front page. She'd get photos based on what information she was allowed to use. Damn, she wished she could verify the crime scene locale. Get it out of that barn, but she couldn't. All the wishing in the world wouldn't allow it yet.

One thing she would omit was Dal's peculiar way of solving crimes. It was always the talk of the town and needed no embellishment. It had been a while since he'd had to deal with that weird type of investigation. How she wished he never had to go into the minds of killers. She'd seen how hard it was on him, especially when it came to dealing with the suffering of the victims. Thankfully not a lot of hardcore crime went on out here. Still, it was destructive for him.

He never talked too much about it to her, other than the link to his Cherokee grandfather who was a shaman. In Cherokee she thought it was called something else, but she didn't know for sure. And Dal wasn't just about to educate her concerning his heritage. He wished the weird ability would go away. Talking to ghosts and spirits, especially those of victims or evil ones, wouldn't be on her wish list either, so she never pushed him about it.

She was deeply in her draft when someone arrived. With a sigh she saved the story and rose to see who it was. Mac crawled out of his patrol

SUV and strolled to the house like nothing was up at all. She pushed open the screen door. Saw he was wearing a pair of brand new Justin boots.

"Hey, Mac. Like the boots. Dal's out on the deck interviewing Parker. Want some tea?"

"What I want is an explanation. I'm only gone a couple hours over to Oklahoma to pick me up this fine footwear and everything goes nuts. I did tell Tinker, and where is she? I get back to the station and there's a brand new wet-behind-the-ears deputy taking her place arming the door and the phones." Voice growing, he waved his arms. "He can't tell me what's going on. Or won't. Where in thunder is everyone? And what the hell is a Texas Ranger doing sitting in my office? And why is Dal interviewing Parker? In short what in thunderation's going on here?"

Struck dumb by the stacked questions, Jessie took him by the hand and sat him in the front porch swing, then joined him. Where to start?

It took two glasses of tea to tell him the answers she knew. That Texas Ranger thing she left till the end, hoping he'd want in on the crime detecting, and she could sort of let it go on by. But it didn't work.

"Well, it seems everyone's got things in hand, so, I ask again, what's a Texas—"

"I don't know."

"Have you met him?"

She nodded.

"Then start there."

She tried, but he stopped her before she finished getting everyone back to town including the prisoner, the tiger thief involved in trying to steal Maizie.

"Whoa! Down there, gal. There's no one in the holding cell. What'd y'all do with this tiger thief? And where's the tiger?"

"She—uh, Maizie—got away from them and went back home."

He lowered his gaze. *"Them?* You ought to learn to tell a story better, gal. Now we got two thieves, no maybe three, missing. Lord have mercy. Can't I take half a day off without the town coming apart?"

"Sure doesn't look like it, does it?" She jumped up from the swing, grabbed both empty glasses, and went inside, him following mumbling under his breath. Sometimes that man was impossible.

Dal came in at the same time. She gave him one glowering look, folded her computer up, grabbed her backpack, and went to the door. "I'm going somewhere where I can concentrate and write a halfway decent story. You can handle this bunch." She stopped in the doorway. "Oh, and there's a school board meeting tonight I have to cover, so don't expect me to be your little cuddle bunny, cause I'll probably work half the night. And please tell Mac what you did with Tiger Thief. I myself would like to know."

Dal spread his hands as if to ask what he'd done, but she went out, letting the screen slam behind her. Just as she opened the door of the Jeep he hollered, "You got any Honey Buns?"

She didn't even bother to answer. Just muttered under her breath. "I'll honey your buns."

Now, a school board meeting in a town with only one school was not typical except unto itself. The board was made up of ten business owners and a few church pastors who tossed their names into a special election. Ten winners ran to fill the five slots open each election year. The entire town voted, and the winners served two years alternately so that only half the board changed each election year, which was every two years. Yeah, and if that sounded confusing, it was. Arguments arose when the results of the election were presented. A great lover of confrontation, Parker always covered that particular meeting, except with Loren lying dead in his barn, Jessie stepped up, even though she dreaded it. Disgraceful things were known to occur, which he enjoyed immensely. She would not.

Last election, the pastor of the Ever Faithful Free Will Church hit the winner in his slot over the head with his Bible and accused him of buying votes. The winner, who owned a slightly tacky clothing store and grew a good-sized marijuana patch outside town, made an off-color joke about the pastor's wife, and the two held an exciting wrestling match on the gymnasium floor where the meeting was held, with bets being placed. Things were not always that exciting, and she hoped for the best. Parker thrived on such antics, and everyone bought a paper that week just to read what he had to say in his editorial.

However tempted she was, she took the .38 out of her backpack and left it home.

Seating herself in a shadowy corner of the bleachers, Jessie took out her notepad. It would be much too noisy to use the recorder. The place filled to capacity and then some, everyone hoping for some sort of shenanigans. They'd never been disappointed on election year.

After a fervent prayer and the pledge, the noise of settling finally rattled to an end. The outgoing president of the board rose and announced the murder of an unknown woman which effectively killed any high-jinx during the reading of the winners of the five slots open on the board. It became impossible to quell the shouting of the crowd following the swearing-in of the new board members. Everyone had loud opinions and listened to no one else. One of the ladies from the Baptist Church, whom she didn't recognize, called the new president a horse's patootie to which he replied, "the word is ass, woman" and so it went. Finally, business was postponed until the next month. Hopefully Parker would return and write something wildly crazy about their shenanigans which she managed to jot down, more or less. Outside she clutched her stomach and laughed till she was sore.

What she would do was save the notes for Parker and dredge up biographies of each of the new board members and write them to include something humorous but non-slanderous about each of the family members. That would increase sales effectively to make up for the upheaval of this week's meeting. It wasn't as clever as Parker's op-ed could be, but she didn't give a flip considering what was going on in town the past few days.

Maybe four or five families and the newly elected board members remained when a storm hit with such fury someone announced in a loud voice that it was the rapture. Thunder cracked the skies wide open, and sheets of water swept back and forth across the school grounds. People ran every which way, and one man trotting past her proclaimed it was punishment for city council considering a permit for The Purple Raven, that blasted English pub.

Oh dear, that's all they needed. She was glad there were only a few nuts in Cedarton, but they could sure stir up trouble. And she would bet trouble was coming in spades.

CHAPTER 4

Dal took Parker home where he insisted on going to the barn, saying he needed to be with her a while longer. There the two men perched side by side on a hay-strewn bench a few stanchions away from where the body was found. Parker gave Dal what little information he knew about Loren. Even though he'd been seeing her for a short time, he admitted to not knowing much about her except that she was a fine woman. She'd moved to the area about six months earlier. Where from he didn't know.

"Where did she live? We need to investigate her belongings, find out more about her."

Parker gazed at him. "I don't know."

"You've never been to her place?"

His eyes got that brittle look again. "I only met her a while ago. I don't push women. What difference does that make? All I know, she's a pretty fine woman." His words grew terse, and anger tightened his features. What little he said brought a sad, distant expression, so he stared past Dal's shoulder toward the stall where they'd found Loren's body for a long moment before going on. "Or *was* a fine woman. You know, I like women of mystery or unusual careers, so I don't question them too much. My question is why can't I keep one?"

Dal ignored the rhetorical question. How odd. He fell for women a lot faster than most. "Ah, what sort of unusual career?"

He shook his head, hunched, and covered his face with a spread hand. "Didn't ask."

Enough was enough, and Dal didn't pursue it. Maybe later if it turned out to be important. The man was suffering and close to shock. Obviously he'd fallen hard for the dead woman. For now, he would concentrate on what they did know.

Parker had never been coy about admitting to his unusual life. One wife had been an actress, another a member of Cirque de Solei—a tiny little thing who tied herself up in ribbons high above the stage then rolled down through them. Another sang opera and traveled all over Europe. As for four, Dal couldn't remember. He thought Loren would've been number five. If it became important, he'd ask. No one knew how in the world Parker managed to meet such unusual ladies. There were strange guesses. Fudge was sure one was a trilaquist, in his words, "one of those folk who throw'd their voice all over the blamed place till you got no idea where to look for them."

Best to let Fudge's weird tales go over your head. Besides none of this brought him any closer to learning about Loren. Hard to solve the murder of someone with an unknown past.

"Her being a woman of mystery, I never found out what her career was." Parker's words brought Dal out of his reverie. The glint in his eyes might have been a memory rather than tears. Hard to tell.

If Dal wasn't so fond of this man, unusual as he was, he'd have risen and left him sitting there in the silence of the barn, wrapped in misery, and stalked off. His fondness outweighed the frustration of forcing information from him. Howie, one of the deputies, had been around a while after appearing one day out of the backwoods to show off his computer talents. He could sit down at a computer and uncover just about anything that existed in today's world. He could check her out and dig up her information in no time. No one could hide for long anymore. Howie had been hired for precisely that reason.

This poor man had had enough. "Parker, we're done for now. You look beat, why don't you go on up to the house, and I'll get back to work? I'll do everything I can to find out who did this. You need anything you just let me know. Okay? A couple of my deputies will bring your Rover home."

The unshed tears finally broke through, trailing down his face. He nodded, turned, and strode away from the barn, not once glancing toward the place where they'd found Loren's body.

Dal watched him for a moment. Damned shame something like this had to happen to someone so kind and generous. The cruel ways of the world sometimes made life too harsh. Dal certainly had his share of sadness. He went back to search for more clues.

Doc peered up from his work over the body, the light reflecting from his round-lensed glasses. "Young lady was rapped hard on the head and choked something fierce. Maybe with a length of leather of some sort. In a barn could be a belly latigo or a leather belt. She has on jeans, no belt. I'm not prepared to say which caused her demise, though. Happened round about midnight." His slow remark was enough to pronounce her death a homicide. Time would tell whether they'd call in the State Police or not. The body would go to Little Rock to the medical examiner. Final results could take weeks.

But all things going well, Dal'd have it figured out before that was necessary. He usually did. There was that one time when he found himself lying on the side of a mountain, half dead, and the killer still running loose after doing the pushing. But that was the only time he fell behind figuring out the killer, and he tried not to think of that. This one no doubt would be a doozy to solve too. Not knowing the victim or her background would slow things down a lot. He found some tack in the barn, but nothing Kathy could be sure was the right width to match the raw mark on her throat. Maybe when the swelling went down. She bagged the latigo found nearby.

Dal leaned close. Whoever did this had touched it. Again, that sweet fragrance.

Damn, he needed to find out where she lived. Without some idea of the motive, knowing opportunity and means would not be enough.

Grandfather warned him to beware the woman with the torn spirit. Was that how he put it, and what in hell could that mean? Ordinarily the old man would show up with answers to his silent wonderings. But nothing this night.

Time to call in Bloodhound Howie. Put him on the job. Dal would have more help with leg work as well as solving crimes from now on. They'd hired three more deputies. Hank Horton, immediately christened The Who, Eugene Bellamy known as Bell, and Neal Neilson, a skinny kid who could shimmy up a tree or climb a bluff quick as a mountain goat. Added to Howie, Colby, Dal, Tink, and Burt, this brought the total to eight which should have lightened the load, but the crime rate would soon climb exponentially. All because of that danged new highway that managed to haul one or two bad ones in every once in a while. Most of the crime was not murder. This one promised a bad year, he feared.

Mac's old-school attitude, "scoop up lawbreakers, toss 'em in jail, put 'em to work on county projects till their time was served, let 'em go," kept offenses under control pretty well. That was talking minor burglaries, arson, diamond thefts, and the like.

"Make good use of the free labor. Teach 'em to stay away from Grace County if they wanted to break the law." That was Mac's preaching to his deputies.

The crew from the jail had painted three iron bridges so far this past summer. One ole boy got bit by a rattler down by Wisdom Holler bridge. Lucky for him, they got him to Doc quick like and saved his fingers. By the time that bunch were sent on their way, word got out about the snake bite. Hopefully it kept the crime rate down a bit.

You could leave keys in your car on the square, not lock your house, park a bike anywhere, stuff like that, and nothing would happen. Soon he was afraid it would be too easy for someone to come along on the Interstate exit, park in the edge of the trees, and make their way into unlocked houses. Clean them out and be gone before you knew it. What a sad state of affairs but still not as bad as big city life. Some were seriously considering toll gates on each side of town to prevent such.

And like Mac said, "we can keep teaching 'em lessons they won't forget. It ain't exactly like a chain gang."

To Dal's amazement, life went on much as it had since his arrival a few years earlier. Cedarton remained a quiet little town with more good than bad. Maybe a tad more excitement, roads and bridges in much better shape, and a few more stRangers wandering about. One thing about being a lawman, there wasn't a shortage of anything to do.

Husbands beat wives, women ran off with lovers, etc. He sure hated it about Loren and poor Parker's loss, and he'd catch who did this, one way or another.

New people in town automatically became suspects, and he sure liked that long, tall Lone Ranger for this one, only because it would be... well, a doozy. And food for tons of jokes. Amazing how death could produce jokes. Folks who worked with dead bodies could tell you why real quick. It made dealing with death that much easier to handle.

Headlights swept across the pasture at his back just as Dal slid the small door to the barn open.

"Well, shit." Just as he was looking forward to some quiet meditation and sifting through the tiniest of clues. Oh well, he'd run them off. It was, after all, a crime scene.

A flashlight came his way, swinging and bobbing along ahead of whoever got out of the vehicle. They had to know he was here and that he was a deputy having parked right next to him.

"Don't come any closer, this is a crime scene." He tilted his light toward whoever it was. "Didn't you see the tape?"

"You that deputy I met today? The one who helped me out when I had a flat?"

"That's me. If you're that Ranger—in which case you'd know not to come out here. We're still working the scene."

"Thought you could use a hand."

"Thanks, but no thanks. This ain't Texas. I'll be busy here for an hour or two. If you want to talk to someone about the case, go on down to the square to the sheriff's office. Someone there will help you out. Or go to the Red Bird. Always good gossip about our small town's business there."

"I'd really like to talk to you about something might be related to this." The lanky lawman scratched up under his Stetson. "Least I think it is, but you know you never can tell."

"Looks like you'd know better than to hold anything back relating to a case. Perhaps you'd better come on into the office in the morning. Catch me there, and we can discuss this. I'll be in by eight or so, and I can decide if it has anything to do with this matter."

The Ranger just stood there, as if he hadn't heard a word Dal had said.

"Did you hear me?"

"Sure did."

"Well, then. I'm gonna have to ask you to leave now."

A low chuckle. "We're both lawmen, can't we just discuss this here? I have to be somewhere else in the morning, and it's pretty important."

Muttering under his breath, Dal closed the barn door and headed toward the flashlight. Maybe ten feet or so from it, a shot sounded, and the light went out.

"Goddammit." The Ranger ducked.

Dal cut his light. "You hit?"

"Nope. Got my light, though."

"Get down."

"That already occurred to me."

"You okay?"

"I appear to be. You people have one hell of a way of welcoming visitors. First someone shoots out my tire, now this. They keep it up, maybe they won't miss."

Interesting, that about his tire getting shot. Wonder if that was what he wanted to tell Dal. While the man blathered on, Dal worked his way to his side, said under his breath, "If I were being shot at, I'd stop talking. Stay low, be quiet, and let's work our way to my car. Whoever it is seems to be after you."

"You think?"

He led the Ranger to the far side of his car where they slid down to sit on the rain-soaked ground side by side. "Let's stay here, put the car between us and the shooter. Could be he's took off or he'd a tried again, is what I think. Where you parked?"

"Around front of the house."

They waited in the silence. Ranger pulled a stalk of grass, chewed on it a while. "Maybe you could call in the cavalry."

"Like this is a John Wayne movie? The walkie doesn't work out here. And I'm not gonna open the car door and give this idiot another target. Just be patient, he'll either give up or work his way around and pick us off, one at a time. Or make a run for your vehicle, and good luck with that."

"Ah, hell, good plan. Wouldn't hurt to return fire, but a'course that's entirely up to you. Believe I'll just light out and catch you another time. Sort of like you suggested."

Before Dal could stop him, the Ranger scuttled away, Soon the sound of a door closing. There wasn't another shot. He started the car and took off, tires throwing clods of grass and rocks.

"A few bullets and he skedaddles. First, he's clueless, then he high-tails it. I heard better about the Rangers. Course he might be the smarter of us two." Hell, here he was talking to himself.

From out of the dark floated a voice he knew well. *"Had you noticed, Grandson, that I am here with you? Thus a reason for your palaver. Or do you prefer talking to yourself?"*

Dal leaned against the side of his car. "You been hanging around white men too long. Palaver, is that a Cherokee word?"

"Who's taking shots at us?"

"Better question is why. Just what do you know?"

"That is not the way this works. I warn you in puzzling words, you have to figure it out. You have the word. She will find you. Take heed when she does."

Before Dal could reply, the world tilted just a bit, and a conversation replayed itself. Two men talking, standing in this very spot.

"It's the woman we want, not these assholes."

"Thought we could just clean up their mess, rather than horsing around."

"You're going to the house if you don't start making some sense."

He waited through the following silence, but there was no more from the ghostly visitors. Damn place had turned quiet as a tomb.

"Grandfather?"

Nothing there either. Stubborn old coot. Carefully he rose and made his way inside and turned on the barn lights.

He was in there for a long time, poking around in every nook and cranny. At last he headed for the department, several plastic bags marked and stuck in his pack. Stuff that didn't belong in a horse barn. A small comb, a package of Kleenex in a plastic container with a mirror, and to his senses added the fragrance of something sweet, matching that in the animal compound.

He drove slowly past *The Observer*. Jessie's car was still there, a single light burning inside. He went on by, made a quick stop to leave the murder clues in a locked safe at the sheriff's office, then drove on home, parked under the trees at his apartment over the garage of the Five B's Bed & Breakfast, and hurried up the steps. In spite of comforting Parker instead of nosing her way into the crime scene, Jessie'd be at the story half the night, and he needed to get some sleep. Things should be more clear in the morning.

Without turning on the light he went inside. Something hit him hard, everything flashed bright then went out.

Jessie slopped through a puddle at the doorway of the office, keyed the lock, and went inside. The rain had been heavy but brief, and she shook her hair free of its ponytail to let it dry. She had to write the story about the school board meeting first, then she'd delve into the murder. That would mean a lot of time on the computer running down information on the dead girl. A Coke and some sweating put the short article into draft mode for Parker. She knew better than to leave out the brawl—Parker would have a fit—so she wrote it in all its glory, quoted some fine verbiage, and left it in his computer, not sparing anyone involved. He'd play around with it. Would love it.

Or maybe coming up with his usual op-ed using the school board antics would help him feel a bit better.

With a second Coke in hand, she slid back into her chair to begin her search for Loren Jasper online. An hour later, she had her face and shouted *whoopee*. For a long while, she stared at the photograph on her computer screen. Yep, that was her. Loren Jasper. Turned out she was on Facebook, after all, just harder to find because of so many of the same names. Said here she was a cashier at a bank. Not hardly strange enough for Parker. Course we always expected people to tell the truth on Facebook. For all anyone knew, the woman could be a bank robber and that was as close as she could come to telling the truth.

She'd seen Parker with the woman a couple of times but hadn't mentioned it to Dal or Parker. He was so private, and it was no one's business.

Odd, she was usually nosier than that. What was coming over her? She expanded the photo and squinted to stare at the pretty face. So that was the woman Parker loved. Now a poor crumpled body in his barn, though she hadn't had a chance yet to see the crime scene or take a close look at the dead face. Not her favorite thing, and she could cover the story without doing so, she would go to the barn now that the body had been removed to get a feel for being there. Bodies were one thing she didn't do well. The ID came from Parker though, they'd do a formal one down in Little Rock.

Wait. This gal was from Dallas. Dal's hometown. Getting interesting. She clicked to get more information. Pictures and lots of them. People never took stuff down or updated it. She closed in on one picture of Loren and her best friend, someone who looked mighty familiar. Must be her imagination. She didn't know anyone in Dallas. Crap. She printed the photo of Loren and her friend. The two could be sisters, but they had a pretty average look, so that didn't mean much. She'd sure like to know what this woman was doing with Parker. From Dallas, the same as Dal. Coincidence? Could be.

What was Loren doing here getting close to Parker? Had she mentioned where she was from to him? And who had killed her? The biggest question was why? How long would it take Dal to find out? Why didn't he know already? Should she show this to him? Well of course she should. It was a connection that needed checking.

Damn, she'd rather be doing a story on Maizie. Yesterday was the second time that tiger had been loose since July opened the animal compound, and it didn't portend a good future for her or for her owner. Even though this time was not in any way the fault of either of them, something needed to be done before the worst happened. She put that possibility out of her mind without forming it well.

She tossed the information on Loren Jasper in her in-basket for the next morning when she'd find out if Dal had it or if she could stick it in his hand with a big ole grin. He might just poo poo her. Lots of people from Dallas. Howie probably would come up with more, he was so good at searching the Internet.

All she needed for her story was whatever the sheriff would release for this week plus her on-the-spot reporting. She would not keep this from him, for she'd learned a harsh lesson a long time ago about that kind of reporting and wanted nothing to do with it. Secrets and lies would only turn around and bite you. Ruin your life. Turned out some reporters wrote stuff that hurt others, and there was no point to it. Yellow journalism it was once called, now it was pretty much accepted.

Worn to a nubbin, she gathered her stuff, straightened the desk, and left the office. Stepping out into the black of night, with only the light around the nearby firehouse to show her the way, she bent over and locked the door.

"Good evening, ma'am." The voice scared a squeal from her lips, and she jumped, dropping the keys. Never had she understood women screaming when frightened, but her backbone literally felt like a snake had crawled up it. A wonder she didn't wet her pants.

"Sorry, so sorry. It's just me. James Jameson. We met the other day."

Fist doubled, she hammered on his shoulder. "Do that again, I swear I'll shoot you."

"I am truly sorry. However, are you in the habit of shooting anything that scares you? Cause I'll start wearing a bell around my neck if that's the case." He bent and picked up her keys, holding them out.

Still shaking, she opened the door of her Jeep and sank back against the seat. "What do you want?"

"I was strolling around town, taking in everything, and saw your Jeep. I remembered it from up in the woods and thought I'd ask you a few questions. You being a reporter and everything."

"I'm the one who asks questions. You answer them. Strolling around in the dark of night? Just how much can you see?"

"Okay. Let's see. A better story. I couldn't sleep and so decided to take a walk. Is that any better?"

"Not really. Tell me, where are you staying?"

"Ozarka Inn."

"Out on the Interstate Cedarton Exit?"

He nodded. "Uh-huh."

"And so you took a two-mile hike to come over here and stroll around?"

"Okay. Truth. I saw you go in here after we left the crime scene, so I waited for you cause I wanted to scare your keys out of your hand." He eyed her doubled fist. "No, really, I wanted to ask you some questions. Well, actually needed to ask them of your deputy person, but he won't talk to me right now."

"Deputy person meaning Dal Starr?"

"I reckon. Not very good at names."

"For instance?" She leaned her head back and took some deep breaths.

"I'm looking for this woman. She's been missing now for some time, and her family is concerned." He placed a 5x7 photo in her lap. "Got a flashlight? Mine got shot earlier."

"What'd you do, sneak up on it in the dark?"

"Funny. You folks have a strange sense of humor."

"I really hadn't noticed." She gazed at the picture, a woman half turned to look into the camera, her eyes and mouth reflecting unhappiness at being photographed. It could be Loren, but.... "Maybe it's just the light or lack of it. She sort of looks familiar, but it's not a very good likeness. Have you shown it to the sheriff?" She wasn't telling him, one way or the other, but it was the Loren on Facebook.

"Oh, no. She isn't wanted. She disappeared a few months ago, and her family is looking for her. I ran across this Dal person and tried to ask him, but he wasn't talking."

"Any chance that's when your light got shot."

He snapped his fingers. "That's what they call intuitive."

Jessie stuck her key in the ignition and started the Jeep. "When did Rangers take up working for missing persons?"

"Ah, well to tell the truth, we don't." He studied her for a minute. "A friend wanted me to check it out while I was here on vacation. Seems she intended to come over here into the Ozarks looking for someone, and they haven't seen her since. Afraid she might've got hurt."

She clutched the Jeep and shifted into reverse. "Go over there first thing in the morning, and I'm sure they'll take a report from you. Good luck."

"That right there is like reading minds. Exactly what your friend Dal told me. Y'all blamed good at keeping your thoughts close to your vest. Er, chest. Umm. Appreciate the help, and I apologize for scaring you, uh… what's your name again?"

"Jessie."

"Goodnight, Jessie."

"Goodnight, Ranger."

His laughter followed her down the road.

Before heading out toward her place, she drove around to the Five B's to see if Dal was awake. The place was dark, so she decided to look in on Parker in case he couldn't sleep and needed company. He was pretty depressed, and that worried her. He might not welcome her company, but she took the chance anyway.

Driving around the square, her lights caught a sign that read *"Open Soon."* An honest to goodness English pub. No official sign with a name on it yet. Purple Raven was everyone's guess from what they'd heard. Hmm, it was beginning to look like that bit of gossip was true. Be interesting to know more about it. Last month's city council meeting hadn't mentioned anything about a permit being approved for a pub serving beer. Wendy had attended and written the article for the newspaper. She'd have to ask her what she knew. It could have come up in the closed session, so no one would know about it yet. By the time it was voted in or out by the council, it would be too late for the general population to attend a meeting and disagree vocally.

Her thoughts faded away when she parked under the broad canopy of trees around Parker's house. The barn where the body was found stood a good hundred yards out back, surrounded by pasture hemmed in by white board fencing. Without a moon it was too dark to make out much of anything. Odd, the yard light was out. None inside either, so rather than waking him up she turned around and went home.

Brad, her little pit bull buddy, turned himself inside out he was so happy to see her. She loved on him, fed and watered, then let him outside for a run while she found something to eat in the fridge. There wasn't much in there. A limp stalk of celery, one dill pickle slice in a jar, a few things she couldn't identify and threw in the garbage, a package of cream cheese, and on the counter some crackers. Definitely time to go shopping.

Standing over the sink, staring out the window, she smeared cream cheese on crackers and ate till she was full. A glass of ice-cold water washed everything down, and she went off to bed promising herself a shower first thing in the morning, plus a trip to Walmart.

When she woke up it was to thunder and a steady rain. The storm front hadn't moved away after all. Hmm. Trip to get groceries, then home for the day. Head down, pushing the cart across the soggy Walmart parking lot, she ran broadside into a man in a long black coat. He staggered two or three steps backward into the side of a car, letting out a whoof.

"Hey, whoa, little lady. Wait a minute. Jessie? You got something against me or what?" He gathered his feet under him.

"Oh, shoot. I'm sorry." She helped the Ranger get his footing, holding onto his arm, hard corded with muscles.

"Strange you should use that expletive considering. You out to shoot me, or what?"

He gazed down at her out of eyes that looked like they brought the rainstorm. Blue or gray or silver, all combined, with a bit of lightning sparking them. Rain dripped off the brim of his hat, and his hair hung in a mass of curls along the nape of his neck

Good Lord, woman. Get a hold of yourself. You sound like the pages of a romance novel. With a grin bordering on laughter, she picked up a plastic bag he'd dropped. Handed it to him. She might've said his touch sent an electric charge through her, but that was probably the storm.

"I have no idea why you'd think I want to shoot you. Unless you might be stalking me." She studied his expression. This man knew way more about Loren than he was sharing. And he sure as heck was following her. So maybe let's just find out what the heck he wanted. "Sorry, I was daydreaming. We reporters often do crazy stuff like that. I was trying to figure out who killed poor Loren and why. Who she came here looking for. Maybe it was unrequited love. Someone she dropped, maybe for Parker?" She gazed into his eyes, trying to pick up on his hidden thoughts. The woman in the picture is Loren, she'd already seen her on Facebook.

"Could very well be. Lost love is right up there at the top of reasons to kill. Tell me, Miss Jessie, do you always try to solve the crimes you write stories about?"

She turned her face up into the rain. "Not always. Mostly to get under Dal's skin."

"Ah, a deliberately annoying woman."

"Tell me, what do you consider the most annoying thing a woman can do?"

"I give up. Just about anything?" His grin came and went.

"And what do your women think of that attitude?"

"My women? What makes you think I have 'women?' But you know what? I'd like to get out of this rain before we both drown. I'm on my way to see the sheriff, so guess I'd better get on over there. It was interesting discussing women with you."

"Oh, is that what we were talking about? See you around."

"Yep." He tipped his hat, tilting a sheet of water off the brim over his face.

She tried to hold back her laughter but couldn't.

He shook a finger at her. "Beware the next time you see me." He fitted the wet hat back onto his head and walked off.

She watched him for a ways. What the heck? All the way home she tried to figure out the Ranger's real reason for being here. She'd just drive by Dal's place and talk to him. He was not at the station, though he was on duty. Something must've come up. Odd she hadn't heard from him. Usually when he took a day off he got in touch. Wonder what was going on. Maybe she plumb wore him out the previous night.

Well, no, she doubted that. It had to be something else.

Running through the rain and up the steps, she knocked on his door. When he didn't answer, she turned the knob and stepped inside. His car sat where he always parked it. Two or three times she called his name while moving around through the rooms. The place was quiet except for the fridge running. Crap. Where was he?

Clothes piled on the floor from yesterday. Eerie. Way too eerie. A sign that he'd been here.

She pulled her phone out to call the sheriff's office. Howie answered.

"Is Dal there? Or Colby?"

"Nope, sorry. Colby, he's out on 23, some blamed fool went off the road into the creek, and they're having to get a wrecker out there to pull him out. No one was hurt, I don't reckon."

"Thanks, Howie. You're a fountain of information. Unfortunately, not what I need."

"Well, I'm plumb sorry about that, ma'am."

"I'm sure you are. Is Mac there?"

"Is this Miss Jessie?"

"Yes, it is."

"I thought I recognized your voice. No Mac, he ain't here neither. You might try their cells is all I know."

"By golly, that's a good idea."

"Thanks. You want to leave a message?"

"No, Howie, I'll leave it on their cells."

"Good idea, have a good one."

Mac needed to get that one some socializing education. She would've laughed if she wasn't so concerned about Dal. And she wouldn't even have been concerned about him had his car not been sitting in his drive.

She stared down at his clothes on the floor, then bent over to pick up the t-shirt. Something dark smeared over the back. Still a bit wet. She stepped over to the window to see better in the dim light.

Oh my God. Blood.

Knees giving out under her, she sat shakily on the edge of the bed. Tried to still her fingers to hit the right button on her phone and reach the sheriff's office. Howie picked up again.

"I need—let me speak… give me Mac, goddammit, right this minute."

"Is that you, Miss Jessie?"

"Mac now, or I'll shoot you dead next time I— "

"Contacting him now, ma'am. Hold on."

5
CHAPTER

Clutching Dal's bloody shirt, Jessie sat on the steps leading to his apartment till two patrol units raced into the drive and skidded to a stop, sending mud clods in all directions. Mac came out of one, Colby the other. Leaping to her feet, she held the shirt out to Mac and led him and Colby upstairs.

Betsy Baker stood on the porch, arms crossed over her breasts. Hollered. "I heard 'em, Sheriff, way into the night it was. Should'a called, but it happens a lot, night callers I mean. They left off, and I went back to sleep. So sorry. Is the sheriff okay?"

"Colby." Without replying to her, Mac threw the deputy's name over his shoulder and followed Jessie into Dal's apartment.

"A lot of blood, still wet." She stuck out the shirt, sobbed his name.

"Easy girl. Sit. Wait." Mac tossed the room quickly—in the closet, under the bed, threw back a wad of covers. "Check his clothes, girl. See what's missing. He didn't go out of here naked."

She hurried to do as he asked. It would only waste time to ask why.

All his uniforms there. Just three, that's all he had. A western shirt and dress slacks. So he was wearing jeans. Maybe a t-shirt. No, his blue flannel shirt was gone. He wasn't a clothes horse. His Cherokee leather outfit hung in the back. Stetson on the high shelf. Snakeskin boots, Doc Martins, and Adidas on the floor. Barefoot? No, he had those old slip-on sandals. Not here.

She followed him into the living room where he searched. Laptop? On the desk. Phone on the floor. He pulled out his own phone and put out an APB. Said "wearing?" and looked up at her.

"Jeans, blue flannel shirt, brown sandals." Jessie supplied the information quickly, and Mac repeated into the phone. "No vehicle yet. Hang on."

She burst into tears.

"Jessie, girl. Ask Colby. Now."

She dragged in a huge sigh and ran down to where the deputy was taking notes from Betsy. "Car?" She stammered out the word. He hollered loud enough for Mac to hear. "Pickup, she thinks. Too dark to tell color, but it has a taillight burned out."

Mac came barrel-assing down the steps, going almost too fast for an old man. He shouted into his phone. "I want this danged county shut down now, you hear me? Notify Staties. If they have to stop every blamed pickup with a burnt out taillight. Call all the deputies as well." He blew past Jessie muttering. "Be durned if anyone's gonna start this sort of shit in my county or my state. Could be whoever killed that poor little girl, and we're having none of it. Ay God, they won't get outta this state alive."

Jessie ran after him. "Mac. Mac!"

"Speak." He kept moving, and so did she.

"She was from Dallas, same as Dal. I saw her picture on Facebook. Do you think…?"

"A connection? Could very well be." He didn't take the time to ask her how she knew, just leaped in his unit, flipped on the siren and lights, and lit out. He went out of sight, and she climbed in her Jeep and took off, Colby right behind her.

Tears flowing to blur what lights were burning in town, she followed Mac.

She had to talk to Dal about the picture. Something nagged at her, but his bloody shirt drove it from her mind.

A couple more squad cars joined them, cutting in two directions off the square. Within ten minutes, the hills echoed the whine of sirens.

Still she couldn't let go a nagging feeling about the picture of the women. The only place she could think of to maybe get some answers was Parker's farm. Lights kept coming on all over town, illuminating the ashy, pink-tinged sky.

He waited on the porch, hands on his hips. When she slid to a stop, he ran to her through the wet grass. He had to already know about Dal cause he had a police radio at home as well as at the paper. Before she could get out, he jumped in the Jeep with her.

"Heard it. Let's get down to the office where we can keep up better than out here."

She stared at him for a moment. "Parker, I can't— What if…? His shirt looked like he'd cleaned up a bloody crime scene with it."

"Get over, I'll drive."

She scrambled across him and into the other seat, broke down when he grabbed the wheel. He drove in silence, let her cry it out, till by the time they were at *The Observer*, she was mad enough to stop crying and start cursing. Something she seldom did but was adept at when called upon.

Inside the office, he started a pot of coffee and turned on the police radio. She sat at her own desk, rolling her chair aimlessly round and round, not saying another word till he brought in two steaming cups. Then she shot the question at him. "Did you know that Loren was from Dallas?"

He stopped, mug halfway to his lips. Shook his head. "And what does that have to do with this?"

She only stared at him, gave him time to think before answering. "I need to show you something."

Stopping the twirling chair, she turned on her computer, opened Facebook, and typed in *"Loren Jasper."* One of those blank faces came up. Immediately, she opened the picture album and stopped on a photo of Loren and put her finger on one of the women with her.

"Dal's wife, Leanne. From Dallas, Texas. I'm sorry, but something's bad wrong here."

Parker let out a sharp gasp, and she glanced his way.

Definitely something bothering him, too. "What are you getting at?"

"I'm not sure. Just thought it an odd coincidence. Her and Dal and his dead wife. And now her dead, just like Leanne."

"That's what they are. Odd. Even so, what do you think it means?"

"He's been hurt and grabbed, she's been murdered. Same twenty-four hours. His wife died of an overdose, self-administered, before he came here. They knew each other. More odd coincidences?"

The police scanner staticked. *"In pursuit blue pickup burnt out tail-lights. Arkansas tag, mud covered. Pulled over ten miles north of Cedarton."* White noise interrupted while the deputy left his unit and walked toward the pickup. A few minutes later he was back. *"Couple only. Issued warning for taillights and tag. No wants, no warrants."*

Parker rose and paced the small room. "This could go on all night. Half the pickups in the county have at least one light burnt out. Damn, Jess. You are jumping to a huge conclusion here. I can't see the women up to something together."

She cupped her face in both palms. "I know, but it could be a connection, you know that. Not much goes on here, and it's possible. Parker, there was so much blood. What if he...?"

He moved to her side, put an arm around her. "You know how bloody some wounds are, Sweetie. Just don't make any assumptions. Mac will find him if he has to tear up the state."

"I'm sorry. I know you're hurting, too, and I know he'll find who killed your Loren. The entire episode just seems way too connected."

Parker rubbed his temples with thumb and fingers. "I know. They just have to be careful about it, that's all. Not head in the wrong direction. Target fixation. You know how that works."

Lightning brightened the sky, thunder rumbled, and rain slashed at the front windows of the office. The scanner blurted a shout. *"We've got him. Picked Dallas up on the side of highway 23. He's conscious, and we're taking him to the hospital."*

Jessie jumped to her feet. "Oh, thank God!. I'm going there. I'm going."

"Let me take you. You're liable to run in a ditch or worse." She didn't object, just raced out into the pouring rain and climbed in the passenger side of the Jeep. Jittered up and down, gasping for air. Parker got in and started the engine. Relief poured through her, and she settled down.

The local clinic was small but well equipped to handle most emergencies except trauma. Since they hadn't said for sure if they were going there or down to Harrison, she phoned Colby, who had made the call to learn that Dal was on his way to the clinic. In his words, "he took a good knock on the head, but he's conscious and making sense."

Slumped in the seat, she took more slow breaths, clasped both hands, and tried not to bail from the Jeep when Parker zoomed into the emergency parking, slammed on the brakes, and jumped out.

Without badges, they were held up till she screamed loud enough for the entire place to hear her. "I'm his wife, let me through."

Little lies usually worked. Since he was the only emergency patient at the time, without further questions, she was taken to the cubicle where he was being treated.

"You'll need to wait here just a few minutes, ma'am. Perhaps you could fill out some papers."

Parker shoved his way through. "I'll take care of the paperwork, she's too upset at the moment."

Mac took her arm. "He's safe, girl. Everyone's out chasing down these yahoos. We'll get 'em." He caught Parker's glance. "And the scum who killed your Loren, too. I won't quit till we do."

Through slitted eyes and past a roaring headache, the first thing that appeared floating in the haze was Jessie's worried face. He managed a grin, but it made everything hurt, so he quit, relaxed into her gentle embrace and lips that planted a feathery touch to one cheek. Her hands snugged around one of his. In his ears nothing but strange sounds and one of those flying dreams. Soaring, soaring, then blackness.

He stretched his body against hers. Lying on a beach. Strange because neither of them were beach lovers. What were they doing here? And where was here? Side by side in warm sand, ocean waves kissed the shore. Birds sailed overhead, yelling and diving into the water. The sky a deep blue reached into space. He held up a finger, touched... the face of an angel. She whispered words he didn't understand, but they eased his spirit.

"What are we doing here?" He ran a hand over her nude body.

She grinned. "I'm not sure, but I think I know." She patted his belly, then headed south toward another realm. Her fingers closed around him, his eyes flew open, and he sat up. Groaned.

"Oh, *fuck,* that hurts."

The young lady taking his blood pressure cleared her throat. "I'm sorry. You should lie down and not move around so much."

"Then tell her not to do that." He gestured toward Jessie who bugged her eyes in innocence but did what she asked and even that sent an aching desire through him.

Jessie's face appeared over him. "Hi, Sweetie. How do you feel?"

"Where you been? Last time I saw you we were on the beach." Even he couldn't understand the words, so he quit trying to talk, closed his eyes, and relaxed with her hand on the side of his face.

Like they said in the movies, time passed and... and what? It was dark outside, but a dim light burned in the room. Again he tried to carry on a conversation. Something was definitely wrong with his tongue or his hearing, one or the other. He could think the right words, but they didn't come out. Two or three somber looking people stood over him gazing down. He might be dead, and they were viewing him. That definitely hadn't been in his plans when he got out of bed this morning. This morning? No, it was another time.

"Jessie? Jessie, you here?" It took some work to get that out, but it sounded nearly normal.

Must've made sense, cause she appeared over him. Course, he could still be dead.

"You're going to be okay, Dal. I'll be here, talking to you. They want you to stay awake."

"Mmm, if all we do is talk, it'll be sort of boring. But I can get through it." It was, but he did.

Finally, they let him sleep, and so he did that for a while. Then, by God it was time to get up, get dressed, and go to work. Time was a wasting while he could be looking for Loren's killer. Parker came to see him, and he felt so bad for the man's loss. Hard to know what to say.

A bit later, Jessie and Parker came to take him home, but they told him he had to take it easy for a while. Jessie'd hang around to make sure he did.

"Guess those old boys clocked me a good one, huh?"

"Did you know them?" That was Jessie, no doubt working on an article for the paper. The victim appeared to be groggy but is expected to recover.

He still felt groggy. The ride home was a bit like floating on a cloud. But he tried to answer their questions.

"Three of them. Two of them wanted something. The other one didn't say a word, just drove. I think they got it, cause they threw me out, but I'm not sure. It's still foggy."

"You left the crime scene in my barn and went home. That's where they grabbed you. What did you have with you from the barn?" Parker asked.

Thinking didn't help. In fact, it made his head hurt. "I can't remember. It must've been something they wanted though. Hell, they stripped all my clothes off looking for it. Why else would they do that? Maybe to look at my gorgeous body?"

No one laughed.

Parker glared at him. "My question though is why didn't they take what they wanted and leave you there where they conked you at your place instead of tossing you in the ditch on Highway 23?"

"Who said I was missing? I mean someone must've realized I wasn't where I belonged."

They arrived at his apartment and helped him upstairs and onto the couch before the conversation resumed.

"So," Dal finally said, "they were smart enough to take me away to give themselves plenty of time to escape but dumb enough not to clean up the blood in my apartment, so Jessie figured out right away I was in trouble. They probably didn't think anyone would show up there till I didn't report in for my shift."

An upset Mac came by later to update them. They hadn't found the truck or the men. "Do you have any idea who they are? Did you hear any names?" He touched his temple. "Or that thing you do in your head?"

Dal ground his palms into his eyes. "No, but maybe when my brain clears up I will. Are we thinking these are the ole boys—wait, a woman—who killed Loren?"

"Heck if I know. Did you see or hear a woman? In that thing that you do? It'd be good to have a blasted guess at least." When Dal didn't reply Mac slapped his thighs and stood up. "Damned odd if they aren't involved, more confusing if they are. Whether or not, they need catching. Tomorrow's another day, and we'll get back at it hard. Maybe your memory will improve. Meanwhile roadblocks are set up with one lawman at each. Staties are helping out."

Jessie finished up a report on a school board meeting where Leon GRanger had picked up a notebook and smacked the coach over the head for not putting his kid in the last half of the game the previous Friday night, which caused the new deputy, Neal, to cuff him like a criminal whereby GRanger kicked the deputy in the shins. His hearing would be next Thursday.

On her way home, she spotted Dal's unit parked at the sheriff's station and pulled in. It was time they had a talk about Loren and the pictures that proved her connection to Leanne. She wasn't looking forward to the conversation, but, oh, well. He was kicked back at his desk, a fistful of papers in one hand, a Pepsi in the other. Looking beautiful, as always. The bruise on his forehead only added to the attraction.

Seeing her, he rolled the chair forward. "Jess, thank goodness. About thought everyone was dead but me and Tink. Let's go out and take a walk. Sitting inside all the time is not much fun."

She kissed him on the cheek and pulled over a chair. "In just a minute. I need to talk to you about something first."

"What? You can't walk and talk same time?"

"It's about Loren Jasper, and I only know one way to say this, but, well, she was a friend of Leanne's."

His face paled. "I don't... what are you saying? Jess, goddammit, what's going on? How do you know this? And why are you bringing it up now?"

"Because someone killed Loren, and she was here for a reason, and I didn't want you to find out from someone else that her and Leanne were friends on Facebook."

He frowned and studied his hands for a minute. "And so you think…
what? And why? Leanne's been gone now five years, six is more like it.
Tell me how you found out they were friends."

She moved beside him, brought up Facebook on his computer, then
Loren's pages and picture albums. Pointed at one of the photos with both
women, arms locked, smiles on their faces.

Not remembering he'd already seen it while he was half-out, he
stared, said nothing. Tears filled his eyes, and he touched a finger to her
smiling face. "That's how she looked before the drugs."

Jessie laid a hand on his shoulder. "Sweetie. There must be a reason
for Loren to be here. It's not like this is a popular place to visit or move
to. From Dallas? Maybe, but Loren is murdered, someone knocks you
in the head and supposedly takes something from her murder scene.
I'm scared for you and Parker, too. Have you been able to remember
what they took?"

"Let's check the evidence locker. I have no memory of what I did
with it when I left the barn. Put it in the trunk? I don't think I'd do that.
It should be here." He looked away, sniffed, and wiped his face. "So long
ago, you'd think I could handle it." He stopped. "If I did remember, it
would be something I'd need to share with Mac, not your newspaper."

"Whoa. Touchy. Well, you check it out. Won't hurt."

"Yeah, well. I'm not exactly in a terrific mood." She was right. Damn
if he wanted to admit it, but he was right too. He couldn't share the
evidence with her.

"Can't say as I blame you. I'll just be on my way and let you figure
this out without interruptions." She touched his head, the dark hair like
silk. "I'm so sorry, Dal. So sorry."

Studying him for a moment, she tried to reason what was happening. What if he couldn't handle the reason Loren came here or why she was killed? He just might light out for high timber again. It had to all be connected. Somehow. And he was already unhappy.

He pulled her hand down to his lips and kissed it. "Me, too—sorry I mean. Didn't mean to be a grouch. I care a lot for you, Jessie, you know that, don't you?"

She staggered, froze. Must be the concussion. Oh, sometimes before, in a joking way, just after a heated climax he might declare his feelings in a muted way, but there he sat looking into her eyes, sincere as all get out, saying what she'd feared she'd never hear. And his dead wife staring out at them from the photo on Facebook.

He wrapped his arms around her waist and held her tight till someone came stomping into the office humming under his breath. They broke apart. Tink's husband, deputy Burt Sample, rustled around in his desk acting as if he didn't see them, then joined them.

"Tink's taking a second shift in the field later tonight. Hope your head's better, Dal."

"Thanks, I'm getting out of this chair real soon and back to work. Bout set here long as I can." He stood. "Want to go with me to the evidence locker, make sure I don't goof up? I may have put something in there before they conked me nutty. I need a witness."

Burt laughed. "Sure thing. I get that."

Jess put her hands on her waist, stared at the two of them. "I'm off today, maybe I'll go scrub the kitchen floor or something."

The two men left to check the evidence locker. Jessie wandered out to Tink's desk, not really in the mood to scrub floors. They talked for a little while about the job, then Burt and Dal returned. She was dying to ask if they'd recovered the evidence from the barn but didn't. Dal wasn't in a good mood, and she didn't want to make it worse. Howie showed up to replace Tink, and she and Burt left to go home together.

Dal rose, plucked his hat off the top of a shelf. "I've had all this I can take. Didn't mean to snap at you. Going back out and find those scumbags." He gave Jessie a quick kiss and left.

"Be careful, Sweetie," she called before the door closed behind him.

Mind wandering from one occurrence to another, she played with a pen lying on Tink's desk. So much didn't make sense, especially the whys. It was still her day off, and she paused at Howie's desk for a minute. "Has anyone found out where Loren was living?"

Howie lifted a gaze, looking a bit puzzled.

"I take that for a no." Might be a good idea to check with someone more in the loop. She pulled out her cell phone and called Mac. Asked him the same question, and he was quiet for a moment.

When he did speak, he sounded a bit embarrassed. "Been so busy looking for the perps, no idea where she lived. Figured Parker knew, and we'd get to it. Everyone's after these yahoos. Wait. Jessie. Git on back to the paper and don't be investigating this. It's our job. Jessie?" His voice reached out even as she clicked off.

On her way to the Jeep, she called Parker. He sounded sleepy when he answered. "Sorry to bother you, didn't I hear you say you didn't know where Loren lived?"

"Yes, you did."

"When you went somewhere together where did you meet?"

"What are you up to?"

"Never mind. Where'd you meet?"

"At the park."

"And how do you think she got there? Walked? Bike? Car?"

"I never thought of it."

"Well, Parker, if you took her back late at night didn't you worry about her?"

He was silent a long time. Finally, *"Well, Miss Nosy, if you must know, she always spent the night with me and didn't go home till the next day. Or maybe even the next. Satisfied?"* He hung up, and she stared out the car window for a while. He must've half broke his finger on that one.

Practically living with him. Oh, Parker, I'm so sorry. We were friends, and I didn't know.

So starting with the park. Stuff within walking distance. Pretty day for a stroll. A few apartments carved out of older houses, then on the south side a few new ones. It took the rest of the day for her to knock on doors, ask her questions, then go on to the next. When she finished, there were four where no one was home. She wrote down those addresses for further investigation and headed for home.

A brisk wind stirred the carpet of colored leaves and cooled Dal's brow. A deep breath, and he felt better. Easier to ignore the persistent headache and ride with the windows down. He'd made some rounds of the roadblocks, just to be out and about. He could've used the radio, but he'd missed the usual morning jawing with the men and needed to get up to date on the case. Something might pop up. But it hadn't, and with the headache continuing, he took off for Jessie's. She could take care of it in short order.

Her Jeep sat under the maple tree, and when he slammed the car door, she hollered at him from the deck.

"Grab some lemonade from the fridge and come on back. It's too pretty to stay inside, and you're forgiven." Her hair was loose, the wind twisting it so the sunlight turned it in flashes of gold. His groin tightened. He didn't want a lemonade, he wanted her in his arms in bed. He chuckled. Chances were, she'd want to do it on the deck or in the yard or under a tree in the woods. For Jessie, making love was meant to be exciting, certainly not ordinary. But he stopped at the fridge, poured himself a tall glass and headed for the deck and her, ready to take her any way he could get her.

She rose from the chaise lounge, bare back moist and brown in the sunlight. Holy shit. She wore next to nothing. She turned toward him, shade from a nearby tree dappling her naked breasts and tanned skin.

"I thought you'd never come."

He barely found a place for his drink before she unbuttoned his shirt, fingers going to his belt and zipper. Hand tapping the swelling in his pants, she made sounds down in her throat. Purring? Maybe. Tap tap, like petting on the rise in his pants. Oh, God. He ached for her to move on, but she kept that up till he thought he might bust right out of his britches. Round and round the gentle touching with the flat of her palm. He reached for something, anything to touch or rub or even just hang on. A breast, the flat of her warm tummy. She kept it all out of reach, teasing, dodging away, laughing. Lowered a cheek against the denim over the sensitive tip of his penis bucking to get out, open mouth blowing through the fabric, giving a blow job a new name. He needed to, had to, must get inside her. Crawl up between her legs and snuggle there. But she was having none of it. In a flirtatious mood. She liked him so hot he could hardly stay put. And knew how to get him there.

Moans escaped his throat, grew frantic. He fought to get out of his pants, to have her skin to skin. Not yet. She would, and that's what excited him. Thinking of when she did want it. Her all but naked, him dressed.

"Lay still, Sweetie." She put her mouth around his clothed penis again, nibbled. Blew through the fabric.

Jesus, how good that felt. "I need... I want...."

"Not yet, my love. I know exactly what you need and want. Just one minute more."

He was so hard, and huge, and throbbing he feared he might rip a hole in the denim. Could that happen? What would it be like to just bust free with sheer and fantastical ecstasy? Something like that would have to happen and soon if only to release the pressure.

"Jessie, could we just maybe tuck it inside. Sort of quick like?" He chuckled. "Tuck and fuck before something happens?"

She giggled at his words. "What do you reckon will happen?" She opened her mouth and nibbled some more through the cloth.

"Holy night and day."

"Just a second, I'm trying an experiment. Hang in there, it won't run away."

"Well, your experiment is about to explode like a chemical mixture gone bad. Come on, babe."

"Does it still feel good?"

"Not sure. Ah, crap. Hard to tell, but I'm putting it in whether you're ready or not. You gotta be ready."

She fell down across him laughing. "I love you, Dal, and now I know you love me."

"Because of this?" He struggled to get out of his pants, but his hard-on kept him trapped and her laughing.

"Yes, you put up with my nonsense." She skinned him free of both pants and jockey shorts, hands rubbing him all over so chill bumps broke out. "Hurry, hurry."

"Now she wants to hurry."

At last bare, he leaped astraddle, plunged all the way, so deep he feared getting stuck in there. The world tilted, heaved, caught fire, and he found the source of his bliss.

"There you go, my sweet, sweet man. Oh, umm, what a ride, does that ever feel good. Got us hot, hot, hotter. Come on, let's get moving. It's friction that builds fires."

"Good God, woman, I think we're gonna catch the deck on fire."

"Explore, my darling. Take your time."

"I would but, oooh too late. Shit." He rocked and rolled with each moan, and she matched them till they lay in a tangle of limbs, gasping and trying for one more and then one more, just for good measure.

His secret fear? Failing Jessie like he failed Leanne, but Jessie was stronger. Still the guilt that he'd let Leanne kill herself with drugs would not completely go away. He could never forgive himself for that. It amazed him that Jessie could. Why did he always think of that failure at a time like this? He was a damned fool. He shoved it away, settled against her. How good it felt, lying with her in the sunlight, her loving him in a way he would never quite understand.

It was a long time before either of them moved from the quilt or got dressed. Over coffee later, they discussed the puzzling case that had everyone befuddled.

"You haven't had any response to your story asking for information?"

She turned to face him to answer his question. "No, not even the ones who usually respond just to get their name in the paper."

"What about the Lone Ranger? What's he up to?"

"Funny about that. He disappeared. No one knows what happened to him. Mac thinks he's probably involved in the killing, or else why would he just up and go?"

"I've tried and tried to picture him as one of those. I know I don't remember much, but I don't think they were that tall. I keep thinking how small they were. Ah, well, probably just a concussive dream." He ran a finger along her bare thigh. "I guess Maizie and July are back to normal though. Does anyone know why those morons tried to catnap her?"

"Nope, and Parker gave me a full page three spot for the story. But listen to this. The other forty percent of the page was an ad for The Quinton Furniture Company. A special sale of their leather chairs and couches."

"Oh, hell, he didn't? Right there with Maizie's story when everyone is pretty sure she was taken for her beautiful hide. Your boss has a warped sense of humor.

"If you ask me, the Ranger was just having fun with us." Dal eyed her. "You know, over here on vacation and having it on with us dumb Arkies? Texans like to mess with us. Bad enough when it comes to football, but he ought to stay home unless he wants some real trouble."

"Well, I know you'd have come up with this if you were back to normal, but I think I know a way to find where Loren was living, and that might give us more clues to what she was up to."

"Oh, yeah. How?"

She told him about Parker always picking Loren up at the park and how she thought they might find her house by grid searching. If the sheriff had already put Howie onto the search using the Internet, no one had told her, but they wouldn't, so she kept her mouth shut. "I've already checked out a lot of places, but we can go on over tomorrow and spread out some more, if you feel up to it."

He grinned. "Great idea. If I recover from this afternoon, we can do just that."

"Meanwhile, there's always tonight. You don't have to go home, do you?" She gazed up at him.

He took her in his arms. "I think I can manage another night with you if you go easy on me. That is if you've got Honey Buns for breakfast."

"Oh, I do, and I'll try to be easy, I surely will."

6
CHAPTER

Jessie lay in bed listening to every move Dal made. First water running for a pot of coffee, then rattling around for Honey Buns he tossed on the table. While the coffee made, he padded barefoot into the bathroom to shower. It was all she could do to remain where she was and not sneak in there, pull back the curtain, reach through the steam, and touch him, laugh when he jumped and took her in his arms. Before it got out of hand she backed away, but he stood naked in front of the mirror, silken ebony hair over one cheek, skin a dark golden honey hue. From behind, she wrapped her arms around him, tucked herself up against his butt. Stop this instant.

He'd finally hinted that he loved her, but did he mean it? Or had it just been an emotional release of the moment? Men had a tendency to love whoever made them happy in bed, but it went away as time passed.

They'd been lovers almost six years. The first two battling over turf that led to hot sex in forbidden places and noisy discussions at crime scenes. Stuff they both enjoyed. Then while Dal disappeared for a year with no one knowing where he was, she took part in a passing fancy with Parker. And Dal never bothered to explain where he'd been or why, just acted like nothing different had happened. But then, so had she. No more was ever said about it. Their personal lives returned to normal, if one could call their style of life with each other "normal." If that was good or bad remained to be seen.

The shower shut off. Out the window, morning caressed the treetops with its golden light and chased away the mist hanging over the damp ground. The bathroom door opened, and she waited another few moments for him to dress and return to the kitchen. She didn't trust her emotions to be with him at the moment. So much was changing for them. Time to think about it some more. Soon, very soon, he would declare his feelings for good. She could feel the change coming like you can feel the vibration of an approaching train with an ear to the tracks.

Cups rattled in the kitchen, and she gathered her clothes and went into the steamy bathroom that smelled of his cologne. Like the deep woods on a spring morning. While she dried her hair, the front door closed, and Brad barked. The house was empty when she went through. A note lay on the table. *Late for work. See you later? D*

She wadded it up and tossed it toward the trash. Still no *love U* signature. He would continue to be a tough one to pin down. But she could wait. He was worth it.

In the Jeep, Brad riding shotgun and her pack on the floor, she headed for city park. It was a beautiful day to scout out a hidden cabin. Three hours later, sweaty and tired and not a clue as to any place worth living in, just a couple of dilapidated shacks and an empty barn, sagging so precariously it could collapse at any moment, she sat on a fallen tree and shared the last of her water with the panting pit bull.

Crap. She headed back to the Jeep, took the county map from the glove compartment, and marked off the areas she had searched. Time to get serious. Keying the ignition, she drove to Parker's, found him sitting in the barn staring at the spot where Loren's body had been found.

A hand on his shoulder, she lowered herself beside him. "You okay?"

Startled, he swung around, rubbed under his eyes. Drying tears no doubt. "Not really, I mean, goddamn it, why her? She was sweet and thoughtful, and we were having a great time together."

Best not to say anything, that would only upset him further, so she lay her cheek on his back. After a while, he sighed and stirred. "Want some lunch?"

"Sure. Whatcha got?"

"Nothing. Let's go to Grandma's on the square. Not in the mood for the gossip at the Red Bird."

"Me neither. I'll need to drop Brad home. Want to meet me there or go with me?"

"I'll just ride with you. Where you been today?"

She waited to fill him in till they loaded up with an unhappy Brad in the back seat. "I had an idea how to find where Loren lived. There's a map marked with where I searched already in the glove compartment. If we can find her cabin, we might discover clues as to what she was doing here."

He took it out, unfolded it on his knees. "Best to leave that to Mac and his boys. Searching those woods can be mighty dangerous." He ran a finger over her marks. "Wait, this isn't right." Flipping the map over, he pointed. "You're looking at the new city park. I was talking about where the old park was. On the other side of town."

She leaned over him. "You mean I spent the entire morning in the wrong park? When did they build the new one?"

"Goodness, way before you came back. You need to go out 23. Here, see." Refolding the map, he handed it to her. "Let's go get lunch, then go out that way. Where is Mac?"

She shook her head without saying anything. How could she explain that the deputies were involved in finding who had grabbed Dal? It would upset him to know they weren't looking for Loren's killer yet. They left Brad at her place and headed for town.

"If we can go horseback, it'll be easier. It'll be a long walk. Did you ever see a car parked where you met? If she came in by car, we've got a lot more area to cover but accessible by a road. If you think of anything, that would help. There must be reasons for her living like that, for her coming here. Try to remember anything she might have said or asked about."

"I can't think of a thing. No car that I noticed. I did see her looking around once in a while like she might be worried about something. But I thought it was just the actions of a woman alone. What we need first is to look at Google Earth for buildings in that area. Though they're easily hidden in the wilderness."

She smacked her forehead. "Well, I'm really on the ball. Never thought of that. I'm so old fashioned. Okay, Google Earth first. Wait, you said "we." You want to go along, help me?"

"Does Mac know you're doing this?"

She pulled into parking in front of Grandma's and shut off the key. "Uh, well, no, but they think whoever grabbed Dal had a hand in Loren's murder. I think finding where she lived will give us more clues. Both will help, don't you think?"

Parker frowned and shook his head. "No idea, but if we find the cabin, we let Mac know. We're not messing up what might be part of a crime scene."

She stared at him a minute. "But I can take pictures first. Mac always lets me do that, anyway. I save them a lot of work, and I'm careful."

"Jessie, we're going to do this right. Let Mac know what we're doing. He may want to send a deputy with us."

Crap. She shouldn't have told Parker, should've just gone on her way. But if she had, she'd have spent wasted time looking in the wrong place. If they got a deputy, they'd piss ass around for hours, even days. Shaking her head, she climbed out of the Jeep and followed him into Grandma's. Seated at their table, she excused herself to go to the bathroom, slipped down the hallway, and out the back door. Parker was sitting face to the wall. She crawled into the Jeep, released the brake, and let it roll out into the street before starting it. She'd go to his ranch, take a quick look at Google, then saddle up and be ready to go before he realized what was going on. Then he'd have to get a ride home, and she'd be gone. By nightfall, if she was lucky, she'd contact Mac with the location of Loren's cabin.

Parker was going to be ultimate pissed at her for sneaking off, but if she found what she hoped to find, he'd get over it.

There wasn't much on Google Earth. Most of the area had been logged a few years back, but then some regrowth took over. A few places looked promising.

Time to go. Out back of the barn, she tossed some oats in a bucket and headed across the pasture to find her favorite gelding. Star Brite perked his ears when she shook the bucket, then tossed his beautiful red-streaked mane and trotted to her. While he slurped up the oats, she swung the saddle onto his back, tightened the latigo around his belly, and tied down her pack. He crooked his neck to gaze at her with soft brown eyes, and she spoke his name, rubbed his nose, and slid the bit between his teeth, worked the leathers of the bridle over his ears and climbed on.

He liked her, and he loved to run, so she let him go flat out across the pasture till they reached the back gate. Once through and in the woods, Star Brite stepped delicately over twigs, branches, and rocks. He was a perfect mount for the wilderness.

She began the search where the logging road terminated and an old trail headed through some thick, virgin timber. The eastern section dropped sharply into deep canyons where not even a fool would have a cabin. Every mile or so she checked the map. If she didn't find anything by sundown, she'd head back so as not to be caught out after dark.

Already thirsty on the unusually warm fall day, she reached into her pack for the bottle of water, pulled it out. Held it in front of disbelieving eyes. Now she remembered her and Brad drinking the last of it right before she headed for Parker's this morning. She'd forgotten to refill it.

Well, she wasn't going back. It was a few hours before dark, and by then she'd be in bed waiting for Dal. There'd be a spring when she needed a drink. They were abundant in the Ozarks, some walled up for those who wanted to haul the crystal clear water home. Or at least she hoped so.

Dal was at his desk when Parker raced into the sheriff's office. "He here yet? You seen Jessie?"

"He who? And no." Dal was pretty sure he knew what this was about. Jessie couldn't stay out of trouble for even one day, especially with her boss. Still he let Parker get it out of his system.

"Mac. I'm waiting for Mac."

Well, okay. He'd keep his mouth shut for now, wait for the sheriff. Find out what Jessie'd been up to in good time.

In the office, Parker paced back and forth, clearly upset and obviously eager for Mac or someone to show up. "I had Duggan bring the sheriff up to date about that girl's current craziness." He muttered something more at the deputy behind the desk.

Dal was tired of waiting for someone to tell him what was going on. "Parker, where's Jessie?"

"Hell if I know. She snuck away from me and took off to search for Loren's cabin. Determined, that woman is. She'll be the death of all of us yet. Her and her rampages always get her in trouble, yet she never learns, just goes out on her wild escapades and does it all over again. Then expects to come through unscathed. And what about the time she got shot, or when she went in that cave after a lunatic and he threw a skull at her, for God's sake? I could go on, I tell you, I could. And I'd fire her if she didn't write such exciting stories." He paced, another arm-flinging round before settling down.

Where does he think she gets those stories? Dal kept his thoughts to himself. "Wherever she is, I'm sure she'll be okay." She *did* get lost easy, though.

Mac slammed his way through the door, long strides carrying him to Parker's side. "Exactly what is she up to this time?" Without waiting for an answer, he headed for the break room. "Come on, we might as well have some of this godawful coffee while we figger this out."

Curiosity piqued, Dal scuffed along behind them. "Where is she?"

Parker threw his arms wide. "Who knows? Took one of my horses and lit out on some kind of a wild hunt for Loren's cabin."

"Well, hell. How does she know where to look?"

Parker gave him a shamed look. "I'm afraid I told her. Showed her on the map just where Loren used to meet me."

Howie appeared in the doorway interrupting the conversation. "Sheriff, a guy on the phone says he found that cabin he heard we been looking for. Fudge passed it around at the Red Bird. Ain't nothin' goes on in this town Fudge don't know about. Reckon that gal had to have a place to live, and it sure wouldn't be a tent. Well, anyways this guy run across this cabin yesterday, but he knew where it was at, something about his grandpa, just forgot about it."

Mac stomped a foot. "Get to the point, boy fore I grow white-headed."

Howie nodded. "Uh-huh. Anyway, he claims he's run across it while he was out hunting an ivory billed woodpecker. What's an ivory billed woodpecker anyway?"

"Ah, dang it, boy. How does he know it's hers?"

"What? The woodpecker? Don't know. Want me to ask him?"

"Shitfire." Mac ran his fingers through already wild hair. "Hell, no. Put him on my phone."

"Okay, hang on just a minute." Howie disappeared, and Dal went to talk to Parker.

"So what in the world is going on? This place sounds like a comedy routine from Abbott and Costello. Isn't it a hanging offense to steal someone's horse?"

Parker shook his head at Dal. "I'm thinking seriously about it."

"I don't think we have much to worry about. You know how she always manages to get herself out of any scrapes. I'd just bet she'll come riding in along about dark, a grin on her face and a long story to tell about how she can take us right to that cabin. Then we'll wander around for a month and won't find it." Dal studied Parker's weary features. "You got that map. The one you showed her?"

Parker nodded and pulled it from his pocket.

Dal took it. "Why don't you go on home and get some rest? I'll make sure we keep you updated on all that's going on."

How he wished he didn't have to be concerned about Jessie's absence. But it was important to keep Parker calmed down by making light of it. There were three men loose who'd bonked him on the head. No doubt the same ones who'd tried to steal Maizie so they could skin her and sell her striped coat. Hell, he wouldn't even want to be out there alone today himself.

Mac returned, putting his phone in his pocket. He gestured at Dal. "Everyone else is out looking for them yahoos, you can come with me."

He didn't say where, and Dal didn't ask. Didn't sound like they were going looking for them yahoos. He climbed in the sheriff's SUV and buckled the seat belt. Mac wasn't known for careful driving. He fulfilled that reputation by taking the corners of the square sliding sideways, headed up Sloan Street, and skidded to a stop at the Red Bird. A thin, gangly man wearing an ear-flap hat that emphasized his bony nose, scurried out, waited while Mac unlocked the back door, and hopped in. He put his face against the wire cage making throat clearing noises but said nothing.

"Where to?" Mac glared at the rearview mirror.

The man jumped. Pointed off to their left. "Wanta take Sloan out to 23, then at where the old park used to be, it's all growed up now, head west on a logging road into the deep woods. I'll show you." The tires squealed, and off they went.

"You might want to slow down, cause I have to hunt for the turn."

The radio blared. *"Unit Nine, in pursuit, red and sorta orange pickup, gotta cage in the bed. No tags. He's turning off on County 10. Oh, shit—he slammed into that big boulder alongside there. Lost the cage. It landed in the top of that big tree a ways down the road. He's lost it. We got ourselves a TA."* A minute or so later. *"Two in custody. NHI."*

"Sounds like we might have our tiger nappers. That could well be those old boys that bonked you, Dal. Not to mention Missus Loren's killer."

"And don't forget, Jessie's loose, too. By the way, did you ever figure out that Ranger fella? What he was up to, and why he suddenly disappeared?"

Before Mac could answer, Flap Ear piped up. "Hey, what's NHI mean?" Their passenger sure was curious.

Mac laughed, and so did Dal. "No humans involved." Both spoke over one another.

"Huh?"

They ignored him.

"I'm not sure that Ranger fella was important." Mac slowed.

The guy in the back seat hollered, "Turn right up yonder. Left, I mean."

"Sure you know where you're at?"

"I meant you was right, not *turn* right. You want to go left."

Mac went to the left. "This is more or less west. Are we still okay?"

"Yep. It's a ways now, follow this old road deep into the woods nearly plumb through old park. We'll be going to the waterfall where they once had picnics and skinny dipped in the swimming hole when this was a nice park. Always wondered why they built that little park near town and let this one go. My old maid aunt lived there, and years ago, she give the land to the city for a park when she died. We'll run out of road right quick then, and it'll mean walking. The cabin is ahead and to the right of town, then down. There's a deep gully divides old park and new. There's the waterfall."

Mac glanced at Dal, drove through mud-filled potholes that covered the windshield. He jammed on the brakes.

"You'll have to park here." Flap Ear hammered on the seat back.

They crawled out of the SUV and stood on the rim of a deep gulley. At its mouth, a stream tumbled noisily over the edge, rainbow colors dancing above the waterfall. Their leader took off around some large boulders to a path that led to the bottom of the gulley. A mist from the falls wet their skin and clothing while they worked carefully down the muddy descent. Wild pink roses clung to the banks, glistening with tear drops. If it were not for the rocky footholds, it would have been too slippery to manage.

Mac stared at the man in amazement. "I've been all over this country but never saw this."

They headed into what looked like a tropical rain forest. A place mighty easy to get lost in.

Their leader took up his yakking. "Be good to take care here. Back in 1998, Little Eileen Kimble fell down this path and into the swimming hole. Knocked her out, and she drowned."

Dal glanced at Mac. "Might be why they shut down the old park, you reckon?"

"Heck yes, I do remember that. Her momma tried to kill the woman who gave the property, and they finally shut down the park. Said she would get back at her one day." I wasn't sheriff here then, was over to Fayetteville taking a law course at the University of Arkansas."

"That was my aunt." Once in the bottom, Flap Ear pointed to a trail leading up to thick woods then along the side of the mountain. "It's an old logging road goes around the new park and up the mountain. My granddaddy owned this property at one time, and when it come up about that poor little gal maybe living in the woods, it jest occurred to me about the old place. I do hope you got good walking shoes. It's a fur piece. Driving in is easier from off to the other side. But I can take you, and you ain't never seen nothing more beautiful. Hardly anyone ever comes back in here. Claim it's haunted. With the ghost of that little girl. She was related to that sheriff somehow. You know the one what run off when y'all was chasin' them kid stealers?"

Confused by the strange tale Flap Ear told, Dal refrained from asking why they hadn't come through the easy way in the first place. No doubt the way Loren would've come. He wasn't in the mood for another geography lesson. Under the waterfall they came out on the other side to see a small cabin in a clearing. It was a good thing too, cause Dal was fixing to go back.

Even though Star Brite was good picking his way through wilderness, Jessie searched for the first evident trail, for if Loren walked out every time, chances are she'd take a beaten path. Puzzling why the woman was so intent on hiding her residence. Usually criminals wanted by the law were the only ones to be so careful. And there was nothing on the records to show she was a criminal.

Up ahead, grass and weeds were beaten down going off the road. Narrow but well used, the path followed the easiest route through the woods. Keeping the gelding to a slow walk she scanned the trees on either side, being careful to look for recent prints cutting off the main trail. The slope slowly changed and flattened, a good place for a house, but there wasn't one. Instead there were signs of logging here in the past.

Piles of sawdust indicated an old sawmill had been used to cut timber into planks right here, which meant there had to be a way to haul timber out. If the road hadn't deteriorated too badly a car could use it.

She dug out her camera and remaining on horseback moved along taking photos that included close-ups of an occasional tire track in patches of mud. The road curved sharply and started down. After a few minutes Star Brite nickered, tossed his head, and drew up. A draw carrying water cut the trail, and the car tracks petered out under some trees. Whoever was driving didn't want to chance getting through the water-filled draw. Clearly animals leaped the narrow gulley as the slope continued to go downhill. There were signs of their hoof prints in the dirt.

Reining in the gelding, she dismounted and led the horse up a ways where it looked like they could cross, and sure enough they could. In fact, she'd found the way out of this wilderness. Nothing but slopes steep as a cow's face to the east, but west the road curled through the forest, still clearly visible. A car could use it easily, but where did it come out? She'd have to mount up again. One foot in the stirrup, she was startled by the appearance of the Lone Ranger. Damn if he didn't get around.

"Holy crap. Wanta get shot?"

The man stood there big as you please, one hand tucking the coat up off his hip, the other hanging at his side. "That all you Arkies do is go around shooting people?"

Her heart liked to leaped right out of her throat. "I'm coming awful close where you're concerned."

He chuckled. "Imagine running into you out here."

"Oh indeed imagine. Certainly didn't expect it, but you never know who you'll meet nowadays."

"Just out for a ride? That's a beautiful roan you've got there."

"Thanks." Craning her neck, she looked all around them. "Where's your mount?"

"In yonder trees." He pointed, and when she looked in that direction, sunlight reflected off glass.

"A house? Who lives there?"

"I think the poor soul found in your friend's barn lived there. Did you find out who she is?"

"Is it locked?"

He shrugged. "I was out for a ride in that lovely little park when I spied it. I've only peered through the windows. It's certainly not located where it could be found easy. Are you interested in going inside?"

This was one of the strangest men she had ever met, but he was beginning to get on her good side. He acted as if he was from another world, and it intrigued her, which was understandable when you thought about it. Being who she was and doing what she loved to do, write about unusual exotic subjects she couldn't resist.

"We would have to be very careful not to touch anything, in case it's a crime scene."

He moved closer, carefully took hold of Star Brite's halter. The roan blew through his nose and crow hopped backward.

"Watch it." He didn't have good sense around horses.

He smiled up at her in a charming way. "Sorry, he's so beautiful. I was mesmerized."

"You practice that Clint Eastwood grin and squint?"

He spread a hand flat on his chest and widened his eyes.

The horse curled his upper lip and knocked Ranger's hat into the mud. His startled expression was priceless, and she laughed, threw a leg up over the cantle, and slid to the ground. She picked up the Stetson and handed it to him. "Let's walk over and check it out. Everyone's hunting the place, it would be fun if we're the ones that found it."

"We? I beg your pardon, but I saw it first."

"That you did, that you did."

They headed for the house, stopped when off in the woods someone laughed, and conversation carried into the clearing.

"We're a hundred miles from nowhere and be darned if it isn't getting crowded. And here I'd hoped to have you all to myself." He shrugged. "Ah, well, that's the way it goes. Suppose we'd better let them know we're here. Folks around here tend to shoot first and ask questions later."

Mac came striding out of the treeline, followed by an odd-looking fellow wearing an ear flap hat like he might be expecting a blizzard. Dal wandered along behind them looking a bit befuddled.

Ranger took long strides in their direction, one hand out in a shaking offer. "We come in peace. James Jameson, and this is my most recent companion." He swung a quick look her way. "Sorry I've misplaced your name."

"Jessie West. Glad to meet you. I should say fancy meeting you here." She giggled, and Ranger chuckled.

"Good Lord, child. Have you been drinking?" Mac gave her a quizzical look.

"No, but it's good to find out I can feel this way without it."

"Marijuana?" Dal raised a brow. "Looks like we've stumbled onto a party. And what about the house? Have you been in it?"

"No, but you interrupted our plans to do so. It's just too tempting. Do you suppose it's Miss Jasper's? Jameson here rode in from the new city park."

"Oh, he did, did he?" Dal appeared ready to take a shot at the Ranger, or the flap-eared guide, whichever one he could aim at first. She didn't much blame him.

He and Mac both shot Ranger a look that might kill on its own.

"Oops, my bad," Jameson said. "I'm not supposed to know her ID, however it was an inadvertent slip-up. I recognized her but wanted to do some investigating on the side before coming to you with the information.

Ear Flap, who had been following the conversation avidly, piped up. "Who is this man? Ain't there some reason you can arrest him? Trespassing or something?"

Ranger grinned. "Probably. I wouldn't doubt it one bit. Perhaps for pretending to be a lawman?"

The skinny man's wide grin left his nose out in thin air. "I don't think that's agin the law, is it?"

Mac shook his head. "Lord have mercy. This is like some kind of Punch and Judy show. If no one minds, me and my deputy here are gonna search the house." He waved a hand around. "Y'all just stay outta there and go on with whatever it was you were doing. Oh, and by the way, Miss Jessie. You are under arrest for horse thieving. Could be the owner can save you from being hung, we'll have to see. Don't leave town."

Ranger walked beside Jessie, hat in hand. "It's been a good long while since I've had such a rip snorting good time. And I can't recall ever knowing a horse thief in person. I must take advantage of this friendship. I hope we can do it again real soon. Oh, and if you need to be bailed out, let me know. I'll be in town a while yet."

"Y'all get through joshing around, I could use some water. I'm out." Jessie made a face at all the men in general.

Before they could produce the water, from out of the woods came the nicker of a horse. Jessie's gelding answered back. A rider all in black, including a watch cap, rode out on a coyote dun. One beautiful animal. It slowed for a moment, the rider lifted a hand in greeting, then went on before anyone could stop him or ask any questions.

They looked at each other as if asking "what the hell?" shrugged and went on. Jessie admired the coyote dun. She'd never seen the horse or its rider before.

As if there'd been no interruption, Ranger and Mac produced unopened bottles of water for Jessie. She glared at Ranger who was getting on her last nerve, acting so proprietary where she was concerned. And here she was just fixin' to like him. She took the water Mac proffered. Screwing it open she drank deeply, held it out to him.

"No, you keep it. Since when do you go hiking unprepared?" Mac studied her, then strolled along beside Ear Flap. "I don't see how you found this place, even knowing where it is."

"I didn't, it'us the woodpecker. I almost tumbled into that holler following that bird. Once I got my bird pictures, I began to recognize stuff from when I was younger, and we played around here. Like certain big rocks and the like. When I went past that gulley and waterfall, I know'd my way. It'us right there where that little gal drowned. Everone thought her momma was gonna murder my aunt. And here you are. It's obvious someone lives in there, or did until recently, and I couldn't resist checking it out. I'm sure it's the one you've been huntin. There are some photographs of that purty lady whut's passed."

"Too much to hope you hadn't gone inside. Now we'll have to print you. I'm really obliged to you, but we'd appreciate it if you remained out here." Mac gestured to Dal. "Would you come on in with me? We'll probably gather a lot of evidence."

And indeed they did gather evidence. The inside of the rustic cabin surprised Dal, and Mac let out a hooting sound. Pulling gloves from their pockets they put them on.

"Did you ever? Just look." The small single room was arranged with a few pieces of nice furniture. Against one wall was a cabinet with a plate, bowl, mug, glass, and silverware, a small wood cook-stove with a skillet, cookpot, coffeepot, and aluminum pitcher. It was a perfect playhouse with a bed in one corner along with a dresser and a few clothes hanging from a hook on the wall. A desk in the opposite corner promised what they searched for, though they took their time checking everything for any sign the murder had taken place there. When that didn't turn up anything, Mac eyed the desk and dresser.

"Best places for her to have kept personal things, pictures, stuff like that. You take the desk. Bag anything of interest. Good Lord, why do you reckon that gal was living way out here? And how in tarnation did she get all this stuff here?"

Dal shrugged. "No doubt she took the shortcut. Sure no accounting for what folks do sometimes or how they do it. I just hope we get it all straightened out... for Parker's sake, at least"

Mac watched them carefully to make sure they carried out the search properly. The old man still thought he had to instruct everyone on crime scene techniques.

Dal wished he was alone so he could work his own way. Listen to the spirits. But no doing it now, for Mac would leave cause it made him so nervous to watch Dal's odd actions when dealing with the spirits.

"What about fingerprints? Perp might've been here."

"We'll go ahead with our search. Call Colby and have him get down here with a print kit. Can you direct him, do you think?" Mac checked a picture on the wall, nodded but said nothing more.

Dal scooted closer to Mac, keeping his voice low. Darned if he'd admit he didn't know someone who'd lived here all his life. Getting bonked in the head wasn't exactly good for the memory. "What's that fella's name with the flap-eared hat? Bet he can give him those drive-in directions he was talking about. And Colby, he don't get lost."

Mac nodded, and Dal pulled out his phone. Glanced up. "No signal."

"Probably trying to take the long way around. Okay, it can wait till we finish taking prints inside and get outta here. Doubt we'll find any helpful prints. Place doesn't look like our killer was ever here. Nothing out of place. But we never know."

After printing, they both began a search. Dal sat down at the desk and pulled open a drawer while Mac searched the dresser.

There was no laptop or tablet. But in the top drawer over the knee-hole Dal found a small photo album. One of those that holds only one 4x5 photo per plastic page. Dates on the lower left corner of each helped tell their story. The first few were dated years earlier. A nice-looking man with a woman he thought resembled Loren. Dead people took on a different look than when they were alive, still… she had a familiar look. He paged past a few more. Background buildings placed them in Dallas. Same woman, definitely Loren Jasper, but different companions, both male and female. Curious but pressed for time, he went to the last page. There Loren sat on the top rail of a fence near Parker's barn, one arm lifted in a wave while she laughed.

He dropped the album in a paper evidence bag and continued to search. Together they carried out quite a few of the bags to be gone through back at the station.

Mac called from the open door. "It's getting late, let's get back. I'm anxious to put Miss Prissy Pants in jail."

"Shoot. I was going to ask if it's okay for me to arrest her." Dal glared at her through the window.

"Either way suits me, but let's wait till she hauls these bags out on her horse before we do that.

7

CHAPTER

Back at the office, Mac opened one of the cell doors, took Jessie by the arm, and led her inside.

"Hey. What're you doing? Surely you aren't going to arrest me."

"You may be kin, girl, but in my county, you can't go around stealing horses. Sorry, gonna have to hold you till the judge comes in the morning."

"Parker, come on. Tell him I have permission to ride Star Brite."

He laughed for the first time since Loren's death. "Well, I like to know ahead of time when you're going to take him so I'm sure no one did steal him. I was about to report the theft so they could put out an APB."

Ranger took in the shenanigans with a wide grin, so she couldn't expect help from him either.

Mac chuckled into his chest and closed the cell door. The latch thunked, sealing her fate. How could Mac and Parker do this to her? It had to be a joke, and they'd let her out soon.

The men stood around outside, studying her as if she were really a criminal. Even Ranger didn't come to her rescue, so why had he tagged along? Just to see her suffer? Maybe they'd had too much to drink. This was way past funny. Surely they weren't actually going to lock her up and go away? If she had to spend the night in this dark, dirty, stinky place, she'd surely never forgive every one of them.

"I don't like it. She looks awful pathetic."

Well, at least Dal had a bit of sympathy for her. But that wouldn't get him off the hook unless he rescued her. It was time this stopped. She really wasn't in the mood.

Were they truly going to make her spend the night here? She grabbed the bars, planted her chin on the cross piece, and tried to look pitiful. "Guys, I need a shower. Please don't make me sleep in this stinky cell in dirty clothes and skin. I promise I'll not ever do it again."

"Whoa now, just a minute. You saying my cells are dirty?"

Dal and Ranger were about to roll on the floor.

Tinker strolled in about then. "What's so funny in here? I'd like in on it." She spied Jessie peering through the bars. Pointed. "I knew one of these days she'd go too far. What'd she do, anyway? Hey, girlfriend, what can I bring you to make you more comfortable?"

"Wait till I get out of here, a whole bunch of you will be darned uncomfortable. Now come on, this has gone too far."

Dal managed to stop laughing. "Hey, let's go get burgers. I'm starved. Can we bring you anything, Jess?"

"This is your very last chance to redeem yourselves. You don't know what it's like to be hunted by me, just wait and see." They were really going to do this.

Their snickering and footsteps receded. She tilted her head and listened. They were gone. Honest to goodness gone. She dropped onto the hard cot. The sun set, and darkness crept into every corner. Thankfully someone turned on the lights. But that wouldn't redeem any one of them. She spent some time hollering in a forlorn voice, but no one answered.

This was getting serious and beyond a joke. She shook the bars. "Come on, I'm tired. Let me out of here. You know I can come up with some scary ways to get back at all of you."

The worst thing she could do would be get really mad, but tears burned the backs of her eyes, simply because she was so tired, and she'd spent most of the day on a useless search. She didn't even get to take a peek inside the cabin, so there went a lot of her story. This was too little a joke and too much trying to teach her a lesson. They had no business doing that. They were hanging around, their whispering and chuckling evident.

Best to just give up and apologize, so she slumped her shoulders and sagged down to the cot. Raised her voice so they could hear her. "Okay, go on. I know you're still out there. Have your fun, and when you come in and find me in this awful place, half dead with no food or water, you'll all be sorry. Just you wait and see."

"Okay, she's right." Parker peeked in. "Tell you what, I won't press charges against you for stealing my roan if you'll agree to help dispense bundles of papers to the boxes Wednesday. With Bobby Ray out, I'm short a man."

"You're making a big mistake letting her get away with stealing your horse and only a meager punishment like that." Dal poked his head around Parker's shoulder, winked, and she stuck out her tongue at him. "As a result of such weak punishment there'll be one heck of a crime wave. Horse stealing, car thefts. You watch."

"No, No, it's okay." She sat on the cot staring at the floor. "I'd rather stay in jail than lug those bundles around all over town."

Mac stuck his head in. "Up to you. Anyone coming with me to the Red Bird?"

Everyone filed out, leaving her in the silence of the empty jailhouse. She waited for them to return, but they didn't. This time they were really gone. Odd how quiet empty cells could get. Even a drunk slumped in a corner snoring would be better than this. Hard to believe they were going to carry through with such a mean joke.

She sat there for a long while, arms hanging between her legs, expecting someone to come back and let her out. When it didn't happen, she lay down, curled her knees up to her chest, and closed her eyes. They'd be sorry, she'd see to that.

On the verge of sleep, she stirred when a door opened and shut with a great deal of stealth. Someone breaking into the jail? Doubtful. It was probably Dal coming back to let her out. He was a pushover. She kept still and tried to breathe so she looked dead or at least fast asleep. Someone was crying, little, soft hiccuppy sounds like they'd been at it a for a long while. Not any one of the men.

Squinting one eye open, she studied a woman slumped in one of the deputy's chairs. Head down on her arms, her crying was sad enough to break your heart.

All Jessie could see was a shape in the scattering of empty desks and chairs. Someone had left a computer on, and the light from the screen scarcely outlined her shape. Jessie rolled from the cot and went to the bars where she could get a better look.

Did she dare speak, maybe scare her off? "Honey, are you okay?"

The woman jumped up, overturned the chair, and fell back against the wall.

"It's all right. I'm not going to hurt you."

"You… you're in jail."

Jessie chuckled. "Well, it's sort of a joke, believe it or not. But you can tell me what's wrong. Maybe I really can help. My friends did this to me. They'll be back pretty soon and turn me loose."

The woman clattered to her feet. "Oh, no, I can't be here when they get back. I don't know who they are, but someone is trying to kill me in this town, and I'm not sure who. Could be you for all I know. Loren was first. I'll be next. Please, just leave me alone. I'll go somewhere else."

Loren? Oh shit. She knew Loren. What was going on any way? Jessie stuck her nose through the bars. "No, no. Don't leave. See those keys hanging on the wall behind the desk? Grab them and unlock this cell. I'll take you somewhere safe till you can figure out who and why someone is trying to kill you. It's not me. My name is Jessie, and I'm a reporter. I can help you."

The woman studied the keys, then eyed Jessie. "How do I know I can trust you? You're in jail, and worse, you're a reporter."

"Well, yeah, but like I said, it's a joke, and I'm not that kind of reporter." Jessie swung her gaze all around the room. She didn't much blame the woman. She herself had once been a reporter who couldn't be trusted. "Look, I will help you. It looks like you don't have much choice."

She wanted this woman and her story desperately.

Outside someone laughed, a woman squealed, yelled something Jessie couldn't understand. She snapped her fingers at the intruder. "Keys. Unlock. We're gone. I'm not the law, and I'm sure not a killer."

A louder shout from outside, and the woman made up her mind, grabbed the keys, fumbled them into the keyhole of the cell, forced it open, and headed toward the front door.

Jessie grabbed her arm. "No, here. Come this way. We'll go out back.

My car's there." Good Lord what was she going to do with this woman now that she had her? Hide her first, since she was afraid someone would kill her. What if that were really true and not her imagination? She did know about Loren who already lay dead in the morgue in Little Rock. Could she save this one from an honest to goodness killer?

Afraid her jittery companion would bolt and try to get away once outside, Jessie gripped her arm and headed toward the Jeep, parked in plain view in a circle of light from a streetlamp. Good choice, girl. Right out in the open. Leave it to her to do something so dumb. She shoved her companion into the passenger seat, slammed the door, ran around the hood, and leaped in. Under the front seat she found a set of keys, one of three she kept handy, poked them until they connected with the keyhole and started the engine.

Everyone gathered outside the jailhouse, divided up, and climbed into three vehicles, laughing at a few protests about leaving Jessie. The entire, dusty, sweaty, dirty group invaded the Red Bird to eat and discuss the case. Already feeling guilty, Dal looked for a way to escape and rescue Jessie.

At a large table seating all of them, including James Jameson, the Texas Ranger who'd inserted himself into the group, Colby asked for some Handi-Wipes, and they were passed all around before platters filled with a gigantic burger and still-sizzling French fries were delivered by Wanda.

Chatter discussing their day's work stopped while ketchup and mustard coated meat and fries. Eating quieted the crew while enjoyment of the food took precedence over conversation. Everything put a stop to Dal leaving, but he kept thinking of her lying on that hard cot. When slices of apple pie and mugs of coffee were delivered all around, he changed his mind. Let her sleep, she was as well off on the cot in the cell as here, and she was exhausted. It was time to make some suppositions and share some information.

Mac chewed his hamburger and swallowed. "Dal, you have anything to add to our crime scene ideas? Anything come to you you want to discuss?"

Dal stared at the floor to get his thoughts gathered. "The girl who came by riding a coyote dun, not a real common horse. She didn't do the killing, but I'm pretty sure she knows something if we could find her."

Mac nodded. "Her? I—uh—take it there was no other witness?"

Dal shook his head. "It felt like a girl, but I'm not sure. We were all there, but...."

A drawn-out silence.

Some of those at the table had no knowledge of his shadowy talent. Would Mac stop to explain?

He didn't. "Colby, you get on that. See if you can run down the owner of that horse. Anything else? Bell, you pick up the clues from the evidence locker, and you and Neal sit down with them. See what you can come up with." He glanced around. "Everyone okay?"

Dal shook his head. "Once Kathy and Dave are done with forensics, I'd like to have a go at them along with what Bell and Neal are working with. See if I can pick up anything."

"Will do." This was always his request of Dal, and he usually ran across stuff no one else would see. Mostly because it was spiritual and something only he could understand. And he insisted on being alone during this process.

By now it was clear that Ranger and a couple of the newer deputies were a bit confused, but Dal kept his mouth shut. Until he could get a feel for the facts surrounding this killing, he'd do well to keep it shut. Bringing all these stRangers in to jumble up everything wasn't a good idea.

"Okay, usual stuff. Talk to people, find who was doing what, when, and where. Don't forget stRangers. Three p.m. today in the conference room, see how far we are. And someone go get Jessie out of jail. Okay?"

It was to everyone's surprise when the Lone Ranger stood. He ought to stop thinking of him by that name, but it wasn't easy.

"Just a word before you all go. We understand the importance of your recent murder, believe me we do, and you'll soon see why. In fact, another lawman from Dallas has just joined us. I understand most of you know him from a previous case here."

US Deputy Marshal Trey Ledger emerged from the shadows. Jameson acknowledged him. "Trey came in when Wanda and her husband closed up and went home. He wants to talk to us."

Jameson went on. "First I want to explain what I'm doing out of my jurisdiction and perhaps we can work together. I remained in the background because I've been working undercover in the cartel and still don't want anyone out of this room knowing it."

That announcement knocked Dal for a loop. This man was good, though he hated to admit it.

Ranger went on. "We have a cold case in Dallas, the death of a CI who had worked for several years sniffing out drug dealers. She had good reasons for being so dedicated, and her death was tragic. We only learned recently in going back to reinvestigate her murder that she had a connection to one of your lawmen here in Grace County."

He might as well hit Dal between the eyes. Was he talking about Leanne? She'd been murdered? Holy shit, could it be true?

Ranger was looking right at him, so it must be. Ranger went on. "Before we're through, this case will involve all three of our organizations and both states, so I have been officially assigned to work with Grace County deputies and US Deputy Marshal Ledger, who is acquainted with your area. Should we need a warrant to search a Dallas locale, I can obtain what we need, while Trey here has federal jurisdiction when necessary. We are determined to close this case which could also shut down a major drug supplier. Let's show those guys on those television shows that we can work together and solve this without a hassle. We're afraid that more victims may emerge. I'd like to ask Deputy Ledger to take just a bit of your time tonight."

It was difficult for Dal to concentrate. All he could think of was talking to Jameson about this murdered CI. It had to be Leanne, such a coincidence just wasn't possible.

Trey chose a chair facing them. "Folks, there's been a lot of concern about the possibility of a pub being opened in Cedarton. I am more concerned about the man and wife involved in ownership for reasons we're not able to divulge right now."

Everyone nodded. WITSEC, under the auspices of the Marshals Service, kept plenty of their business close to their chest. He went on. "We understand this is a dry county. Is there any chance the city can okay a license for this pub? It could help keep our persons of interest close while we carry out our investigation. They may or may not be involved."

Parker spoke up. "I don't see how that can happen. At the last city council meeting, the request for a license was turned down."

"Did Mister and Missus Captree attend that meeting?"

Parker again addressed the question. "Yes, they presented their hopes for licensing and left with no comments when it was voted down."

Trey scratched his chin. "What can they do to change the vote?"

Mac laughed and added his two cents worth. "First they'd have to get a majority vote from at least the city, to go 'wet,' then they'd have to convince city council members that a pub wouldn't mean the end of life as we know it. Have they considered a tea shop or house? The Brits are big on tea, which I understand means a full meal."

"In other words, sometime within the next year or two they might get their pub, but a tidy café would be possible right away? Then they would become well recognized citizens of your fair town of Cedarton. Perhaps volunteering and joining organizations? A good way for them to become well-admired citizens of our fine town," Parker said.

Dal leaned over and whispered in Mac's ear. "I'm going to let you and your pals take care of this. I'm going to spring Jessie out of jail. Bring me up to date later." If he didn't get out of here, see if he could learn more about Leanne's death and turn poor Jessie loose as well, he was going to create a scene that would send everyone on their way.

Jessie might never forgive them. Time to get her out of there. What she needed, what they all needed, was at least eight hours sleep in their own beds. Well maybe an exception for him. He had to find out about the mysterious CI.

Parker had overheard and scooted closer to him. "She's going to be pissed as all get out. Whatever came over us to do that?"

Dal frowned. "It's like they say, get a bunch of idiots together and they'll all agree to do something idiotic every time." He turned for the door. "Sorry, but I'm going to go let her out and see she gets home."

Parker ran fingers through his mussed hair. "Best you duck. You can tell her I won't be pressing charges. I don't know where my brain was. I were you, I'd be real careful she doesn't half kill you before you can apologize. And, oh, I wouldn't take her home expecting to crawl in bed with her, either."

"Ain't that the truth?" He left without saying anything to the others. Jessie was generally a good sport and had pulled some jokes in her time. He could hope for the best.

Lights were still on at the sheriff's office. He parked in his reserved space, which he'd insisted upon after one windy winter morning when he'd had to walk halfway round the square to get to work. Up to that point Mac was the only one with one of those pretentious reserved signs. He scooted through the glass door. Howie sat at the entry desk. Dal raised a hand and headed for the cells only to find them empty. Good, the deputy must've let her out when he came on duty.

Going back to Howie's desk, he hooked a thumb toward the empty cells. "Pretty pissed, was she?"

The blank look was not that unusual. One had to obtain the young man's total attention before a conversation could begin. It wasn't that he was slow or dumb, he simply existed in the electronic world and seldom came out. He could, however, make a computer do just about anything in the world. That's why his duty was at a desk, so he would be available immediately.

"Jessie? Locked in that cell." Dal pointed. "You let her out?"

"Cells were empty when I come in. That one was standing open, made me wonder. Someone escape?" His expression revealed fear that he'd done something wrong.

Dal hurried to reassure him. "Nah, it's okay. Anybody asks about Jessie, you tell 'em she went home. Got that?"

Howie looked perplexed, but he nodded. "Sure, of course."

Dal left before the nerd could think of anything to ask. He had a few questions of his own, but he'd let it go for now. He went straight home. Could of gone by Jessie's, but under the circumstances, he'd better not. Besides, it was out of his way, and if he swung by, he'd want to stay. Make up and stay. Not a good idea at all. Especially since she might hogtie him to teach him a lesson.

The next morning, deputies drifted in to work almost as if they anticipated a big row. Of course, Jessie didn't work at the sheriff's office, but she usually dropped by first thing to see if anything was going on worth a story in the paper. This morning she never showed.

But Jameson, formerly Ranger, along with Dal, Ledger, Parker, and Mac gathered in the coffee room. Kathy and Dave Spacey, the forensics people, joined the deputies in going over the clues from the evidence locker. The photos that Jessie took were strangely missing from Parker and Howie's computers where they should've been. Jessie, too, was missing and there weren't any messages from her.

Mac poured a cup of coffee and started for his office. "Anyone heard from Jessie? Dal?"

He shook his head. "She might be pretty mad. Somehow she got out of the cell yesterday evening when all of us were at the Red Bird. Any ideas?"

"Not any I can repeat." This from Parker, the one the closest to her except for Dal.

A nervous chuckle went around the room. "Ain't that the truth?"

Kathy set down her cup. "Dave and I can drop by the paper on our way back to CJC. Save you an extra trip."

Parker stared out the window and spoke as if his audience was out in the square. "This isn't a day she needs to come into the paper. She may have just overslept after yesterday. Go ahead and check on her, uh, have her send the photos to us, if you don't mind, Kathy." His eyes moved to take in the entire room. "Probably best ones to do it, considering the mood she might be in. Best to avoid her for a while, give her a chance to get over her incarceration."

Everyone would know what Parker was talking about except Kathy and Dave, and they all looked embarrassed. As they should. Whatever possessed them to lock her up like that after such a long, hard day? The miscreants, including himself, deserved whatever she decided to do to them. Dal wouldn't blame her one bit for whatever she did. He needed to get a private audience with Jameson, find out more about the cold case he brought up last night, but it would have to wait.

"I'll do that first off." Dal grabbed his Stetson and left. He headed for the alley that ran behind the office. Her Jeep had been parked there last night when everyone went to the Red Bird. On one knee, he examined the tire tracks that turned left. Strange. Wrong direction for her to be headed home. For a while the mud off her tires marked the pavement, but soon the last wore off. Going out of town toward highway 23. He parked in the Walmart lot and fingered his county map from the glove box to make sure what all lay in that direction.

He marked the road to Red Rock Mountain. Guessing where she was headed and why wasn't an easy task. Then put an X on the cutoff to the ruins of old Hermitage House that had burned the previous year, and further on, the abandoned road to SEFOR, still standing even though it was supposed to have been cleaned up and torn down the year after he moved to Cedarton. The Southwest Experimental Fast Oxide Reactor— a breeder reactor—was rumored to still bleed radiation and chemicals into the ground. Jessie had located a cache of stolen diamonds there a few years back. And if Dal headed the other way on 23, he'd wind up at July's new animal farm.

All three seemed good places to hide, if that's what she had in mind for a day off. Often she went driving, hiking, or searching for fill photos for the paper. Wouldn't surprise him if she just wanted to be alone for the day. Sort out her thoughts. He ought to leave it at that. But something told him not to. And he always listened to the somethings. Despite knowing the countryside, she often got turned around and spent hours trying to get back where she belonged. And she had a phone. And there were black holes. He shouldn't ignore that warning. He didn't.

Dammit, hard to decide whether to go after her or go on his way digging into the murder investigation and that tempting Dallas cold case. Would she pull a stunt like hiding out, making them all worry about her? Yep, she would. Darn her, she had that kind of ornery streak. She was way pissed off at all of them, and he felt bad about the entire episode. Frankly they deserved almost anything she could come up with. Almost. He shuddered at the possibilities.

SEFOR and Hermitage House beckoned. He couldn't exactly explain that decision except that he just felt it like he felt other stuff. Which, if Mac found out he was out chasing Jessie down, he'd be in trouble. He needed to be out at Parker's barn getting a feel for the crime scene and Loren's killer. But something told him he'd better look for Jessie first, though he wasn't sure why.

He needed to follow those feelings. All these thoughts revolved through his head while he drove like a maniac, choosing the most distant location first. Trees had grown up around the dome of SEFOR, the red and white paint mostly flaked off, till it could barely be spotted from the overgrown road. He had no plans to go inside the breeder plant. Just drive a circle looking for her Jeep. No way would he expose his boys to any sort of radiation.

Weeds slapped the undercarriage of his SUV, grasshoppers thickened the air, and riding the bucking treetops, a murder of black crows cawed as if urging him on. Some of the branches, already bared for autumn, resembled skeletal fingers clawing at dark clouds boiling into the sky on wings of black. One heck of a storm brewing. No sign of Jessie's Jeep. He smiled at a memory, like a vision, he and Jessie back in the woods, her beautiful body naked in the shadows, skin soaked with rain. Him reaching out for her, a passion so exquisite he yearned to keep her forever in his arms.

Time to move on. Where the hell are you hiding, Jess? The Spaceys would be done with the evidence soon, and he needed to get a feel for it. Hopefully Jessie would be in town when he got back. If not, he'd run on up to Hermitage House, sort of on the way to Parker's. Mac was going to rip him a new one for sure.

The storm hit with a fury the moment he pulled out onto 23 and turned toward town. The SUV rocked with the wind and a curtain of rain blocked his vision even as he sped up. Already late, he reached to turn on the lights, and out of the waterfall, a box truck rushed onto the road directly in his path. There was no stopping in time. He slammed under the double wheels, foot standing on the brake. The windshield burst into deadly shards of glass, the seatbelt tightened painfully across his ribs, and the world exploded in darkness.

Grandfather held out his arms, spoke his name, and led him off into a bright and sunny day.

The Spacey's red pickup sat at Parker's when Jessie pulled up and stopped under a huge tree. To the west a rumbling storm turned day into night, flashes of lightning temporarily blinded her. She had to discuss something important with Mac and the rest of the crew about the woman she'd picked up at the jail and left at her house. Yet, the only vehicle here belonged to the Spaceys. Where was everyone?

She leaped out and ran through the downpour and up on the porch, blinded by the rain. There was no answer to her hammering on the door, so she turned the knob, and it opened. Shouting, first Parker's then Dal's name, she ran through the house, but no one was there.

"Come on. Where is everybody?" Strange.

Soaked from head to toe, she took refuge out of the storm in the Jeep and called the sheriff's office. Voicemail came on, urged caller to call 911 if it was an emergency. That she knew would connect directly to the fire department first responders. Normally someone was at the sheriff's office to answer 24/7. What was going on?

She dialed 911 and Mike, one of the first responders, answered.

"Hey, this is Jessie. What's going on?"

"Oh, uh. Been looking for you. Bad wreck out near SEFOR."

"Wow, must've been a bad one for sure to shut down the sheriff's department. What happened? Who was it?"

"Jessie, it was… uh, shit. Where you at?"

"Leaving Parker's now. Why?"

"I'll meet you at the sheriff's office. You wait. I'll take you."

"Dammit, Mike. What's going on? Is it Mac? It is, isn't it?"

"No, it's not. I'm on my way."

On his way, he was only a block away.

His pickup rolled up soon after she did, and he shoved open the door. "Come on, get in. I'm taking you."

Grabbing her pack, she splattered through the mud, clambered in, her stomach clutching. "Who is it? What's happened?"

He stomped the accelerator, fishtailed onto the street. "It's Dal, Jessie. They took him down to the hospital in Harrison. He run under a truck."

Her world turned upside down. She groaned "no, no, no'" over and over. It was bad or they wouldn't have taken him down there. Her mouth clamped shut over the scream that went back and forth through her brain. It deafened her with its shattering denial. Knuckles crammed in her mouth, she bit down hard and stared out into the rain. A mantra, *"don't be dead, don't be dead, don't be dead,"* would not stop reverberating, bouncing, hammering through her brain.

Would this be the one he didn't survive? So many second chances. The shooting in Dallas that nearly killed him, then threatened his physical ability. The shove off Red Rock Mountain where he lay alone in a cave until she found him over a day later. Only a couple weeks ago the knock on his head. Now this. For a man with a guardian shaman, he sure had his share of nearly fatal accidents. What if this was the one he didn't walk away from?

She couldn't live without him. The realization hit her like a bolt of lightning cutting zig zags through the roiling clouds. She shivered and hugged herself violently.

"Don't take him, don't take him, don't."

"He'll be okay, Jess. They'll take good care of him." The words like echoes from a distant plain.

"Hurry, I have to be with him when…."

Oh, God, what was she thinking?

The road curved up, then down. The rain blocked any view. Fog draped the valley below, hiding crevices and bluffs. She rode the seat as if she could urge the truck forward. Visions flashed through her mind. Him laughing at her, the wind whipping his black hair, him turning to look at her over his shoulder, as if he had someplace else to go.

Her heart thrummed, her stomach clutched. She saw him leaving her. As clearly as the sun rose and set, he was gone, swallowed up by a boiling cauldron of clouds.

In horrified silence, she hugged herself, head low, tears flowing.

8
CHAPTER

Good God, there he lay out in the open, naked as a jaybird right in the middle of the day. No one around, but it still was weird. All inches, every inch bare. Wait, where was he? If anyone was watching, they were getting quite a show. Worth a laugh, so he gave it one. Squinting into a brilliant sun, he sat up, covered his genitals with one hand, tried to figure out what to do with the other. Maybe put it over his eyes so he couldn't see anything.

Out front there was an empty field with not even a clump of brush to hide behind. How embarrassing. Caught running around like this. Shameful. Odd thing was, why did it bother him so? Especially since there was no one around. Another minute and he'd get up, make a wild dash for cover just in case someone showed up. One arm across his forehead as if that might keep him from being seen, he sneaked a quick look. No one, far as he could make out. Something kept blurring his vision, like a thin scarf over his eyes.

Run, fool, run. Get up and get out of here.

But on his feet, he teetered back and forth like a damned pendulum on a clock. Not getting anywhere. So all he could do was work to keep his balance, never mind hiding his bare skin and hairy places. Held steady in a vice so it was like his naked body swayed back and forth, round and round. Someone beat on his head with a drumstick. A big one with a fat padded end on it that bounced and thrummed. Hurt like the very devil every time he got smacked with it.

Stop, dammit, stop. I've got the mother of a headache, and you keep hammering on it.

"Do you love me?" A woman's voice asking.

"Yes, I love you." Him. Definitely him answering. But who would be foolish enough to love someone who hammered on his head, over and over?

He needed to finish writing this song to give to Jessie. *"Love you more,"* Okay, so far it was sort of shitty. How dumb. There was that song, *"till the oceans all run dry... ta dah."* Can't recall anymore, that damn drumstick. But he didn't know anything about oceans.

Where's Jessie? She was here just a minute ago, now she's gone. Tears burned his eyes, so he couldn't see the field anymore. Only something white. On and on, all around him, white sheets blowing in the wind. That was a song. Well part of it. Wrapped all around him, cool and rain-washed. Covered and proper now, trussed up like a mummy. Wrapped all over so he couldn't move his arms or legs or head or feet. At least he wasn't naked.

To sit up meant he had to bend and fold every bound inch, but he had to go. Go hide. Cause that woman was coming. Seen her before, but where? Why did she keep after him? Everywhere he went he saw her face, but who was she? He ought to know her, was supposed to know her. But he wanted to escape, for Grandfather warned him about her. But what? He smacked his forehead with one palm. Damn that hurt. Plumb stupid.

His head hammered trying to remember who she was and what she wanted. Needed.

Think. Let's see. Not that many women in his life, so this should be easy. He rolled over and came eye to eye with one, her eyes milky, her skin pale as his sheets that were no longer wrapped around him. Oh, God, she was dead, and he was naked again. This was getting to be annoying as hell.

"I want some clothes. Put me on some clothes." His shout reverberated in the air. Cupping his face, he cried out, *"Take her away."*

She faded, replaced by another and another. Twins? Sisters? What the hell? Asking one thing only. Find who did this. Stop them. Do it for me, for us. At least that made sense.

Hands on his shoulders, her voice repeated his name. Though echoing, it must be his name because she kept looking at him while she said it, soft like to a child, her pretty lips pursed. Perhaps she expected him to reply, so he tried. Made an O of his mouth, blew out so a sound came. Not much of one, but still, he was quite proud of himself. He waited, then waited some more. Least she could do was answer. If she didn't, he wasn't going to talk to her anymore.

Well, that did it. The bed was a bit lumpy, and his feet hung off, and what were those ding dong noises that never stopped?

And then he knew. Knowledge hit him like a basket of bricks. It was a hospital. If the constant bonging stopped, he had died.

"Sweetheart, I'm here." Jessie took his hand, careful not to disturb the tubes and needles. "You're going to be okay." Tears dripped, and she ignored them, watched the jagged lines and blinking lights and flashing numbers, as if she understood what they meant.

As long as they flashed and zigzagged across the machine, he was alive. It had to be enough. She had loved him all of the best part of her life. The only time that mattered. All that went before meant nothing. If only it were the same for him. Her heart settled into a beat as if trying to match the pinging. It hurt to look at him helpless, tied down like this, but she couldn't turn away. Her existence became this place—the few feet that surrounded where she huddled over him.

A hand brushed her shoulder. "I'm sorry, you need to step out for a few minutes."

No, I can't, I won't. What if he goes while I'm not touching him? Then he can't take my love with him. He won't know, he can't know, he'll go without knowing.

And I'll be left behind without him, without knowing either.

The nurse touched her shoulder again. "He's not going anywhere. He's going to be all right. I need to take care of a few things. Your friends are right outside. Why don't you join them and have something to drink? It'll only be a few minutes." The face addressing her appeared blurred with only a mouth. Someone to be with him, help him. It needed to be her.

"What are you going to do to him?" Tears spurted, tears she couldn't stop. "Is he going to die?"

The young woman hesitated before answering. It was too much.

"No, you promise me he won't. I'm not leaving him." Her raised voice brought someone into the room. Colby, who wrapped an arm around her. "Jessie, we need to let them take care of him. Let's get a cup of coffee. Okay?"

Defeated, Jessie nodded, agreed, but her hand would not come away from touching him. Why were we so stupid? If only she had told him. And he her. "I will, okay? Don't let anything happen to him, please?" She managed to drag her fingers from his. Leaned into Colby's embrace when she stood. He steadied her, guiding her from the room. She watched Dal for as long as she could see him before the door sucked closed.

"They don't know yet about his injuries. His back and leg. What if he can't walk again only this time he never can? He'll hate it."

"Jessie, you need to be strong for him. He'll be okay, and so will you."

"Yes, okay, I'm okay." She nodded so hard her teeth rattled. What a liar she was. Okay? Not till he climbed out of that bed and gave her that magnificent smile of his. Somehow she shuffled along in Colby's grip, reached out to Mac and Tink and all the others gathered around. Their eyes filled with caring sympathy.

Tink handed her a cup of ice water, sat with her while she drank it. Mac stood at the floor-to-ceiling windows staring outside. Parker huddled in the shadowy corner, watching.

"He'll be all right. The doctors all say he will." Tink lay a hand on hers.

"I know, it's just, well. I thought he was dead, and I couldn't take another breath without him."

"Well, he isn't, and the best thing you can do for the two of you is believe he'll be okay. You need to drink and eat something. Stay strong."

Jessie nodded. "I will. I've never been so scared in my life." She managed a small grin. "And some scary things have happened to me, you know that. Never like this, though. I didn't know how much I loved him till I thought I'd lost him." She nodded fiercely. "I know, I know, what a cliché, but it is precisely that because of the truth to the words."

Parker came to sit beside her. His recent loss still showing in the dark circles under his eyes and the faraway look, but he took her hand in both his. "You'll get through this, Jess, and so will Dal. He's tough as a knot. You'll see."

"They say he was fortunate that the earlier injury from that shooting in Dallas suffered no further damage. Back then he was told he'd never walk again, but he did."

Parker patted her knee. "The seat belt and front and side airbags protected him. He must have seen it coming last minute and thrown himself down on the seat. Otherwise he'd have been decapitated when the roof was ripped off. I have pictures of his car. How he lived through that I'll never know. Jess, he was meant to survive this."

From the other side Tink put an arm around her. "And he did. They said all the way in, in the ambulance, he kept telling his grandfather about you and how much he loves you."

"He did?" Jessie sobbed, then smiled through her tears. "You do know his grandfather is dead, but he talks to him a lot."

Tink snickered. "Well, there's no explaining some men, honey. All I know is he's going to be okay, and he loves you."

"Just wish he'd tell me that, I truly do." She grabbed Tink's hand. "We almost lost him. I don't know what I'd do without him, I truly don't."

The nurse came from Dal's room. "You can go in now. He's awake, so it would be good to talk to him. But he's on a morphine drip, so he'll be in and out for a few days. Don't expect too much yet."

Mac moved from the window. "See, honey, that's good news. We're going now. Gotta catch the bad guys. If you need anything at all, you call one of us, and we'll be right here. You understand? I mean anything. A drink, a hamburger, a teddy bear." He rubbed her shoulder. "Okay?"

She managed a grin before going into Dal's room.

He lay on his back, tubes connected to an IV. Bandages covered one side of his head, and it was easy to see his hair had been shaved off there. When she said his name and took his hand, he slanted a look in her direction. Seeing him like this terrified her. He was always so strong and stubborn about what he could do.

He whispered something and she leaned down close to hear. "What happened to me?"

Planting a kiss on his chin, she told him in a joking tone. "You got run over by a truck."

His eyes widened. "Feels more like I was in a train wreck."

They held on to one another, and he soon relaxed into a deep sleep. Staring out the window, she came to herself long after sunset and the onset of darkness. She could only imagine what must be going through his mind. Hers was filled with turmoil. What if he didn't walk again? Could he come through something like that one more time?

Almost seven years ago he'd been ambushed in an alley in Dallas, his lower body ripped open by gunfire. During that time his wife Leanne died of an overdose, which nearly destroyed him. He'd fooled everyone by getting out of his wheelchair a year later to receive a medal of valor for creating a huge dent in a major drug gang while working undercover.

That's when he retired and moved to Cedarton to take a job with the peaceful sheriff's department in Grace County.

For the next few days she remained with him several hours a day. Parker urged her to take the time away from work, and so she did. She read to him, played music, and discussed what the deputies were up to every day. And he simply lay there, sometimes watching her, other times appearing as if sleeping. Never talking or responding to her touch or voice.

Within a week a physical therapist was working with him. He did what he was told but never spoke to anyone. Slowly she lost hope. Her world had crumbled around her, and she could hardly stand it. The man she loved had withdrawn to some secret place, a place she could not go to, and her heart lay inside her chest in tiny pieces.

One day after she had returned to work to keep from going insane, Mac called her.

"Colby is coming over to pick you up. Be ready."

"What is it, Mac?" Fear muted her voice.

"It's good, sweetheart. It's good. He's asking for you."

She squealed at Parker, told him she had to go, and ran outside when the patrol unit slithered to a stop outside. At the hospital she found Dal sitting in a wheelchair at the window, watching for her. He pulled her down into his arms.

"I love you, Jessie. I always will. I'm sorry I never told you. This has made me take a good long look at my feelings for you. But I had to wait to make sure I'll recover. Please forgive me."

She held two fingers over his lips. "Now, one more time. Say it." Smiling, she took away her fingers.

He cocked his head. "Say what?"

"Stop that. You know what, and you'd better be quick."

"I love you, I love you, I love you. Is that enough?"

"And you'll come home with me when they release you. Okay?"

"Only if you have plenty of Honey Buns."

She took him home to her place a few days later and went to bed with him, vowing to never let him out of her sight. But of course, that was ridiculous. Life made its way slowly back to normal.

One morning he turned over and touched her, smiled and kissed the bare shoulder peeking from under the covers. "You taste good in the morning, like dew on honeysuckle."

Snuggling into his arms, she nibbled at his throat. "You don't taste so bad yourself. I'm thinking like honey on a bun. Best I can do. How do you feel?"

His fingers moved over her ribs, crawled to enclose one bare breast. "You mean like this?"

"Well, looks like you're feeling better. I'm going to get up before you break doctor's rules. That's obviously about to happen." She eyed the tent in the sheet over him

His lips moved downward to brush the other breast. "Hmm, what do doctors know, anyway? I don't suppose you'd give me just a bit?"

"Correct. Not one damn bit. Obviously doctors know how to heal their patients." She kicked away the covers, gave him a kiss, and crawled out of bed.

"Aw, come on back. Look what you did to me." He sat up slowly, dragged his legs over the edge of the bed.

"Doing good, mister. I'm going to fix something to eat besides Honey Buns. Need any help? No fudging now. You keep wanting to put your hands on my butt."

"Nah, I'm okay. Besides, if I'm reading the calendar right, I'm going into the station today. Take a shower with me?"

"Desk duty only. Give you time to figure out the case. Shower first, then breakfast. I think Colby has been assigned to ride with you the first week. But that will be a while."

"Never mind that. Gotta get up. Play real." He grabbed the cane near the bed and headed for the bathroom.

She leaned against the door frame and took a deep breath. Her world had stopped a few weeks ago, weeks that had at times terrified her, but he was back except for the bad leg with scar tissue from earlier injuries.

It was time for him to get back to work and catch up on the happenings since the accident. If only he would resign, but he wouldn't, and she wouldn't pester him about it.

She stepped into the shower at his back and wrapped her arms around him, his skin soft under her touch. They made slow gentle love, and it felt as wonderful as anything in her life. He was hard and hot and slick with soap. Inside her, he moved about with an ease that set her afire, and she returned the tenderness producing a trio of gripping orgasms. He came with joyous laughter, perhaps happy to be alive. So far, he hadn't said.

Chin on her shoulder he growled, low and contented. "It's good to be alive, isn't it?"

There, he'd finally said it. Read her mind. "You bet it is. And let's not ever forget it."

He rode to the station with her. Mac had called the day before and said his new vehicle was waiting whenever he was ready. Would he ever be able to crawl behind the wheel again? If it were her, she'd be frozen with terror.

Everyone was there waiting for him when he limped through the door. "Oh, look. The law's all here. Hope the bad guys don't hear about this and go into hiding." His remark brought laughter all around. Finally everyone drifted away for their assignments or to go off duty.

Jessie leaned over Colby's shoulder and whispered, "You keep an eye on him, you hear?" She smiled and left to write an article for the paper.

Colby grinned and nodded, remained sitting beside Dal. "My duty is to bring you up to date. I know Jessie has told you some stuff, so bear with me, and we'll get through it. I'll try not to bore you. Questions when I'm finished.

"After we got you safely tucked away in the hospital, Mac arrested the driver of the truck, which by the way, ironically was carrying a load of liquor for the anticipated pub, known by the hideous name of The Purple Raven. Then our angry sheriff sent us out to get serious about catching our murder suspects who have still managed to dodge all efforts to bring them in. We've conducted statewide searches with no luck. Mac's afraid they've left Arkansas. But we think they've holed up."

"What about—"

"Tut, tut, tut. Questions later."

Dal nodded, drank the last of his coffee. "Proceed."

"Now, where was Miss Jessie after she escaped the jail?" Colby pointed at Dal. "Was gonna be your next question, wasn't it?"

Dal nodded. "She refused to tell me much of what went on. Didn't want to upset me."

"Seems like Jessie took the mystery woman you've been seeing around town to her place to hide from someone who she said was gonna kill her. Said she came over here to find you, buddy."

Dal spread his palm over his chest. "Me?" His brain jolted, but he missed the connection.

"That's right. Do you know her? She is—was—a friend of Loren's, and when she learned Miss Loren had been killed she panicked. Her and Loren knew stuff they weren't supposed to know about drug lords too. And some woman acquainted with them who was murdered back in Dallas seven or more years ago. It's a confounded mess if you ask me, cause before we could get her together with Deputy Marshal Ledger and Jameson, why this woman, she took off again. Slippery as can be, she is. So once more everyone's looking for her. She said she'd be in touch with you when you could be of help. She's scared bad. Until then, she's hid out good and proper. I know these parts, and I've spent hours and hours searching but to no avail whatsoever."

"Question." Dal's mind shifted into gear. "Did anyone get a picture of her? I need the photograph album from my apartment to show you a picture. My God, if it's who I think, I…. No, no. It can't be. No way. If she knows me, then I should know her. Not that it will help finding her, but it might if I knew who she is. Her habits, maybe some kin, you know?"

"You're right there. Mac is concentrating on catching the suspects he thinks killed Loren, but want to know what I think? Someone who worked for Miss July is involved. Otherwise they couldn't have planned it so well. Get Maizie kidnapped, so to speak. Do the murder while everyone is out looking for the big kitty cat. Move the body to Parker's so he'll be suspected. That didn't work, and the kitty cat escaped, so they had to skedaddle while they're getting rid of Miss Loren at the compound. We know that much. I have a hunch, but I want you to form your own ideas."

"Okay, that's good. We're going over to the apartment for my album first, then to the newspaper. If anyone got a picture of her, it'd be Jessie. Or there's all the forensics from the cabin. I could look at the photos from there and see if I recognize anyone. I never got a chance to look at that picture album when we found it in her cabin. The only picture

I recognized was Loren Jasper, but we were in a hurry, and I flipped to the last page and a photo of Loren out at Parker's ranch. I need to see all those pictures. I'm betting this gal is in there. Jessie hid her out, so she'd recognize her picture, too. But all she sees right now is me. I'm who she knows. But I'm not sure from where. Has to be Dallas. Just wish I could place her definitely. She might well know who we're looking for I hope."

"Well, it's a place to start. Feel up to doing it now?"

"Sure. You drive. I'm not up to that yet. I'm sure curious who it could be that I knew back in those days."

But he wasn't. Not really. Not up to that for sure. There's absolutely no way it could be who he thought it was. And if it was, his whole world would crack wide open. But it couldn't be. If it was, then WITSEC was involved. They did some fabulous things hiding witnesses, but no, she wouldn't be out wandering around exposing herself. She only resembled Leanne to his jumbled brain.

That had to be it.

And what was that business about hauling liquor to The Purple Raven? Last he knew, the city hadn't approved the pub. With a deputy marshal and a Texas Ranger busy with their own case as well, he might never catch up.

Jessie finished the article in time to break for lunch. Wendy had a bowl of mixed fruit, so they fetched cold drinks and together went out back to sit in the shade at the picnic table.

Sandwiches unwrapped, they settled down to talk about some of the funny items they'd received for the columns. Nervous about Dal's first day, Jessie couldn't keep her gaze away from the back door of the office. Wendy gave up holding a conversation alone.

She opened a pack of Oreos, waved one around. "Double stuffed. He's going to be okay, you know."

"I know. It's not that. It's... well we take everything for granted and then so fast it can be snatched away. Do you have anyone special in your life, Wendy?"

The pretty blonde flushed, nodded. "Well, yes but...."

"No, yes, but. Tell him now. Do it, and don't be afraid to build a life together."

Wendy chewed for a while, staring at her Coke. "What if he doesn't return the feelings? Kill myself?"

"Of course not. What I'm getting at is live your life. Don't hang back waiting for something to happen. Make things happen. Do something positive. Regretting things you didn't do can make you forever sorry about what you missed out on."

Wendy looked solemn. Took a bite of her sandwich. "Is that what you're gonna do with Dallas? Cause if he was mine, I'd have him wrapped up in big bows and never let him go."

Darn, she hoped Wendy didn't try that with her man. The quickest way to lose a man was tie him down. Meanwhile, she was going to finish her lunch and go find her man. Hard not to smother him after seeing Parker's news photo of him tangled in what was left of his patrol car, not sure if he was alive or dead.

But she'd try real hard not to.

"It's Howie. He's not completely done yet, but he's a good man."

Concentrating on Dallas, Jessie didn't hear for a minute, then Wendy's admission got through to her. Howie? Hmm. Not quite done yet.

What a funny way to say it. Like he was a cake baking in the oven. Good choice, though.

Wendy waved a hand. "Oh, don't worry, I know he'd never look at me twice, but I just get goose bumps when I'm around him. He's a nice, thoughtful guy."

"Then go for him. You'll always be sorry, always wonder if you don't let him know how you feel. He'll be well worth the effort."

"Oh, I know that. It's just... what if he laughs at me?"

"If he's that kind of guy, then you don't want him anyway. Besides, knowing him, he won't laugh."

She shrugged. "I just don't know."

"I do. Ask him to go to War Eagle with you. Or if you like to ride, invite him to take one of the fall wilderness riding trips. They're fabulous. You can use Parker's horses. He likes them to be taken out. Some of the trips are all weekend. You could really get to know each other."

"That all sounds so exciting, but thinking about it makes me nervous. I haven't dated much for a long time. Not since... well, I lost my fiancé in a forest fire three years ago. That's when I came here to work and... I don't know. It's been so hard to even think about another man."

"Oh, honey, I'm so sorry. I didn't know. If you feel ready, you couldn't do better than Howie. Tell you what. If you'd like, I'll ask Dal if he'd like to go to War Eagle, and we can invite you and Howie to go along. Then if you hit it off, you could sign up for one of the wilderness rides. What do you think? Romantic." Jessie wiggled her hips and hugged herself.

Wendy laughed and gathered up her lunch leavings. "I'll think about it. Better get back to work."

"Yeah. I've got to go over to Blue Eye to do an interview. Let me know how things go and what you decide."

Wendy went ahead into the office, stopped. "How's Dal today?"

"Acting better than he is, but he's doing fine. If we can just keep him on desk duty for a few more weeks. Men can be so stubborn."

When Jessie went out the door, Wendy was still chuckling. It would be sad if she didn't approach Howie. They'd be good for each other. Stabilizing, even.

In the Jeep, she remembered to plug in her cell to recharge it, even though she'd probably go out of the coverage area before reaching her destination—a buffalo farm. What was it with all these unusual animals? Take lots of pictures, Parker had said, urging her to ride one of the animals for the camera if she got a chance. Sometimes news coverage was really freaky out here in the Ozarks, but she liked it. She'd never go back to Los Angeles and the madness that had driven her to do terrible things. Not much chance here she'd have to stick a microphone in the face of a grieving mother who'd lost a child to a gunman. Or lose a friend because she'd gone behind his back to steal a news story and ruined his career as well as her own.

Shaking her head, Jessie pushed away the bad memories and drove southeast toward the Arkansas Grand Canyon and her destination.

Her phone rang before she was a few miles out of town. It was Wendy. Dal and Colby were there wanting to see the pictures she took at the doll house cabin. She told her they were in her computer, that she'd downloaded them from her camera before she left.

"Put Dal on." She plugged her earbuds in and lay the phone in the seat in order to navigate the curves and hills.

"Hey Babe. I'm thinking I may know this gal you lost for us the other night."

"Hey, I didn't know she'd run out. Thought she'd be safe and sound. Who do you think she is?"

"I kept seeing her in town for the last few weeks but couldn't place her. I'm not sure yet, but she may be a CI who worked with us when I was undercover in Dallas. I just want to check it out."

"The file reads Doll House. And you be careful. If you know them, they'll know you. Make sure you stay with Colby today, okay? Promise?"

"Yes, Mom. You take care now, and what do you want for supper? I'm cooking tonight."

"Steak and salad would be fine. Love you."

"Me, too."

He was gone. Well, "me, too" was better than *bye, now* or something like that. One of these days, she'd get him to tell her he loved her just as naturally as he'd say goodbye. Foolish to fuss over such a little thing. Since the accident and his release from the hospital, he'd been living with her. That in itself had been tough enough to arrange with him, but he had little choice the first couple of weeks, unless he wanted rehab over in Harrison. Rehab in Cedarton did not include a room, and he couldn't be by himself for a while.

Now he could, but nothing had come up on his side or hers to suggest he return to his apartment. They got along well, probably because she was gone nearly every day, and once he got back on full duty, he would be too. Why pay for an extra place when she owned the little cabin Mac had given her when she came home from California with her tail between her legs? When Dal packed a bag, it contained most all his worldly goods, so it was an easy move.

She arrived in Blue Eye by two thirty and she tried to program her GPS. It had no idea where her destination was, and she pulled over into a service station bay laughing. Inside a young fella in coveralls with grease across his nose told her how to find the Buffalo ranch.

"I know exactly where it is. Looks sorta like the old West out yonder. We hear it's the coming meat, no fat. You ever taste a steak with the fat all trimmed off? Couldn't give me one. Well, anyways, just go on out this road yer on till you come to a field full of dirty white cows with bumps on their necks. This part of the woods is getting popular for raising unusual animals." He grinned great big like he'd told the funniest joke, then scratched his nose adding another smear of grease. "Turn at the end of the fence row, only one way, and that's right. After you cross the low water bridge, go slow till you see this big ole watering tank and windmill. Turn right there, and you'll be surrounded by them big, brown, furry buffalo, all of 'em watching you like you're prey. You're at their place. It's still a ways to the house, but you can see it from there."

She thanked him and drove off, laughing so hard she could hardly see the road. God, she loved this part of the world. Where else could you get such entertainment just by asking directions?

She made it through the interview and some hilarious pictures of her astraddle one of the smaller animals, sure that at any moment she would take the ride of a lifetime. But the animal behaved very well. Legs trembling a bit, she climbed in the car and sorted through the photos. Parker would be pleased.

She'd kept some of those she'd taken of family pictures hanging on the walls and propped on tabletops at the dollhouse after Mac let her in. She flipped through them. Besides some groups there were a few couples and families. One of the women was Loren sitting next to the one she'd helped hide and another who looked so familiar she studied her for the longest time. She had seen her somewhere, but not recently. She couldn't come up with an ID for her. The three of them looked like sisters, or at least relatives, with that blond hair and those blue eyes, high cheekbones and so skinny you could count their ribs.

She lay the camera in the seat and started back home. After she'd gone a few miles and didn't find the water trough and windmill she stopped. She'd turned the wrong way, not unusual for her. The GPS was lost too. No telling where she'd end up, so she drove slow on the narrowing road looking for a drive where she could turn around and retrace her steps to familiar surroundings.

Good God, she was in the tail end of nowhere. A sign hanging on a boulder next to the road read, *"This property protected by Smith & Wesson."* Bless Arkansawyers and their desire for the right to privacy.

Shit. Now she was in real trouble. The ditches had closed in on either side of the narrow, overgrown track, as had huge trees. It was time she decided whether to back all the way out or take a chance on tangling with Smith or Wesson.

Dal liked Colby as well as he liked anyone, but he was used to working alone. So by the time they'd downloaded Jessie's copies to a flash drive and Colby made a quick run up the stairs to pick up Dal's album from his apartment, Dal was ready for some alone time. Colby wasn't about to turn him loose, so after lunch at the Red Bird he asked for a couple hours to take a nap.

"Pick me up at three, and we can work on these pictures."

Colby studied him for a minute. "No funny stuff, okay?"

"Hey, I'm not yet up to shenanigans. Just drop me at Jessie's. No car for me to escape in." He chuckled.

Colby gave him a harsh glare. "Okay. Three o'clock on the dot. Get some rest."

"Oh, and when you get back, I want to hear how in the world those Brits talked our city council into okaying a pub in Cedarton."

Colby stood beside the open door. "Oh, it's quite a story. You'll like it."

After the patrol car disappeared down the lane, he went to the fridge and took out a Pepsi. Tucking the album under one arm, he limped out on the deck, found a chaise lounge in a shady spot, dropped the album on a nearby table, and eased down into the chair.

The leg ached, and he leaned back for a while, eyes closed, taking deep breaths. Bird songs and insect chirps filled the otherwise quiet afternoon. How lucky he'd been not to get killed. Grandfather would claim he had important things yet to do. Who was he to think otherwise?

So, might as well figure out what those important things were, even though he'd rather not delve into his past in that other life. To remind himself, he opened his own album, paged past the newspaper clippings to photos of people gathered to watch him accept the medal of valor. After a brief search in which he located Loren sitting at a table with several officers he knew, he ran across the woman he'd spotted in Cedarton. He stopped, put a finger under her chin. Yes, definitely her. He didn't know any of those with her and flipped the page. Leanne laughed up at him until his heart thundered in his chest. Another page, again his wife between two other women, with their arms around each other, again that laugh of hers. Tears filled his eyes. He wiped them, and when the moisture cleared, he recognized the other two. Loren Jasper on one side, the woman he'd been seeing in Cedarton on the other.

No, not possible. Totally not possible. How could the woman who killed herself six years and eight months ago be sitting there with a woman who was murdered a few weeks ago in Cedarton and another one who, dear God, looked so much like Leanne it hurt to look at her. And why hadn't he seen the resemblance between the two before this very moment? No, he must be losing his mind. Again, he wiped his eyes, tilted the album so the gleam of sunlight stopped blurring the photo. Shook his head and ripped out the one of Leanne alone to lay it beside the group. Both were his Leanne, taken before she overdosed, in the center a somewhat younger Loren Jasper smiled at the one on the right. All three so resembled one another they had to be sisters. Now he was going crazy, for his Leanne had no sisters. Not that he knew of, and why would she keep that a secret?

With a shout of distress, he threw the album across the deck. Fool. You're imagining things. It simply isn't possible. Face buried in both hands, he sobbed. Sobbed for the loss of his wife and for his own stupidity knowing far too late, how important that relationship was.

CHAPTER 9

With only one way to escape the narrow road, Jessie shifted into reverse, checked the rearview mirror, then the one Parker had installed outside the left door, and jammed down the accelerator. Brush on the left side of the narrow track screeched across the paint on the door. She cringed. Parker would have a fit. So stop. Try again. Turn the wheel. Remember going backward is opposite forward steering but the mirror makes it another opposite. Okay, here we go. Who's that in the rearview mirror? Standing in the middle of the path? Familiar yet not. He stood spread-legged knee-deep in the overgrowth.

Slam on the brakes or hit him. Some choice. The fool pranced about like he didn't care one bit if she ran right over him. Of course she wouldn't, but she ought to.

Instead she yelled at him. "Idiot, want to get run over?" Once she came to a stop he strolled alongside, the yellow golden rod whipping around his hips. At her door he leaned into the open window, forefinger over his lips in a shushing motion.

Of course it was him. Why not? He was everywhere. The infamous Ranger Jameson. This time the gunfighter's coat was missing. He wore a pale blue dress shirt open at the collar to reveal a gold chain around his neck and black, tight-legged trousers. A gold ring shimmered on his right hand. The man was clearly a changeling. Was that the word for it? Have to look that one up.

What was he doing out here dressed like that? Struck dumb and nose to nose with him, she stared into his blue eyes. "What are you playing at today? An LA gangster?"

He smiled, his blond hair tousling in the wind. Finger over his lips wanting her to be quiet? Good grief. For a man wandering around in the wilderness, he was immaculately clean down to the shiny boots.

"Expect you either dinna see the sign or you canna read."

What? A dreadful Irish brogue. If she didn't know better, she'd believe she was dreaming. He definitely didn't have his Texas accent. Mouth open, she pointed at the sign. "You're going to shoot me?"

"Ah, so you ken its meanin?"

"Oh, my God, stop that before I throw up." If he didn't have his elbows planted in the window, she'd boogie right out of there.

"Did it say stop, no trespassing, or private property? Crap no. Smith & Wesson indeed."

"Lassie, what air you doin back here in the end of nowhere?"

"Guess you're going to keep that up. Did I wander into another universe? And who are all these men?" They'd emerged out of the brush like magic, trying to look menacing. More like a bunch of hillbillies, got up that way on purpose.

He leaned closer, spoke in a low tone so the onlookers who were chattering among themselves, wouldn't hear. "Let's see if we can get you out of here before trouble arises." With a charming grin, he raised his voice. "I'd be pleased to turn this"—he slapped the top of the door frame—"beautiful car around for you and see you on your way."

"No, thank you. I prefer to do so myself." She leaned close. "They doing tryouts for a play?"

He stepped back, then whirled to face her. "Then I would suggest you hasten to do so as in immediately, Lassie."

"Keep calling me that." A dog indeed.

Before he could reply, a shot rang out and pinged on the rear fender. She yelped.

He opened the door, grabbed her arm. "I fear you did not move in time. I must ask that you step out now, if you value your life. My partner isn't as friendly as I, and despite our looks, he runs things around here."

The man who stepped into view from the trees nearby, a rifle all but pointing at her, was dressed in overalls, red long-sleeved undershirt, unlaced work boots, and a cap pulled low on muddy colored hair. A character straight from Hollywood's imagination.

Yanked from the car seat by Jameson, who had warned her not to recognize him, she searched her surroundings wildly. She was in Eastern Grace County right on the line beyond which some very odd happenings often occurred. As long as they remained in the very wildest of the area bothering no one, they were left alone. And she hadn't been privy to the meetings held between the lawmen while she was in jail, so to speak. Obviously things had moved on, leaving her behind. Catching up on what might endanger the remainder of the county hadn't happened because of her time spent caring for Dal. It really wasn't her business what these men were up to, but it sure galled that she didn't know.

If Jameson was who he earlier claimed to be, he wouldn't allow her to be hurt or killed. Would he? One could only hope. For now she had no choice but to go along. Things were getting interesting. If she got through this, it would make one hell of a story. Provided they'd let her write it.

"I'll drive the lass out of here. She has no idea where she is. Meet you down at the camp."

Sounded good to her. She hurried to climb back into the Jeep, and with a shudder took the shotgun seat, the intonation clear.

"Go along with what I say and keep your head down." Jameson cranked up the Jeep, popped the clutch, and spun dirt and clods when the next shot clanged into the front fender. Apparently they'd changed their minds about letting him haul her off. Cowering under the dash, she hung on with all fours, swore they did a one-eighty right there before speeding off, small tree limbs smacking fenders, hood, and windshield.

If the front wheels hadn't left the ground like a horse rearing, she'd be surprised. Near to magically it dug its way out of there gunshots cutting chips out of trees on every side. Cursing under his breath, words Jessie only knew existed, Jameson floor-boarded the gallant vehicle, that in its former life had seen plenty of unfriendly gunfire, until the only sounds behind them were echoes of pounding feet and the ping of bullets. Sucking in a rattling breath, he slowed and downshifted to a comforting speed, though still being swacked by tree limbs on both sides.

He hammered the steering wheel with both hands. "Do you have any idea what you've done? I ought to've let them shoot you or in the least hung you out to dry, which is one of their favorite customs. Upside down like butchering a hog. Sheriff Richards might ought to put you back in jail permanently."

Still hunkered under the dash, she trembled at his threat. "I got lost, that's all. How could that possibly have damaged your crazy plan, whatever it was? Next time you're going to play Secret Agent Man let me know, and I'll go round the other way."

"You have no business wandering around like a lost goose. Especially not out here in God's Little Acre. Lord woman, you almost got us both killed. And now I won't dare try to get back in with them."

"Well, from the looks of 'them' I'd say you're lucky I came along. Besides, till you left Texas to come here, I wandered where I pleased."

Once more he socked the wheel, this time with both fists. And there came that indistinguishable dialog again. "So I've heard."

"Watch your damn mouth and stop beating on my car, you insidious wild man."

"Kindly don't use such words. Wild man is sufficient."

"Do you suppose you could calm down enough to take me home? I have no idea where I am."

No one appeared to be chasing them, but he kept up a good pace after the road widened, muttering under his breath all the while. It was probably a good thing she couldn't make out what he was saying, so she didn't try.

When he reached the windmill, she sat back and pointed. "I was here, see the buffalo, and then when I came out that road right there, I guess I turned the wrong way."

He stopped, set the brake, and left the car running. "She's yours if you think you can manage to get home. Oh, by the way, you're welcome." Before she could say anything, he took a deep breath and went on. "I swore you said you were a native around these parts, and then you go and pull such a crazy stunt."

He swung out over the closed door and headed up the road.

She yelled at him. "Well, I've never run across the likes of you, so how would I know you dragged danger around like a skunk's tail? All cute and smelly."

He swung an arm in the air to dismiss her remark.

She was not in the mood to let it go at that and stood hip-deep in brush, hands on her hips and yelled some more. "Wait. Where are you going now? It's miles out of here, you can't walk. What if they come after you?"

"Well, they won't, and I can walk. For your information, I have to go tell my boss I lost our connection. I may lose my job, but don't you worry about it. We'll have to start all over cleaning up this backcountry." He just kept walking, didn't even look back.

Tired of trying to keep up, she jumped in the car, reversed, and crept along beside him. "Look, I didn't mean to cause you trouble. But since when do Texas Rangers go under cover in Arkansas? I seem to recall you saying you're on vacation. And for your information we have our own Rangers. Never mind answering me. It'd just be another exaggeration. Let me take you wherever it is you're going."

"No thank you. I'd appreciate it if you'd go where you're going, and let me do the same. It's only about twenty miles. I can make it in no time. And it'd do you well to educate yourself on what's going on out in the world before you get yourself killed." He glared at her. "Lassie."

She sniffed. "Again I'm sorry. Hope you have a nice day."

A trail of dust rose in the air at the crossroads ahead of them, and a black SUV with dark windows skidded to a stop. He hollered something to them, then climbed in the opened door. The vehicle pulled around her. He rolled down the window and held up a Sat phone, grinning like an angry ape.

Next time she saw him, she'd shoot without warning. She ground the gears and sped off, making sure to head the right way at the crossing.

What an asshole.

Dal had his display of pictures ready when Colby came back at noon. Together they compared each one, sorting out any that contained one or more of the three women. Both were convinced that the women were so alike they might well be related. How that lent clues to the case, he had no idea. They both agreed on Loren, the one who was the body in Parker's barn, and the one unknown Dal had seen around town was the same one Jessie had rescued at the jail. The third was Leanne, Dal's wife, standing arm in arm with the other two women. She'd overdosed seven years earlier. His stomach turned over like he'd eaten something dreadful. Shaken, he stared for a long time at the young Leanne who had been his wife. Be damned if he'd let that throw him. How would they learn the connection between the three? It had to be connected to drugs. The best and worst guess, but how and why and what now? He did his best not to show Colby how he felt. His heart was broken, but he swallowed the pain. They needed to learn what had happened, that's all. Once they agreed on the IDs, Colby marked each picture with initials and lay them aside.

Doing his best to keep his gaze off the image of a younger, laughing Leanne, Dal swallowed hard and scanned the pictures for one last look. Straightening them, he cleared his throat and touched her image one last time.

"They have a connection, I'm not sure what it is. Jameson is tight lipped so far, but he knows more than he's shared with us. I'm losing my patience, but Mac assures me not to worry. Everything will work out. I have to believe him since I've not been involved the past few weeks. He gave me a quick update, but it's not the same as sitting in on an interrogation. When we find out where they're at, then we'll know where to start."

Mad with a desire to hit the ground running, find those involved, and get busy with interviews, Dal couldn't stop chattering. "Obtain means, motive, opportunity, alibis. Maybe someone saw them commit the murders, but I tend not to rely on eyewitnesses. People see the craziest things when they're running on adrenaline. Plumb stupid to rely on eyewitnesses."

Dal continued to pace, pulled out his phone, and punched in Jessie's number. It went straight to voicemail. He muttered, tried Mac. Stared at the array spread on the table while it rang.

Mac picked up, the sound of machinery clattering in the background. Dal hollered in the mouthpiece. "What's going on?"

"Dragging the wreck off the road. Tried to get some help earlier but blamed if everone ain't busy. Been one heck of a week. Git back away from that… you wanta git your head took off? Whatcha need, Dal?"

"Sounds like you got your hands full. We can handle this. Stay with it. I'll talk to you later about what Kathy and Dave came up with at the cabin."

Mac cleared his throat. *"That'll work, but we're gonna have a long day and night. You need to go on home and remember you're on desk duty for a while yet. Do wish we could find that other gal, though."*

Dal nodded. "Find her soon, or she's going to be dead. I can guarantee you she's in bad danger." Touching the other girl's picture told him so, but he kept quiet to Mac, who knew of his abilities but often remained skeptical.

"You know something for sure?"

"As for sure as I know things. Get her found, and I'd say do it now."

He'd do it himself, but it was best not to argue with the old Sheriff about desk duty. His head was close to feeling better, certainly good enough to do more than sit at the station. Colby was watching him when he disconnected and turned around. "Mac figures we oughta see if we can find out more about that other woman, find her fore she ends up dead. He's got his hands full. We'll put together all we know so some of the boys can help handle the investigation."

Not wanting to explain further where the idea that the other woman was in danger came from, Dal gathered up the pictures, went to the copy machine, and duplicated a stack. "Let's start with handing them out on the streets and to the deputies. Our chances of finding someone whose seen one of them are better that way. We'll send copies to the Staties as well so they can all be on the lookout for this little gal. Sure don't want her to turn up dead like that Loren girl." He shook his head, mind on Leanne and how she'd died. "We need to find this girl and get her in custody. Now."

Couldn't save his wife or Loren Jasper, but by God he'd do his best to save this gal. To hell with a dumb thing like a concussion.

Colby stared at him. "You need to go home, lay down. Those concussions can be bad if you don't take care."

He shook his head. Stopped when the room whirled. "Dammit, no time for that now, let's get these pictures handed out. Someone may have seen her or know where she is." Just thinking of her out there alone made his heart jerk like it'd been hit with a ten-pound hammer. Someone was out to kill her.

Colby frowned when he took the stack of pictures that included both the dead girl and the girl who had run away. "Why we hunting this dead girl? Loren?"

"We aren't. We're hunting someone who might have known any one of these girls including her. We know the first one died in Dallas, the second one here." He turned away, wiped his face with the flat of his hand. "Someone may recognize any one of them. Door to door, people walking. Kids. Anyone who'll take a look. Okay?"

Colby nodded. "Yeah, okay. But you better take it easy for a while. You get dizzy or anything, hike your butt back to the station. Mac'll have my hide I let anything happen to you." He picked up a picture. "Beautiful girl. I'm sorry, what happened to her. Must be tough."

Dal turned and headed for the door. "Yeah, tough."

Forgetting about Colby, he slammed the door behind himself, leaving the deputy to catch up to him on his own, which he managed in a hurry. He no more than rounded the corner than the two of them came upon Shilo and Marvin Captree, hand in hand and in a big hurry, so that they all tangled on the narrow sidewalk. The two big deputies carried more weight, and the Captree couple sort of bounced off them. Two piles of pictures fluttered to the sidewalk. Shilo slammed back against the wall, and Marvin hit the telephone pole planted on the corner. Colby went down to scoop up the pictures. While Colby knelt gathering the photos, Dal steadied Shilo, handed her over to her husband. Muttered "sorry."

After the "are you hurts" were over, Marvin noticed a photo still on the sidewalk. He grabbed it up, took a long look before handing it over.

"Do you know this girl?" Dal watched Marvin's odd tugging of his lip, the sliding sideways of his glance, and not looking too long at any one thing. "Sir, if you do you could be a great help."

The man glanced toward his wife then down to the sidewalk, held the picture up to her. "Doesn't this look like that one who came in the pub in Dallas looking for a job? This was a couple years ago. Right after we came to the US. She—"

When Shilo nodded, Dal handed them another photo of all three girls "Do you know any of them?"

They both took a long look. "Just the one, because of the mark. They all do resemble each other, but that's not unusual when girls are looking to work in a pub or strip club or the like. They all go for the same look."

Colby looked closer. "The mark looks like a tattoo. But you don't know the other two? Or remember her name?"

The couple looked at each other once more. "Sorry, no," both said at the same time. They agreed to take copies to keep on hand at the pub.

Colby turned to pass a strolling man a copy. Dal didn't want to let the British couple go yet. It just seemed like they might know something, just didn't know they knew it. But they offered no more.

He changed the subject. "You folks actually get a permit for the pub? What is it? The Purple Raven. Is there really such a thing?"

Both laughed. "Not exactly." Marvin appeared to do most of the talking. "We have a permit to open up as a tearoom serving tea, coffee, muffins, cakes, biscuits, sandwiches, and the like. In another month or so we will go back before the council, and they will have it sorted."

"And you're happy with that?" Dal nodded at a woman passing by who took a copy of his pictures.

"Well, it gives us a chance to get sorted to the ways of you Yanks. After all, we might decide we don't like it here. Or a tearoom is extremely pleasant. Who knows? It's okay for the present, so we shall wait and see how things go. We really like your wee village so far."

Dal stopped to answer his phone. Parker on the other end. *"Heard from Jessie lately? She's not picking up."*

"Nope, where'd she go?"

"Over to the rim of the canyon. Pretty country over there. Some odd folks have brought in a herd of buffalo, and she wants to write a story. She might be in a black hole for the phone. I'll wait a little bit and try again."

"More likely she's off riding one of those brutes. You know Jessie." Dal hung up and shook his head. Parker never worried about Jessie this much before Loren was killed. He couldn't blame him. A man should protect the woman he loved, and when he couldn't, he knew he'd failed.

He stared down at the photo in his hand and the image of the wife he'd failed to protect. Someone else was wandering around in danger too. Jessie needed to keep in mind that a lot of that country was wild and wooly. Dammit, now Parker had him stewing about her as well. Odd how that county line area was allowed to remain long. But let heroin and murder into the civilized part of the county, and Mac had just had enough. And rightly so.

"You okay, Dal?" Colby paused on the sidewalk,

"Huh? Yeah." The question brought him out of his reverie.

"You know I can finish up distributing these, you best go on back to the station. There's plenty of paperwork to do, and I don't want to end up having to do it."

"Yep, you just want to get out of it all." He was worn out but hated to admit it. Yet he gave in and headed for the station. Colby's laughter followed him around the corner and up to the entrance.

Before burying himself in the files stacked on his desk, Dal tried to reach Jessie again.

A rap on the door and Jameson strode in, dressed in raggedy jeans and t-shirt, bare feet stuck in sneakers.

Dal laughed. "One of these days you'll get shot for a stranger, Ranger. You've got one heck of a wardrobe."

"What? This? My relaxation outfit. Heard talk about a woman who moved into a shack over on Greasy Creek. Gonna go take a look. Need to be dressed for the part. Thought you might want to come. Could be our missing woman."

Forgetting about the headache, Dal eyed the files on the corner of his desk, rose, and fetched his hat. "Long as I don't have to look like you do. Reckon I can hide till you make contact. Better send Colby a text. You know he's my keeper." Maybe this'd stop him from worrying about Jessie.

But it wouldn't.

Jessie eyed the flat-as-a-pancake tire. Still thirty miles from home on roads that only allowed for twenty-mile-an-hour speed, at the most. Well, okay. She'd changed a tire once or twice in her lifetime. Usually someone came along, stopped, and lent a hand, which she was always willing to accept with thanks.

The spare hung on the back of the Jeep, and it'd never been off since Parker turned his baby over to her when she fell in love with it. The tire iron was under some stuff in the back, so she dragged out a jug of anti-freeze, two cans of oil, four bottles of water, and a tattered denim jacket to get to the thing. Now she had to get it off the rear end. Most spares lay within a trunk and didn't have to be manually removed by taking bolts loose. She fitted the iron on the first one, heavy with dust, leaned into it with all her might. It didn't budge.

After four hard tries, she planted her butt on the rear bumper, opened a bottle of water, poured some over her head and drank some. Rested there a while and tried again. No luck. The thing wouldn't budge.

"Enough of this." Panting, she trudged to the door, reached in, and fetched the phone from her pack. No signal. Standing on the seat, balancing on top of the window frame, the blasted thing above her head, or walking round and round on the ground. Nothing.

"Grrr, what good are you if you don't work?" She pitched it into the seat. Peered up and down the road. She hadn't been in this area of the county a whole lot, and given her propensity for getting turned around, she could well end up walking into Tennessee.

Reaching for the pack, she spied her camera. Digital, it hooked up to the phone and in turn sent pictures to her tablet which she'd left on her desk at the office. And the GPS in it told the receiver her location. So, okay. Best to remain here, send out a visual SOS, and wait to be rescued. Plenty of water, always bags of cookies and chips stowed somewhere. And it wasn't all that hot, being mid-October.

Yep, that was the smart thing to do.

Two hours later with no result. Still the smart thing? Well, maybe not.

Leaned up against the back, she stared down the road. Something moved, stirred dust. Coming toward her. Not a car. Motorcycle? Closer? The sun hung low in the west, doing its best to blind her, but the vehicle looked like a farm wagon being pulled by a team. By standing in the middle of the road, she spied it. Sure enough, a farm wagon, two large jacks in harness and a man slumped in the seat like he might've been there for hours.

Well, it was better than nothing. She raised an arm.

He tightened the reins. "Whoa, boys. Whoa." The command was deep and guttural. "Where ye headed little lady?"

"First town you can take me to, if you don't mind."

He spit over the side away from her. "That'd be Round Mountain, I reckon. But they ain't nuthin there but a mercantile. Looks like you might need more than that."

"Think they have a telephone?"

"Believe so, and they've got cold pop, bologna, and bread. Mustard too, I believe."

He was right. Inside the place might as well been that long-ago memory. Her mouth watered.

Years ago, she was with her grandpa, Mac's best friend, and they stopped at a small town mercantile. Inside behind a glass window in a cooler was a big roll of baloney. The old man behind the counter sliced off some of the meat, and grandpa bought a loaf of Rainbow bread and bottles of cold RC. They ate sandwiches sitting on a bench outside the store in the warm sun, nodding once in a while when someone walked by. Nothing had ever tasted that good then as now. And at that moment, sitting there waiting for Dal, nothing seemed so real, so treasured as that memory.

A deputy's car skidded up to a stop, and she opened her eyes, the vision fading. Scowling, Dal burst out of the car like one of those Jack-in-the-box clowns.

"Goddammit, Jessie, you had me out of my mind with worry. Then I saw your car empty. If my GPS signal hadn't been on I'd a had a fit. How the hell did you get here? And what are you eating?"

By this time, she was on her feet. "Back off, buster. First off, I didn't ask your permission to come over here, and I sure as hell don't have to do so. I've been on my own for a lot of years, so don't go hooking a leash to me. Not now, and not ever." Nothing annoyed her more.

Fists against his thighs he stared at her in silence, eyes sparking with anger. "Well, then I reckon I'll just go on my way and let you solve this little problem all on your own. This fella have a spare or a way to fix that tire? I'll just leave you to it and be on my way."

Her rescuer tossed down the crust of his sandwich and strode to the car. "That ain't no way to talk to a lady, Mister. Even you being the law and big as you are."

And he was. The fella had to crick his neck to look him in the eye. But he was doing just that. Dal went at him toe to toe to show just how big he was. "I'd thank you to stay out of this. I haven't had a good few days."

This was fast building up to a fistfight. Jessie let go her anger and laid a hand on Dal's arm. Last thing he needed so soon after the wreck was a rough and tumble backwoods match.

"I'm sorry, Dal, he's helping me, that's all"

"While the two of you have a blamed picnic, we're all running around scared to death what might've happened to you. Shit, woman." He whirled, snatched his radio, and mumbled something into it she couldn't understand.

Turning back, he grabbed her arm, propelled her around the hood, and placed her in the passenger side. "Sit, Stay." He slammed the door, kicked his way through the dust back to the other side where he stuck out his hand. "Thanks for helping her, sir. Someone will pick up the car by dark."

Jessie grabbed hold of the door handle, but he'd locked it. She shook it. "Let me out of here, you big ape. What's wrong with you? You never treat me this way."

He sat in the seat, started the car, glanced at her. "Seat belt," he said and fastened his.

Before she could do the same, he took off so fast she was glued to the back of the seat.

The car fishtailed, tires spitting gravel. Fingers fumbling, she fastened the buckle. "What in the holy crap is wrong with you, Dallas Starr? You know better than to treat anyone this way." Tears filled her eyes but be damned if she'd shed them. She looked away, staring out the window at the field of huge hay bales lined up in neat rows as far as she could see till the tears dried.

Out of the corner of her eye, she took a quick peek at him. He rubbed his eyes with the fingers of one hand. He was crying. Well, by God he ought to. Treating her like that. But what was going on? In all their time together, even when he did lose his temper, he never took it out on her. Sure didn't cry.

"Stop." He didn't, so she said it louder. "Stop this car right now."

He slammed on the brakes, sending the car sliding sideways to fill the wide gravel road. This reminded her of something that happened right after they first met, and she argued with him about locals making a living growing marijuana. He'd acted the same way, and when he stopped, had bailed out, and got himself tangled up in a barbed wire fence.

She spread her hand on his thigh. The muscles tightened. "You're not gonna bail on me, are you?"

Bringing the vehicle under control, he turned off the engine and leaned back, rubbed his eyes. "She's dead because I let it happen. I didn't watch out for her like I should've, and now something terrible is happening because of it, and I don't know how to stop it. We can't find that other little gal anywhere. Ranger and I been hunting, then he bailed on me to check out some holler he knows, and so I come over here to find you. Hell of a day, Jess, trying to keep up with wayward women. And you... you... act just like it means nothing."

Her heart trembled with despair, and she wanted to cry. "I'm sorry, Dal."

He grappled to hug her with the loaded console between them. One hand behind her head he kissed her on the tip of the nose. "I'm sorry, so sorry. If anything ever happened to you, I don't know what I'd do. I truly don't."

"Oh, shit, I didn't mean it, Dal. I didn't think."

Then with doubled fists she hit him on the shoulder. "Don't ever treat me that way again. Just talk to me. You hear? I don't read minds."

He nodded, kissed her again, and started the car.

Times like this she hated consoles and bucket seats. She wanted to scoot over against him, lay her head on his shoulder, kiss the bare warm spot on his neck. Instead she placed her hand high up on his thigh. Kneaded until he grew huge under the jeans.

"Up there, behind those trees. Pull over." She circled her fingers around his swollen penis.

He barely made it to the shelter of trees hiding them from the road before he skidded to a stop, jacked open the door and scrambled to the ground. She pawed in the back, dragged out the quilt kept there for just such emergencies, jumped to her feet, and ran around to his side. He grabbed it, spread it on the ground, and took her hand. They were both on their knees, unfastening clothing, not waiting till they were totally undressed before they threw their arms around each other. and started a frantic search for erotic zones. His mouth found a breast still inside the bra, and he sucked while she worked him clear of the zipper of his jeans.

For some reason his sucking on her nipple through the cloth of her bra was about the sexiest thing he could do for foreplay. Perhaps it was because that's what he had done the first time they'd made love. Fearful they'd be caught, they didn't undress. Just found gaps in clothing where they could touch bare skin.

Now as if he feared losing her for good, his lovemaking went from frantic through tender, wild, and sweet. all in the matter of a few minutes. A sob escaped from deep in his throat.

Terrible of her to frighten him so. She would never do that to him again. Spread palms buried beneath the seat of her jeans he peeled the fabric down a bit, till he could work his way inside, slide the anxious, searching member between her legs. Like a creature making its crawling way along her leg headed for its nest. Hot, hard, moist, slippery. She went mad with desire, wiggled and squirmed to give him entrance. Every time he missed, she tightened her legs around him and shivered with an orgasm, and he would begin again.

Good heavens, she was about to fly apart. "Dal, sweetie. Slow down. Let me pull my jeans down so you can get in."

"Uh." A grunt of sorts before he tried again, only to slide along the warm slippery access and miss, which set her off once more. She tightened her thighs and gasped, driving him a little more wild.

This time his efforts succeeded, and in that very instant he came with such a joyous growl and a whoop that she joined him. Counting orgasms wasn't copacetic, but she could've sworn she had half a dozen while he tried to manage one through their tangle of clothing. After that she did not count.

His shout turned into a deep chuckle she could barely hear over her own outcry. "Guess you'll want to do that more often, huh?"

He was still inside her, though fading fast. Shoving tight against him, she laughed. "You betcha. Wanta go at it now?"

"With a little urging, I could, but I think I hear someone coming. We might ought to get tucked back in and try to look like we're just enjoying the shade.

She rolled free, zipping his jeans, then hers. "You always were a chicken. It's more fun when you almost get caught. Leaves you wanting it so bad you can't hardly wait."

The passing car slowed, a man yelled out the window. "Y'all need help?"

Dal laughed "See?"

"Naw, we're okay." She giggled into her fist. "Okay, you win. Let's go to my place and try something else."

"Just promise me you'll never do something so crazy as taking off like that again. Surely it wasn't just to put a bit of excitement in our sex life."

"A bit? Holy crap. Well, if it was, it worked."

"It did, but there are other ways, believe me. Just promise me."

She nodded, but could she?

10
CHAPTER

The next morning Dal paid for his actions of the previous day with a furious headache, but there wasn't time to dwell on it. Mac came out of his office, grabbed his arm, and guided him into the detective's room. Colby was busy rearranging the murder wall.

"What happened? Who'd we get?" Jerked away from worrying about the woman who was still missing to the present, Dal concentrated on the changes.

"Colby here decided to make one more swipe of empty places where our perps might be holed up before he went to bed last night, and—"

"Lo and behold he found a definite hidey-hole in the barn up at the Hermitage house." Colby finished for him. "Built theirselves a fine place behind some bales of hay hauled in yesterday."

Mac slapped the deputy on the back. "Great thinking. Jake Brown down the road rented the barn this summer to store some of his smaller bales, and no one thought one thing about it when he plumb filled that ole barn and the loft. These guys squirreled their way in, probly in the night."

Colby grinned great big, pure dee proud of himself. "It just oc-curred to me, like a flash of lightning when I noticed the baler sitting out back there."

"Got 'em in the interrogation room, Dal." Mac couldn't have looked more proud. "I'd like you to take a run at them first. Work your magic see what you can come up with. Only jest two of 'em, but you might get something out of one of 'em. Talk to 'em one at a time, and don't let 'em share a cell afterward to compare notes. And don't mention we got Tiger Thief. Once you're done, they don't confess, then me and Colby will go at 'em." He pounded Dal's shoulder, laid the files on the corner of his desk. "You up for it, boy?"

"You bet. Had my fill of this damn chair." He rose and stretched out the kinks.

Mac filled everyone in quickly. "Leon Gross worked earlier at the animal farm for six months and was a suspect when Maizie got loose be-fore. The white donkey was blamed for unlocking the gate, but later, Dal and Colby both doubted the small animal could've unlocked the gate and let her free. That little donkey just liked to look guilty of the crime at the time. Proud of herself, I reckon."

The gathered deputies laughed.

"Well, ole Leon quit his job to take a better one. He had a key to the locked gate when Colby rounded 'em up. We're waiting for forensics. Let's try to put these ones with Loren when she was killed. All we got is the three guys who set a tiger loose. I myself figure they did that to cover up the murder of that purty little gal. Give themselves time to get her body placed up at Parker's and get away. But a lot of this is guesswork. Meanwhile let's get ourselves a confession or two."

Colby studied the file a moment. "I'm going out to talk to July, there's some gaps here, and maybe she can remember more now. I'll get back to you."

Mac nodded. "See if you can get more, but Dal here can talk to these two in the meantime."

About time he was turned loose to get back to some serious work. Dal picked up a copy of the file and stepped inside the interview room.

These men could very well be killers, and he needed to get close to them, though he hated the thought. Their evil would come off on him, no matter what he did to avoid it. Grandfather had taught him some tricks for avoiding the pain of such a thing, but he still dreaded it.

Tucking the case file under his arm, he asked for the youngest of the two. The one who might be coerced into coming clean for a deal. He wanted to close this case before anyone else was killed.

Talking to them separately would be best. Easier to convince each they were in deep shit. Alone—except for Grandfather. It could be a long day's work. A shaggy little man sat across from Dal, fear washing over him. Seldom did Dal have to say much in a situation like this, so he stared until the guy started to tremble. And it worked. A tumble of thoughts, how he was paid to steal the tiger. "Never saw no tiger before, but shit a cat is a cat." His words died, but his thoughts didn't. He and two friends knew when July would be inside, and they took the cage to the farm, baited Maizie into it with the dead deer, and took off.

"That's not the end of it. Who paid you, and why?"

Shaggy shrugged. "Didn't care why. Money is why."

"How'd you know when it was safe to go after Maizie?"

"Huh-uh. He'd kill me. All I knowed was what time to take the cat, and that was all. I don't want to know nothing more, and if you're smart you won't either. She—uh—they one mean bunch."

Dal kicked the chair out from under himself and hovered over Shaggy. "I'm the one you ought to be scared of, I'm meaner than they are."

Shaggy cowered, threw both arms over his head.

Someone rapped on the glass. A signal to come out.

On the other side of the door Colby waited with Mac.

He grinned. "Miss July remembered something when I showed her Loren's picture. She visited with Miss July on a few occasions. Always come by on foot. Say, did you know that her cabin is just down over the hill from Miss July's farm?"

"Oh, shit. I'm going back in there. Did you see the report came in this morning from Kathy Spacey? I just glanced at it before you sent me in there. There were hulls of feed Miss July gives those big birds, what are they? They found them in Loren's hair. She was killed at the animal farm."

"You think them boys did it?"

Dal studied Mac for a minute. "Nope, they're too dumb to carry it off. They took Maizie so someone else could kill her. Not sure all the whys yet, but I'd bet I can get some of them. I'm going back in there."

Mac didn't object.

Dal dragged the shivering Shaggy to his feet, held him close so he had to look into his eyes. He said not a word to the poor guy. When he dropped him into the chair Shaggy's thoughts ran rampant, and Dal heard everything. He knew nothing about a murder. He and his friends were paid to take the tiger, and when it got away, they went into hiding for fear of what might happen to them. They'd been in the hay barn since, sneaking out at night to steal food and liquor and cigarettes from surrounding farms.

"Who paid you? You know you could go to prison for stealing an endangered species?"

"A what? We didn't steal no whatever that is. We took a blamed cat and couldn't even keep it. Durned thing run off first chance it got."

"All I need to know is who paid you, and if you tell me that, I can get you out of trouble over the cat, since it came home and all." Dal pinned the terrified Shaggy with a dark-eyed stare.

Fear from the young man washed over Dal. Whoever hired those boys was one mean son of a bitch. Or the bitch herself. While he saw shadows in the kid's mind, he never got a good look at the faces of more than one responsible for Loren's death. Obviously the kid didn't know why she'd been killed, or Dal would've got that from his frightened thoughts.

He did, however, pick up something that maybe the kid had over-heard, he wasn't sure. He kept hearing whispers of finding the other one, getting rid of her too. She knew too much.

He finally sent Shaggy back to his cell and went out to talk to Mac and Colby some more.

"Mac, I think the other woman is in great danger. This goes way deeper than a single killing. We need to try to find her before those others do. Ranger is out there looking, but I haven't heard from him. Besides, he makes me a bit nervous. Hard to tell whose side he's on sometimes. It keeps bugging me that those two in black July spotted might be women or very young boys. I'd put my money on women, though. It's way big, and they're out to get this young woman I saw a few times in town. Tiger thief and his pals have nothing to do with anything but a cat snatch."

"Okay, let's put a BOLO out on her before she gets herself hurt. We'll keep looking for those responsible for killing Loren Jasper. I hear Jameson and Ledger will be by tomorrow. We need to correlate info with them. I agree they aren't telling us all they know. You go on home and get some sleep. Come in tomorrow at ten, and we'll exchange information with them."

Dal nodded, glad to leave this place. He wanted to see Jessie, sit with her, and enjoy an evening together. Go to bed and make love. Forget the images that played in his mind.

For more than three hours Jessie sat at her computer. She had Googled Loren's and Leanne's names and dug her way through line after line of information flowing up the screen. She had already done the same on Facebook with no luck. With Howie needed in the field, she took a run at finding something that might help locate the other woman.

Why weren't these people on social media? What was wrong with them? Everyone who was anyone was on Facebook, for goodness sake. She'd ruled out uncountable listings.

Come on, ladies. Surely you don't both live in a tree house in Bolivia.

What she needed was a cop who could get her inside their tree house, wherever it was.

No, what I need is a good hot shower.

She turned off the laptop and peeled out of her shirt and jeans, leaving a trail into the bathroom. Just as she closed the door, Brad barked, and someone knocked.

Well, crap.

"Just a minute! I'll get decent."

She turned, bent over to pick up her britches, and arms enclosed her around the waist.

"Dal, sweetie."

"Not Dal." The hands made their way up her bare ribcage to cup her breasts.

"Parker, uhm." She'd recognize that cologne anywhere. But the rest? What was going on?

He lifted her, turned her, and wrapped her in both arms. Burying his face against her shoulder, he took a deep breath.

"Jessie, I can't take this a minute longer. I loved her, and she's gone, just like that. It's like being smashed in the gut with a cannon ball to know I'll never hold her again. She's all I can think of."

Shivering under his touch, she covered his hand, turned, and led him into the bedroom. "Close the door and come here."

Sitting on the edge of the bed, him facing her, she slowly undressed him, touching him with gentleness. Having been with him intimately she knew what he needed, and she crawled behind him to rub the back of his neck, then pulled him onto the bed on his stomach where she straddled him and massaged his shoulders, then his back until he relaxed under her touch.

"That better?" It was just a tad too good for Jessie, and she slid off him, breaking contact that was getting a bit too hot.

"Yes. Don't go."

"You relax now. Just stay right here, and I'll take my shower. Then you think about this. Do you really want this to go further when it's Loren you're thinking of? I'm not her, you know. I never can be. You're hurting, and believe me, if you do this, you'll hurt more."

His shoulders quivered, then began to shake as he sobbed. "I came here wanting you, thinking I wanted you, remembering how good we were together. Now I don't know. My body says I need you, even though my heart and spirit say that's not true."

"What your body wants is entirely different from what you truly want. You listen close to your conscience till I get back, then we'll talk."

She remained under the shower for a long time, giving him a chance to think. As for her, she needed comforting, too. But she needed it from Dal, and so far that hadn't happened. Parker was so vulnerable. What would he do if she turned him down? She had to make him see that this was not what he truly wanted. Somehow, someway. She returned wrapped in a towel just in time to come face to face with Dal.

He smiled, reached out to put an arm around her. "Uhm, hello, darlin. Looks like I timed it just right."

From the bedroom came a voice. "I've decided, Jessie."

She swiveled to meet Dal's shocked expression. "Good God, it's a romance novel."

He stood between her and the door, arms held wide. "Is that who I think it is?"

Nodding, she took hold of his arm. "It is who, but it's not what you think."

The door swung open, and a naked Parker stood there, looking as surprised as Dal must've felt.

The two men stared at one another for an instant, then Parker backed into the bedroom.. "I'll get dressed."

Looking shocked Dal, dropped down onto the couch. "Anything you want to say?"

"I can't think of anything."

"Well, that surprises me."

"You wouldn't believe the truth, and I can't think of a way to tell it."

He ran his fingers through tousled black hair. "Why don't you try, Jessie? Right now. I need the truth more than anything else."

Remembering what he'd been through and the possible involvement of Leanne in the murder case they were working on, she moved to sit beside him on the couch. "I know how foolish or made-up this will sound, but I was giving him a massage."

He slanted an astonished look her way, then laughed, laughed some more. "You've got more imagination than that, surely."

"Precisely, so if I were going to lie, I'd use that imagination, come up with something you might believe. Like I was going to remove a cactus thorn from his butt. Something like that. Don't you think?

"So, since we're on a roll with unbelievable excuses, why are you wrapped in a towel, Miss Masseuse?"

"While he dressed, I went to take a shower, which is what I was about to do when he showed up."

"This gets better all the time. Sure didn't look like he was getting dressed to me."

The bedroom door opened, and Parker crept out as if expecting to be hit or shot at.

She opened her mouth.

Dal raised one hand toward her like a traffic cop stopping cars.

She closed her mouth.

Dal opened his. "So Parker, you give me your version of what's going on here."

Jessie rose, the towel falling away. Scrabbling to cover herself, she blurted out her feelings. "This has gone far enough. Number one—I'm free, over twenty-one, and can do what I want short of breaking the law, which is tempting about now. So, let's take a step back. No matter what, I can still do what I please, as can Parker or even you, Dallas.

"My explanation stands, and even if it didn't, evidently I'm not committed to any sort of relationship as of right now, so...." She lifted her shoulders and glared the statement in Dal's direction. "I'm going to dress. Don't kill each other."

Without waiting for another word, she left them staring at her. Slipping into a pair of shorts and a t-shirt, she didn't hear any outcries, so she took her time. Hopefully both men would be gone by the time she finished. What she'd have to deal with tomorrow was another question entirely.

For a few minutes Dal stared at the closed bathroom door, then a few more at Parker before he could bring himself to say anything. When he tried, so did Parker, so they both shook their heads.

"Go ahead."

"You first."

The words came out together.

"I'm leaving now." Dal picked up his hat, screwed it onto his head, and stomped out, ignoring the dancing pit bull trying to get his attention.

At his back, Parker muttered his own thoughts, and they weren't worth considering, so Dal didn't. Though not buddies, him and Parker had always been friends. On the other hand, Jessie and Parker were close. Let's not forget that brief affair while he was gone getting himself back together. She never knew he found out.

Hell, in his mind, he'd been faithful to Leanne all the while he was with Jessie. No matter how strange that was, he felt the truth of it, strong inside himself. Wonder how she felt about it.

The next morning, Dal returned to the office, totally confused and wanting something to take his mind off that episode with Jessie and Parker. The forensics report was on his desk. Looked like Loren had been strangled with a latigo belly strap. The size was right, but they hadn't found one in the barn that might have been used. She had sustained bruises prior to death, as if someone might have beaten her with their fists. She had died approximately four to six hours before Parker found her body in his barn. Dal flipped the page, saw only a few more medical notes as to her physical history prior to death. She had needle marks on her arms, but they were old, so she had obviously stopped using, and her body showed she had no drugs in her system. There was not much else. The body was in Little Rock as of a week earlier.

Once more he studied the photos, then lay the file aside. She did look familiar, but he sure couldn't place her. No sense thinking about who she reminded him of. It was just the body size and coloring, that's all. Leanne looked much the same. That was all, dammit. All. Did Parker know she was a junkie? None of his business, though it could matter to the investigation. It could've caused a fight between the two of them and would make him a suspect.

The search of her neat cabin had brought forth several bags that he hadn't gone through yet other than the photographs which yielded most of the clues.

What he needed now more than anything else was to tie the two women to Leanne and see where that led. Even though it would hurt to go in that direction. The photo of them together had to be at least seven years old, because his wife had been dead that long. But at one time the two women had been together like friends.

Pushing aside the other files, he went to Colby's desk and fetched the original photos of Loren, the unknown woman, and Leanne together. He took them to the scanner and worked a while blowing up sections that showed particular backgrounds. If the pictures were taken somewhere in Dallas, he might be familiar with the place. That could help him learn where those women had been together. It was worth a try.

He sat at his desk studying them using a magnifying glass, so engrossed that when Colby stopped by and leaned beside him, he jumped like he was shot.

"Hey, you were deep into that." He studied what Dal was looking at. "Finding anything new that might help us?"

"Maybe, maybe not. Tell me what you think this is, right there behind Loren's shoulder."

Colby took the glass and peered at the blown-up copy. "Looks like the bottom of a *C* or *O*. I'm not sure if that helps. What's up?"

He put a finger on Leanne's figure. "This is my wife. She died seven years ago, and I was hoping to place these other two women by maybe seeing where this picture was taken, but I'm not getting anywhere yet."

Colby studied the photo a long while. "The background through the window is definitely a nightclub. The tables and dance floor, but don't they mostly look alike?"

"I was hoping I'd recognize it from my club hopping days, but nothing stands out."

"Have we run fingerprints on Loren Jasper yet?"

"Hey, maybe not since we already have an ID on her. Let's check just in case she is someone else."

Colby took the prints from the file and began by running them through local records. "Meanwhile, I'll check the pic of the unidentified one. So far nothing. I'm going to send it to the Staties to see if they can come up with an ID on her. Jameson and Ledger need copies if they don't already have them."

"Say, didn't she have a cell phone, right? Did we check all the contacts in there?"

"We went through it, came up with nothing definitive." Colby glanced up.

"Why don't you let me have a go at it? I just might spot someone I know or someone I remember being with my wife or someone she mentioned. Since I'm just sitting here at my desk why don't I call all of them?"

Colby nodded. "It needs doing. One of the many things we've listed is to try to ID the middle woman. You'd be just the man for that." Colby patted him on the shoulder and grinned. "Good luck, old son."

"Oh, shut up and bring me a cold Coke, would you?"

"Yes, sir, at your beck and call, seeing as how you're injured."

Two hours and four Cokes later, Dal reached a woman from the cell phone contacts who said she had lived in a condo near Loren for a few months back in those years. She now lived in Austin. He identified himself and asked her a few questions, but she didn't know a lot. She didn't remember ever meeting Leanne, and he was about to hang up when she stopped him.

"Wait a minute. I just thought of this. Her best friend was a woman from Dallas who worked for the police department there. I think her name was Leslie something, and she told me once that her sister and her best friend all had names beginning with an L. I think the three of them were close at one time. Does that help?"

"It does indeed." His heart beat faster. "Tell me, do you know where any one of the three might be? Just a clue or idea would help. This is very important."

"Okay, let me think. Wait. Her sister died a few years before I met her. But there was a guy who came around them for a while. His name was real odd, so I ought to remember it. Give me a minute. Uh, no, no. Darn, I can't remember it. Wait, he was British, that I do remember because of his accent. The name I can't come up with. But I'll let you know if I think of it. I promise."

His heart sped up again. Unbelievable. "It wouldn't be Captree, would it?" He held his breath.

"Uhm, that sounds… uh, nope, not quite right. If I think of it, I'll call you back. Can you be reached at the number you're calling from?"

Too much to hope for, but he'd hit on something anyway. Leanne and Loren and now Leslie. Too good to be true? No last name though. Where to go with that.

He'd drop in on Jessie, maybe she'd have some ideas.

Shit, she probably wouldn't let him in the door after their earlier squabble. Maybe he could take flowers or a pizza or a sad looking apology. Hell, he knew she wouldn't mess around with Parker, not in that way. Maybe to soothe his broken heart. Well, he'd go over anyway. It was worth a try. She was a damned good investigator because of the research she had to do on newspaper articles. She might come up with some ideas.

He reached for his hat, and his phone rang. A blocked number, but he picked up anyway.

"Is this Dallas Starr?"

He dropped back into his chair. "Yes."

"This is Leslie Younger. I'm who you've been looking for. I need your help. Where are you? Please hurry. I'm afraid they'll kill me."

He leaped from his chair. "I'm on my way." No one in the office, so he scribbled a quick note and took off.

Following her directions for she'd warned GPS didn't work properly, he found the logging road, went to the T, and followed the creek. He lost the phone signal when he started down into a narrow valley, but her directions took him through thick virgin timber along a game trail that forced him to walk till he came to a shack. The sun set behind him, and a lamp came on ahead, flickering behind tree limbs that tossed in a slight breeze. That had to be the place. Being extra careful, he crept up to the one window without glass. Bending low, he peered over the sill. Inside looked deserted, the lamp no longer shining. The door hung on leather hinges. He pushed it open a few feet and slipped inside, hugging the wall.

Against bars of late sunlight breaking through slits in the wall, a silhouette held perfectly still. When she turned, her features captured by that golden sun, he caught his breath.

No, it couldn't be. His head swam, the knot of the concussion aching like fury.

"Leanne? My God, Leanne?" His voice like broken glass.

"Leslie. I'm Leslie Younger. Are you sure no one followed you?"

He held out his arms, and she rushed to him, let him hold her till they both trembled and cried.

At last she spoke. "I was so afraid you wouldn't come. They spotted me in town, and I had to leave, come deeper into the woods. I found this place. Terrible, isn't it? I've been so afraid someone would've known her. Then me. We're so much alike."

With an extreme effort, he drew himself together. It was like being thrust backward in time. His head spun, and he could barely breathe or stand without clinging to her. "Why are they after you? And who are *they?*"

"It's a long story."

"This is a dump. Let me take you somewhere safe. Clean and safe. You can't stay out here like this."

"Okay, but we have to be careful. They'll kill me, and you as well, if they get a chance, just like they killed Loren."

Unable to think of her as anyone but Leanne, he continued to hold her trembling body against his, wanting her in ways he could not explain. What if she were lying? What if she was Leanne, and somehow he was experiencing a spiritual moment in time. Grandfather could be at work here, and he could have her back? Whole and young and beautiful? At least briefly.

Fool. He had to listen to his own conscience, do what made sense. *Stop. Stop such nonsense. Get her somewhere safe, and get this mess straightened out.* She was Leanne's friend and a CI, and she needed help.

Dogs barked and beams of light slashed through the woods. She cried out, grabbed his arm.

"Oh, God, they're here, they've found us."

"Come on." He pulled her by one hand out the yawning door and into the dark side of the woods. Crashing and tripping over fallen limbs and brambles they fled the pursuit of vicious dogs. Something no one could outrun. God, where could he take her? They were cut off from the car.

Ahead, woods so thick they appeared like an impenetrable wall. Yet he found a way to slither between the huge trunks, drag her along by one hand, leap clumps of brambles, dodge limbs reaching like claws to grab them and throw them into the jaws of the yapping animals hot on their trail. Each step evaded their hot breath by seconds. She stumbled, and he caught her arm, literally pulled her out of reach of the lead animal.

Together they rolled and tumbled into a depression and landed in a leaf strewn bottom. The dogs raced on, their barking fading into the distance. And they were safe, at least for the moment. He held her close, hearts hammering to the rhythm of their gasping.

Caught up in the otherworldly feelings he couldn't yet deny, he held her in a lover's embrace. But he could not do this, had to return to the real world. Otherwise how would he explain his foolish actions to her or to Jessie?

But the needs of his body, fed by the fear of death, betrayed any doubts he might have, and he unbuttoned her shirt. Hand cupping the perfect pink aureole, he circled his lips around its twin that rose to his searching tongue. She wore no bra, and he pulled the sleeves of the shirt free of her arms to taste deeply of her flesh. His kiss brought her alert, her eyes going wide. Nipples hard as pebbles she rose into his kiss, giving until her cries of pleasure matched his.

As if mesmerized, her body moved from the thick matting of grass and leaves, and he slipped her pants off while she arced on her shoulders and heels. Supporting her that way, he licked downward, nibbling, sucking, then licking till he reached the vee between her legs. She cried aloud then, grabbed him around the neck and held him tightly till he couldn't move away. She took what he gave her, sounding like a small child crying then laughing in turn. His tongue explored the soft, sweet, honey-dewed laps until she collapsed to her back, breathing heavily.

Dear God, what if she was a virgin? He had to stop, not do this to a young girl who could very well be his Leanne from the past. Would Grandfather do this to him, to her? Though he had no answer, his body throbbed with a desire so strong he grew large and hard. He wanted this one last time with the woman he loved.

His voice low, he asked what he dreaded to hear the answer to. "Are you a virgin, sweet baby?"

She clung all the harder, shaking her head up and down. "But do it, please. It feels so good. It would be okay, really."

He held her in his arms, hand cradling the back of her head. "No, I can't do that. I won't. Leanne would never forgive me." Biting his lips, he held her for a long moment, relishing her fragrance, silken touch, lovely taste, then lay her back in the grass, kissed her forehead and settled just out of reach, staring up into the starlit sky. Her sobbing slowly died away, and he sensed she slept.

Tears dripped from the corners of his eyes. *I miss you so much, Leanne. I'm so sorry I failed you. I'll never forgive myself.*

You haven't failed me. Now you must let me go. Please, I have to leave, and I can't until you let me.

A voice out of the mists. He reached for her, but she disappeared into the darkness.

He awoke surprised that he too had slept. There was no sign of Grandfather, the dogs, or their followers. His tears had dried, leaving stiff trails on the skin of his cheeks.

Nor were they in a cave, but lay on a thick covering of sweet grasses near a burbling creek in the shade of huge trees, their clothing in a pile next to them. Her head nestled on his shoulder. He kissed her cheek, the soft young skin sweet as nectar against his lips. Then he dressed her, surprised she didn't awaken. Perhaps she wasn't supposed to.

Would she remember her vague experience with orgasms? Probably, it wasn't something easily forgotten. Maybe it would be best if she didn't.

He hoped someday he could forget it. It wasn't often one was offered the chance to relive a moment in time that held so many sweet memories and had the good sense to turn it down. Relieved that he hadn't gone through with what he'd wanted so badly, he stared up into the twinkling of sunlight through the leaves. The girl deserved more than that memory of her first experience with sex. And Jessie deserved his honor.

Well, Grandfather, you've outdone yourself this time. Pleased with himself, he smiled into the blue sky. Sometimes things were just too much to be explained. But he truly wished Grandfather would stop messing about with him. It was almost too much to handle.

11
CHAPTER

Leslie awoke slowly, looking puzzled rather than frightened.

"You okay?" He was afraid to say anything for fear of how it would come out. Once Grandfather had given him the voice of a fox for half a day because he sassed him. Dal was twelve, and it never happened again.

She nodded and sat up. "Where are we?"

"Not far from home."

"Is that your car?"

The patrol unit sat on a dirt path that was merely tire tracks in the grass. Great. Grandfather often managed to surprise him. He recognized the area. They were less than five miles from town and not far off Center Road, which was a part of the regular patrol. He'd driven it on several occasions when they were short of duty deputies. Grandfather had pulled another one of his tricks. Whatever his reasoning, there wasn't time to figure it out. Worse, how would he explain his unit being out here all night? Or, for that matter, maybe it had been brought here by magic. Yeah, sure. Tell Mac that.

Perhaps him having found Leslie would be enough.

She interrupted his thoughts. "I had the strangest dream last night." She let him pull her to her feet.

"Oh, yeah?" Couldn't have been any stranger than his.

"I was terrified. We were being chased by dogs and people with guns."

He shook his head. What was the point of putting her through that? Or himself either, for that matter. Knowing Grandfather, he might never learn what the old man was trying to teach him with this entire episode. Perhaps it was connected with his earlier warning to beware of a woman. He could well have made an ass out of himself with Leslie when she crawled into his arms and begged him to make love to her. Sometimes he needed guideposts with Grandfather's puzzling lessons.

He opened the car door and helped her in.

She wrinkled her forehead. "How did we get out here, anyway? The last I remember you came to pick me up. I don't know where we were going."

"I'm not so sure of that myself. This has been one crazy few days. What do you remember?"

She studied him as if he were nuts. There was a good chance he was.

"You called me, asked me to meet you, said someone was trying to kill you." Maybe if he prodded her, she'd recall more.

But she didn't. Her eyes opened wide. "I did? I'm sure I must've been drunk or something. Do you think you could take me home?"

"You mean to that run-down playhouse in the woods? I don't think so. I don't like having my time wasted, especially when someone has been murdered. Now what's up?" Good, get on the offensive.

"Who was murdered?"

"Oh, for god's sake, this isn't funny anymore. I heard Loren Jasper is a good friend of yours. She was found murdered in the barn at Seth

Parker's place over this past weekend. Figuring you were next, we've been searching for you ever since we learned you were in the area."

She stared at him, batted her eyes. The news broke through her consciousness, and her appearance changed to that of a distraught woman. One who might tear at her hair or scream at any moment. Instead she collapsed like a balloon with the air let out.

Soft words trailed from her mouth. "Loren is dead?"

He had to prop her up to keep her from tumbling off the seat to the ground.

She struggled to speak, finally managed in a hoarse voice. "No, that's not possible. I came to find her, to save her. Where is she? How did they find her? Why didn't you stop them?"

"We were hoping you could tell us that." Clearly she had some knowledge of what was going on, of who was after Loren. Else why had she hidden away after coming to Cedarton? Why in hell didn't she simply come to the law? He was pretty fed up with the entire situation. "Look, I'm taking you to the station. We'll need to question you concerning her death." Hope to God she believed their time together was all a dream.

"No, please, I don't know anything. I just need to lie down and rest. I feel like I've been running a marathon. Please, she and I are—uh, were— friends. I didn't kill her, and I don't know who did."

Exhausted from the long night spent God only knew where since Grandfather obviously had messed with both their minds, but why? Dal fastened the seatbelt around her and stumbled to the driver's seat. He'd had quite enough, and she looked totally exhausted. Maybe she'd remain as confused as he was.

"Let's take you where you'll be safe. Sooner or later you'll have to talk to us. You must realize that. Withholding information about a murder is a felony, and we can hold you, at least until we can figure out what's going on. You could go to prison."

She broke down, sobbed so hard he thought her heart might break. Crying women usually left him helpless to do anything, so he didn't. He had his car, though he wasn't sure how, so he closed the door and started the engine. Mac would kill him for not bringing her right in, but he couldn't. She'd end up in a cell. She was confused and wiped out, and she wasn't going anywhere. He could use a shower and a nap about as much as she could. Yet if he took her home with him all hell might break loose. He had to find a neutral place for her until she could deal with what was going on. Somehow she and Leanne were connected, though they were not sisters. Leanne was an orphan with no kin, she'd made that clear to him from the beginning. Still, he had an obligation to protect this woman.

Truth be known, the last he remembered clearly was setting out to go to Jessie's. The rest was fading like a fuzzy dream. Either Grandfather's doing or the concussion. No telling when that was. Following the beaten tracks, he headed toward Center Street. His phone rang startling him from his near trance.

Leslie made a funny sound as if it frightened her.

The minute he picked it up, he wished he hadn't. Mac shouted. *"Dal, where in God's name are you? We've been looking everywhere. Why'd you turn off your phone with an active case?"*

The old man was furious, and he didn't really blame him. "Sorry, I guess I overslept."

"Overslept? I reckon you did. Two days overslept. Missed the meeting this morning. Where the heck you been dilly-dallying? I sent someone by your place twice, and no sign of you or your vehicle. Not answering your phone.

Jessie doesn't know where you are. You pass out somewhere from that head injury? If so, get your butt to the hospital. Otherwise, plant it back here, the sooner the better. This case is about to blow wide open. I need every man I can get. US Marshals and the DEA will descend on us soon. Seems we've got fugitives and dope dealers roaming around in our fair county. We need 'em gone. They expect cooperation."

Holy shit. Now he was in it up to his eyeballs. He spun the wheel, stomped the accelerator, and see-sawed along the vague road, trees flying by on both sides. Leslie shrieked, hid her eyes, and hunkered between hunched shoulders.

"Shut up, or I'll toss you out the door." Front tires hit the pavement, squealed, and the back ones chittered, sending the car in a fishtail that threw her against the side door.

"Let me out, you madman!"

Instead he turned on the lights and siren and increased his speed, not slowing till he got to the school zone on the east side of town. At a small house clinging to the lower incline of the street, he slammed on the brakes. Mac would sure kill him now, leaving her at his place, but it couldn't be helped.

He turned to the frightened woman. "Go in there. Key's under that flowerpot. Take a shower, make yourself at home. Sheriff lives there alone, so no one will bother you. Someone will be by to pick you up soon as possible. Do not answer the door till you see a badge. Do not call anyone. Got me? You leave, I'll have real dogs after you. Now go."

He shoved her out the door, paused to see she stayed on her feet till she followed his instructions and disappeared inside, then he pulled away. He didn't bother to look back but took a deep breath. Steered around the corner and up three streets to the square and the sheriff's office. Kept the speed down adhering to Mac's rules. One thing for sure, he was in no hurry to get his butt reamed out.

How could the case have broken so soon? Mac said two days and nights. So he'd been immersed in a dream, what the Cherokee called a vision quest, for much longer than he'd realized. Grandfather often felt Dal needed time to think since he'd lived most of his life in the white world. He sure hoped he learned something from the time given him because he was in a heap of trouble back in that white world.

Nosing the car into his saved spot, he leaped out and hurried inside. The office was abuzz with activity. Looked like just about every deputy was there, night and day shift. Couldn't stir them with a stick. What could've happened?

From across the room, Mac waved and pointed toward his office. Uh-oh. That meant trouble. Maybe the fact that he had the missing woman stashed in Mac's very own house would help soften the blow. He'd save it for when things got really hot. Sliding through the door, back against the frame, he waited, hat in hand, to find out how bad it was.

Mac burst through, didn't bother to close the door, just inspected Dal up and down, frowning at the wrinkled uniform, then held up a hand. "Whatever it is, save it. I put you down as on injury leave. You're back now. You *are* back?" Their eyes met.

"Yes. Yes, sir, I am."

Mac nodded so hard his teeth rattled. "Into the meeting room. Everyone awaits with bated breath. What do you have for us?"

This was his chance to get back into Mac's good graces. "Leslie Younger, the woman we've been looking for. I told you she was in danger. I put her at your place."

Mac's shaggy eyebrows climbed so high on his forehead they tangled with his white hair. "Why in tarnation didn't you say so?" He gave no chance for a reply, just moved on. "And why is she at *my* house?" Teeth ground as his tone rose. His shouts carried into the meeting room, the crowd staring.

Dal leaned close to his ear. "To keep her safe."

Mac's face bloomed like a spring flower. His reply bounced cross the room. "JC on a crutch, how'd you manage that?"

"Honestly, you don't want to know."

Lips pinched. "You mean it's gonna be one of those many instances you can't put in a report?"

Dal nodded. "Fraid so. Now, what's all the excitement going on around here?"

Mac grinned. "Any minute. Once we're done here you might want to call Jessie before she tears down half the town looking for you. Meanwhile I think everyone is here, so let's be seated and pipe down." He moved to the murder board, rubbed his hands together. "Can't wait to announce we have that little lady, thanks to Dal here. What's her name? Perhaps you'd care to tell us how—"

Dal shook his head. "No, I wouldn't. I couldn't. No time now. You'll have to trust me on this. Name's Leslie Younger, only I don't—"

"Just thought I'd try." Mac grinned and strode up front chest out. "We're pleased he's returned with the missing lady. Uh, Miz Younger. The one I spoke about yesterday. She is currently stashed away, so no questions yet."

A few whoops and hollers and hand clapping sprouted, then faded. Dal dropped into a chair, tipped his hat, then settled it on a nearby desk. Boy, he'd sure slid by that one easy like. Be good if he could at least explain how it had happened. Later, maybe.

Jessie ate a burger and fries sometime during the long two days while no one could find Dal. Convinced he'd left her because of the misunderstanding between her and Parker, she finally wore out looking for him and went home, so hungry her stomach growled like a bear. Standing in front of the fridge, she gazed at the puny offerings. One day she needed to take a class on shopping or cooking—or maybe both. Shrugging, she headed for the shower, dirty jeans and t-shirt discarded as she went.

The next morning, she awoke lying naked on the bed not sure what she'd done or how she'd gotten there. Dawn draped along the peaks like a silver skirt. She snatched up the phone. No messages. She dialed the sheriff's office. Tink picked up.

"Hey girlfriend. The disappeared returns. Where you been?"

"Looking for Dal. Did anyone ever find him?"

"You sure do have trouble keeping up with that boy. He showed just as I came on duty this evening. There's one heck of a meeting going on."

Relief made her dizzy. They'd parted on such lousy terms. Her and him. Seeing as how she'd lost most everyone she loved, it made her nervous when someone just flat disappeared. Especially him. Their life had been rocky, and she wanted nothing more than for it to settle down. It was time, but she didn't know how to go about it.

"Did he say where he'd been?"

Tink snapped her gum. *"Sweetie. You ought to stop trying to put him on a leash."*

"Sorry? What?"

"Start trusting him. He's a big boy, and nothing makes a man more upset than to be tracked all the time."

"Tinker. Where is this coming from? I thought you were my friend, and now you come out with advice like you're Oprah or someone."

"I didn't mean to, honey. It's just that I know he loves you and you him, but I see you both struggling to make it work. The way he looks at you is like he could just eat you up, and you don't see it. What do you want from him?"

"I guess that's the problem. We don't either one know what we want. He's always dodging away just when we get really close."

"You know what? You need to talk. That's usually the problem in any relationship. I read in Oprah's magazine—you know O?—how she said just that."

Tink could always make her laugh, and this time was no different, though her chuckle was weak. "Okay, I deserved that. I'll just curl up and wait right here for him like a good little lapdog. He's bound to drop by just any old time to talk. I promise, I won't even ask him where he's been. Love you, girl."

Tinker was laughing when she returned the endearment and hung up.

And so there you are. Talk is the answer.

But how much truth? How she almost made love with Parker? Perhaps borrow his handcuffs, hook him to the bedpost. Yes, a bed is always a good place to talk. Why don't I call him this very minute, and if he just happens to answer the phone, ask him to come over to talk? Yeah, he'd appreciate that in the middle of an important law gathering. Lying on the bed air drying her body, she snickered. A sound that turned into a teary-eyed sigh. She came this close, she really did, to soothing Parker by making love with him. A temporary fix at best. Good thing she didn't. He was so needful, and she loved him but not like she loved Dal... but she couldn't even explain it to herself. So why didn't she give him what he needed? Because. Because what she needed was to be held, to be wanted, to be valued by the man she truly loved. That stubborn but gorgeous Cherokee deputy. She wouldn't hurt him for the world.

Just imagine calling Dal and telling him that. Just like Oprah advised.

While she thought of such a thing, the phone rang. She glared at it. *Go away, leave me alone.* But it didn't, and after a while, she picked up.

"Jess?"

Dal? It was like someone plugged her heart into an electrical current. Hopeless, that's what she was.

"You there, Jess?"

"Where else would I be? Thought you were in a meeting."

A long pause. Had he hung up? *"Had to let you know, we found Leslie Younger, the missing woman, and she's stashed away till we figure everything out. Have to get back to the meeting. Where are you?"*

"I'm here. Home."

"Would you...?"

"I wondered...?"

"You first."

"Go ahead."

"Jess?"

"Yes?"

"Would you mind having a guest for a couple of days?"

"Sounds good to me. I was afraid you were going back to your place." Maybe they could talk.

He pushed on as if he hadn't heard her. *"She won't be any trouble, and we don't want to put her up in a jail cell."*

"What? *Who* she?" He didn't mean himself at all. Maybe she'd just leave town, become a hermit or a nun.

"You know this case? Well Leslie Younger, her life has been threatened. I've got her over at Mac's now, but you know how small and dinky his place is. And since I've been staying with you—"

"Excuse me, when you're in town."

"Uh, sure. Okay. I mean we thought maybe you wouldn't mind just till we can... well, actually they're looking to get her in WITSEC, but Ledger won't be able to pick her up for a couple of days."

By the time he finished, she was biting her tongue. But then a little birdie pecked away at her brain. An interview with the only survivor of three friends who must've witnessed or been involved in something horrendous to have killers after them. Ought to make a heck of a story, even if she had to use fake names.

"Okay, bring her over, but you'll have to pick up something to eat. My cupboard is bare."

He laughed. *"When isn't it? I'll bring something."*

"Dal?"

"What, darlin?"

Oh, good grief, how he could drawl that out. She gulped, struggled to speak. "Don't forget, I don't cook." *And don't you darlin me. At least, not till you're standing next to my bed near naked.*

"I will take care of that. We'll be there in an hour or so. And thanks."

"Oh, you are welcome." She threw the phone across the room. "So very welcome."

Dal stuck his head in Mac's office. "It's okay with Jess. I'll run Leslie over since you won't put me to work. Jess sounded sort of put out, though. Probably just tired. I may spend the evening with them. You're putting a guard on the house while she's there, right?"

"Yep, till Marshal Ledger picks her up. Boy, you're looking a bit wan. You feeling okay?" Mac got up close, stared into his eyes.

If he told the whole truth, Mac might shut him off being involved. It was bothering him a lot that Leanne was a part of all this. Since coming here, he'd managed to let go of her tragic overdose death, now he had to face the fact that he hadn't known the half of what she was involved in. Still didn't. He did intend to find out everything before this was over so he could finally put the loss behind him. It wasn't something he wanted to discuss with Mac or anyone else for that matter. He wasn't even sure how much the sheriff knew about Leanne's involvement.

"You sure you're okay, boy?"

"I'm fine."

"Well, you get you some rest, and don't you worry about none of this. We've got some of the finest help around. It'll all come clean in the wash."

That might be, but not this day. More bad times were coming before this was said and done, but he had to go with the flow. There were plenty of experts on this case, and it would all wash out just like Mac said. Maybe not to everyone's satisfaction, but everyone would learn to live with it.

At the Red Bird he ordered three burgers, a triple order of French fries, and three large Cokes. Wanda fitted the items in a tray. "Having supper with Jessie tonight? She'll sure be happy to see you. Almost drove everyone nuts chasing around hunting you the last couple of days." She grinned up at him. "Sweetie, you look sorta peaked, you okay? Looks like you could use some tender loving care. You go along now, and the two of you have a fine evening." Her grin morphed into a teasing wink. "You might ought to get some breakfast."

He passed her a bill, told her to keep the change, and left, almost running into Fudge who acted like he wanted to talk, but Dal pushed on past him. At his back Wanda said, "Don't worry, he's had a hard—" and the closing door cut her off.

In front of Mac's, he honked a couple of times. The porch light came on, and Mac escorted Leslie across the small lawn. Dal unlocked the car door. Mac swung it open and reached to help her inside.

Later when he thought about it, he was well aware that he didn't hear the shot, only a single grunt from deep inside her, a grip that tightened, glass shattering, and a screech of tires fading into the dark. At the moment, it occurred though it was like something out of a bad movie.

Without another sound, Leslie sprawled halfway across the seat, blood spurting from her neck, raining on him and Mac. It was the two of them making all the noise, dreadful, inexplicable outcries from men who knew they had failed to protect this woman.

He rode with her in the ambulance, but she didn't know it. Still in a trance of sorts, he waited at the hospital and accompanied her body to the morgue. Her hand slipped off the gurney, and he captured it, his large one swallowing her smaller one. He felt like her spirit passed through him and into the cool night. Though he hadn't known her, sorrow at her loss filled him with anguish, a regret that he couldn't save her. The last connection he knew to his dead wife.

Goddammit. How did they find out she was there? His breath hitched, he could hardly swallow, like someone was squeezing his heart. Life had gone out of her while he held her. Odd how achingly sad death of the young could be. Lips on her limp hand, he cried for her. She needed someone to care, and he had allowed this to happen. Assumed the looming dark of the peaceful town held no danger. But evil had slipped into town on the skin of a shapeshifter, the wicked making themselves at home. They would regret this.

Guilt. What a dreadful human emotion. What did it say about us? Perhaps that we needed to feel we were important enough to carry the blame for things that really couldn't be helped? Not by us. It lay on the shoulders of the unknown.

Grandfather had warned him that a woman of great meaning to his life would come along. That she would bring harm to him. Would it be through others? He hoped not. No doubt he would soon see.

After the short trip, Doc met the ambulance, accompanied the body into the morgue where he would ready it for transport to Little Rock. Dal called Jessie, told her briefly what had happened and asked her to please come pick him up. Then he slumped into a chair in the waiting room to do just that. Wait. He would not tell her what had happened between him and Leslie. Odd how it meant nothing, and yet it meant everything for Leanne had forgiven him during that strange interlude, and he'd forgiven himself. Right now, it didn't seem to matter.

God, he needed to sleep. His head hurt, and he wished that everything would go away.

Jessie came through the door, looking worried. He stood, and she went into his arms.

"I'm sorry. Do you want to go home or come with me?"

"I think I'd better go home. I'm not fit company, and all I want to do is sleep."

She nodded without disagreeing, slipped her hand in his and led him out the door to the Jeep. All the way to the B&B she was quiet. He sat upright, taking the bouncy ride without complaint. At the bottom of the stairs leading to his apartment, she stepped out and walked up with him still saying nothing.

"It's okay. I'm okay," he told her as if she had asked, which she hadn't.

"Get some rest, and I'll see you soon. Where's your car?"

First he'd thought of it. "Mac's. Yes that's where. I think." Dal felt a bit like an idiot.

"Call one of the guys in the morning to pick you up if you feel like going in."

With a weary nod, he took hold of the rail. "Yes. Okay. Take care."

He climbed the stairs slowly and when he turned at the top, all he saw were the red taillights of her car.

He'd never felt so alone.

She drove out of town and to her cabin. Brad met her outside the door. "Oh, sweetie, I'm sorry. I didn't mean to leave you outside. Come on." She knelt and swept him up into her arms, unlocked the door while he licked the tears from her face. First she'd known she was crying. For whom it was hard to tell. Leslie, Dal, or herself? Probably all three.

She put Brad down, added food to his dish, and tossed her keys onto the counter. Something was missing. Damn, she'd left her bag in the car. Everything in it including her laptop, and she needed to get to work on her story. One moment standing at the door and something moved in the tree line. Just a shadow passing from one pale spot to another. A deer? No, taller. Before she could get a better look, the lights around her blinked off plunging the surroundings into pitch black. Okay, no games tonight. Three steps took her to the table where she kept the .38. She slid it free of the drawer and holding it down at her side, remained very still, gazing at the spot where she'd seen movement.

What was going on? Were the killers trying to ambush them one by one? Shooting at shadows was not advisable, but she was pretty fed up with recent events. The county was crawling with lawmen searching for a killer, actually three or more bad ones, and she wasn't about to be a victim, but she sure wasn't going to shoot at someone she couldn't see.

"Tell you what," she shouted. "Let me know who you are, get the hell out, or we'll see if you're bulletproof. I'm easy, I'll count to five. One...."

"It's me, Trey. No need for two or three." He appeared, his feet scuffing fallen leaves. "What happened to the lights?"

"Oh, they do that. I saw you move. What are you doing here?"

"Mac is nervous about you being alone. Someone talked to Dal. I was on hand. Just arrived in town, so he wanted me to come out and keep an eye on you." He chuckled as if the idea of being a bodyguard was alien to him. "Everyone else is out patrolling for that son of a bitch who shot Leslie. I thought you might appreciate some alone time, so I settled in out here." While talking, he drew near enough to take her hand. His firm touch gave her renewed strength.

She gestured toward the front door. "Come on in, I'm getting my bag out of the car, and I'll make some coffee."

"I'll get it, you step inside. You sure you're up for company?"

"Sure, it's been a while. Maybe we can talk about this case, whatever you're allowed to say."

He chuckled and took long steps to get her bag and stepped up onto the porch to follow her inside. "Always working, huh? I'm not sure what I can tell you."

"Well, maybe just the part you guys play in this sort of situation, nothing personal. Like research. I am curious what details you and Jameson play in murders committed in our county. Just general stuff."

He handed her the backpack. "You fix me a cup of coffee, and I'll see what I can help you with. Long as it's not connected to this case. That you'll have to wait a while for." He went tense, his voice low. "Might be good the power's off. We're not a target that way."

Her shoulders tightened. He sensed something out there in the dark. "I understand. Being related to Mac has taught me a lot about the release of information."

"Glad you didn't get to five out there. You a good shot?"

"Depends on how close I am to the target. Sorry, no coffee, but let's light a few candles." She fetched two from a drawer, lit them, and carried both into the far corner away from the windows. "I'll be right back. Ladies room.

"Jess? Stay down. I'm just going to look around a bit."

His unusual care was beginning to frighten her. Did he hear or see something? "You be careful, too."

"Oh, I'm good at being invisible. If someone is out there, they won't see me. Stay out of the light."

In the cave-like darkness of the bathroom, something crawled up her spine, and she shivered from her toes to the top of her head. Shaking off the feeling, she finished and ran down the hall, dragging her fingers along the wall.

Shaking, she sank into a dark corner of the room.

"It's me." Trey slipped in the door.

There were Cokes in the Jeep. She whirled to tell him that. Something cracked through the window, smashed into the open cabinet door, and sent shards of broken dishes in every direction, sharp bits and pieces cutting her face.

Not one to scream easily, she clawed at the blinding pain, then fell to her knees just as another bullet slashed through the room. Hot blood dripped between her fingers, and she pulled them away, crying with the pain.

A touch on her shoulder terrified her till Trey said her name under his breath. "Where's the bathroom? At the back of the house?"

The calm tone of his voice settled her thumping heart. "Yes."

"Crawl there. I'll be with you. Steady on, just keep moving."

She obeyed, though her cheeks burned. Into the bathroom, and he closed the door behind them. "Window?"

She gestured toward it, then took his hand and pointed.

"Towel, big heavy one."

Sobbing with pain, she crawled to the small linen cupboard and pulled at the stack, handed him two.

Noises, not too loud, while more bullets sliced through the front half of the house. Glass crashed, bullets contacted the log siding like someone hitting it over and over with a jack-hammer, the noise unbearable.

They were destroying her cabin. Trey literally hefted her into the bathtub. "Lay down, stay there." She obeyed, shaking all over. Another minute or so, the scratch of a match, a quick flare of light. The window was covered with the towel.

"First Aid kit, meds, bandages?" His voice sounded so calm.

She could barely answer him. "Below the sink, a first aid kit."

Noises, then he held another match up and squinted at her. "We're going to need some light so we can get that glass out."

It didn't seem possible with people shooting at them and the power out that he could stay focused on taking care of her. "I'd rather get out of here. These aren't fatal cuts."

He remained quiet for a while. "Maybe you're right. This window is standard size rather than small like most bathrooms. Think we can crawl through it?"

"Yeah, well, I can. Long story. Me first?"

"Nope. I'll make sure it's safe first. They may have someone out back waiting for us to try to get away. Odd they're only shooting from the front. On the other hand a lot of criminals are stupid. Sure hate to count on that with them. You wait here?"

"I'm with you. Wish I knew where Brad is."

"Who's Brad?"

"My dog. I haven't seen him since we got home."

Trey whistled through his teeth and a whine replied. "There, that's him. Can you tell where he is?"

"Brad, come on."

Claws clicked across the floor, and the little pit bull shoved against her. She gathered him in her arms. Trey lifted the corner of the towel, shoved the window open, and she dropped Brad outside.

Trey followed. "You wait here, I'll be back. Do *not* come out here until I say it's safe, got it?"

She nodded, the cuts on her face aching. Waiting there, hugging the wall beneath the window, some weird thoughts went through her head. What if he left her here? What if the men came in the house and took her away? It was all she could do to stay there and trust him to come back.

Gunfire from out back. Blat. Blat. Blat. Then silence, no yelling as if someone were hit. She held her breath, listened.

Tap, tap, tap. Psst.

Maybe a strange signal only he would make? Hoping, she gripped the windowsill, hoisted herself up, and fell through. It didn't hurt much more than the godawful pain in her face.

"Go, and don't wait for me. Take off for the woods. I'll be right behind you."

She couldn't breathe or see or swallow, but she could run, and run she did, legs stretching, feet slapping the ground, into the first of the trees, limbs scraping her face to cause more torture. Her toe caught on a widow maker, and she sprawled on the ground where she lay, no intention of getting up. Brad jumped on her, then off, not barking as if he sensed the danger. It was all she could manage, and she lay there, knees pulled up to her chin quivering like a fox hiding from hounds.

While they made their escape, bullets continued to hit the house in fits and spurts as if the ammo was running short or the attackers were simply tired of the battle. Brad skinned into the bushes, belly on the ground. Trey loped through brambles to crouch next to her.

"You hurt?"

"Damn right, I'm hurt. Those bastards. They better pray you catch them before me." The firing slowed then stopped. In a few minutes, the lights came on, including the yard light. A couple of figures darted in and out, and back and forth across the windows.

"Wonder what they're looking for? I don't have anything of value. Sure don't now." She sniffed and tried to change position. "If not for you, I wouldn't be alive."

He lay an arm over her shoulder. "Sorry about your house."

"Me, too." If she had a bed at the moment, then she'd curl right up and go to sleep. But she appeared to be homeless.

12
CHAPTER

Awakening, afraid he'd set the headache off again, Dal sat up in bed carefully, but the drums were gone. He nodded, shook, gazed across the room, but still no pain. About time. A concussion was a dangerous nuisance, and he was tired of babying it. Aches and pain he could put up with. He drew the line at doing nothing. There was so much to do he was raring to get back to work and curious he might have missed something.

Trey Ledger and James Jameson were convinced that Leanne's death—as well as that of Loren and Leslie—were connected to the current case. To have her death solved after such a long time should cure his feelings of guilt. Even if he had to return to Dallas, he was anxious to learn the truth. It wasn't like Texas Rangers or US Marshals to make that kind of mistake.

What he wanted today was to get Mac to assign him to the Dallas investigation. That would be tough, but maybe Ledger and Jameson could be convinced to request his help. After he finished two Honey Buns and three cups of coffee, he took out his cell and called Jessie. It went straight to voicemail. Hmm. Not like her to not be up and about by now. She should be getting ready to go into the newspaper office to file her stories for the week. Might drop by at lunchtime and sit with her out back at the picnic table and chat awhile. Hopefully he could then leave for Dallas with a clear conscience. He wouldn't go without talking to her, explaining his reasons. She would surely understand.

Before he could start the car, his phone buzzed. It was Mac. He let go the keys and answered.

"You need to drop by the clinic. Jessie and Trey were attacked last night, and I think she needs you."

Dammit. Attacked? When would this end? Hands shaking, he fumbled to start the car without disconnecting. "How bad is she hurt?"

Mac's voice rattled on, but he could hardly make out but a few words, glass in her face. Holy shit, what next? On the way to the clinic, he broke Mac's rule about using the siren and speeding around the square and leaped from the car. He shoved on the clinic door, but for some reason it was stuck shut. He kicked it open, sending a gurney flying. A male nurse grabbed his arm, but he easily shook him loose.

"What the hell have you got the door blocked for? Where's Jessie? Jessie West?"

The nurse shrugged, pointed toward the front desk, and took off with the gurney. A nurse, this time a woman, stood behind it, shuffling through some files. She hadn't even looked up, so she must be used to disruptions.

He quickly faced her, and she glanced up as if she'd just then seen him. "Sorry, who is it you want?"

Irritated, he flashed his badge. "Jessie West, brought in with glass in her face."

The nurse, her badge read *Judith*, kept shuffling. "When?"

"How many people have been brought in today with glass embedded in their face?"

"Let me check."

Losing all patience, he turned his back to control his temper.

"Dallas, hey. Glad you're here." Trey Ledger came out carrying two steaming cups. The doors into the "inner sanctum" swung open, and Jess came through with bandages over most of her face. The male nurse he'd met earlier hustled after her. Jessie saw Trey first and went to him, took a cup, and kissed his cheek.

"Somebody's messing with me, I swear they are." She saw Dal and tried for a wink. Always one to make out like things weren't as bad as they were.

He touched her hand. "You okay?"

"Other than looking like a mummy? Sure. I'm pissed. They shot up my house." Tears finally came, and she patted them away carefully.

He found a spot on one cheek to kiss, then locked an arm around her shoulder. "Just glad they didn't shoot you."

Lips firm, she nodded. "I'm hungry."

Thirty minutes later, sitting at Grandma's cafe eating breakfast, Trey and Jess filled Dallas in on the previous night's happenings, sometimes talking one over the other in their excitement.

He finished his pancakes and washed them down with coffee. "Too damn bad we didn't have some deputies out there. Did you get a look at any of them?"

"Nope, sorry. We were too busy running for our lives."

Yeah right. If it'd been him, he'd a winged at least one of them. This marshal wasn't much of a shot.

Jessie glanced over her coffee, nodded toward Trey. "He saved my life."

Dal wished he'd been with her but didn't say so. Just finished off his coffee. "Where you gonna stay now your place is all shot up?

She shrugged, eyes filling with tears. "This is the second time my cabin has been destroyed. I'm wondering if it's not hexed."

"Aw, Jess, you surely don't believe that nonsense, do you?"

She tried a grin, but the stitches on her face pulled at her skin. "No, of course not. I'm just feeling sorry for myself."

"You know you'd be welcome at my place, but it's barely big enough for me." He glanced over her shoulder at the station house, thoughts drifting. They had to put a stop to this. Was the harm Grandfather promised coming to Jessie? Had he misunderstood him? Maybe he ought to stay here, not go to Dallas, so he could make sure she didn't get hurt again.

Trey, who had been quiet during the conversation spoke up. "Don't you have a victim's fund here that would pay for her a place to stay until she could make arrangements?"

"Oh, my, that would be nice, wouldn't it?" The bandages prevented a coy look. "I do remember one thing." She glanced at Trey. "I'm sure I saw two people darting around, but it was pretty dark. Just flashes here and there."

Trey shook his head, grabbed the bill, and paid it, and the three of them left together.

"I'm going over to my house and see what can be salvaged."

Trey shook his head. "Sorry, Jess, but it's a crime scene. You can't disturb anything till a crew goes through it."

"What? No one was killed there. They didn't even get in."

"But those guys spent some time there, we have to search for anything that might give us a clue as to who they are or what they're up to."

"Surely you're joking. Everyone knows who it was. Those assholes who killed Loren and Leslie. This town isn't full of criminals. No one else it could be. You telling me I can't even go in and rescue my backpack and computer?"

They both shook their heads. "But we don't yet know who they are."

Trey halted. "Wait a minute, we can take a good look, and let her get her stuff, can't we?"

Dal wasn't sure, but this guy was a fed, he probably could push it through. He nodded toward Trey. "Whatever he says. You go on to work, and we'll do the search. Should be done time you finish at the paper."

She hugged them each in turn. "Danged good thing I make copies on a flash drive the end of each day and leave it at the newspaper. Might as well get on over to the office. I can use the computer there to work on my stories for the week. Then I'll go get me a room out at that new motel on the Interstate. You can find me there should either of you care. I feel like I'm starring in one of those thrillers so popular today. Hope I'm the star."

Dal couldn't help chuckling. "You are most definitely the star, and a lovely one at that, even with all those bandages. Hey, Jess, if you need any britches or anything, let me know. I might have something in your size."

"Yeah, twice my size."

He'd made her laugh, and that was good.

The two men strolled away, leaving her to go to work. At least they could keep everything light. Dal was right about one thing, she was going to have to go shopping for something to wear real soon. Wearing clothes filled with glass slivers and ragged holes wasn't appealing. On the other hand, she might be looking for a reason to get a new wardrobe. Wardrobe, yeah. Jeans and t-shirts for the most part. Thank goodness she wasn't hurt badly, but whatever those guys wanted, they could come back.

She headed across the square. First was write a story on her attack. Parker would expect that for his precious front page. She'd get it outlined, then drop in on Mac to get some comments. Even with bandages like a mummy, her day would have to be carried on as normal as possible.

The office door was locked, which meant no one was there, and she could write in peace and quiet, or so she thought. However, inside the door, just as she started to lock up to keep out nosy visitors, a high voice shouted from across the way. A woman in a purple dress waved a hand and crossed the street. Running her way. Oh, great. Hopefully just someone delivering a community news item. Shouldn't be too hard to get rid of her.

She waited to greet the woman whose face was heavily made up to hide wrinkles. It wasn't successful. An obvious red dye job on frizzy hair covered the gray. A forced smile hurt Jessie's cuts.

The woman stopped and stared openly. "Oh, my dear. Whatever happened to you? Some cheeky sod knock you around?"

Hand to her bandaged cheek, Jess laughed at the woman's British slang. "Oh, no, nothing like that. I tangled with a broken window. It looks worse than it is. You must be our newest business owner. We met earlier, Missus. Captree. I didn't have these." She pointed at her bandages

"Oh, my. I was warned about small town gossip. Shilo, please. My husband and I bought the boutique on the square. We shall remodel it, turn it into a pub as soon as your city council okays the license. Meanwhile, I was hoping we could run a small ad to hire some help to get the place sorted out."

Jess had to smile at the woman's interesting accent. "Of course, come on in. I'll give you a form, and we can get it published this week if that would suit you." Shilo? As far from a British name as is possible.

She found a form for a classified ad in Wendy's desk, sat Shilo there with a pen, and seated herself to get to work.

Shilo sank down and thanked her but kept staring. "You seem very young to own a newspaper."

"Oh, I'm sorry I should've introduced myself. I'mJessie West, a reporter, feature writer—I wear nearly all the hats. Just dropped in to work on a story for next week's issue. I'm sure you'll soon meet Seth Parker, he's the owner, publisher, and editor of *The Observer.*"

"Ah, interesting. What is your circulation, dear?"

"Around three thousand. We deliver about twenty-eight hundred through the mail, and the rest are sold from boxes around town."

"And the population of the village, I believe is five thousand eight hundred. I should think everyone would buy a copy of the local paper."

Jessie smiled. The woman was well-informed. "Those numbers will fool you. The population of the county is about eight thousand. Cedarton is the county seat, and the remainder of the population is rural with small communities scattered about. You have to look at it this way. The average family contains seven members, so each family subscribes to one copy of the paper. Well, of course some families don't take the paper for one reason or the other. Our circulation is pretty good considering."

Shilo thought about the explanation for a while, then filled out the classified ad questionnaire and handed it back to Jessie. "I included the name of our business in the ad. How much do I owe you?"

"Classified ads are free." Checking the ad for content she saw the name of the pub was indeed The Purple Raven. Must have a meaning to the British. All she could think of was Poe's *Quoth the raven, nevermore.* And she thought ravens were black and very similar to crows. Dal once explained the difference. It had something to do with the placement and amount of feathers. That reminded her that the business once in that spot was a boutique shop called The Crow's Nest, a sort of quaint coincidence.

Drawn-on brows raised, Mrs. Captree interrupted Jessie's train of thought. "Why that is very kind of you. I sincerely hope that doesn't mean we should serve free biscuits with our tea."

I really don't give a hoot what you serve with your tea. Biscuits go better with gravy, anyhow. Jessie kept that thought to herself but suggested that she might want to interview the woman and her husband when they actually opened the pub.

"Why that would be kind of you, dearie."

"It's customary with all new businesses." Jessie kept as much of a smile on her face as possible until the woman left.

Relocking the door, she went to work and soon finished a draft of her story and filed it ready to finish when she could get something from Mac and maybe Trey who had been with her during the destruction of her cabin. She deliberately kept herself out of it personally, just referred to herself as a member of the local newspaper. Gossip would supply her identity.

The square remained a buzz of activity such as it had never seen, with patrol units, state police, and several important looking civilians including Mayor Hodges coming and going to the sheriff's department. A story occurred to her covering Cedarton and so much activity. Mac's fear had come true that the new highway would cause an increase in crime in Grace County. Perhaps that was the cause of all this hubbub, or maybe not. She decided to write an editorial about that subject, and maybe

Parker would publish it. It was an interesting thought and should elicit some "dear editor" letters—always a good thing for the paper.

She had just finished the draft when a noise in the morgue caught her attention. No one should be in there today. The outside door should be locked. A bit uneasy following the shoot-out, she had kept her gun in her pocket after using it, and it was still there. She slipped it out and padded silently to the door to the morgue. It was kept cracked open, but she could see little through the few inches. Without breathing she eased the door open a bit further. A shadow flitted across the far wall. Hard to tell if she had been seen. She waited.

A bundle of papers fell to the floor. Enough. Shoving the door wide, she stepped through and shouted. "Put your hands up." The gun in her hand shook as if palsied.

"It's just me, Jessie." Burke stepped into the open from behind a stack of bound papers. "Geeze, I hope you ain't a gonna shoot me. Jest looking for a back issue for Phil. For some reason he missed that story about the pig and blind calf. Thinks I'm makin' it up." Hands shaking above his head, he went on. "I'd sure appreciate it if you'd quit a pointin' that gun at me."

Embarrassed but still shaking, she lowered the weapon. "I'm sorry Burke. Didn't expect you to be here with ads till tomorrow. We had quite a scare yesterday."

"Yeah, I heered. You okay? All them bandages. Who got at you?"

With knees wobbling, she dropped into Wendy's chair and lay down the gun. "I thought I was okay till right now." She held her hands out, shaking badly.

"I think you ourght to go home and lay down fore you fall down. You might have that PT and SD they talk about. Can I take you?"

She chuckled wryly. "Afraid not, my house was all shot up, and now it's a crime scene."

"Shoot, I'm sorry. Where you gonna stay?"

Covering her face with both hands, she started to cry. And she couldn't stop.

Dal and Trey joined Jameson in the breakroom, and he was still discussing the Dallas possibilities with them when Mac gathered the deputies coming on duty.

"I'd think if we requested you to accompany us for a specific reason, you'd have no trouble coming over." Trey appeared eager to have Dal along.

Dal nodded. "It might help for you to know I was once an undercover narc in Dallas till I got shot on duty, so I know the lay of the land."

Jameson scratched his head, found a seat, and they joined him. "Probably be a little while since we don't have a reason for going over there just yet. Most of our duties are here just now. We suspect that one of the biggest drug distributers is prepared to nestle down right here in your Ozarks. I was getting in with them as a dealer from Dallas wanting to get a line on a good supply up from Mexico when your darlin little reporter almost broke my cover. But I got back in. It looks like they're looking for someone to set up a connection here for an east-to-west delivery. The marshal here got well known when he went undercover and broke that child trafficking case last year, so he can't do it. Damn reporters, anyway." He grinned and punched Dal on the arm. "Try to handle that pretty blonde from your local paper. I spect she's worth the effort."

Dal glared at Jameson but didn't reply. The Ranger shrugged and shut up.

Chairs screeched on the floor and laughter died down when Mac stood and hollered for them to pay attention. A few throats cleared, and the room quieted.

"We got a couple of outside lawmen with us today, and it looks like they are able to remain and give us a hand, since this operation is affecting their jurisdiction. Most of y'all know Texas Ranger James Jameson and US Deputy Marshal Trey Ledger. Until we round up these killers and drug dealers, they'll be giving us a hand. I'm told a DEA agent may join up in a few days." He looked around, hitched up his pants, and went on. "Looks like it might be true what ole Fudge said when he predicted crime would rise here in Grace County when they built the Walmart and that blamed highway."

Laughter rippled around the room.

"Well, I tell you what. We're fixin to show them they've come to the wrong place."

Applause drowned out the laughter.

"There's some pictures I want you all to take copies of. Some fellas identified with the help of Marshal Ledger and some DEA fellas from over at the Federal building as being in the drug trade. They could be involved in the killing of those poor ladies this past week. At least they are suspects and a place to start. You find 'em, bring 'em in for questioning. No gunplay now fellas, just get 'em by the ear and drag 'em down here to the station. Right now they are people of interest. Names are on the photos."

Conversation swelled again. "Keep it down, we're about done here for the day. Y'all know about the gunplay out to Jessie's. She got cut up pretty bad, but thanks to Ledger there, both got out without any other injuries. He got a look at one of them, and there's a sketch of him in the photos. Take care, he sort of resembles a couple of us."

Again laughter. "Right now we're cracking down on arrests of anyone suspicious but no shootin or hangin just yet. Okay, that's it. Overtime for them who can handle it till this is over. See Tinker at the input desk to be assigned."

Dal shoved his way through the crowd to Tinker. "I'm back on duty, and you can put me down for overtime. At least till I find out if I can assist in Dallas. I want these bastards caught before it gets any worse. Sorry to see this happening here. Well, anyplace else either. We can't go to Mexico and wipe out these cartels, but by damn we can protect our people in this county."

Tink assigned him his usual car and a section in the county on call 24/7, which meant he would be on call even when he wasn't out and about. When he left, a line had formed to sign up for overtime. Instead of three cars pulling out for night duty, he counted eight, which meant some deputies would use their own vehicles, mostly pickups. In addition, there were two Federal SUVs, black with tinted windows. That'd be Trey and James. So far one deputy to a vehicle, but if things got worse, they'd go to two.

Bastards better hunker down.

Two a.m. and Dal had just finished a round through Hackmore Ridge, a popular hangout for drunks and the like, when his radio went off. He keyed it on.

"Starr 32 here."

"Call for you."

He said okay and waited. Who the hell was awake this time of the night? Must be one of the guys on duty. He'd been in a black hole for the cell phone.

Static. *"Starr, that you?"*

He replied. "Who is this?"

"Name's Kimble, Robert."

Holy shit. "Okay."

"Remember me?"

"Yep, sure do. What are you doing on the police band?"

Laughter. *"Jest cause I'm hiding out don't mean I can't remember how to get ahold of one of my old buddies. Bet you thought I'd left the country."*

"You know what? I hadn't thought anything about you. Say, while I've got you, why don't you turn yourself in?"

"Shit. You know what it's like being a cop in prison. I ain't goin that route."

"Only one other choice then."

"I got something to trade."

"I'll just bet you do." Dal got an itch where he couldn't scratch. Meant this could be important. "Well?"

"Not on the radio. I didn't get stupid all of a sudden."

"You did that when you took bribes to turn your head and let those cultists steal all those little kids and sell them 'cross the border."

"Didn't get caught, did I?"

Dal sighed. "Might not, but you got stopped. Enough of this. What do you want?"

"To talk, in private. I know some stuff you could use."

"Okay. When and where?"

"Nothing specific. Remember where you and me used to go fishing? Where you hooked that big catfish and had to go in the water to land him? Don't repeat the name."

Dal thought a moment. "Yes." Not sure he wanted to be out there alone with this owl hoot, but he might know something good.

"Tomorrow, midnight."

If he said *come alone,* Dal was going to hang up.

He didn't. He clicked off.

Dal had no more than disconnected when his cell buzzed, causing him to jerk the wheel and stop on the side of the road. Guess he'd been out too long. The phone buzzed again. He dug it from some stuff in the passenger seat. Didn't even know he had a signal out here. He picked up, said hello. Broken words he couldn't understand.

"Say again."

"—it's me, Jes—can—?"

Damn these damn things, anyway. What good are they when they don't work?

He keyed in his radio. "This is Starr 32. Would you try to reach Jessie West for me? I think she's in trouble."

"Dal, this is Tink. She called here first, and she's in trouble."

"Where's she at?" He pressed the accelerator and skidded onto the road. He was a good twenty miles from town.

"Said she's at The Observer.*"*

He squealed around a curve. "This time of night? You sure?"

"What she said."

"Say what kind of trouble?"

"Something about a coyote?"

"A coyote? In town?"

"What she said."

"Not exactly a dangerous predator, but I'll go over there." Could be Tink misheard.

"When I couldn't reach you, I got Colby. Think he's on his way, him being known around here now as the animal man."

Tink disconnected still laughing. He had a hunch this wasn't funny at all. Jessie didn't panic over tigers or snakes, so certainly not a coyote. But what was she doing at the newspaper? With her house being all shot up, she was supposed to have gotten a room at the Ozarka Motel. Why the hell wasn't she there at this time of night?

Better question. What was a coyote doing visiting a newspaper?

Even though Colby was on his way, he'd go anyhow. A few minutes later, he slid sideways into the gravel drive at *The Observer*. There was no sign of Colby's vehicle or Jessie's. What the hell?

Lights were on across the road at the fire department, so he hopped out and trotted over. Fred was playing solitaire in the lunchroom, and Dana was snoozing in a recliner.

"Hey, you guys seen Jess or Colby over at the newspaper?

Both looked up like they thought he was crazy.

"Yep. Wildest thing. Jess came out the door," Fred said.

"…and this horse came running down the middle of the road." Dana finished the sentence.

Fred took it up. "She jumped in her Jeep, you know that old thing she drives?"

"Yeah, yeah. What about a horse? You sure it wasn't a coyote?"

"Reckon we'd know a horse from a coyote. Had some person on its back. Anyway, she started after it."

"Wait. Person? Man or woman?"

A shrug. "Couldn't really tell the sex. All in black." Dana pointed down the road. "And here comes Colby in his deputy's car, and he takes off after them."

"Something about a skunk?" Dal raised his brows and glanced from one to the other.

Both laughed. "Aw, no. It was one of those coyote duns that's got a stripe down it's back. I hollered it looked like a skunk. Sorta. Kinda."

"She yelled 'it's not a skunk' or something like that. Then they were all gone out of sight. What do you reckon was going on, sheriff?"

Dal sighed. He wasn't the sheriff, but he was tired of saying it out loud. He just drove off in the direction they pointed.

Didn't sound like she was in trouble. Where did he remember a coyote dun being mentioned lately? He couldn't recall. They did have a stripe down their back, but they looked nothing like a skunk. It was a stripe of brown hair against the dun color. Beautiful animals. Maybe those two firemen had been tossing back a few.

He drove slowly up and down a few curly streets, but he never saw a horse or Colby or Jessie anywhere, or for that matter a coyote or a skunk. Maybe he was in another universe. Finally, he turned around and drove over to the sheriff's station.

Tink looked up when he went in.

"Find her?"

"Nope. I'm beginning to think I'm in another world or something. Coyote Duns, skunks, cops chasing horses in town."

Tink snapped her fingers. "That's what she said, coyote dun. The connection wasn't too good. Sorry."

"Have any idea why Jess was at *The Observer*?"

Tink shrugged. "Nope. Working I'd guess."

"Well, nothing's going on in the real world. I'm going home and get some sleep. Call me if you need me."

On the way home he thought of the call from Robert Kimble and the appointment he'd set up. Hope that made more sense than what had just happened.

In the middle of the night he sat straight up, eyes wide. The blamed coyote dun. Someone riding one, and it was important to a case that he find them, but when, where, and who?

Damn if anything in this case made sense.

Jessie trailed slowly after the coyote dun. Pretty strange if you thought about it. Riding a horse in the middle of the night without a reflector or lights or anything. Course this was Cedarton, Arkansas, so most any-thing was possible. But they were looking for this person as a witness. He rode by the cabin where Loren had been staying when they were all out there poking around for evidence. Mac made a comment that he might live nearby and could know something about the woman who might live there. For one reason or another, they'd never tried to run him down. Could be things just plain got too harried and someone forgot.

Anyway, she hesitated to follow him alone, considering what was going on, but when she couldn't reach anyone, she took off after him. Caught him, funny as it might seem, in the Walmart parking lot. Some Walmarts stayed open all night, but theirs didn't. Appeared no one liked to shop all night in Cedarton, so it closed at ten p.m. That meant the sprawling tarmac lot was empty. But lights burned. Another thing about a small town like Cedarton with such a low crime rate had no cameras like you saw in towns on television crime shows.

Jess took a look around the silent, empty acreage and hesitated to approach the slow-moving animal who had almost reached the wooded area out to the north side of the store. Could spook a horse, put the rider in danger. But then Colby's unit crept around the corner to move along at hers and the dun's pace.

So she blipped her siren quick like so as not to wake anyone up, then nosed up close to the standing horse, who crow hopped sideways, and shrieked. A light came on in the nearest house. Oh, well, she'd tried to be quiet, but at least now they had an audience. She and Colby brought their units to a halt simultaneously. To match that, the rider swung a leg over back of the saddle and dismounted. Turning to face the two cars in the headlights of their vehicles. The rider wore a hat and what looked like a cape.

Once with two feet on the ground he swept them both off.

Jess came out of the car and so did Colby, both ready to face they knew not what. They didn't have to wait long, for the rider stepped forward. She might have been a young teen, but she acted younger.

"I'm ready to go to jail. Long as you keep me safe. My brother said nothing could happen to me there."

"It's a—a girl." Colby moved closer and was finally able to make that identification.

"Your brother is right, sweetie." Jessie was always quick to grab control, or maybe she was just more curious.

"I was just trying to get off the street and get back home without getting caught."

He took a few steps closer. "Caught? What's your name?"

"I'm Shirley Lee Hunt. And I was there when everyone was looking for that lady. She broke into that house, and I should'a told someone first time I saw her there, but I was afraid."

"Afraid of who? What?"

"The people who live there. The man, he told me if I ever said anything about them, he'd come to my house and kill all my brothers and sisters, so I... you won't tell him I said anything, will you? Please just take me to jail and lock me up."

Colby stood right next to her by then, and Jess, being wary considering what had been going on lately, had remained a good distance. Best to get her off the street and notify her parents.

Obviously, Colby agreed. He took her arm. "No one is killing anyone or locking you up. I'll take you home, so we can talk about this with your parents."

She leaned against Colby. "No. Please just take me to jail. Please." She raised her voice at least two octaves, bringing more house lights on across the street.

Colby stared at Jess. She moved to the girl. "Okay, okay, I'll take you to jail."

"Is that okay? What about Coyote here?" She gazed up into Colby's face.

Jess chuckled under her breath. Of course, its name was Coyote. That's the way things were going lately. Weird and strange.

He shrugged. "Okay, yes. And I'll get someone to come get him. They'll put him in a stable where he'll be safe."

Jess smiled sweetly at Colby. "I'll see she has the nicest cell in the jail where she'll be safe. Come on, darling."

The girl grinned and took Jessie's hand as if they were the best of friends. "Will you stay and play with me?"

"Sure, why not?" Jess seated the girl in the front, helped her with her seatbelt, and without a word to Colby, climbed behind the wheel and drove off toward the jail.

13
CHAPTER

By the time she and Colby deposited Sally with Tinker, who promised to play with her till her parents could be reached, the sun lightened the sky like peaches and cream.

Headed out the door, Jessie suppressed a giggle. "Well, it's been quite a day or night or whatever. At least no one has shot at me. And my stomach feels like it's in touch with my backbone."

Colby agreed. "How about a steak and eggs with pancakes on the side?"

She nodded at him. "Grandma's it is, then."

Colby lay down his fork and leaned back with a satisfied groan. Jess drank the last of her coffee, having put away two eggs, ham, biscuits and gravy.

He grinned at her. "Oughta do us for a spell."

The grin gave Jessie a tickle way down deep. Why in the world hadn't this man been grabbed up by a smart woman? He was gorgeous, smart, and a very nice catch.

Of course, it was really none of her business.

Just the thought of gorgeous men made her long for Dal's arms around her. When things got to going fast, she missed their normal love making. Too much else going on.

"Reckon we ought to move on." Colby rose. "I've got this." He took some bills from his pocket and lay them on the table. "Good job with that little girl. Have a nice day."

"Thanks. Guess I'll see you later."

He touched the brim of his hat and strode off, looking a lot like a young Burt Reynolds.

That does it. Damn if it doesn't. She took out her cell and punched a well-used number. He answered in a sleepy tone. She was about to have that nice day Colby wished her.

"Got room in your bed for a body that's aching like the very devil for a certain fella?"

He growled down deep in his throat. "And just who might this be? Uhm, Melody, Crystal, or just maybe Jess?"

"Good thing you got it right. I was about to hang up."

"Well?"

"Well, what?"

"When will you be here?"

"Can you be ready in five?"

"I'm turning back the covers."

A few minutes later, headlights out, she pulled in under the trees at the back of the B&B. Hopefully the Five Bs was closed and the couple still asleep. She parked on the far side of the garage where they wouldn't see her Jeep. Such a funny pair. Best if they didn't know she was here. Tiptoeing up the steps like a sneaky teenager, she met Dal in the opened door at the top. His naked figure a Greek God shadow in early rays of sunlight sent a jolt through her that missed not one single erotic spot as it traveled from head to toe.

While she ached to leap into his arms, she stood there a moment wishing that what had passed in the last few hours was a crazy dream and life would be perfect the moment she went into his arms. For a brief moment pause, she stood in front of him, the heat from his body washing over her.

There must be something she could say, should say, but she couldn't think what it might be. So she placed one hand on his arm, ran the other up to his bare shoulder. His touch tingled over her skin like lightning on a hot summer night.

Oh God, how she loved this man.

Pulling her close so their bodies embraced, he gently brushed her hair back, found some spots bare of bandages, and kissed the exposed skin. Stretching the neck of her shirt he eased it off over her head without touching the cuts. She wore no bra, and he bent to kiss each bare breast in a sweet homage, knelt on the floor in front of her, unfastened the zipper, and skinned down her jeans. Mouth and tongue followed the clothing till the pant legs rolled all the way down to the tops of her Keds. By this time, he had developed quite a hard-on that seemed to reach out for her. And there they were, squirming to solve the knotty problems of entanglement with limbs and clothing.

She laughed, then dropped to her knees, wrapping both arms around him and rolling them to the floor like a ball till she was under him, his legs locked around her. Both were laughing so hard they could barely untangle their tangles.

"Wait, I got it." He slipped off her shoes, helped her kick free of the jeans. "Now, do this." He wound her limbs around his neck placed one ankle across the other. "Hang on."

Magic and more hilarity to unfasten her grip around his neck so more could be accomplished. He wiggled this way and that, raised enough to ease his lips around the swollen aureole of one nipple even as he slipped deep inside her.

And away she swooped, hanging on for dear life in an imaginary world of zooming lights and soaring flight. Raising her hips, she took him even deeper into that sweet, secret welcoming darkness, hung on tight, and sailed off into infinity.

As if lost, he searched frantically to find the tiny heart that fluttered beneath his swollen desire. That was too much. Her imagination went wild, and she suppressed adding more impossible words. He was the butterfly, she was the flower. And that should be good enough for anyone. Gazing into her sea-blue eyes, he tickled her breasts with strands of her long hair.

"Oh, God, I love you, magic man."

To her dismay, he didn't reply but teased her with the touch of his tongue along her belly, played his fingers over her bare flesh, down her tummy and into the V of her thighs, made a sound down in his throat, revealing a growing wildness, and murmured in Cherokee words she couldn't fathom.

And then she understood a word, a name that nearly stopped her heart. "Leanne, Leanne." Slipping an arm beneath her hips he lifted her, shifted their bare bodies tighter together. She came once, twice, three times, with a sick feeling of loss while he reached a climax murmuring his dead wife's name.

What was going on? Was he saying goodbye? She couldn't bear the thought. Would he never let go of the woman who trapped him in a web of guilt while wrapping him in her arms?

Despite his apparent memories, he continued to make love to her. But it could be driven by remorse. He did not want to let go, though her sadness made her want to pull away. End this now. Yet she continued to honor her own desire. He joined her agitated attempt, trying to ask her something but failing with a noise close to sobbing. She would keep this going, not give him a chance to say what she was afraid of.

Orgasms rolled over her till she could scarcely breathe, but she couldn't slow one bit. If he wanted her enough, enjoyed her enough, perhaps he wouldn't leave. She should be ashamed, for herself and for him. But she continued to entice him, in spite of that shame. What else could she do?

Following a final dual explosion, they wrapped up limb for limb and lying that way fell asleep, small, indistinguishable murmurs coming from both.

Full daylight and she moved just enough to tantalize him and shut the alarm off. "Just slide this way a bit, then push." She would have him one more time, trapped within her by his own desire.

He did, and they were off. He came fast with a satisfied moan, kissed the corner of her mouth, raised to gaze down into her eyes. "I don't think I'm ever done with you."

"Me, either." There. At last he had come close to saying what she needed. She sighed and curled into his arms. Perhaps if she worked this right, she could prevent his leaving forever, embracing the ghost of his long gone wife, even if he wouldn't declare his love for her. That would truly be enough, wouldn't it? It wasn't healthy for him to continue loving a ghost, a dead woman. Given the chance, she could help him forget.

He touched her cheek. "I'm so sorry, Jess. I am, but there are… there's something I have to do. I've put it off too long. I know something… I mean there's something I have to take care of in Dallas. I'm going there as part of this investigation that Jameson and Ledger are involved in. Mac needs some of us to go, and since I'm familiar with Dallas, guess it'll be me for sure. Don't know who else."

There it was, and she couldn't prevent it after all. With an excuse to leave, he was going. Given this excuse he'd go back there to be with the memories of his dead wife, and she couldn't stop him. If he felt that way, did she really want to stop him? There could be more reasons for him to return to Dallas. Perhaps revenge for what had happened to him in that dark alley all those years ago. Drug dealers were at the source of it, and he might suspect they were the same as those involved in the move by the cartel into the Ozarks. But Leanne died of an overdose, and he still couldn't face that without feeling it was his fault for ignoring her.

His news didn't surprise her. There was nothing she could do but ask how long he'd be gone.

"Not sure, Jess. We'll just have to wait and see. Something may come up that will keep me there quite a while. It seems... well, you can talk to Mac about it. We can't discuss it. I'm so sorry."

Even though she'd expected it, he might as well have hit her with a whip. Over and over. Her heart cracked apart. She rolled into his arms.

"Last night was so good. Sounds like it was a farewell good." She could scarcely utter the words. Perhaps he would deny their truth.

When he remained silent, she prodded. Needing to know. "And now, after all we've had together, you're just walking away?"

He didn't say no.

She covered her mouth, eyes wide when she finally had to say it aloud, make him admit to the truth. "It's her, isn't it? It's always been her. She's dead, and you still can't leave it alone. How can Mac even let you get involved? She was your wife. Dammit, Dal, will you never let her go? Perhaps you should crawl in her grave with her."

Words that should have shocked him had no effect. He only shifted enough that they were no longer touching. "I have to know what happened. Why can't you understand that?"

"Understand? You took off for almost a year, me not knowing where you were, and I was right here when you finally came back. I understood. How can you keep doing this to me, to yourself?"

Without another word he slipped out of bed, Michaelangelo body outlined against the window. She could scarcely breathe, fearful of the wail that would pour from her mouth. Impossible to keep her hands off him, yet they slipped away when he rose.

"I'm going to take a shower, better to keep those cuts dry. Be out in a jif."

A way to keep her from joining him like usual. She could barely speak. "I'll get dressed. I need to go to work." Zombie-like words.

He studied her for a long while, and she met the stare. "Okay. What?"

"You sure you ought to go back to work? Parker'd give you time off if you needed it."

"I'm okay. This is turning into a huge story. I'm going to ask Parker if I can have it. I don't see why you care anyway. Just go. Do what you have to, and I'll do the same."

He shook his head, frowned. "Don't, Jessie. Don't do that. You know how the story went the first time around. Are you willing to go that route, rake muck all over Leanne's memory for the sake of a big story? I thought you were done with shit like that."

Furious, she pointed a finger at him. Words rose in her throat, but she swallowed. She would not do this, not let him do it to her. Shrugging she climbed into her jeans, pounded on the legs. "Crap, these are dirty. I don't have any…." Tears filled her eyes, and he tried to take her in his arms.

She shoved him away. Fists balled against her thighs. "Go on, do whatever you have to do. But you just remember, *she's* dead, and *I'm* alive." A pause. Then, "And you are, too."

Though she wanted to hit him, throw things, scream and shout, she lay down with her back to him, held her body stiff to ward off the rage. He went into the bathroom and shut the door.

When he came out of the shower, she was gone, no sign of her having been there except the rumpled bed and pillow. Pain at the loss shot through him, but he couldn't turn back now. He had to know how Leanne had died and why he hadn't known about her involvement in the drug trade while he fought them in dark alleys. It was outrageous that his wife could have been a junkie CI while he worked undercover to put a stop to the heroin trade. And him not know it. So wrapped up in other junkies he didn't have time to save his wife. And now he was on the verge of learning what had really caused her death. He could not back down. Why couldn't she see that?

Jess might be right that he had no business being involved in the investigation, but Mac couldn't stop him. If a man could love two women, well then, he did but be damned if he knew what to do about it. He'd never been good at making his feelings known with words, and this situation made it all the more impossible, since he didn't truly understand why he was willing to leave her. He had no way to explain to her how he felt about the situation with Leanne. Couldn't even explain it to himself. To try would only hurt her worse than his leaving. He had to deal with one thing at a time, and for now that was Leanne.

When he arrived at the station, Jameson had parked in his spot.

You'd think he would know better. He said nothing when those going on special duty gathered in the meeting room for the afternoon meeting. Mac took one look at him and frowned. "What in tarnation you been doing, boy?"

"Working. I got a few hours' sleep, and I can catch a nap on the way to Dallas." Still concerned Mac might try to send other deputies with Ledger and Jameson, he stood straight and forced a smile. He could only concentrate on one thing and that was clearing up Leanne's death by arresting those involved. Seeing every last one of them jailed. Though he knew better than to believe that, this assignment promised to at least help. He couldn't lose the opportunity. The remote possibility that she didn't kill herself with an overdose took a huge load of guilt off his mind. Loren and Leslie were CIs all involved with the cartel as well as Leanne, so it could be all three were killed for the same reason. At least he had to believe that to make Leanne's death a bit easier to take. Now all he had to do was avenge her murder. There would still be other problems to deal with but not nearly so many.

Jessie would come to understand that. She surely would. He could not lose her, but right now he didn't know how to keep her.

As head of the station in charge, Mac stood up front for the briefing. "Reckon we need to discuss going to Texas a bit. Working in Texas is something none of our men have done, with the exception of Dal. With Ranger Jameson's approval, I've also assigned Colby who will assist in the investigation, and Howie will handle communications and computer searches from this end. Sat phones on the table for Colby and Starr so everyone can stay in touch. Ranger Jameson will acquire any search warrants necessary in Texas. Deputy Marshal Ledger will be in charge of locating and detaining suspects. Starr will assist in both since he's familiar with the territory. Howie Duggan and his computer will come in mighty handy. Use him, you'll be surprised what he can do.

"I don't want to hear one word about squabbles between y'all. This ain't a television show or a movie. Questions?"

Colby's hand went up. Everyone chuckled, and he glanced around like he was embarrassed. Ever the joker, he kept everyone in a good mood.

"Colby?"

"I just want to know if we're sharing a hotel room or what?"

"Depends on how much money you have." Mac watched the reaction with a big smile. "Yep, single room if you want to pay for it, share if you can all get along sharing the rooms provided."

"Well, I don't mind sharing, but the rest of 'em might. Man, I snore like thunder on the mountain."

"Y'all can work that out. Actually, we've got two bedrooms at one of those apartment motels on the Interstate where your comings and goings won't attract so much attention. You'll be pleased to know you're traveling by SUV courtesy of the US Marshal service who has quite a stake in this as they are also hunting down some wanted fugitives suspected to be working with the drug dealers we're after.

"This is thought to be directly connected to the death of three CIs, Loren Jasper and Leslie Younger, who were murdered here in the past two weeks, and Leanne Starr, killed six years ago. We'll continue to work this end. No discussing with friends and neighbors or other deputies on this. Keep it quiet.

"Good luck and be careful. These men are armed and dangerous."

"Well, heck yeah, Sheriff. We are going to Texas, ain't we?" Everyone looked around, and Colby tipped his hat and grinned. He moved to Dal's side. "Don't you worry none, we'll get the bastards."

Unable to speak, Dal nodded and accompanied the men from the room and to their lockers.

Despite his desire to get this done, he remained removed from the others. Returning to Dallas after all this time forced him to face memories of the shooting and rehab from several years ago. Shaking them off, he went to the locker room with Colby to fetch their go bags.

Colby kept up his chatter. "Have to admit I'm kind of nervous about this. Only time I was ever out of Arkansas is when I was in the Marines, and that didn't turn out real well. People kept shooting at me."

Dal chuckled. He couldn't help but like the former marine. "Well, as long as we can find humor in what happens, we'll be okay."

"Yeah, we can always die laughing. But damn, I hate big cities. They're dangerous, man."

"You're crazy, you know that?"

Colby sobered. "It helps, man. It helps."

The blinking cursor was about to drive Jessie nuts. Parker had agreed she should stay home—correction, at the motel—because of her injuries, said he'd begin work on the huge story about the drug dealers and the two murders. This could be the story of a lifetime, and she wanted it. More because of her anger at Dal. Foolish and stupid, she admitted, but only to herself.

She drove to the office, ran her boss down in his little corner of that world, and asked to talk. He leaned back, hands locked behind his head. "What is it? Having trouble with the story of Maizie's kidnapping and escape?"

Without sitting, she cleared her throat and dove right in. "I want this story. The drug dealers and murders right here in our backyard."

He peered up at her through dark eyebrows. "I've been wondering how long it would take you to ask for it. You sure about this?" He caught her gaze, his own eyes glistening.

Nodding, lower lip caught in her teeth, she sat in the chair opposite him. "Are you sure you're okay about the entire episode? We really haven't had time to talk it out. How you want Loren's death handled in this story, I mean. I can take care of it if you want to go on home. Rest."

He never took his gaze from hers. "I do that, I'll fall apart. Sitting there thinking about her and what happened. Jessie, thank you. I appreciate how you handled the other night. And I'm sorry about this deal with Dal. I know how hurt you are."

A knot rose in her throat. That he could think of her hurt and anger in the midst of his despair told her just what a good friend he was. "Thank you so much." She paused, shuffled some notes.

"I'm thinking I can conduct some interviews here to set the tone for the piece. Any ideas you have, please share them. Because we're not going to have much information this first week, we can concentrate on the way folks here in town see what happened. Since no one knew Loren or Leslie, and Mac hasn't issued a release yet, we can get comments from locals on drug dealers discovered so close by. Mac will surely release some photos, if not we can set some interviews in the foreground of the barn where Loren's body was found and over at the house that looks so peaceful, yet Leslie walked out to the car and she was gunned down. This is the biggest thing to happen in Cedarton ever, isn't it? And we all hate it."

Parker raised his hand. "We can't always like what we have to do. Let's be careful here. As far as we know the drug dealers have not been tied to the murders, and so we can't insinuate that."

"Okay, we know that the Texas Ranger is here investigating former Dallas drug dealers setting up headquarters in Grace County." She checked a page of notes. "And the deputy marshal has a list of wanteds he suspects are tied to the dope dealers, so…?

"Jameson's undercover," Parker reminded her. "We'd better not reveal who he is and what he's doing."

She let out a huge sigh. "But he said I'd ruined that already."

"He was razzing you. He covered that little episode nicely, and according to Ledger he's back with the cartel."

A relief settled within her. She'd done that once already, to a man who loved her. Now he hated her, had even tried to kill her once after she came home to begin her new life. She wouldn't do it to the Ranger.

"Okay, then what are we going to write about? Cute puppies, or hey, maybe we could run pictures of heroin addicts or some poor prostitute being arrested for dealing to feed her kids."

He stared at her. "That's exactly what we'll do. Talk to people in jail for using, dealing, etc. Find out why they do it, how they got started, what they're on, when their life changed, where and how they get their dope. Then we'll research how many recovery houses there are in the state helping them kick the habit. It'll be a helluva feature."

"Okay, but we need news, too. What about the three suspects? Surely Mac can give us a release of some sort on them. What if we wrote a follow-up about Maizie's kidnapping and how the law is on to that being a ruse to misguide deputies?"

After Parker gave her the go-ahead with Mac's approval, she sat at her desk staring out the window in silence. What would be wrong with writing what really goes on instead of having to tip toe around? It's a free press. If she wrote what she'd really seen up to date and sent it anonymously to the Gazette or some other newspaper in the state, would they publish it without vetting the story? She wouldn't put her name on it or anything. But that was cowardly and not standing up for what she believed and certainly not honest journalism. Irritated, she tapped her fingers on the desktop.

So, a better idea. She knew where the dealers had come out of hiding when she was with the Ranger. The few photos she'd taken of surrounding scenery had GPS coordinates on them. What if she sneaked in there at night, took a couple of cameras, and set them up to take snapshots all night long right in the midst of their secret hideout, then sent them to the Little Rock newspaper anonymously? Give coordinates for the pictures. There'd be no way that would reveal undercover guys, but it sure could bust the drug dealers wide open even though she couldn't claim credit.

Okay. An idea worth trying. First she'd write the story Parker wanted. She dialed the county jail and asked Tink if they had any junkies currently awaiting charges or waiting to be sent on over to start serving time.

Luckily, a couple were still at Grace County, and they would do for her purposes. She needed something she could turn out quick so the story could go to press this week, then she'd have time to get her cameras set up at one of their camps and prepare for the big story. There was a chance Parker would fire her, a big chance. But she didn't care. The publicity would get her a job of her choice. And it wouldn't do harm to *The Observer,* for when things cooled down, the circulation of the paper could easily double.

Of course she could get killed, but she doubted that too, because she wouldn't get caught. Besides, the mood she was in, let 'em try to kill her, she'd take a few with her.

By that evening she had her first interview for the series Parker wanted. A young kid who had been fed opioids by his parents from the age of five to keep him pretty much out while they went about their life of crime. He was a showoff and eager to tell recollections of his life. Sick to her stomach, she recorded an unbelievable story of child abuse, then wrote a touching article for the current issue without revealing the kid's identity. Parker was more than satisfied, said he'd come up with a header and told her to go home.

Then she drove out to her temporary home, the motel on the Interstate where she'd remain until she could decide what her next step would be. Now she had a next step, and she began preparations for her nightly mission. It might take several trips to get what she wanted from the drug camps, situated far off the hiking trail around the lake, but it would take her mind off Dal and his disappearance into the Texas nightlife of crime. If she let herself think about it, she might come apart.

But she didn't, she wouldn't, she couldn't. It was time she became the sort of reporter she'd always wanted. Time she got out of this rinky-dink one-horse town and proved she could be a real reporter. She would show Dallas Starr and all the rest of them.

The sports outlet store in Harrison had everything she needed. Took some of her savings, but it was going to be worth it. She returned to the motel with the equipment Google advised. Two Cloak Pro IR Trail

Camera Packages—14MP 24 high-intensity infrared lights for capturing images. She wanted the cameras to take a picture and immediately send that picture to her cell phone or email, so she purchased cellular trail cameras. She wanted two angles to make sure she got most of what was going on in the hidden camp. Sound was the real problem. The cameras were to capture game or trespassers, but how was she going to record what was said? Turned out to be simpler than she'd thought. She found voice activated HD quality USB flash drive audio recorders on sale and bought two to help balance the sound.

She hooked up one of the cameras and a sound flash drive on a wall in her room, then sneaked across the room with all the lights off and the equipment running. She remembered sound and sang "Ain't We Got Fun" and tripped over the chair in the dark, barking her shin and shedding tears of remorse. The equipment captured it all.

The image playback on her cell phone was perfect, and the sound from the flash drive as well if you consider some idiot singing and prancing around in the dark and taking a nosedive perfect.

Righting the turned-over chair, she sat on her heels and considered what she was about to do. If caught, she would be lucky to be charged with trespassing or less lucky if the criminals decided to just shoot her with a Smith and Wesson and bury her somewhere.

The next thing was the dangerous part. Making her way to the camp where she had stumbled across the dope dealer's hangout and ran into Jameson. She hoped it was still in the same place. Hooking up the equipment would be touchy and dangerous, probably at night when all were asleep. If that didn't work, then wait till they left to carry out some nefarious deeds so she could sneak in and hook everything up.

She drove and parked deep in the thickest of woods as close as she felt safe, relaxed, and prepared for a long wait. Occasionally a bit of noisy revelry was carried on the wind. Hopefully she would be lucky and they would all fall asleep, but she wasn't too optimistic.

After the sun set, she pulled out a plastic bag with some vegetables, cheese, and crackers for a snack. In the back a small cooler held several bottles of water and a few Pepsis. Phone turned off held a message that she had gone to visit her aunt over at Bee Rock to get away from it all for a few days. Determined to succeed, she had prepared well.

A bit later she took out her laptop, plugged it in to the charger, and went to work on her story about Maizie's kidnapping and escape that she had promised Parker she'd finish in time for this week's issue. He was writing a piece from Mac's release on the death of Loren Jasper and Leslie Younger to go on the front page with her feature about the cause and effects of drug use she'd turned in before leaving for Aunt Annie's in Bee Rock.

In spite of all her planning, she couldn't help thinking about Dal and his betrayal. Just when it looked like she and he could get together, he upped and took off on some lunatic manhunt. And what does he tell her? He didn't know when or if he'd be coming back. Well FU, you cheating, underhanded liar. Oh well, she'd only been in love with him for more than five years, closer to six. How could he do this to her?

Stop, stop. Forget him and pay attention to what's at hand. The woods faded into dark shadows and twinkling stars sprinkled the purpled sky. She leaned back and closed her eyes. Just nap for an hour or so till it's time for all bad guys to be in bed asleep, then on with the action.

Something cold and wet slobbered around on her hand. Jerking awake, she cringed away from the intruder, a half-grown raccoon watching her quizzically while it licked her palm. "Shh, shh, git. *Git.*" She'd read somewhere that a whisper could be heard more clear than a low spoken word. Not sure what she believed, she decided against either one and waved the cute little animal away.

Through the distant darkness, a flickering campfire burned low. Not a sound came from the gang. She had opted for wire to fasten the cameras so there would be little noise installing them. Though it was suggested that they be hung far above eye level, she wasn't up for skinning a tree so had decided to find thick shrubbery where the cameras could be hidden well and pointed toward the center fire which seemed to be a gathering place.

The first one was no problem since she approached from the outer rim. Camera and sound equipment well in place, she was doing her best to see well enough to get around to the other side and place the second units when a voice nearby scared her so bad she almost wet her pants.

"What the hell are you doing?"

Interestingly, it was whispered.

Deputy Marshal Ledger drove the Cadillac Escalade competently, but who wouldn't? It sorta drove itself, the ride soft as silk. Dal stretched his long legs without bumping anything, the leather seat hugging him like a smooth-skinned woman. Damn, a fella could live well in one of these. Music, TV, telephones, computers, maps, bed, cooler. He didn't see one but wouldn't be surprised if there were a microwave as well. The marshals had it made and then some.

He nodded off after a while and didn't wake up till they stopped for food somewhere in western Oklahoma. He dreamed about Jess except instead of being pleasant, she was chasing him around shooting at him with her .38, so it wasn't enjoyable, though no doubt a deserved result. Ledger bought, and they had huge steaks at some place with a sign of a cowboy in a Stetson hugging the roof. A smaller sign advertised they had the best steaks this side of Texas. They did.

They stayed in a motel somewhere outside Amarillo, and Colby hadn't lied. He snored big time. Everyone vowed they were buying ear plugs, but Dal just laughed. "If y'all think plugs are gonna keep out that noise, you're crazy. What we need are those noise killing earmuffs men who work jackhammers wear."

"Aw, hell, I'm just gonna sleep in the car." Colby's declaration met with total agreement.

It was good the four were getting along well. Dal just hoped the camaraderie continued during the investigation. He hated working with someone who caused trouble all the time.

During the trip, Duggan kept them up to date on the manhunt in Arkansas for the unknown murder suspects. No one had been able to get any one of the three cat nappers to name names. Dal had his suspicions though, after having heard from Robert Kimble. That man was definitely involved, and he hated he'd missed meeting up with him. Mac had feelers out but so far nothing.

Then on the second day of the trip, Duggan came through on the computer with news that Kathy Spacey had found that the latigo belly strap found with Loren's body had not been what strangled her. It had been strapped tightly about her neck postmortem to cover signs of the real murder weapon. She had been strangled by two strong hands. No fingerprints so far, so someone knew a bit about cleaning up a crime scene. It remained to be seen who had killed Leanne, but the motivation for killing the other two women was just too much. All three deaths had to be connected. No such thing as a coincidence like that. At last Dal knew in his heart that his wife had not overdosed herself. News that could be printed was sparse with Mac holding back almost all pertinent information.

The trip to Dallas in the Escalade went smooth as if it were a jet plane ride. But Dal wasn't fooled. Things were about to get western, and he was ready.

14
CHAPTER

At the gruff challenge in the darkness of the woods, Jessie almost wet her pants. She'd been caught planting her cameras and sound recorders without even getting started. Afraid to say anything, she raised her hands and waited, knees ready to fold.

From the other side of a huge tree, a male voice stopped her cold. "Just taking a piss. You bout made me do worse. Whatcha doing out here?"

"Thought I heard someone sneaking round." Another male voice in reply. "Guess it was you. Best we all get a good night's sleep. Lots coming up to get done in the next few days."

Knees locking, she hugged the tree with all her might. Holy crap. They hadn't seen her.

The men continued to visit. "Yeah, well, I'd ten times druther do it from a comfortable house with all the facilities and such. What's the point of living like homeless fools?"

Something crackled through the leaves around her feet, and she covered her nose and mouth to keep from making a sound. Could be a snake or one of those ugly possums with teeth like a vampire. Frozen, she let it walk over her foot.

Would you guys get done with your business and go on back to bed? I've got work to do. The thought appeared to reach them, and they zipped up and crept off toward the dim light of the fire.

Good Lord, what a fright. For a few minutes, she couldn't move. Slowly, she felt her way out around the camp, clinging to small saplings till the fire appeared to be between her and the other camera. A brief stirring while the two men settled. Again she waited till it was totally quiet except for some snoring in the camp. The night was dark as the inside of an alligator's belly, but despite that, if she was patient, her night vision made out clumps of brush. It took a lot longer to make her way out around the camp to the other side, find another angle for the camera, and get it and sound pick-up placed, and she was soaked with sweat. At last a patch of paw-paw trees offered the perfect hiding place. Wired securely head-high to one of the finger-thick trunks, its lens peered between the huge leaves. The infrared lights showed several men sleeping on the ground and lanterns hanging in the trees. If only the sound worked as promised, she'd get what she wanted for an exclusive story. Then one of the men snorted, and she let out a squeak.

Oh, God, she had to get out of here before she came apart and ruined everything. *Stop worrying.* The unit worked fine at the motel. She double-checked that it was on and backed up to lean against a hickory nut tree. On the ground, their hard shells poked into the soles of her shoes making popping sounds. Fear of being caught kept her knees trembling. Sweat ran down her back, bugs crawled around on her skin, but she remained there until her heart went back to a normal rhythm so she wouldn't trip and fall. Be crap if after all this she got caught leaving.

All the way back to the Jeep every stick and leaf underfoot crackled and snapped, birds and wildlife screamed and pointed at her so she could be found easily. Low-hanging limbs smacked her in the face or snagged her clothing. It took ages to get out, and when she did, she slumped in the seat of the Jeep for a long time, shaking like the wind-blown leaves before heading back to Cedarton.

Just as she drove onto the pavement, relief clearing her vision, another thought hit her. She had to come back and gather all the equipment, or at least check it to see if she needed new batteries or the like. Worse, if she got nothing, she'd have to keep it up no telling how long. Good Grief. What had she gotten herself into?

All the way back to the motel she worked at making what she had done okay. Well, perhaps it was, but it was also dangerous. And that wasn't all of it either. When she wrote the article and sent it down to Little Rock, she would effectively put herself in a position of having betrayed Parker and everyone at *The Observer*. If she turned the story in to him, then what? She had absolutely no idea. Editors didn't care for the tail wagging the dog style of journalism. A term used when a reporter went out on her own, gathered information, and wrote a story. For obvious reasons, editors wanted to be boss, choose the stories, and assign them.

Well, what was done couldn't be undone at the moment. She didn't want to admit it, but she had done it as a direct reaction to Dal going to Dallas to work on a story about his dead wife who was a junkie six years dead. She felt bad for his loss, but why couldn't he just forget the past, let it go? She had put much worse behind her after Steven tried to kill her resulting in her shooting him.

Still mulling over the decision she'd made, she parked at the motel and sat there staring at what was now her home. Tears filled her eyes. Her home was gone, the man she loved was gone, and she might just have set something in motion that would ruin her career or at least make an unholy jumble of her life. She could stop right now. Silence in her head, then the moment of truth. She needed this like she needed to breathe. Why? Because despite the past, she'd do almost anything for a story. That almost being the key. She refused to hurt innocent people, but that's where she stopped. And that fire is what made her a good journalist. And often somewhat careless.

Lord. She'd probably end up living in a trailer park somewhere in the dregs of a big city working at Walmart unless she could bring this off. But in truth, she could not betray Parker or Mac. So, she'd see when the time came how far she would go chasing a story.

After a while, she dried her eyes, scolded herself, gathered her pack, and let herself into the motel room. After a long shower, she dressed and drove up to the Red Bird. There was always something going on there to help cheer her up. Fudge with a joke, his uncle Theron with a rich piece of gossip or stories about someone's latest escapade. She was inside the door before it hit her that there would also be all sorts of questions about the whereabouts of Dallas and Colby. Too late, everyone spotted her, so she took a seat alone at a table hoping to avoid questions, but that didn't work either.

Betsy Black rose, wohooed, and waved. "Come join us, Jessie. Have you met the Claptrees?"

Leave it to Betsy to want to be first. First at anything and everything. Jess tried to wave her off, but Betsy was having none of it and hustled over. "Come on, Jessie, you need to meet them. They are absolutely delightful."

Unable to figure a way out, she stood and followed the noisy woman through occupied tables. Was there a way she could correct Betsy before she called the new couple by the wrong name again, or should she just let her do it? Weighing who it might embarrass the most, she whispered to Betsy, "It's Captree, not Claptree."

"Oh, dear, are you sure? I'm convinced I heard it right."

Jess smiled sweetly and shrugged. Betsy held Jessie's hand and introduced her to Marvin and Shilo Claptree. She shook their hands in turn, saying only their first names. "Marvin and Shilo, we've met." She kept Shilo's hand for a moment. "I'm so pleased to see you both."

The British couple graciously did not correct Betsy on their last name, and she had the nerve to smirk at Jessie.

"Do join us." Shilo indicated a chair, and Jessie sat next to her. "We met at the newspaper office."

"Yes. How are you liking Cedarton?"

"I'm finding it a charming village."

"Shilo was just telling us about The Purple Raven and their attempts to obtain a liquor license." Betsy was bright-eyed and bushy-tailed when performing before an audience. She had to bring up the hot topic loud enough for most everyone in the place. Her tone announced God forbid, a liquor license for a business in Grace County.

Marvin stepped right in. "For now we have agreed to go under the identification of a tea house until your city council gets it sorted." Shilo added that didn't mean all they served was tea and crumpets.

Betsy gushed forth before anyone else could speak. "Shilo explained that in Britain, tea means a full meal."

The gracious woman smiled. "You see, we serve tea at 4 p.m., and tis a full meal. But no one would think of offering tea without a good malt liquor. A pub is not a bar nor tis it a tea house. A pub is… well, tis a pub, which is our goal."

Everyone laughed and commented among themselves. Jessie took out her pad and paper to take notes. She immediately liked the British couple. The Purple Raven could indeed be an interesting addition to Cedarton, and she was going to write an editorial she hoped would convince members of the city council to pass a bill allowing this pub to serve liquor. As a reporter, she could not write news or feature articles that took sides, but an Op-Ed was different. It should stir up a lot of discussion amidst the voters of the city and hopefully bring in stacks of letters to the editors. Parker would love it.

A bit later, with her time well spent at the Red Bird, Jessie headed back to the motel a bit more relaxed. After she finished the editorial, she went to bed. The next day she and Wendy were going shopping for clothes. The perky blonde insisted that it wouldn't all be jeans and t-shirts, either.

In spite of, or maybe because of, severe unhappiness over the change in her relationship with Dal, Jess looked forward to a shopping spree plus eating out at the new Mexican restaurant in Fayetteville. Elegant margaritas were a specialty of the house. Fayetteville had gone "wet" a few years ago, though a portion of the county was still "dry."

Grieving was not one of her favorite things, and she avoided taking part in it as much as possible. One recovered from disappointment quicker by having a grand time. When Dal took off a couple of years ago, she had a fantastic short affair with Parker. It sure helped her recovery. She had never told Dal, but he probably knew. Might even have indulged in the same type of recovery while away from her. This was the twenty-first century, and casual sex was entertainment. No telling what she might do to recover this time, but she'd not sit home and mope, that's for sure. That tall, lanky James Jameson was obviously available, though his antics were at times annoying. One never could tell. And of course there was Colby and Deputy Marshal Ledger. No shortage of available men.

Once settled at the Fairway Motel Apartments west of Dallas, Dal opened his computer and studied the digital copies of all the pictures they'd found at Loren's cabin. Interesting comparing the backgrounds. Crow's Nest Boutique was lettered neatly in an arc above the heads of three beautiful women who could've been sisters. Sadly all deceased because of drugs. A young Leanne gazed at him, and he touched her face with a fingertip.

Ledger dropped down onto the couch beside him and studied the photo. "Taken in Cedarton? Does it have a date?"

Dal shifted down to the corner. "There. 2011. The Crow's Nest was where The Purple Raven is located. All three women were here together then." He paused, then clicked on to the next photo. "Odd. Wonder if they lived here? If not, what were they doing here? Leanne lived in Dallas in 2012 when she was killed. She never mentioned Cedarton."

His voice cracked. So sad to realize all of them were dead.

"You moved to Cedarton later. Was it because of them?"

Dal scratched his head. "I never thought so, but some things happen mysteriously." Especially when your grandfather is a shaman. Had the old man been behind this ever since Leanne died? Guiding Dal toward an inevitable conclusion. Or perhaps a crossroads where he would finally find the truth and make his own choices.

How could he possibly believe in that sort of superstitious nonsense? Shit. He could because as a Cherokee, Grandfather had made sure his life had been structured around it.

Ledger studied the next image. "These girls. Are they sisters?"

"As far as I know, they were childhood friends. But I don't know as much as I thought I did when Leanne and I were married." He paused. "Hell, turns out I didn't know much of anything about her. I've learned most of this since I got involved with your investigation."

Jameson came in from the kitchen carrying three cups of coffee on a tray. "I think it's time we compiled our information. See where we're at before we tackle the Dallas end of it."

Ledger took a cup. "I agree. Who wants to go first?"

"I think Jameson probably since he's our Dallas link."

Nodding, the Ranger pulled out a tablet and turned it on. "Here's what we know. It began when one of our CIs"—he nodded toward Dal— "that would be Leanne, contacted us about a lot of talk on the street concerning a drug cartel bringing heroin in by private planes from Mexico. Big surprise, huh? In the beginning, Mexico imported mostly brown heroin, very impure, low quality, and cheap. As Afghan drug producers began importing more high-quality heroin into the US, Mexico created black tar heroin. It's still only twenty-five, thirty percent pure, much less than white heroin powder, but again, cheaper. A hugely popular product for the masses. These guys from over in the Ozarks got into the trade when the law cracked down on meth so hard. Next to marijuana, it was a best seller. They saw a big market opening up. An already organized group in the meth trade switched to heroin, seeing a huge profit. Thinking they could dodge the law, they've centralized in the Ozarks, using I40 and I44 to transport coast to coast. It got out of hand fast. In 2012,

Leanne, a CI for me for about a year, came to me with a story I found hard to believe. A good friend of hers had died of an overdose of black tar heroin. My CI's husband, Dal here, worked undercover at the time, and I guess she thought she might sort of help out."

He glanced at Dal. "Sorry, buddy. Besides, she wanted to avenge her friend's death. She'd gone undercover and soon learned a lot from dealers. She quickly realized what she'd found."

Jameson stopped. "You may not want to hear this, Dal."

He swallowed hard, fingers balled into fists. "No, go on."

"When she turned up missing, not keeping an arranged meet, we sent an undercover in, and he found her. She'd been overdosed and then posed on her bed as if she'd done it to herself."

Dal leaped to his feet. "Goddammit, why wasn't I told? You knew I was on the street. You let me believe all these years I'd been married to an addict. Worse, you put her in harm's way then let her die. Jesus." He stormed from the room and slammed the door on them. "Bastards."

He dropped to his knees, sobbing. The way he felt, she might as well have died this day, for his mourning had begun again.

An urge to kill grew. He'd find someone, anyone involved and do the same to him as had been done to her. Then to hell with all of them.

I'm sorry, love. So damned sorry. I should have been there. Why didn't you tell me?" He wanted to run but had nowhere to go. It was time to stop trying to escape or to hide.

With the pain came a bittersweet forgiveness. An emotion he'd never expected. He'd always been angry that she'd turned into an addict and betrayed all he stood for. Yet it wasn't true at all. She believed in the same thing he did. The knowing released his pent-up anger. She was still dead, always would be, but her death had a purpose, wasn't useless.

He rose, went in the bathroom, and washed his face. Combing his hair back, he went to join the others. The best thing he could do for her now was put a stop to the cruel deaths from heroin addiction. They'd never completely take drugs off the streets, but they could honestly say they'd done everything they could.

He sat in one of the chairs. "Sorry. Okay, where do we begin?"

Jess would never have bought the damn dress had it not been for Wendy. It was a brilliant blue that, as Wendy put it, popped her eyes. Whatever the hell *that* meant. She would've guessed it did more for her boobs, revealing the top half till one could almost see the peachy glow of her nipples.

Standing behind her, Wendy cupped her hands and lifted her breasts so she looked very well developed. "We'll need an uplift bra," she murmured to the salesgirl.

The girl trotted off and Jess studied her reflection. "What happens if I bend over? Do I grab them so they don't fall out? I don't even know where half of this came from."

Wendy laughed. "You know what would be tantalizing?"

"This isn't?"

Chewing her lip, Wendy shook her head. "More-so if you get one of those camisoles you can see through and wear it under. Then they just get a glimpse. Wait here, I'll find one."

Jessie lifted her shoulders and sighed. "What have I done? That isn't me."

She slipped into the changing room, shed the dress, and took down the next hanger containing a pair of Wrangler jeans and a men's undershirt. She had them on when Wendy returned with three camisoles draped over one arm.

Throwing her arms out, Jessie exclaimed quite loudly. "Ta-Dah. Jessie West returns."

"Oh, good grief." Wendy looked stricken.

Behind her the salesgirl appeared with an uplift bra. "These are quite out of date. Today women go more for the natural look, just letting them hang out there without any help. Which of course yours don't need." She turned her toward the mirror. "Hmm, yes. I like it. Could I show you a pair of Tony Llama boots?"

"She just wanted to make a sale. You do realize that, don't you?" Wendy marched along beside Jessie, both carrying several bags from the store.

"That's her job, and she's good at it. She saw what I really wanted and made sure I had it. I bought the dress too, so what are you complaining about?"

"Six pairs of jeans, ten various colors of tops, long-and-short-sleeved and sleeveless. Those ones look like what my father used to wear under his white dress shirt."

Jessie laughed. "Well, I did give in and buy the blue outfit and the camisole along with some sling sandals."

"Yes, but what about the uplift bra?"

"You heard the woman, they're out of style. My girls will remain right where they belong, thank you."

"Sure, hanging down to your waist."

"I beg your pardon?"

Wendy hugged her and laughed. "Guess what?"

"You've got a date?"

"How'd you know?"

"Who?"

"It's Howie Duggan."

"Oh, my, how did you get him out of his shell long enough to ask?"

"I asked him to take a look at my computer cause it's broken. He's a real sweetie, just takes some easy-going talk. He's shy but really smart. He has a PhD in digital communications. Speaks five languages. And I like him. He's going to teach me French."

"Oh, well, then. I thought you'd never get together. That is so great. I wish you both well."

"Thanks."

"So, what are you wearing?"

"Well, it won't be jeans."

Sitting in the car, they broke up laughing. Wendy let her out at the motel. "Let me know how things come out," she said. That brought on another bout of laughter.

"Well, it won't be my girls."

"Oh, by the way, my cousin has a double-wide he wants to sell, and I thought of you. It would be so simple to take it out to your place, hook some stuff up, and move in. And it's real nice. All the furniture comes with. He's getting married, and they're buying a house. It's really roomy and fancy."

"Hmm, let me think about it."

"Don't think too long, they go quick here, you know. And he has a good price on it."

When the motel room door swung open, Jessie dumped her packages in the middle of the bed, hit her toe on a chair leg, went in the bathroom and bumped her elbows getting on the toilet. "Sheesh. That'll do with the nerves."

Back in the room, she dug her phone out and dialed Wendy. "Ask your cousin when I can come look at the trailer." She remembered she was going out to the camp tonight to check on the cameras. "How about Sunday afternoon?"

"Great. We're having a barbecue, and we can take you out there after."

"Oh, are you sure you want me nosing in?"

"It's the whole family, and I know they'd love to meet you. They all quote things you write all the time, and I've promised for a long time to introduce you, it just never came up. But I'm asking Howie, so he can get acquainted with everyone too. It'll be great fun."

"Okay, if I can wear my Wranglers and Tony Llama boots."

"You are a real hoot, Jessie."

She hung up, still chuckling. Why in the world had she never gotten better acquainted with Wendy? They saw each other only occasionally at *The Observer*, working odd hours like they did. The girl was so much fun, and it had been a long time since she'd pursued a new friend. Hell, she hadn't made many friends in all the time she'd been back in Cedarton. Dave and Kathy, Parker, and her childhood friend Tinker of course, and the deputies. Dal was something else entirely, and without him life would be mighty stale. She brushed away tears. It would all work out. It had to.

Tonight promised some excitement though. She lay on the bed and rested a while, then went out to Grandma's and bought something to eat. An enormous Cobb salad and a glass of sweet tea. Afterward, she parked on the back roads, her tablet turned on to focus on the farthest camera. Nothing. No images of trees, of curious animals, or men milling about. Just a snowy screen. Fumbling about on the keys, she finally pulled up the nearest camera. Ran the images back to the beginning. Whatever had happened had occurred while she and Wendy were shopping. But no matter what, it would be on the tablet and on her email.

On the screen, out of the shadowy woods, lumbered a black bear, a bit large for the species. Toddling along behind came two cubs. The mother stood on her hind legs, snorted, checked out the perimeter. Took two or three steps, checked again.

Come on, come on, get out of there. Hurry.

Closer to her hidden camera, nose wet, tongue pink when it came out to lick her lips, then the lens, slobbers distorting the picture.

No, no. Don't do that. Go on, git.

She dare not speak her thoughts aloud. Maybe a rock tossed just hard enough to scare the animal. She picked one up, weighed it in her hand. Did she dare? One of the cubs rose to its feet, pawed at the camera. It swung, looked like it might come loose.

"You little shit, go on, *git!*"

Suddenly, before Jessie could really think what was happening, the mama bear opened her mouth, closed her jaws around the camera, ripped it loose, and turned and ran.

She shouted out loud. Couldn't help it, the sow went out of sight with her camera, followed closely by the two cubs.

Someone behind her spoke. "Lucky she didn't take you along. Just hold real still. Don't think of running. This is a gun barrel you feel in your back, and it's loaded with real bullets. You don't look like a buyer or a dealer. So we're just gonna settle down and wait a spell." He gestured with the gun. "And you can shut that thing down real easy and put it on the ground. Evil damned things anyways."

All the while that darkness crept into the woods, she mulled a way out. Ought to be something she could do. This was worse than waiting for a pot to boil. Obviously they were all off somewhere, probably selling that deadly black tar to everyone. All but the one holding her at gunpoint.

Lowering her butt to a fallen log, she hugged her knees to keep them from trembling.

Her captor sat on his heels and studied her real close, like he wanted to have her for dinner. "What in Tom Thumb was you thinking? Poking about like that?"

Play it innocent. "Just curious what a bunch of fellas were doing camping out in the woods like this." She swept an arm around to include the entire camp. "Don't you know it's not hunting season yet? You're liable to have to go to jail."

The man chuckled under his breath. "And so you come in here to tell us that? What? You a Fish & Game fella?"

Best if she didn't say anything to that. Besides from off a ways came the sound of big footed men walking. Stomping like they had no fear of being caught doing whatever it was they were doing. Damn, she wanted badly to be the one who stopped them, but she couldn't come up with anything. Worst of all, what would they do to her? The woods were filled with places where a body might not ever be found. Would they go that far? For now there was nothing she could do but meekly let her keeper clip her wrists together with those plastic things they used now instead of handcuffs. Not fight back when he shoved her into one of the tents and hit her hard enough she knew only star blazing darkness and excruciating pain.

For the third time that night, Dal tried to reach Jessie with no answer, and she didn't call him back. Tomorrow they were going all out to round up the bastards putting together this heroin crew, and he didn't want to go without talking to her. Where could she possibly be without her phone? Not usual at all. Shame filled him over the way he'd treated her. He had been so cruel, cutting her to the bone, then walking away as if it didn't matter. And it did. So very much.

Time to call Parker, see if he knew where she was. Just a message there too. Not unusual, this being Wednesday. They were getting the week's issue of the paper out, and Parker usually turned off his phone. But the office phone should be on. He clicked off and dialed the landline of *The Observer*. Wendy answered. He took a grateful breath.

"Have you seen Jessie?"

"Dal? No, she… I'm not sure what's up. She's usually here laying out her page, but she called in earlier, Parker talked to her, then said she wouldn't be in, and he'd lay out her page. She turned in an Op-ed that he enjoyed a lot, but I haven't read it yet. And her story about abused children as a result of drugs is excellent. As always, her column is in too. I'll see if I can reach her and have her call you. Okay? How is Dallas?"

He finally cut into her long diatribe. "It's okay. Fine. Do you know what she was up to? You know, don't you?"

Silence. In the background, chatter from everyone while they worked on each page and discussed the best spot for the ads. He'd been there enough to know the process.

"Wendy?"

"You know what, Dal. She was really upset after you left. I don't know what you said to her, but it must've hurt her bad. And it's not my place to try to smooth things over. She'll get in touch with you, I'm sure, as soon as she forgives you. I will call her, though. Let her know. Now, I'll have to go."

And she slammed down the phone. The one that sat on her desk up front in the office. The one she used to talk to people who called to complain or ask questions. He had a vision of her scratching back thick blonde hair with her long pink nails and going on setting type, maybe muttering just a bit, telling him off.

He put down his phone, took a shower, and crawled in bed. In spite of not being able to talk to Jessie, he was excited about the plans for tomorrow. He would accompany Jameson along with Colby to serve a warrant on one of the three fugitives on Ledger's warrants. They'd located an address for him. The man was dangerous, and he found himself wishing he would come out shooting so they could solve the problem of his existence right on the spot.

But they needed him alive in the hopes he could lead them to the others. And speaking of those killers still running loose in Grace County, Howie was working from Cedarton to run them down, and Ledger was assisting with information needed to help in the search.

What excited Dal the most was those still in hiding, including ex-sheriff of Nolton County Robert Kimble and one of his deputies, Jason Gold. Regrettably, he'd missed his arranged meeting with Kimble by taking off for Dallas. He probably wouldn't get another chance since things were heating up in his area. It now appeared they'd been involved with a man called Bainbridge in a scam run on the department of human services regarding foster children taken and sold in Mexico last spring. It was an ugly crime, and those two escaped a wide net after the Grace County deputies and Deputy Marshal Trey Ledger broke up the child trafficking cult six months ago by arresting Bainbridge. Up till now, that had been the largest and longest lasting case since Dal had come on the scene to work as a Criminal Science Investigator for the Grace County sheriff's department.

The way things were going Kimble and Gold should be swept up in the wide net being spread over the entire area around Cedarton. A search also continued for the fugitives wanted for questioning in the murders of Loren Jasper and Leslie Younger. Rounding up all of the fugitives and drug dealers would clean up Grace County, and everyone was on high alert. Mac wanted to prove that having a Walmart and an Interstate in Cedarton would not cause a concentration of criminals in the small town. And by thunder he would see to it before he retired. Mac had already talked to Dal about running for sheriff to replace him.

Early Thursday morning, Texas Ranger James Jameson, Deputy Sheriffs Dallas Starr and Colby Hanson journeyed to the southeast corner of Dallas where they knocked down a door, presented the surprised and fuming residents with a search warrant, and arrested them as well. They went along, though with loud protest, where Ledger joined them, one at a time in a ten by ten room and began a long, drawn out questioning.

Dallas and Colby did a fine job of tearing apart the shack of a house. Finding a filing system in Spanish, Jameson quickly translated it to locate the latest shipment of heroin hidden in a delivery of tortillas that left Mexico a few days earlier headed for a chain of Mexican fast food stores throughout Texas. Just another way to deliver the deadly drug. There would be a bunch of unhappy dealers all over the state when their delivery failed to arrive. And another bunch of Texas Rangers working with the DEA who would be very happy hauling in the dealers.

There was still work ahead of them. A crew remained active in the wilderness of Arkansas. What it still would take to round them up was anybody's guess. But one thing at a time. They might get some information from these guys or not. Dal could hardly wait to catch Kimble and

Gold and put them away. If not for being involved in drugs, at least for their part in the child trafficking last year.

Dallas and Colby rode along with Jameson to the motel where they all took showers and called for an order of four T-bone steaks from The Roadhouse just down the street. The fourth one was for Marshal Ledger who left his unfortunate prisoner sleeping with his head on the table to eat with them.

Ledger slammed through the door laughing. "I promised if he'd give me the source of this black tar shipment, I'd bring him the biggest T-bone The Roadhouse has. Course we have a long way to go to dig out the sources. It's flowing in out of Mexico like eruptions from volcanoes. We let this get a toehold over there in Arkansas, we're liable to choke on the damned stuff. The only thing we can hope is that the wilderness will prove more than they can handle."

"Think he'll talk?"

"No idea, you can't ever tell about these Mexicans. Reckon it depends on how much he likes steak. Or how hungry his family is. Hard to think of it that way, but...." Ledger washed his hands and face.

"Yeah. Or how scared he is of dying," Jameson said.

Dal watched the men josh with each other. At one time, he'd been hip-deep in battling the heroin trade here in Dallas. Seen kids dying in back alleys from using the cheap black tar. Now that he could prove what had happened to Leanne, he couldn't wait to get out of Dallas. He was truly ready to put this behind him. If it wasn't that this cartel business threatened his new hometown, he wouldn't remain involved now. Tomorrow was another day of digging around, trying to find links to the Ozark gang that they could use to haul those hillbillies out of there. Put an end to this before it got started. He'd come to believe that growing marijuana for medicinal purposes was clearly a good thing, this dealing in a drug like the killer heroin was a whole other thing.

God weren't there any places left where kids could be safe from drugs?

Before he closed his eyes, he thought about Jessie. Why hadn't she called him? Had she gone off on one of her crazy trips looking for that one big story? It was a long time before he went to sleep. He should've treated her better.

15
CHAPTER

Well if this wasn't the shits. Too dark to tell if her eyes were open, but her head was still on her shoulders, obvious because it hurt like the very devil. What had she gone and done now? Hard to remember, but it looked like she'd messed up again. Best to lay downright still till she figured out where she was and what the chances were she could do anything about it.

Uh-oh. Gone there for a while. Back now. There wasn't much sound. But there were men about. Men smelled different than women. Farts probably. She wasn't out real long cause she didn't have to pee. Let's see if she remembered her name. Mud. That would probably do. Her age? Old enough to know better than to get in a mess like this. So what the devil was she doing here?

Okay stop criticizing and assess the situation. Something around her wrists was so tight her fingers tingled. Fright and panic crept through the darkness, threatened to smother her. Don't give up. Never give up. Kick and squirm, maybe she could loosen her arms. All that did was bring a load of pain down on her. And told whoever had her she was awake. She lay still. Someone was there with her.

"Please don't hurt me too much. Please, please don't." How awful pathetic she sounded. Begging like that.

"Jest lay where you be, little darlin. You're flat out lucky I'm the one who heard you. Some of these fellas are nothing but bastards. Like to hurt women. My mom taught me better than that. What in thunder did you come messin around in here for?

It was the same guy from earlier who had tried to help her. "Let me go. I won't say anything." How stupid did she think they were? Of course she'd say anything. She'd shout it to the world. Around the world. Put it on Facebook and Google Plus, Messenger. And that would just be the beginning. But let's keep that quiet for now.

He clucked his tongue. "Yep, that's what they all say."

"What are you going to do to me?" He sounded nice enough, might let her go. Right. In a pigs eye.

"Can't downright say for now. Shit, woman, why'd you come in here? It creates a real big problem."

"I know. Don't you think I know? I'm the one with the problem. Look, I have no idea what's going on in here. So what can I tell?"

Outside background noises told her men were real busy with something. Talking, making jokes, grunting like they were working.

He chuckled. "Yeah, but you're a woman. Curious like all of you'ns. Got an idea for you. Keep that pretty little mouth shut and act like you're out. You listen'in to me?"

A shuffling and some noise, then nothing. She held her breath. Yep, he was gone. What was that smell? Something she was familiar with. Vinegar? Well they sure weren't makin pickles.

Aware she'd been out again. This time, laughter and a low hum of conversation brought her back. Her belly told her it'd been a while since she'd eaten 'cause it growled with hunger. Her mouth was so dry her tongue stuck to its inside.

"I'd just bet you it ain't either." A sharp voice from outside was followed by a hack of a laugh.

"And I'm tellin you it is."

"Well I'll just betcha a million dollars."

"You ain't got no million dollars."

"I will have. Soon as Bracken gets here and we hauls this load out. He says so. Lissen, you gonna do it?"

"Do what?"

The voices moved away, faded so she couldn't make out what they were going to do for a million dollars. Too bad the images on her tablet hadn't shown much of anything. Looked like the camp was empty when that ole mama bear and her cubs ripped out the camera. She hadn't had time to check the other one before they caught her. This is probably the worst idea she'd ever had. Dal would kill her. If he ever got the chance.

Sometime during the night someone hustled her upright, gave her water till it dripped down her front. Might've been the man who was so nice to her earlier. But he didn't say anything. A bit later, she couldn't tell how long, she roused a bit to find she was being carried. Men with lanterns walked along as if they had a certain destination, her flopped over the shoulders of this gigantic man who walked like he was running over railroad tracks.

No one would ever find her now.

Pain from the jiggling zig zagged through her temple like strikes of lightning, and she passed out.

Though her head still whirled like crazy, the next time she came to, trussed up on the floor of yet another tent, the horrid movement ceased, she sorted out some thoughts of what she knew. Marijuana was the most popular money making crop in these hills, but something else was going on here. That smell wasn't the popular plant. Her brain wouldn't quite come up with it. Not meth, the one available in the wilds of eastern Grace County where hardly anyone ventured. Her research on drugs wasn't as complete as she'd like. Cocaine was popular but not much around here, and she couldn't think of reading that it smelled like vinegar or could be cooked over a fire in a pot. Could heroin be cooked, and did it smell like vinegar? She couldn't remember. What if they were wrong?

If only she could get loose and take a look around the camp. That might give her some answers. Then what? Anyway what kind of sense did it make coming off here into the wilderness to make and distribute drugs? No roads to haul out the product, whatever it was. And a sudden amount of road building and in and out traffic would attract too much attention and take too much time. In these parts everyone knew a lot about what was going on unless it was kept pretty secret.

What would be ideal was if she could interview one of these men, get her story straight from the horse's mouth. Then somehow escape. Wow, what a scoop that would be.

Time to get her mind on something else before she really went bonkers.

At early dawn, one after another, men with large backpacks came and went, making very little noise. A smell of eggs, bacon, and coffee mixed with campfire smoke hung in the early morning stillness and drifted into the tent, once in a while carrying the stink she couldn't quite place. Sometimes so bad she choked and coughed.

The sun came up and where the flap didn't quite close sent golden bars across the floor so she could make out a few things inside. Nothing there but backpacks, bedrolls, boxes stacked in the corners. Something stenciled on the ends like when you bought a complete box of single things. Meth was all she could think of. It could be cooked on a campfire in a kettle from stuff you could buy at the store. In itself a dreadfully addictive drug, the makings scattered here and there and usually located by law enforcement. It had a definite smell, and it wasn't vinegar. What else could be made the same way?

Put it all together in her head. Or write it down. She scooted across the dirt floor, using her heels, trying to find her tablet. She had it in her hand when she went down, so it was probably lost somewhere behind them and of no use. Still, she had to check. One thing. If it was turned on, Dal or Mac or any of the guys with their computers could find her if they were specifically looking. Her GPS would lead them in. If any of these guys unearthed it though, surely they would know to turn it off.

God, she was in one heck of a mess. Worse than any she'd ever been in. Because not only was she lost, her life was in danger.

Dal sat in the office at a borrowed desk perusing a Fish & Game Department aerial map of Arkansas plus a Google map online. Hopefully Jessie was operating in the trustworthy hands of Parker and Mac, and he could concentrate on getting this drug business out of the way, once and for all. He still had no sense of where those ole boys could be making black tar heroin and hauling it out without being spotted. Where in that wilderness could it be possible to carry out such a project?

Trouble was, black tar heroin could be cooked up much like meth could. Even a campfire would do. But shit, the stench and tromping in and out with the stuff? The law would run it down. No roads, no transportation. Mules? Horses? Nah. It didn't make sense. Still, in a way it did.

The DEA and local law enforcement in Dallas had made it so hot that their distribution and dealers were on the run. Barely keeping ahead of the law. Time to find another solution for selling the cheap black tar. There was the smell from cooking that made it hard to hide, even off on some farm. Wilderness in the Ozarks did make sense for some reasons. But then the traffic hauling in the raw stuff then getting out the final product required transportation and a decent road off where people don't get curious about what's going on.

That and a constant niggling worry about where Jessie could be and what she was doing, and Dal felt like he was bashing his head up against a tree trunk.

Ledger came in the office shaking his head. "All I need is one of 'em pointing to where they're hauling the dope to, but they're scared to talk. That's why they use Mexicans. These guys can't find work, they've got families to feed, and this kind of money makes 'em forget about the danger. It's coming into Texas and disappearing."

Dal glanced up from the paper map. "What do we know for sure? Are they dealing with distributors in our part of the county over in Arkansas? If so, it's not a good idea to use Mexicans. Too unusual there once you are out of Northwest Arkansas. White guys, maybe? Transportation?"

Ledger cracked open a bottle of water and moved to stand behind him. "Why the paper map?"

"Cause this is the very latest aerial release. Some of those online are two or three years old."

"Don't get it."

"Sheds, shacks, old houses. Some burn, others fall in. Camps come and go. Even new trails. Nothing thought that important to issue new maps regular like."

Ledger leaned down, pointed at a thin tan line amid the trees on both maps. "What's this?"

"Ozark Highlands Hiking Trail. It runs from… shit." He scrambled to his feet. "Clear across the damn country. Just took a new set of eyes. Dammit, should've seen it."

Jameson strolled over to join them. "Someone discover gold or something over here =?"

Ledger shrugged. "Got me, I think he's having a stroke or maybe he swallowed a frog. Either way explains that look on his face."

Dal gathered his stuff spread out on the desk. "How soon can I get back to Grace County?"

"Depends on whether you want to fly, drive, or hitchhike. And if you want to let us in on what's up."

"If it's good as it looks, we'll take that Fed SUV out there." Ledger pointed out the door toward the parking. "I'll get someone else to handle the questioning of these two old boys. We've got 'em whether they talk or not. I've got to see how an old Arkie works his cases."

One of the deputy marshals came over from another desk. "I'd like a go at those fellas you got in there. Think I can break them." He then rattled off a sentence in Mexican and grinned. "Maybe they just need someone who can talk their language."

Jameson wandered around, hands in his pockets. "I think I'll stay here. You don't need me over there. Maybe I can help break these Mexicans."

Ledger slapped him on the shoulder. "Go to it. Me and these deputies are going back to Arkansas."

It took less than an hour to pile everything in the Cadillac Escalade and head east. By taking turns driving, all three got good sleep in the large comfortable car, and they pulled into the motel at Cedarton twelve hours later. Easier to have plenty of room there than go to Dal's small apartment or the sheriff's office open to everyone's eyes.

During the trip they concentrated on driving and resting rather than discussing thoughts and ideas about catching these guys. Best to clear their heads for a fresh start. Plenty of time to plan once they were back.

They settled in, and Dal got Parker on the phone. "I'm worried about Jessie. Thought she was busy with a local story. What was she working on?"

"That's the problem. She finished her assignments, and we hadn't really talked about anything for next week."

"Please don't tell me she was working on the murders."

"Not that I know of, but you know her. I really think she shied away from that. It came too close to that case out in California that got her in so much trouble. Still, why would she just disappear? It's not like her. But I felt, well had this... dammit, I'm afraid to tell you this, but she asked to do the murder story but let me talk her out of it way too easy. I had a feeling she was going off half-cocked, but she assured me not. Then we got busy with the paper, and later when I called her, she didn't answer her phone."

He hung up and called Mac. Howie patched him in to the patrol unit's radio. *"Haven't heard from her."* Mac's voice scratched. *"Had a lead on your friend Kimble, so we're out looking around. Nothing yet. Don't worry about Jessie, you know how she is."*

"That's exactly why I'm worried about her. But this deal on Kimble. Do you want me to help there?"

"Nah, you stick to what you're doing." Static interrupted, and the sheriff's voice faded.

Torn between the drug case, chasing after Kimble, and finding Jessie, Dal took a break to build himself a ham sandwich from the stock of groceries they'd bought on the way in. Soon the others joined him.

After all, a fella had to have nourishment.

Colby stood in the doorway for a moment. "I think I'll go see about finding Jessie. Her being missing this long is a bad sign, knowing her. You guys can handle this from here, can't you?"

Dal looked up from smearing bread with mustard. "That's a good idea. I'd feel better if you were helping look for her. I'm really worried about her, but we've got to run this down. I shudder to think what will happen over here if our woods get taken over by heroin distributors. Check with Parker to see if he has a horse missing. Oh, and Colby, keep in touch, would you?"

"Will do, and let us know when you get on the trail of these fellas."

"Yep. You find Jessie, tell her… well, never mind, I'll do it myself."

Later that evening, maps and notes scattered everywhere, Dal stood rubbing his eyes.

Ledger leaned back and groaned. "You still convinced they're using the wilderness for a new distributorship for black tar?"

Dal nodded. "And I think they're making it there too. Haven't figured out all the hows and wherefors yet, but I will."

Dal's phone rang later that evening. The two men were still working on his theory, mapping out possibilities. He grabbed it.

"Hey, Colby. What's up?"

"It's like she dropped off the edge of the earth. No one in town has seen her, so she's left on purpose so no one could report seeing her or talking to her, not even her best friends."

"Why would she do that? Good God, she ought to know better."

"Why would you think that?"

Dal hesitated before going on. "Take it easy. There's sure to be an explanation. She'd leave word for someone. Has anyone checked her online messages? She wouldn't go off like this with no explanation. Remember the fit she had when I was out hiking and Steve shoved me off the mountain? No one knew where I was. She's left a note or voicemail or something. Have all her friends, everyone, check their messages, voicemail, email—hell even look for a note maybe in their door. Could you do that?"

"Done some of that but didn't think of it all. I'll double check with Howie. How's things going on your end?"

"Looks like we might put something together by morning. Can you alert the guys that there may be overtime coming their way? We're gonna need searchers."

"Sure. And I'll get on the Jessie hunt."

"Thanks, Colby."

"You bet."

Back at the map-strewn table, Dal couldn't get his mind off Jessie and what might have happened to her. It gnawed at him. It was important to get these drug guys rounded up, but he couldn't give it priority over finding her.

Though not one to use social media, he picked up the tablet long ago issued to each deputy, plugged it in in case it wasn't charged, then turned it on. Nothing on Facebook Messenger.

He texted Howie. *How do I find out where Jessie is? I know I've heard you talking about some kind of signal from one of these dadblasted things.*

The reply came back a minute later. *Hang on a minute.*

He waited impatiently. Then hammered out, *Howie, dammit.*

Okay, if she's with her tablet, she's right there. A map came up on the screen with a blinking green dot.

Dal stared up it. *That's way on the other side of the lake. What's she doing over there?*

Knowing your Jessie, she's following some kind of a lead for a story. What's she working on right now?

No one knows. Figure out how we get down in there. Someone go up to Nick Snow's place, tell him we need him if he can join us here at the Ozarka. If anyone can find her down in that wilderness, he can. Get a couple of deputies to join us.

Ledger peered over Dal's shoulder. "You going to go in there after her? What about this lead on the heroin dealers?"

Howie messaged him again. *Look here. There's several boat docks around the lake. Here's one about five miles off the hiking trail, and there's an old logging road barely visible here. It'd be my guess you might find your girl and your heroin in about the same place. Knowing her, it's my bet she's after them.*

"Son of a bitch." Ledger got on his radio.

"Did someone leave to get Snow?"

"Yeah, Colby took off a while ago. He ought to be back shortly."

"Okay, gear up. We've got a destination. It's worth checking out, and we don't know much else to do but follow it."

"Come on, girl. Get up." Long strong fingers gripped her wrists, pulled her painfully to her feet. Dirty breath washed over her.

Were they going to kill her now? Toss her off a cliff or throw her in a river? She kicked out at him, bowed up, and tried to fight, but it did little good. He was big and strong, with long hair in a man bun and a day-old beard.

"Let me go. If you kill me, they'll catch you. They will." With her hands behind her back she could do nothing but sass him.

"Be quiet woman and stop fighting. I'm trying to untie you. Who the hell tied these knots, anyway?"

She held still. "Well, don't you have a knife?"

"Nope."

"What kind of hillbilly doesn't carry a knife?"

"Hard to fly on airplanes with a knife in your pocket. It's considered a weapon."

"Oh, shut up and get me loose."

"You'd do well to talk nicer to me, girl, considering that I'm setting you free."

"Well, quit going on about it and do it. Maybe you could find a flint rock or something."

He kept picking at the knots, loosening one. "Okay, getting there."

"Tell me, what's a nice guy like you doing in a place like this?"

"You're gonna get on my last nerve here any minute, and I'll leave you here on your own."

"Might be better than watching your pathetic attempts."

At last the ties came loose. Her limp hands fell to the ground, pain shooting through them like someone had taken a hammer to each one. Moaning she tried to move them, put them together, rub them. Useless.

"There you go."

"Here I go? I can't move my arms. What am I supposed to do now?"

"I don't know. Hide. Run. Get yourself a pile of rocks. There's a logging road down yonder, nearly growed over, but it'll take you to the hiking trail and a boat dock. There you can call someone to come get you. Git moving."

"Come with me. I'll tell them you rescued me, and they'll let you go free."

"Girl, I'm liable to get so mad at you I tie you back up if you don't get the hell out of here. They'll be back, some of them, to get another... go on, git."

She started off, stopped, and turned to him. "Have you seen my tablet? I lost it—"

"Git now fore I throw rocks at you. I ain't seen no tablet."

With one last glower, she scrambled down the incline toward the trail he'd pointed out. Wouldn't do her much good. She had no idea which way to go. She was liable to wander around out here forever trying to find her way home. If she ever got back to Cedarton, she'd never again follow down a lead to this kind of story. She'd stay there and write up the latest recipe for tomato relish, a story from someone who just returned from Russia. Anything but this.

Coming down hard on the weed-strewn trail, she fell on her butt. Kicked up a cloud of yellow pollen from a bunch of shoulder-high goldenrod. Climbing to her feet, she stopped to stare at where the man had turned her loose, wanting to wave a thank you goodbye. But no one was there. Besides her hands were too numb to wave.

Crap. Staring one way, then the other didn't do her a bit of good. She still didn't know right from left or east from west. North from south for that matter. Knowing north, she'd been told a million times, would help her know her directions. Her right would be east. But what good was that when she didn't know which way was north?

Weary and frightened, she plopped down on a good-sized boulder at the edge of a drop-off into a deep gulley. Voices coming toward her. Not in sight yet. Massaging her hands, she slid down off the rock, scrambled behind it and into a growth of paw-paw trees. Might be the very men she'd just escaped from. How would she tell? How would she know if whoever it was might help her?

Wonder what they were up to, men coming and going along this old road. Couldn't be much of anything back here at all. They all carried large backpacks weighting them down. Dangerous as it might seem, she decided to follow a small group as they walked along. They knew where they were going. All she had to do was remain out of sight but keep them in view. After what seemed like forever, her darting from bush to bush, boulder to boulder, they rounded a curve, and there was the camp she'd just escaped from.

She squatted behind a thick growth of blackberry brambles. Now what? Parting the stickery branches, she peered out to see a group of men come out of a large tent while another moved in. All carried large back-packs, the kind hikers carry their tent and all their gear in. What in the world were they up to? One way to find out. Follow one of the outgoing groups, see where they went. Yeah, girl. What happened to that vow to write about tomato relish?

She gazed around, hesitated, then made up her mind. Tomato relish could wait for just a while. These guys weren't innocent hikers, had to be moving drugs this way. How simple to trail along and be real careful. Terrifying though it might be.

The Ozarks Highland Hiking Trail was here somewhere. It circled around the lake on its way northeast and southwest. She'd never been a hiker, but she'd once done a story about a guy walking from California to somewhere on the Eastern coast. He'd used that trail, camping every night. It made her sore all over just thinking of sleeping on the ground every night and walking all day for over a year. She'd wondered at the time who would do that and why.

From the looks of things, lots of people did. But this was odd. The beaten path they were coming in and out on wasn't the famous trail, it was just an overgrown logging road. And this was the very middle of nowhere. Nothing here to attract hikers. Oh, once in a while ragged cliffs overlooked deep gullies, waterfalls under the arch of a colorful rainbow, and breathtaking scenery, but still… no way would this be an exciting vacation.

After a while she got bored watching the small groups, often maybe a quarter of a mile apart, coming and going like there might be a movie or something inside the tent. It was time she decided which group to follow and take off. They had to be going somewhere away from here. And that's where she wanted to be. Since she didn't know how to get home anyway, what could it hurt? One of them might lead her out where she'd recognize something, a way to get home perhaps. After she got her story.

She'd always been pretty good at secretly following someone. Well, here came a small group of four, huge packs on their backs, trudging along, not looking much like they were enjoying their hiking hobby. Why do it if it made you that miserable?

Hidden behind the boulder, she waited till they were gone. Now she could follow them till they came out somewhere she was familiar with. Trails all had a destination, didn't they?

The men were rigging up to leave when someone knocked on the door. Dal yanked it open, expecting the men answering Ledger's call.

Tinker stood there grinning, Howie on her trail. She held up a folded piece of paper. "Is there a prize for being first?"

"Come on in here, girl." With a huge grin on his face, Dal snatched the note. "Good news, I hope. We're just fixing to light out to find her. Whatcha got?"

"Not sure you'll think so, but it is news. Where you going?"

Dal glanced at Howie, who held out his tablet. "Thought I could go with you guys. Help you find her."

He looked up from reading the note.. "Good thinking, Howie." He turned to Tink. "We're getting a signal from her tablet. It looks like a good shot at maybe finding those old boys hauling that heroin around. Leave it to Jessie."

"My suggestion, if you're interested, is to tie her to the bedpost."

Dal laughed heartily, feeling hopeful even though this could be a thin lead. It was sure better than none. And they'd surely run across Jessie, at the least.

"That has some questionable connotations."

She leaned back on her heels. "Whoa, there, big guy. I'm impressed by your big words."

"Just what does she mean by this? *I've gone looking for a tiger.'* Maizie came back."

"I'm not sure, but it's some kind of code. And why would she write a code? She'd expect us to figure it out, wouldn't she?" Tinker gazed at Dal.

He shrugged his shoulders. "Why look at me?"

"You're the one who solves crimes by figuring out stuff like this. Almost like magic." She was referring to Grandfather's cryptic clues and

Dal's connections to a surreal world where visions of evil were revealed to him. But the last clue he'd had was a while back, and it was that a woman had the answers they sought. Could very well be Jessie. He sensed no evil in the open spaces where they were headed, but with Grandfather you never knew.

He stared at the note like that would decipher it. If ever he needed Grandfather and one of his adages, this was the time. "I have the sense that we'll figure this all out if we just keep on this trail. We have two mysteries to solve, but they appear to be intertwined, so let's just follow our noses, so to speak. Yes, Howie, I want you along with your magic screen there. Can you keep her in sight?" He swung an arm around their room as if it were the whole outdoors.

Waiting in the doorway, Tinker chimed in. "Sounds exciting, but if you guys don't mind, I'll go back to the office and mind the store, so to speak." She tilted her head to look at him. "Find our Jessie and run down that nasty black tar while you're at it. And watch your own back, too."

The tablet made a jangling noise, and a message came through from Dallas and the deputy who had stayed behind to question the Mexicans. *Broke one of them, Jorge says they're moving the heroin in by plane, RVs pick it up and carry it into Arkansas where they camp and distribute it to hikers along the Highland Trail. Boat docks around the lake there. There are camps all in the wilderness where they're cooking the stuff, then carrying out the black tar in more RVs along I40 and I44. We promised a free ride home to the first one who broke, and Jorge has a pretty young wife.*

Ledger joined the two of them reading the email, Dal still studying the note from Jessie. "We were right, Ledger. Using the Overland Trail. You about ready to go check out that hiking trail?"

"Huh? Oh, yeah, as soon as Nick Snow gets here. He's former military and a mountain climber. He's helped us out on trails before. We may need him. Looks like Jessie's tablet is close as can be to that trail."

He folded the note and stuck it in his pocket. Dammit all anyway. He wasn't her keeper, but he felt like he ought to track her down. He had no idea where to start finding her from that blasted note. But Howie and his magic could. She knew what she was doing. Dear God, he hoped she did. For that matter, he hoped he did too. What would he do without her? His job, to run down those dangerous guys trying to muck up his county with the filth of drugs took a back seat. At least till he found her."

Many nights all he saw when he fell asleep was Leanne's beautiful but haggard face, needle still hanging from her arm, body filled with the heroin that had killed her. And now that he knew she didn't do it to herself, he was going to catch those bastards who had a hand in it, no matter what it took. All he hoped was that, when it came right down to it, he wouldn't have to choose between the two women he loved.

16
CHAPTER

Nick arrived with climbing gear in a large carry bag. He wasn't very big but strong as an ox, else how could he carry such a load with so little effort? Having spent time with him dangling off high bluffs, Dal trusted him implicitly. He'd come in handy in the rugged wilderness.

With deputies gathered around, Dal asked Ledger to bring them up to speed on what had occurred in Dallas. Then Dal let them in on what he suspected was going on out there in the wilderness.

"We have evidence that this cartel has moved into the Ozarks after the law over there in Dallas made it too hot for them to deliver their product. They think they can hide out in our rugged wilderness, and we can't find them. Looks like we already may have them spotted, so we'll be on their trail soon. That means overtime cause we're staying out there till we get them.

Now that Jorge has broken the Mexicans, we have enough information to get moving. According to his latest contact they move around while cooking the tar, then use several boat docks on the lake to pick the product up and transport it on I40 and I44 in RVs. So grab a go bag, water, and some food. I want you back here within an hour ready to move. We'll be hiking, so dress appropriately, boots included. Nick here has equipment we may need for climbing, so don't worry about that.

"Howie and I are going to run down Jessie's tablet if we can, but it looks like we'll be right in amongst the dealers doing it.

"They're bringing the heroin in from Mexico. There are quite a few of them, but it's not unusual for travelers to park there while they picnic or go boating or hiking. So no one pays attention to that activity. Meanwhile, the heroin can be transferred to backpackers hiking the Ozarks Highland Trail. Again no one pays attention. No one but us, that is. They in turn walk it several miles in all directions from the trail to scattered pre-arranged delivery points deep in the wilderness where it is then cooked into black tar. There's a heck of a lot of wild country out there where that can be done without rousing suspicion cause there's no one around to smell it or notice the activity. The same backpackers can return the cooked product to boat docks all around the lake where RVs pick it up and deliver it all over the country using I40 and I44. Sorry for the repetition, but I can't stress enough the importance of spreading out.

"Right now, this is from intel from our guys over in Dallas, so it could be somewhat off, considering how they got it. It's worth following up. Once we're able to locate and follow the groups, the DEA will come in to round them all up."

"Aw, shit, Dal. We need to be in on that roundup," Colby said.

"I know, and I'm working on that. Don't forget, Jessie is out there either in their hands or following them, so let's be careful. No cowboying. That goes for you, Colby.

Colby spoke up again. "Does she know what's going on, or did they just catch her snooping around?"

"Not sure yet. We figure if she didn't know early on, she does now. So let's get moving. She could be in danger. Finding her is priority, but this is a hunt for heroin dealers. About the worst drug on the market today. We've got to stop it putting down roots here. Let's get moving."

By the allotted hour, groups milled around in the parking lot of the sheriff's station getting assigned to their ride. They would leave out in as few unmarked cars as possible so as not to attract attention and gather under a shelter at the nearest boat dock and picnic area. Everyone dressed in camouflage, weapons in hidden shoulder holsters to look like a group on a trail trip. Heavy armament filled trunks of the cars in case it got really hot. It was very possible there'd be spotters, so they tried to be casual unloading and walking to the hiking trail. It was important they act like a bunch of men out for a hiking trip. Joking and acting like fools. Drinking, playing cards, etc.

Once there, Howie led them, heading for the flashing unmoving dot on his screen. The GPS on Jessie's tablet. After a while, he called a halt at a spot designed for resting and enjoying scenery.

"Howie, what's up?"

"She's remained in the same spot ever since I located her. Could be she's not in possession of her tablet. She may have dropped it, or someone took it away from her. It just doesn't make sense she wouldn't move at all since last night."

Frightened of the worst, that she could be dead, Dal stared out across the breathtaking vista. Inside he knew a pain he hadn't experienced since Leanne died. If Jessie were dead, he would never recover. Nor would he ever forget that last day with her and how he had treated her.

"How far are we from her?" He could barely voice the question.

Howie traced his finger just ahead of their location. "It's about half a mile off the trail just yonder, around the next big curve. But I stress, she may not—"

"I know." Dal turned to Ledger. "What do you think?"

"I don't know these woods, but it might be good if we sent in someone to locate that GPS site. See if they can find her tablet. Doesn't look like she or anyone else may still be there." He paused, clearly not wanting to state the obvious. He swallowed, went on. "They could've took it from her, or she dropped it, or they planted it to throw us off their trail. No sense going in gung-ho till we find out."

Dal nodded. "I agree. The rest of you fan out and take a break, just don't gather up or make lots of noise. Wait here while Howie and I go in to see what's up. Does everyone have a signal on your radio?" He waited while they clicked off and on, then nodded. "Every ten minutes do a radio check starting with Ledger, and we'll be back soonest."

Hunkered low, Dal stuck close to Howie, and they struggled through the underbrush, making as little noise as possible. After a long trek fighting shrubs and low-hanging limbs, Howie raised a fist, and Dal drew up close to him. Ahead, a clearing looked well stomped. He leaned close to Dal and pointed.

He was almost afraid to look. "See anyone?"

Howie shook his head. "It's coming from in there, right in the middle. Want me to go get it?"

"You sure? I mean, you don't see—see a body?"

Howie shook his head. "Nothing."

"Okay, you go that way, I'm going this. Completely circle this clearing, look for any signs of her or anything suspicious. Don't jump the gun, it may be a trap. Be careful, be quiet, don't go out in the open. We could walk right up on one of their camps. Meet you back here." Dal tapped Howie's shoulder, both nodded, and they set off.

Careful of the dried leaves and broken limbs underfoot, Dal made his way with caution. If spotted, it could mean Jessie's life. These guys dealt with killing all the time and wouldn't hesitate. Though he ached to bring them all down and let God sort them out, he knew better. If they'd been camped here, they'd been damned careful to police the grounds before leaving. It was tramped down more than the surrounding area, but nothing there would prove they'd been there. Someone sure as hell had.

His radio clicked twice. A signal to stop and look. Just across from where he stopped to do just that, Howie stood in the edge of the clearing motioning at the ground. He clicked back.

"It's straight in front of me about ten feet. Want me to get it?"

"Any reason to do that?" Dal itched to tell him yes but feared a trap. Someone left behind to keep an eye out.

"She could've left a message, but I doubt it. I think they grabbed her, and she lost it, otherwise she'd have sent a message. I'd leave it."

They both continued, eyes peeled for anyone or anything, until at last they came back together.

"Let's get back to the others." A mix of relief and disappointment filled Dal's chest, making it hard for him to breathe. He'd so hoped she'd be in there somewhere, maybe knocked out but okay. That they'd taken her with them didn't bode well for her chances if he couldn't find her.

Circles of sweat marked Howie's shirt. Dal hadn't noticed, but his was damp all over, as well. It was beginning to look like they'd be out here more than a single day and night. He'd hoped that wouldn't be the case.

"Let's get back to the others and head on out. Our goal remains spotting these guys and, in the end, taking them down. Maybe we can catch up with them making one of their exchanges. Nick's one heck of a tracker. Let's put him to work. They haven't been at it very long down here. Maybe it'll be a case of not having their act in gear yet, and we'll catch up." Though he hoped for that, he was afraid it wouldn't happen.

What he was more afraid of was that Jessie was in great danger. She was never much afraid of anything and just waded right in. It could get her killed. He knew too well the pain of losing someone he loved. If it happened again, he wasn't sure he'd get over it ever.

Somehow being free of that gang of dope smugglers didn't make Jessie feel much better. She had no idea where she was, and the group she'd followed thinking they were a part of them turned out to be some men on a weekend outing. Hiking parts of the highland trail had obviously become a popular two- or three-day event. At the end of the day, they left the trail at a boat dock where they were met by women in cars. Wives of the men, she guessed. No RVs to be seen.

Before she could make a decision that it would be safe to ask them for help, they had all left. The dock was deserted, and there wasn't even a phone booth or marina. It was simply a remote place where boats could be taken in and out of the water after a day of fishing, and everyone was long gone. For a while she lingered along the perimeter of the dock, hoping someone else would come along.

Far across the lake, a man sat in a small boat, the setting sun silhouetting his hunched figure. Behind him the mountains turned deep purple, the last of the sun's rays setting the tops aglow before everything plunged into darkness. Frogs and other night critters filled the silence with their song, making her so lonely she almost cried.

A fear such as she had never felt covered her like the falling darkness. Not so much for what might happen to her but how her death would affect the lives of those around her. Oh, it wasn't that she was so important, it's just that she knew how losing her would hurt Mac and Parker and Dal and Tink. And how disappointed they would be that she'd been so foolish. She had to laugh. Being worried over everyone thinking her inept. How silly. But it's how she felt at the moment. Why hadn't she known better than to walk right into such a dangerous situation? She was furious at herself.

So here she was, alone on a hiking trail with night coming on, everyone settled in, and her without so much as a sleeping bag or food. She did have the water the guy who'd untied her had given her, but that was all. However, she'd been dumb enough to come out here with nothing. This place didn't even have picnic tables or shelters or bathrooms like some of the larger ones, and so, afraid to sleep in the woods where snakes crawled at night, just like the old song said, she curled up on the floating dock. The gentleness of its bobbing finally put her to sleep.

Warmth from the morning sun caressed her cheek and awoke her from a restless dream in which she'd rambled the woods in search of a way home. Scrambling along on trails that ended, sending her scurrying back to where she started.

Feeling grungy, she left the dock and walked to the edge of the water where she knelt and washed her hands and face. The lake water was cool and clear and smelled vaguely of fish. Today she surely would find her way home, or someone would come along she trusted to help her.

Should she remain right here or go back to the trail and walk to the next dock where there might be more facilities?

She would not just sit and wait for something to happen. That would make her feel doubly stupid. She'd watch the sun as it rose into the sky, figure out what direction was which and get out of here. East was more or less where the sun rose, depending on what time of the year it was. She knew that much. So which direction was Cedarton from the lake? How many times had she driven along the highway and looked down upon the glistening water? Not once had she thought which direction was which.

So in the end, she followed the road that led away from the dock, knowing it would take her to another road and yet another till she came to the highway. From there, she'd know her way home or could find someone who did.

The road she found herself on was two tracks of dirt, and it followed the shoreline into a circular route that grew more and more desolate. Obviously, she should've gone in the other direction when the road reached another set of tracks in a *T*. After standing there a few minutes, she picked a turn. The one that dumped her on a dead end where there was a sign that read *Private Property. No Fishing Allowed.* Wrong again.

She dropped down to the ground and sat there a long while staring out across the glistening water. "So just what kind of joke is this?" she asked of the universe in general. "In any case, I don't think it's a bit funny. For two cents, I'd just sit here till I turn to dust."

Now she was talking aloud. She had to get hold of herself and fast. She was out of water and damned hungry, and if she didn't get a shower soon, she was going to turn into a ball of dirty sweat. Maybe she'd just jump in the lake. Then she'd be wet but not so dirty.

The sound of a horse coming reached her long before she saw it. She drew up fast, waited for it to come to her. Instead it halted to study her, tossed its head several times, and whinnied.

Clicking her tongue, she held out a hand. It nodded again, then walked toward her. What was this beautiful, well-cared-for animal doing out here alone in the wilds?

"Come on, boy."

Ears pricked, he moved closer, reached out, and let her touch his nose. He was definitely a gelding the color of the red dunes of the Southwest. And he had a dark stripe down the center of his back. This wasn't possible, but he looked just like the one ridden by the man down at Loren Jasper's abandoned cabin. They'd called it a coyote dun. How far from here had that been? Was she still asleep and dreaming of her struggle to find her way out? Or had it just wandered too far from home?

Who was she kidding? She had no idea where this horse's home was in relation to her location or Cedarton's where she'd last spotted the coyote dun. Or that it was the same horse.

Another look around, but she couldn't place anything in relation to this road. For all she knew, it could all be in the same general area. At least she liked to believe that. Oh sure, and then the animal happened to show up here to take her out of the wilderness. Like a child's storybook. Something really weird was going on here.

The dun nuzzled against her shoulder, whickered, then took a few steps away, swung his head around as if to see if she were coming or not. She decided to follow. Why she had no idea, it just seemed to make sense.

He led her along a narrow winding track not wide enough for cars. After a while, she wished she could climb on his back, but she wasn't that good a bare-back rider. Then he broke through a thick copse into a small clearing under the shelf of a high bluff. Water fell from high above into a circular pool, rays of sunlight reflecting through a rainbow.

She cupped the dun's soft nose, gazed at her reflection in his large brown eyes. Okay, dream or not, she was going in. Stripping off her grungy clothes, she ran to the rim and, without hesitation, leaped in. The water was icy cold and sweet when it washed into her mouth. Drinking her fill, she leaned back and floated, staring up through the leaves into the crystal blue sky.

What seemed hours later, she awoke lying naked in the sunlight on the bobbing boat dock, her bare skin pleasantly warm. How she got back here was anyone's guess. Beside her where she'd fallen asleep was a backpack. A folded note poked up from an outside pocket. On it was a hand-drawn map showing the way to the highway and on to Cedarton. Inside were two bottles of water, several packages of crackers, and an apple. A savior. No one around anywhere.

After drinking, she sat cross-legged and stared at the note. Munching on a cracker, she thought back on the dream or whatever it was. The horse, the lake, even the appearance of food were inexplicable. Okay, sometimes things couldn't be explained. Life was often crazy, and we just had to take stuff for what it was. A sign, perhaps.

Then she pulled on her damp clothes, gathered up the backpack and map, and followed the directions out to the highway. She arrived home in time to learn that the deputies were out hunting down the drug dealers said to be working in the wilderness and looking for her.

Tinker ran to her and hugged her when she walked into the sheriff's office. "Where you been, girl? Everyone's been worried sick. You gotta radio Dal right now." At which time Tinker put her in touch by radio, and she assured him she was fine and told him to be real careful. There wasn't time for more. He had to go.

Tink clicked off. "So, come on, give. Where you been?"

Jessie smiled. "Oh, just out and about. Would you let everyone know I'm okay? What's going on with the search for who killed Loren and Leslie? Looks like that should be important. All they're thinking about now is their precious heroin."

"Not sure, girlfriend. I'll ask next time I talk to them."

Jessie stood and stretched. "Think I'll go to the motel and take a nap. For some reason I'm really worn out."

Howie tagged along behind Dal to where they'd left everyone. The desk-bound deputy evidently wasn't cut out for field work. His face was red, his breathing deep. "Heck of a relief, hearing from Jessie, huh?"

Relief was right. Dal had wanted to whoop and holler like some idiot, and at the same time give her hell. But he held it back. Now that he knew she was home he could concentrate on finding these bastards wandering around in his county and skin their hides. Never mind thinking of what he would have to say to her when he got home.

Daylight faded into darkness while they gathered and planned their next move.

Nick Snow built a campfire in one of the overnight spots along the trail. Fragrant smoke hung in the air. They sat around munching on trail snacks, pretending to be hikers, and discussing their next move.

Colby made coffee and passed around steaming cups. They teased him about toting pot and coffee everywhere he went. "Learned it early on in the Sandbox. There we carried packets of instant coffee. Spoon coffee in your mouth, drink some water, swish it all around, and swallow. Be surprised what a caffeine rush it'll give. Wakes you right up while crouched in a bunker waiting for the next IED to hit."

Howie leaned toward Dal. "What's this sandbox he talks about? Surely he's not going back to when he was a kid."

"Nah. It's Afghanistan. He served over there."

Howie stirred at the dirt a minute. "I hate war. Can't even watch movies or news about it. Guess that's why I don't know what's going on there. Why do we do things like that?"

Not sure he'd heard right, that Howie might put down the service of a Marine, Dal replied rather tersely. "Not sure what you're getting at."

The young deputy shook his head. "Oh, I don't mean anything derogatory. It's just that… well, look up at those stars, think about where they're at. How they came to be there. It's such a beautiful, breathtaking world, yet we humans insist on trying to tear it apart. Too bad we can't spend more time respecting than hating one another."

As if in reply, the flames crackled a shower of sparks that leaped into the surrounding darkness and seemed to disappear among the stars. Dal agreed. He couldn't help but read the worst into everything when pursuing evil men, and he couldn't help but tag drug dealers as the evilest. He hated their souls for what they were doing to the country. But they weren't alone by any means.

Long silence followed, as if each man there considered what had been said. Dal rose and brushed the palms of his hands. One by one the men crawled into their sleeping bags, no doubt each one entertaining his own thoughts about the enemy they would pursue the next day. An enemy determined to ruin their surroundings.

During the night, thunder and lightning rolled in out of the southwest, and by morning, a heavy downpour drowned their plans for pursuit of that enemy. It looked like they were in for a good soaking. There'd be no tracking this day. Huddled under the thick forest, discussion continued while leaves caught the heaviest of the rain. Nick had lit out at dawn and soon returned to tell them of a shelter along the trail.

"Chances are some of them might hole up there. On the other hand, they have their main camps with tents, and I'd figure that's where they'd hang out. There or in the RVs waiting at the boat docks."

Dal didn't agree. "These men stand to make a lot of money the more product they move. I don't think a little rain will slow them down a bit. They don't melt, and neither do we. We might not be able to track them, but we can keep tramping the trail looking for signs. This business moves night and day, rain or shine. So do we. They're making black tar, and it stinks in the making. Smells like vinegar. There'll be smoke off in the wilderness, in hidden valleys or thick forests. They'll do it even when they can't move it for a day or so. And they can move their main camps at a whim."

In the end, they all agreed and set out to hike the trail, Nick leading, everyone keeping an eye out for unusual activity off-trail or signs of odd movement. After another full day of rain, they hiked back to where they'd left the SUVs and returned to Cedarton for a break and some reconnoitering until the weather broke."

Dal climbed out of the shower and sat on the bed naked to call Jessie. Maybe he'd cooled down enough to spend a quiet evening and night with her. Or could be she wanted nothing further to do with him. Either way, he wanted badly to try. He promised himself he would hold his temper no matter what. She had given him a bad scare, and it wouldn't be easy.

She picked up on the first ring, as if she'd been holding the phone waiting for his call.

"Dal?"

"Uhm, Jessie?"

"You okay?"

"Yeah, sure. You?"

"How did it go?"

She was going to play it cool, though she must know how angry he was with her for taking off like she had. "I'd like to see you, that is if you're not too busy traipsing around through the woods."

Watch out, he tried to back down.

"Not doing a thing. Like the good little woman, just sitting here waiting for you to come home and call me."

Oops, she was not happy at all, but still, he had to see her, touch her, know she was definitely not hurt. Maybe he'd get lucky and she'd tell him where she'd been and why without it causing a big fight. The things he wanted to say to her he just couldn't bring himself to say. Not yet. There was still the thing with Leanne to deal with. To make right.

"Come on over then, unless you want me there." He hoped she did so they wouldn't have to deal with the attitude of the B&Bs and her spending the night there.

"I'm still at the motel. It's pretty nice. Small. If you'd like to stop and get us something good to eat. Don't imagine you want to eat out."

"Okay. Anything special?"

"You choose. And Dal?"

He was almost afraid to reply, but he did. "Yep?"

"I'm so glad you're back."

He dressed, trying not to hurry like some little kid going on a first date. Jeans, t-shirt, feet in leather sandals, not trying real hard to impress. He took time to comb his hair despite his desire to rush to her side, grab her in his arms, and try to stop shaking.

The pizza he bought filled the car with a spicy aroma. Would he be able to wait to hold her, to scold her for scaring him, till after they'd eaten it? She never liked it cold, so he would hold back.

She opened the door to his knock, outlined in the light wearing a long, gauzy dress that he could see through. Every line of her exquisite body was visible, sexier than if she wore nothing. In his groin, a signal he did his damndest to ignore. Blue eyes sparkling up at him, skin gleaming from a recent shower, and he was supposed to sit down and eat pizza with her?

He tried, he really did, but by the time she backed up and let him close the door it was too late for anything but his arms around her. Best he could do was drop the pizza box flat in a chair and scoop her into his arms. Her body warm and sweet, her lips seeking and finding his. Fingers raked through his hair, body clung to his till he groaned with the effort to hold on till the backs of his knees reached the bed.

Damn his clothing, his shoes, everything that remained between them. Somehow, he shed them scarcely loosening his hold, and with one movement the thin fabric floated to the floor in a puddle around her feet. Both hands flat on his belly, she shoved him backward, fell on him. Warm and soft, she cuddled until every line of their muscled bodies fit together and he slid inside her.

"Oh sweetheart, hang on, please just hang on. Don't move. It feels so good like this."

So he did as she bid, though he could scarcely wait. Inside her, he rose and grew larger. She stiffened, shoved down hard, and held him fast.

It was okay with him, though the top of his head was ready to blow off. He chuckled. Which head?

She poked him in the ribs. "What's funny?"

"Told myself a joke." Could you do something, please? Anything before it bends or breaks.

He wanted more, to move, to ride her, but he waited for her because when it happened it would be so much crazier than if they just went at it all at once. God, how good it felt every time her muscles contracted then released. Nothing else moved. Just up inside her. She had a way of bringing him to climax as if to surprise him. She would halt all movement, eyes wide, the smallest of a tremble deep inside that excited him. Made him want to climb the wall. Up in there so warm and wet and sweet, and just as he began to come, she'd stop everything, maybe slip away for a few seconds till he wanted a finish so bad it hurt to the very tips of his toes. A good hurt that would be held ever so long, then all hell broke loose, and she rode him to a very edge of forever, till both exploded with a brilliant, shouting joy.

They lay locked in each other's arms, rolled over and over on the king-sized bed, nearly tumbled to the floor before stopping.

When he could speak, which was a while, he tried to say how she made him feel, but there really were no words. So what came out was muffled against her breast. He lay that way, her too, till finally both could move a bit. He spoke finally.

"I smell pizza."

"Yeah, it's cold."

"I suppose that's my fault. Sorry." He apologized because she expected it. "However, you have to admit you started this."

"I what? I did nothing. I opened the door."

"Half naked."

She laughed. "What you expected. Admit it."

"I admit this entire episode is my fault. There."

"I hate cold pizza, you know I do."

"Microwave?"

"Yuck."

He sighed, sat up, and slipped on his jeans. "When I come back, you will be fully clothed. Yes?"

"I will do my best. However, that was so much fun, perhaps—"

"I'll hurry." He was laughing when the door closed behind him.

The pizza was so good and their activity so strenuous, or so he guessed, they polished off the entire pie. With a Pepsi beside each of them, they settled propped on pillows on the bed.

"Now, I want to know what you were up to that you couldn't answer your phone, and no one could find you."

Eyes wide, she stared at him.

"And don't give me that innocent look. Jessie, we were worried sick. I just knew something dreadful had happened. Like perhaps you fell off a mountain."

His reference to the time he'd gone off when he fell off Red Rock Mountain got her full attention. "Okay, I should've let you or someone know I was following a story. I left Tink a note."

He cleared his throat. "To be precise, the murders, which you agreed not to do. And that vague note you went out looking for a tiger?"

"A tiger was a story. Besides, I changed my mind about the murders, and you were busy with that drug thing in Dallas and…."

"Not an excuse. Mac nor Parker nor your best friend knew where you were. What if one of those killers had gotten their hands on you?"

She looked down at the floor for a long time. "I'm not a child. I don't need permission to do my job."

"That won't work either, Jess. We agreed we need to keep in touch, no matter what. It has nothing to do with control or age or gender. I could've lain on that mountain, died, and turned to dust if you hadn't managed to find me, and you were right to be so angry. Now admit I'm right to be angry with you. You gonna tell me what happened and where you were?"

"I'm home and safe, and I won't do it again, but I can't tell you about it. I won't."

"Jessie, dammit." He rolled off the bed, pulled on his boots, and went to the door.

"Wait, where you going?"

"Home. When you decide to tell me what happened then give me a call. Oh, and by the way, we're leaving in the morning to go back after the drug dealers. They've settled into the wilderness. I'll keep in touch with someone. Will Tinker be okay?"

She scooted off the bed and, hands planted on her hips like a child, glared at him in silence. "Dal… you… you all but left me for good, going off hinting you might never come back, but no explanation or anything. Your only excuse, you loved your dead wife. What did you expect, I'd be sitting here twiddling my thumbs if you decided to come back?"

"Well, I didn't want you to do something so dangerous."

"If you knew my plans, you'd think you could tell me not to do it again. And this is something I'm going to follow through on whether you approve or not."

"It's the murders, isn't it?"

"None of your business."

"Oh, but it is. That's tied into the drug business, and they'll kill you at the drop of a hat. Like they killed Leanne. And if you let them do that, I can't answer for what I'll do."

He slammed the door so hard her Pepsi danced across the tabletop.

CHAPTER 17

Immediately Jessie wanted to kick the door open and tackle Dal. Say he was a big oaf who'd never told her he loved her. Oh, he murmured or muttered it like a vague thought sometimes when they made passionate love, but that didn't count, did it? In the end, she took a shower and went to bed, hoping for a better day tomorrow.

And it was. A crystal clear day with a promise that something beautiful this way comes. She had survived very scary times mostly thanks to a rider on a coyote dun. The oddly marked dun had to be one of a kind, and a small girl named Sally had last been on it in Cedarton. Time for her to check and see what had happened with her. The man was obviously part of the drug cartel, yet he had freed her. The two had to be related, but who takes a child into something like that? She'd check it out sometime today.

Time to get some work done. She filled her backpack to last the day, dragged the top off the Jeep, and headed for Parker's to pick up Brad. The little pit bull would enjoy riding shotgun with her for the day.

While she was there, she'd begin interviews with her boss for her story about the murders. She parked in the shade under the old oak beside the house and started toward the barn where he would be with his favorite horses. She no more than stepped from the Jeep than Brad came running around the corner of the barn followed by Parker. Interviewing him would be a challenge, but maybe she could keep him on track with her questions.

She hunkered to greet Brad, and the little dog leaped into her arms, giving her licks to the face and ears.

"Good morning." Parker hugged her, and Brad grunted and wiggled between them, bringing soft laughs. "Hope you've got time for coffee. It's made." He started for the house, presuming she would follow, which she did. He appeared more rested, but his eyes carried a sadness.

Yet this was a perfect time to get her questions out of the way. Inside she set Brad down and washed her hands while Parker filled two large mugs. She settled across from him at the table. Out the window, the red, gold, and bronze leaves of fall rolled across the rolling hills offering a palette for a colorful canvas.

"How have you recovered from your ordeal?" He sipped while eyeing her closely. "Mac filled me in, quite annoyed, I'd say."

She shrugged, not wanting to let him be the interviewer. "I'm good. Mac is protective."

"You still that reporter who throws safety to the wind, or have you learned your lesson?"

"Oh, I'm thinking about being a bit more cautious, considering the past few days. Maybe resort to writing stories about a city hall meeting where folks argue about whether the county goes wet or remains dry. Or wait, maybe I could go to the school board meeting and get a picture when Fudge hits someone he disagrees with over the head with his minutes book. I think I'll just settle for being a bit more cautious."

"Seriously, Jessie. You scared everyone, especially Dal. He almost went crazy hunting you instead of doing his job. You need to think about this."

"You're right. I have decided to go with Mac's releases and some safe interviews on these murders. I have, as you say, learned my lesson. From now on I will be more careful, but I won't stop what I love doing. On the spot research and writing. I'd like to start with you if you don't mind." She reached in her backpack on the floor and took out a recorder.

"Of course. I'd be a fool not to cooperate for a good story in the paper. I am, after all, involved whether I like it or not."

"Okay. Tell me where you first met Loren."

He paused, took several gulps of coffee, then set down the mug and caught her gaze. "I was riding out at the old park when she came jogging out of the woods on one of those paths. Surprised me and Iron Brand too. Smacked right into his shoulder. Good thing Iron doesn't spook easily."

"Wonder what she was doing out at that old overgrown park. It's a long ways from her cabin."

"Said she liked to jog, but she acted like someone might be after her. Kept looking over her shoulder to make sure no one was there."

"Did she ever tell you about it? I mean later on, when you got better acquainted?"

"Just said she enjoyed jogging in the woods."

"Did you have any suspicion that she was hiding from someone?"

"Not really. We hit it off so quickly I guess I just ignored any strange actions she might have. I never went to her house, so I didn't know how remotely she lived."

"And after she was killed and left in your barn, what did you think? I mean any idea who would do that or why?"

He turned away, wiped wet cheeks with his fingertips before going on. "Dal asked me some of these things."

"I know, but I want to write my own story from my questions. Just like you'd want."

"Of course, I'm sorry."

"No need. Do you think they suspect you of killing her?"

"I don't think so. Kathy found some seed husks on the body that came from the ostrich food out at July's animal farm, so they knew right away she wasn't killed in my barn but moved here after she died."

"So do you think they suspect someone who works out there?"

He eyed her closely. "Not a proper question. What I think doesn't mean much."

"But it looks likely, doesn't it?"

He didn't reply but asked, "Do you have any more questions?"

"Yes, just one more. The police seem to link all three murders to the drug problems and the dealers said to be moving into our county. What do you think of that?"

"If they're right, then something has to be done. We can't stop these drug wars, but we sure as heck can kick them out of our county and see it remains free of those evil sons of bitches who ruin lives right and left."

"You sound like Dal. He's dead set on driving them out of here."

"Can't blame him, seeing as how his wife died the way she did."

She turned off the recorder. "This is off the record. You know I'm a bit worried they're spending more time fighting the drug problem than finding who killed those three women, who it looks like were CIs for the Dallas Narcotics Unit."

"You're not putting that in the story, are you?"

"No, that's why I turned off the recorder. The murders are an entirely different story from this fight against the drug cartel, even though they are connected." She put away her recorder and stood. "Besides, a reporter's opinion has no business in a news story."

He walked her to the car, Brad trotting along to claim the shotgun seat the minute he spotted the Jeep. "Be careful, Jessie, it's still dangerous out there till we get all this straightened out."

She kissed his cheek and climbed into the car. "I'll be careful. Just wish I knew if there were any witnesses to the shooting of Leslie Younger, but guess I'll have to wait for a release from Mac on that one. So far no one on the street in that neighborhood will admit to seeing anything. See ya."

He stood in the yard waving, his image disappearing in her rear-view mirror.

Pounding on the door woke Dal. Dim light barely encircled the blinds over the windows when he kicked out from under the covers.

"Get yourself into your britches, Dal." Sounded like Colby.

"You just hold your britches, I'm coming. It's the middle of the danged night."

"It's five a.m., and we've got ourselves a problem." He flung open the door to see Colby and five other deputies crowded around his door. "The DEA is here in full force, and they want to storm the woods to drive these guys out. Their words, not mine. Mac drew down on them, and they put him in jail, which didn't go over real good with anyone. A noisy crowd is gathering."

"Good God. Do they have any idea what this wilderness out here is like? Storm the woods indeed. Colby, you get on back there and settle them down. Get me a mic and loudspeaker set up outside the station. I'll be there in ten. Do your Marine best."

Colby stood straight. *"Oo-rah."* He hurried the group off the porch and back to their units parked in the yard.

Owner of the Five Bs Bed & Breakfast, Betsy Blake stood on her porch, robe clutched under her chin. "What's going on?"

"It's okay, Missus Blake. We'll handle it." Dal waved to her and went back inside.

He put on his uniform which he didn't always wear, hooked on his utility belt, but left his weapon in the gun safe. He wanted no part of playing quick-draw with the damned DEA. This was not a situation where guns were a good idea.

He climbed in his unit and with siren blaring and lights flashing screeched onto the main road, breaking every town speed limit Mac set for deputies. The car slid sideways to a stop near a crowd gathered around city hall. Shoving his way through the angry gathering, he halted where some twenty odd men in bulletproof vests with "DEA" across the back stood on the lawn, fully armed with serious looking Uzis. Deputy Marshal Ledger stood as if holding them back. Grace County Deputies barred the entrance to City Hall.

It was a damned Mexican Standoff.

It was almost funny. At Grandmas, open at 4 a.m. for early workers, the telephone could quickly become a public announcement, and it took very little time for the word to get around that the Feds had arrested Cedarton's sheriff. This would never do, and while the crowd wasn't violent, they weren't happy at all. Dal had known this going into it. Small town southern mentality was indeed something to be admired but often misunderstood.

Without acknowledging the DEA, he took the mic, tapped it with his fingernails till everyone quieted down. Facing the civilians, he spoke loud enough for his voice to echo off the surrounding hills.

"You all know me, but for our guests, I'm Grace County CSI Deputy Dallas Starr. I need you all to settle down. Everything is fine here. No one is under arrest."

"Except Mac." The voice came from a crowd of men out front.

He couldn't tell who said that, but he was quick to address it. "Colby, would you go inside and release our sheriff from custody?"

An angry murmur went through the DEA agents, but no one spoke out.

"I'm sure no one here wants this to turn into a Waco event, so let's go inside and organize. None of us wants drugs in our county, and that's what we're here to take care of. Please everyone but law enforcement go on home. I'll guarantee you everything will be okay."

Damn, he hated to mention that. If the cartel had spies in town, they'd be forewarned, but with the swarming in of the DEA in their expensive Cadillac Escalades, windows so dark they could be carrying just about anything inside, that was already a given. The best they could do would be to organize into groups to cover the boat docks around the lake as quickly and quietly as possible. Put a stop to this before it got out of hand. Who the hell notified the DEA? Some of these men had never worked off cement or tarmac. They'd slosh around making all sorts of noise. But at this point, it couldn't be helped. It would've been best to continue the sweep through the county with deputies familiar with the trails and lakeside camping spots before these bastards knew what hit them.

He stopped to ask Ledger if he'd help get members of DEA inside where they could organize efficiently in private. Maybe he could save some of this debacle from going wild.

Ledger cooperated immediately, practically ordering the nineteen grumbling feds inside city hall and to the large room where Dal gathered every deputy plus Nick Snow and pounded the front desk with his fist.

There he organized the men into groups of five and assigned each group a spot on the large map tacked up front. He placed Nick Snow in charge of the section containing the dangerous high bluffs and had him choose three men he considered able to handle the rough terrain. Each boat dock and surrounding area was numbered as were the copies that Tinker ran off and passed around. Instructions. Collect heroin and black tar for burning. Keep track of it. Again, mumblings.

"At the end of all this we want the dope gone and these men under arrest. Hopefully without any deaths. They'll be in the custody of the DEA." He stared around the crowded room.

"You all know how black tar is made and how goddamned deadly it is. All it takes is a campfire and a pot and a supply of heroin, and you've got hundreds of packets that immediately are addictive and deadly. The boonies are ideal for cooking. There'll be smoke in the air plus that peculiar vinegar stench in the middle of the wilderness where there'll be few to detect the smell. Our intel from an informant is that each boat dock is the location for a drop from RVs, then it's carried deep into the wilderness, cooked, packaged, and carried back out by men who seem to be innocent hikers who in turn deliver it to waiting RVs for transporting on I40 and I44 and delivery across the USA.

"We're gonna see that dog don't hunt, not around here." Dal's raised voice ululated across the square.

A general uproar answered.

"When was the last time you saw RVs pulled over and searched? Let's put a stop to this before it gets a foothold here in our county. We can't go to Mexico and wipe out the cartels sending this filth into our country, but we can protect our people here in Grace County by running these bastards out of here. Make it too hot for them to stay. Show them what it's like to try to invade Arkansas."

There was a great rousing agreement just as Mac rushed out and motioned to Dal. "Excuse me, folks. You go ahead and get yourselves organized, and I'll be right back. And I'd suggest you get rid of some of that gear you're carrying. It'll only hold you back and maybe get you killed. Don't make the mistake of thinking these ole boys aren't armed, cause they are. But they're not dragging all that heavy equipment around with them. Nick can help you with that."

Dal joined Mac, who appeared agitated. "We have a problem. Folks around here are getting real nervous. You know how they are. They're afraid the government is trying to take over our county. Fudge and a bunch of his friends are up at the Red Bird, all are armed and ready to fight. I noticed that the Brits over at the Purple Raven are locked up and fortified as are other businesses on the square. Ain't a one of 'em without a rifle or handgun."

Dal turned his back on the feds to speak to the sheriff. "Most everyone trusts you. Go talk to them. Explain that these guys are just here to help us get rid of the drug dealers and their product. You can calm them down. Same up at the Red Bird. Promise we'll keep them informed. Suggest they leave their guns at home. We can't have people running round shooting at each other. They'll listen to you. Oh, and Mac. Keep an eagle eye on the Brits. Something may be squirrely there."

Mac nodded. "Will do. But I ain't gonna threaten to disarm folks. That'd start World War III. You get this thing organized so it's not a riot with these wild-assed feds, and I'll do the same."

Dal soon had groups of agents ready, each with a deputy leader he felt he could trust. He went over the maps with them, explaining the terrain and how it could cause real problems.

J.C. Dawson, who had earlier introduced himself as the one in charge of the DEA, spoke up. "We'll let you handle it unless something gets out of hand. If we have to come down hard, then we will. This is your county, and you're in charge. I'm glad to see more than two of my men in each group, but I'd like to defer to Deputy Marshal Ledger for any disputes."

Dal nodded. "Howie here will be in charge of communications. Stay in touch with him. I'll let him explain."

The young deputy stood. "Keeping in touch the normal way will be difficult because there are times there's no signal for your phones. The radios do a better job, but sometimes the distance is too much, so if you'll arrange to pass messages along from one group to another when necessary I'd suggest that. Mac and I will be here to try and help handle communications. Leave your phones on at all times, and use your radios if you have a problem. Use clicks over the radios to avoid these guys hearing us talking and planning. One click is yes, two is no, three is move in, four plus your map number is SOS. or need help. And keep the chatter down. That okay, boss?" He glanced at Dal, who gave him a thumbs up. The shy young deputy had outdone himself.

Howie sat down, and within thirty minutes, everyone was raring to go. A surprise they all got things arranged so quickly, and they were ready to move out by the time the rising sun tinted the eastern sky with gold and lavender.

Dal took his group out first, since they were set to handle the boat dock on the farthest side of the lake. Each group was to wait five, then follow and take over their assigned section. Dal could do nothing more but hope these guys, most of them militarily or law enforcement trained, could get the job done without messing up too badly. God forbid any of them was killed.

A final reminder went out to everyone. "Be safe. Use your weapons when necessary, but don't go shooting at anything that moves. Rather one of them goes down than one of you. Keep your group together so you know where everyone is. Let's make sure we don't kill someone with friendly fire. These guys don't care who they kill. So be careful. If you have any problems report in. Any questions?"

"What about medics if someone gets hurt?"

"Use the boat dock in your area, report someone down, and we'll get you help. Mac is going right now to arrange boats as the best way to haul the injured out to the nearest clinic or hospital. Anything else?"

They remained quiet. Someone murmured, "Looks like the DEA could supply a chopper."

He ignored the remark. "Okay. Everyone, come back in one piece."

Dal led his men down the trail toward the distant boat dock assigned number twelve. They'd done the best they could considering such a mix of soldiers. He could only hope no one got killed, but in a situation like this someone would be killed, that was for sure.

Jessie went by the sheriff's office. It sure was quiet. No one around but Tink, Howie, and Mac. She tapped on his door then went in.

"Hey, good to see you all in one piece. I heard you were arrested. Some fun, huh?"

Feeling a bit chagrined, she tried out a grin toward her best friend. It sort of fell flat. "Mac, could you talk to me a bit and give me a release for my article on the investigation into the murders? I need something for this week. Last week was literally a look at what drugs do to users and everyone else as well. I need some news."

He nodded and sorted through some papers. "I printed up a release for you last night." She took it and quickly read it.

"Any questions?"

"Not much here. I was hoping for more. Guess I can research the backgrounds on the three women who are dead as a direct result of the manufacture and sale of drugs. It would be good if you could let our readers know if they might be in danger from the killers who are still wandering around free."

He glanced up at her. "You may quote me. I can't speak on an ongoing investigation. However, I can assure everyone in town that as long as they are not involved in the sale or use of drugs, they are in no danger from these morons who produce, sell, and use drugs themselves. We will hunt them down and take them dead or alive." He stared at her. "How's that?"

She read the brief release that vowed clues were being pursued around the killings of three young women and arrests were expected soon. Anyone with knowledge pursuant to this case was urged to contact the sheriff.

"I guess if this is all you can give me, then I'll have to go with it. I will quote your words which I recorded. Thanks, Mac." On the verge of leaving, she turned. "Say, what did you do with the girl we picked up with the coyote dun over at Walmart?"

"Oh, little Sally. She was able to show us how to get to her folks' trailer, and we took her home. Talk about living in poverty, those folks really do, and they weren't too happy about talking to me either. All the guys were busy, so I took her home."

"Did you meet her dad?"

"Nope, was told he was gone as in deceased, just the mother and a grown son and Sally, who's a bit of a girl but supposedly fifteen."

"What about the horse?"

"Horse?"

"Yea, a coyote dun, real unusual markings. Sally was riding him when we found her. Colby was going to take him home."

"Oh, yeah, I plumb forgot that. He told me that horse followed him and the girl back here, but when he went out to get him, he took off. Just flat wouldn't let him close after he left the girl with me. Said he took off and headed into the wilderness. He followed a while but gave up. He figgered it was going home but it seems nobody claims him."

Should she tell Mac about her rescue and the dun's rider being involved somehow with the drug cartel? Thinking about it, Sally must have been the rider when the dun showed up at Loren's hideout cabin. Just rode right on by, but she didn't forget that coyote dun or how small the rider was.

She left the office feeling pretty good about this week's paper. What with Parker's interview along with Mac's and a bit of personal stuff about Loren, Leslie, and Leanne from their Facebook pages it was a pretty good look at what was going on. She could get maybe a four column by twelve-inch story. And that without putting herself in jeopardy. Once it was all over, the drug cartel banished from Grace County, she would write a feature about her experiences. Could easily get a double-truck in a daily paper.

During a short break at work, Wendy brought Jessie up to date on her and Howie. They'd had a date between his absence while with the guys in Dallas and a short time before they went back out that morning. She was to the moon about how the two of them got along.

"Under that shyness, he's a really nice guy. And real intelligent. Course I'm not foolish enough to think it might always be that way, but it's a good start. I've been a long time without anyone in my life. Even if it doesn't work out in the long run, we're both enjoying it right now."

"I'm so pleased for you. Very few of us are happy being without companionship with the opposite sex. We're just sort of cut out for coupling if you think about it." She laughed, and Wendy joined her.

"Good thing our cutouts fit together so well, almost like it was planned, huh?"

Parker joined them in the break room. "You two are having way too much fun. Bet you're talking about men."

"Oh, shame on you. It's not always about men." Jessie grinned. "Though mostly it is."

Obeying his own rules, he grabbed a Coke and some cookies and sank down in a chair. "Take a break away from work, it always helps you relax more."

They chatted a bit, then drifted back to their jobs of laying out the pages, getting them ready for printing. Sections of pages, laid out in the computers, printed, then pasted onto sheets went to Harrison where the *Harrison Daily* had their printing apparatus. The printed newspapers would be delivered the next afternoon to Cedarton for mailing and delivery to stores all over town.

Bigger dailies were handled in a more up-to-date fashion, but this suited the smaller weekly, and Parker wasn't in any hurry to update.

Jessie waved to Wendy and climbed in the Jeep. With Dal off in the woods somewhere, she would go home to an empty room. Usually on her long night, he would be off duty and would meet her at her place with something to eat. Most of the time, he'd bought it earlier since not much was open in Cedarton that late. They would warm it up and have a nice meal, sometimes making love before the fragrant pie came out of the oven. Many a meal was overdone.

The headlights revealed the long lane to her house, and she was in sight of the ravaged walls before she remembered she didn't live there anymore. Her life was ripped apart by those wicked outlaws who thought nothing of carrying guns and attacking anyone they chose. Parked under the big trees in the front yard, she laid her head on the steering wheel and cried.

Now Dal was somewhere out there in the wilderness gunning for those scum bags. She'd made a solemn promise not to let his career affect their lives, but it wasn't easy.

Let it go. Remember her own propensity to walk in danger that he had to deal with. Somehow they'd make it work, if only he'd be able to put Leanne's death behind him. Finally cried out, she turned around and drove up to the Ozarka Motel, parked outside her unit, and sat there staring at it for a long time remembering the fear she'd experienced under fire. Dal must be putting up with the same feelings. Shaking her head as if clearing cobwebs she crawled out, fetched her backpack, and let herself in with her card.

Showered and dressed in her favorite night shirt, she ate a sandwich and drank a Pepsi. She had once thought nothing would ever be right again after she ruined her career out in California and came running home to lick her wounds and hide out from the results of her own stupidity.

Wrong then. Hopefully wrong now. She could make it so. Dal could too, so hang in there. With him on her mind she fell asleep and dreamed they were making love while battles waged around them.

Morning presented another beautiful day with fall blue skies and cumulus clouds crowding one another along the southern horizon. A great day for hope that life would be good.

First, pick up Brad. They could share this lovely day. Drive out to the house and pack what she could salvage. Staying busy should help take her mind off the danger Dal was in as well as ridding herself of unnecessary stuff from the past. What did they call it? Downsizing. What she wanted now was to fill the emptied spaces with new hopes and dreams. It was time to begin arrangements to buy the double-wide. Living in a ready-made home would be a new adventure. An adventure she could only hope she and Dal would share.

At Walmart she bought some banker boxes, then stopped by the grocery store and picked up what empty cartons they had stacked out back. At Parker's she loaded an ecstatic pit bull in the shotgun seat and hurried out to the small cabin nearly cut in half by bullets.

Note to self—try not to think of the danger Dal was in.

She backed the Jeep up to the front porch littered with shredded logs to make it easy to unload the array of cardboard boxes. Singing loud enough to startle birds from the trees and chase away the uneasy thoughts of why there was no news from the men raiding the drug camps, she made trips until the front room was piled with cartons.

On her way back, a tiny sound from inside caught her attention. Sounded like the mewling of a cat. She followed it. Down the end of the hallway, behind the linen closet door. She leaned an ear to the thin panel. Yes, something crying, but not a cat. Something bigger. On tiptoe, she moved to open the door slowly. Shoved aside a stack of blankets to find a small girl, hunkered up in the corner crying.

"Sweetheart, what's wrong? What are you doing here?"

"My mommy—they took her."

"Who took her?"

The girl sobbed thickly. "Can't... can't tell."

On her knees, Jessie coaxed the girl out to see it was the one who'd ridden the coyote dun into town the night before and probably rode past Loren's cabin.

She put an arm around her. "Why can't you tell? Come on, stop crying and tell me what's wrong."

The girl pulled away, shouted angrily. "No, they'll kill her. Let me go, let go!" She jerked free, ran down the hallway and off the porch. Brad, busy chasing a squirrel in the yard, ran after her. Without a second thought, Jessie took off behind them. She didn't know who might kill who, but she couldn't let it happen. She yanked up her backpack as she ran past it and followed the girl into the woods, a yapping Brad racing between them.

Disguised in the brush around the number twelve boat dock, Dal and the accompanying agents settled down for what might be a long wait. They had to be sure of their prey before closing in, so everything ought to be just right. A family came and went, two men with young boys paddled up in two canoes, tied in their fishing poles and packs, loaded the lightweight canoes on their shoulders, and took off down the trail joking and laughing.

Silence descended. Sunlight flashed across the rippling water from the passing of a motorboat. This waiting was a perfect example of a stakeout. It could take all day and night for the cartel to deliver and pick up their drugs and money. As Dal had said deliveries would happen at boat docks around the lake. Men on foot with backpacks, waiting RVs. Might as well get comfortable, but remain alert. Talking or smoking, coughing or sneezing, moving around too much, all forbidden. It could sure get monotonous. Much as they might despise it this had to be done. It was too important. Everyone had to kick in. Get rid of these evil greedy sons of bitches. And do it now before they got a stranglehold on the beautiful, peaceful Ozark wilderness.

The sun hung low in the western sky when an RV inched up to the boat dock, settled in as if to camp overnight. Two men came out and walked down to the edge of the lake, stretched, and chatted a while. Two women joined them, talked, and laughed. So damned innocent. Evening turned ashy, lights came on in the RV, and two hikers sauntered off the trail. Both checked their surroundings, then one knocked on the door.

Dal motioned to the men, who went on alert. They had to see the actual exchange and let the hikers take possession. It could develop from hikers to campers or the other way around. A solid final exchange had to take place before the law closed in. It would be bad if he had misjudged how many lawmen it would take to bring them down.

Everything came together, Dal signaled to move, and they were on their feet, guns pulled, shouting "Federal Agents, on your knees!" All five surrounded the camper and the hikers. One hiker made to break free and run. A shot rang out, and he went down, grabbing his leg and howling, just like that. Dal was impressed. The agent was on the ball. It only took minutes to cuff the other hiker and the two men and women who made the most noise about being mistreated. You'd think they hadn't done anything wrong.

Shots rang out in the distance, sounded like the boat dock on the west side where two tributaries ran into the lake. A tougher area to police. He let two of the agents take over with their prisoners, locking them up for transport in their own RV, and while a volley of shots rang out, he and DEA agents McCarthy and Jones took off for boat dock number eleven.

Damn, it sounded like heavy-duty automatic fire. Crashing through the underbrush, dodging trees and boulders, they hit the hiking trail on a dead run and took off for that part of the park. On an uphill spurt, Dal wished he'd done more running to keep in shape, but he managed to keep up with the other two. Off to the north, the roar of the RV told him it was moving right along. Trouble being, the gunfire and vehicle noise was bound to alert those doing any business at one of the other boat docks. They might lose them as far as an arrest went, but the hulla-balloo could send them scooting out of the country. Panting, he signaled McCarthy and Jones to head out down the road to the next boat dock. No need to approach in the woods now. There was an all-out war going on, and they needed to be a part of it, quick as they could. He didn't like the sound of heavy automatic gunfire, even though the agents did have new Uzis, which he was itching to get his hands on.

A runner, pack dangling from one shoulder, sprinted up the road, caught sight of them, and quickly rushed into the woods. Dal sent agent White after him, and they went on down toward the boat dock and still more gunfire. Someone was loathe to give up. Bell and Colby had ac-companied DEA agents Taylor and Henson to this site and, though he hated the thought of anyone being shot, if Colby were injured, he'd be doubly upset.

Rounding a curve past a cluster of huge trees, he drew up short. Two men lay on the ground, automatic fire belched from the window of a fancy purple RV as long as a railroad car. Agents were pinned down in the tree line. Hunching, he led the two out of sight toward the front and around the back side. An RV like this would have a second exit.

Without any hesitation, he kicked in the flimsy back door and, followed by deputy Hank Horton and a DEA agent, burst inside, taking down the guy in the window who held an Uzi belching bullets. A sudden quiet descended followed by the screaming of a woman. She burst from the other room, frizzy red hair flying, and launched herself at one of the DEA agents, taking him to the floor. Chaos reigned for a moment before the surprised men dragged her off and cuffed her. She kept kicking till Dal finally subdued her by tying her ankles with a pillowcase.

He headed for the front door. "Who's down out front?" He had no more than reached the downed men when Colby came out of the woods with the escaped carrier in cuffs. Gathering up the wounded, they found deputy Bell with a bullet in his shoulder, the other man, one of the drug dealers, was bleeding badly. Taylor tried to patch him up, and Henson called for help from one of the boats Mac had arranged. But one look told Dal he wouldn't make it. Arterial blood squirted like a pumping fountain. So that was two dead and one wounded.

What a frigging mess. Why didn't the fools just give up? How could something like this be worth a life? Dal knelt down beside Bell to talk to him till the boat arrived to carry him and the two dead druggies away. So far, there'd been nothing from the other boat docks. If all the carriers were this determined, this could go on another few days.

He gathered the men, opting to sit inside the fancy RV. Settling on a comfortable couch, he took in the fancy interior.

"Boy I hope they didn't buy this with plans to pay for it with drug money." Nervous chuckles went around the room. "It belongs to us now," McCarthy said.

"Anyone able to contact any of the others?"

Everyone shook their heads.

"Well, let's hope some of them had a number twelve result. Why they couldn't all be that way is a mystery." He scrubbed both hands down the front of his thighs. "Tell you what, let's reconnoiter, reload, relock, and take this baby a ways closer to number ten. Are the keys in her?" Colby hollered yes.

"Okay. Let's make our way back west, see if we can lend a hand somewhere else. I know it's been a long day, but there's plenty of daylight yet, so let's see if we can get this wound up."

General agreement circled the room, everyone checked their weapons, slapped in loaded magazines, shouldered their packs, and settled in the comfort of the RV. It would do till they came closer to dock number ten, which no one had heard from. With the captives bound in the back room, they drove the road out from dock number eleven and headed for the next dock. It looked like it was going to be a long night.

18
CHAPTER

Ahead of Jessie, Sally picked up speed, shouldering aside the low-hanging limbs as if they were nothing. Once in a while, she'd slow, look back, and urge Jessie on. Whatever was going on she was terrified out of her wits, pretty grey eyes wide with fear. Was Sally rushing her into a trap? Could she even help whoever the child wanted to find? Winded and thirsty, Jessie sank down next to her when she scrunched up against the bank of a creek. A welcome rest in which she could take in the girl's appearance.

Jessie took a chance to question her. "Honey, tell me what's going on."

With a shake of her head, she put her finger to her lips. And so the two of them hunkered there listening and waiting, Jessie wasn't sure what for.

At last Sally stuck her head up and gestured to move forward. "Stay down. Mommy and Lucas, I'm afraid they might be dead. We have to see."

"What about…?"

The girl's shushing silenced her. "Okay, they've gone. Let's go see."

Jessie followed her a ways down the creek where she climbed the bank and scrambled on hands and feet toward the back of a lean-to, invisible in the thick brush, until they were right on top of it.

"Come on, in the back, but be quiet."

Inside, where the gloom of late evening darkened every corner, two covered lumps lay under a ragged quilt on the dirt floor. A third person sat on a stool, a bloody bandage around his head. No matter how she strained, Jessie couldn't make out features. His carriage, the way he was built was familiar, though. She had to help them, friend or foe. A bucket of clean water sat on a handmade wooden table. Grabbing the cloth draped over a rack on the back wall, she wet it and cleaned the man's face, still not prepared to look under the cover on the floor.

"Are you okay? Mom? Lucas?" Sally dropped to her knees, uncovered first one, then the other. A woman and boy were tied and gagged but appeared to be alive. She went to work freeing them.

After Jessie washed the blood away, the man opened his eyes. It was the man who had helped her escape the dopers. At the time he'd acted like one of them.

He nodded weakly. "I found them in the camp and dragged them all out here."

"Who are you? What's going on?"

He held up a hand. "Whoa, wait a minute." His words were slurred, his eyes glazed. "Water."

She filled a coffee cup that looked fairly clean, at least it was only coffee stained, and held it to his lips. He gulped it all down, rubbed his temples between his fingertips, and looked a bit better.

"I'm not part of them. Name's Jackson Delray. I guess it doesn't matter much now who knows this, but I'm working undercover with the DEA. I'd worked my way into their bunch, let them think I was willing to carry drugs over the trail. Meanwhile, big problem. I ran across their trailer." He indicated Sally and the two on the floor. "Hiding in a beat-up trailer from someone, not sure who. They need to be moved out of here while this battle rages. Then I turned you loose cause those dealers were set on killing you. I recognized you right away. After that, they didn't trust me, so they did this." He gestured all around at the destruction in the lean-to, grimaced from pain.

"Once all the uproar and the attacks calm down, those morons think they'll win and can take their time disposing of us." He sighed. "These guys aren't exactly rocket scientists, they believe they'll always come out on top. They plan on coming back and getting rid of us. How are they moving this junk cross country? I need to get in touch with J.C."

"Not sure yet how it's being moved, but J.C. is around. Jameson stayed in Dallas."

"Who?"

"The guy undercover with you. The tall Texas Ranger."

"Lady, I'm the only one undercover. Never heard of this Ranger fella."

Jessie stared at Jackson. "You sure? You took quite a knock on the head."

"Maybe so, but I recall helping you and finding these folks. Nope, no Texas Ranger name of Jameson or anything else involved in this."

"Well, crap. I knew there was something about him I didn't believe. Turns out everything was a lie." Confused and upset, Jessie took in the rugged living conditions. "What's all this?"

Jackson grinned weakly. "My digs, believe it or not. I've had worse. You need to tell J.C. about this guy. Did he meet him?"

She tilted her head. "Nope, come to think of it J.C. arrived after Dal and them came back from Dallas, and Jameson didn't come with them."

"Well, shit. We need to find J.C."

Obviously he wasn't connected to the druggies except being under-cover, and neither were Sally and her mom. And if they didn't get out, they'd probably end up being victims. Anyway the mother and her two kids for sure. The man had a job to do, but helping her had messed that up, so she felt responsible for his plight as well. Lord, what a mess. And what a story.

He dragged himself to his feet. "You know how to get out of here? Where to take them where they'll be safe?" Before she could answer, a noisy approach from out of the woods interrupted. "Too noisy to be one of them." He moved to check it out and came back grinning. Following him was the coyote dun. "Get these two kids on his back, and you all get out of here. Okay? I'm going to hang around for a while, maybe I can lend a hand with your deputies and my guys to see this ends here and now. And I sure need to talk to J.C."

He squinted at Jessie and she nodded. Anxious to get out herself and get these folks safe, she still hated to leave him here. One last glance at the frightened kids made up her mind. "If you're sure you're okay."

"I'm fine. Head's too hard to damage. Now get them out of here."

Lucas mounted, then Jackson lifted the girl up in front of him. Lead-ing the horse, Jessie and Sally's mom bid him thanks and goodbye. Jessie took the motley crew down the path that led to the logging road.

After walking awhile, she asked the woman's name.

"Beth Gold." She had a soft voice and eyes the color of ice. Beneath all the grubbiness was hidden an attractive woman who appeared to be in fear of her own and her children's life.

"Why in the world were you living out here?"

"First place we found to hide from them." They walked a bit longer in silence before she spoke again. "The kids, my husband took them a few months back. Then a friend of mine saw them with him on the streets of Fayetteville. I liked to never found them, you'd never guess how. It's an age old joke around here that if you want to find someone go to Walmart."

"You didn't."

"Did. Took to hanging out at three or four in town before sure enough, there they were with him. I followed them, and he drove off out to a trailer park over in Berryville. I made a dry camp in the woods so I could watch, and the first time he left them there while he went out to move some dope for a friend, I grabbed them, and we've been hiding out ever since. We landed in that ratty trailer a few weeks ago. I want to take them back to live where they can have a good home. My mother has a big house in Blue Eye and would love to have us live there, but he knows about her, watches her place a lot. I don't know what to do."

Beth sobbed, stumbling over a widow maker and grabbing Jessie's arm. "I'm sorry. We need to get out of here. Where did Sally find you?"

Jessie told her. "My car is there. I'll take you into town and our sheriff will see you're protected."

"I'm afraid that'll never happen. Robert Kimble and my husband Jason will never leave me be."

Jessie's heart beat faster. Robert Kimble was the man Dal was after even before they organized this big sweep of the county for drugs. He was involved in the child trafficking for a couple of years before Mac and his deputies arrested the lot of them, save for Kimble and his partner who managed to escape. Must've been this fellow Gold. Maybe Beth could help trap him.

"Did you know his wife?"

"Robert's?"

"Yes, he always claimed she was dead, but I've heard different."

After a long pause during panting strides, Beth spoke softly. "Oh yes, she changed her name and is surely alive. I'm ashamed to say, she talked me into something I've always been sorry for."

Jessie kicked her way through some weeds. "Oh, what's that?"

"She told me who she was and that if I did something for her, she would make sure my husband left me and the kids alone. It sounded harmless. She told me they needed someone to keep an eye on the animal farm, let Robert know the lady's schedule, and so I did."

"You mean July?"

She nodded. "Yep, her. Just had to volunteer to work around the place, so I did. Then one day they asked me to let a tiger out and show Robert how he could get in and back out. He was only going to set some of the tame animals free, she said. I never knew what they did with my information cause it wasn't long before I ran off. I had to get my kids out of there, and so we found the trailer and had been hiding there till that Jackson man found us."

No sense in letting the woman know what happened after she passed on her information about the animal farm. That they'd used her information to lure Loren in when she was out hiking, kill her, then move her body to Parker's barn. They were not only drug smugglers, they were cold blooded killers. No doubt they'd hired some of their kind to shoot Leslie down on the street. Beth felt bad enough as it was, but at least that explained a lot. By killing Loren and blaming Parker they felt they'd gotten rid of two people they thought knew the cartel's plans for Grace County. Then they must've gone on to have Leslie shot or do it themselves.

The Kimbles were alive and so was Jason Gold. Moving from child trafficking to taking part in heroin smuggling and the cooking and sale of black tar. And not to forget, murder as well.

It was a long walk to the bench below Jessie's cabin, and she and Beth lagged farther behind Coyote but finally staggered onto the path below Jessie's shot-up cabin. She'd had adventures there with Dal before, and thank goodness she knew the way home.

Back at the cabin they were greeted by an ecstatic Brad who hadn't managed to follow without becoming distracted and had returned home.

Jessie rushed the three into the Jeep. "Quick, get in, and let's get out of here before your husband comes along. Luck seems always to be with men like him, but it's about time that ran out. We'll go to the jail and lock you up till the men come back from the drug raids. The sheriff and a deputy and lots of townspeople are there. We'll protect you."

Brad leaped in Sally's lap and had her giggling before they got to town. Parker met them at the door on his way out of Mac's office, and when she explained who they were, he turned around and went back in with them. In Mac's office, she had the story to tell again.

Lucas embraced being in jail. "Guess I can tell all my friends I've been in jail, huh?"

Sally plopped down on the mattress-covered cot. "It feels so good. Think I could sleep for a month. No one can get us. Honest?"

"Honest, sweetheart." Jessie turned away with tears in her eyes.

These kids had been through way too much mistreatment for their age. All because of drugs. It was way past time to do something.

Following Dal's instructions, Colby hid the fancy RV, the captives handcuffed inside, in a thick grove of trees barely out of sight of dock number ten, that appeared almost too quiet. He silenced the men, then led them around the back way.

"Looks like the deliveries haven't made it here."

He situated them, watching a small RV near the boat dock. There were no lights, as if campers were in bed. "Let's lay low in the shadows and wait. See what's up."

Colby knelt near him. "Where you reckon our guys are? We don't want to shoot each other."

"Wait and be wary. They're close." Dal promptly clicked the prearranged message in his mic. In a minute, a clicking signal came back. "Pass the word down that our men are in hiding nearby."

He didn't like this one bit. It would take very little for rapid fire to cut loose, no one knowing who they were shooting at. Since it appeared the other guys had it handled, he clicked them he was moving on, then let his guys know to back off up into the trees, to reconnoiter for other plans. Being this close was way too dangerous. Someone could kill their own partner.

Once far enough away from dock ten he radioed those men, happily surprised his signal actually went through. The message was kept short in case hushed voices might carry in the still night air. He did learn that the earlier gunfire was from dock nine, and they had arrested five hikers and two drivers. No one was injured.

Relieved that he had made a correct call on the movement of drugs, he wished they had caught some of those hiding out in the woods cooking the stuff. Believing they were well hidden, they would keep right on cooking till someone figured out a way to identify and stop the raw heroin from getting into the wilderness in the first place. It was enough right now to dry up the black tar leaving the Ozarks and supplying the countryside. Take it a step at a time.

By morning, five of the twelve docks had been shut down. Only three carriers actually escaped. Probably enough to warn the others. The remaining docks were quiet. Of course there was no way for the suppliers to bring in enough heroin in one night to keep all twelve busy transferring to the hikers, so more nights of watching were inevitable.

On the radio, Dal instructed everyone still guarding an unused dock to set up alternate guards and the rest get some sleep. Come morning all would check back in at Cedarton. By nine a.m., a weary group straggled into town to fill all the tables at Grandma's for big breakfasts and discussions on successes and failures of their first night breaking up the drug runners. Evidently it would take more time to shut them all down.

J.C., in charge of the 18 DEA agents, leaned back in his chair. "We keep this up though, it won't take long to send 'em off someplace else."

"I hope you're right, though I'd be happier if we jailed ever last one of 'em." Ledger scrubbed at his short hair. "But these ole boys don't scare off too easy. You could be stirring up a war that'll cost innocent lives. They got men whose only job for the cartel is to fight dirty to keep the product moving. The town could be in for some hard times. If you're serious about this, you might need to call in some deputies from other counties. Maybe even the staties."

Colby nodded. "He's right. They don't think anything of overrunning a town and burning it to the ground. Hard to fight these guys unless we're willing to fight as dirty as they do. Don't reckon we can do that. Back shooting and killing women isn't on our agenda."

The door burst open, and a tall, lean man with a bandage around his head entered. "Sounds like you're expecting it to get western real quick."

Mac came to his feet. "Danged if we ain't attracting the dregs. When did you get in town? This here is an old buddy, Jackson Delray. No one's for sure who he works for, but I can vouch he's one of the good guys. Cut him loose, and we got half an army. Set, Jack, set. You need to have that head tended to?"

"Nah, it's okay. I'm more hungry than anything else."

J.C. came to his feet. "Damn glad to see you, Jackson. We were beginning to worry how you were doing it's been so long since contact." He pulled out an empty chair next to him.

Mac introduced him to Dal and Colby and the others having breakfast. "Sit, Jack. Eat."

The man sat and ordered steak and eggs. Cleaning his plate, he offered some advice. "Only way to get rid of this scum of the earth is to go in and wipe out their camps. As in completely. Ones you can't catch you run off quick as you can. You got enough men right here to do it, you plan it right."

Mac leaned back. "Could be that's agin the law."

Ledger and Jack and J.C. all tilted back their heads and guffawed.

Jack was quiet for a minute, then he grinned. "Well, who's gonna call 'em? Get it done right, and no one would be the wiser. You want your kids to grow up in a town run by gangsters?"

"Course not, but neither can we turn into vigilantes."

Jack was still enjoying himself. Dal liked the guy. "What do you have in mind?" He squinted across the table at Jack. "Looks to me like you've been in a rough skirmish yourself." He pointed at Jack's bandaged head.

"Shit, this? It ain't nothin. How many of your men do you reckon know this wilderness pretty good?"

Dal glanced around. "Hands?" He stuck up his own.

Nick, who had been really quiet since his group had failed to turn up any drugs, reached high. Colby, Burt, and Ledger did the same.

"Looking good." Jack went to work on his steak and eggs.

Dal nodded. "Okay, you got your spotters. You all lawmen? Them that ain't, why Mac here needs to deputize them. That goes for ever one of you who intend to stick this out. Each one gets a badge. Any more who wanta help, are good with weapons and fighting, why do the same. I know the main problem here is signals for phones and radios. You go in at night, locate, send up a bottle rocket or roman candle. Nothin fancy."

Dal shifted his attention to the DEA agents. "Y'all in this?" They nodded, each and every one. "Okay, you got your DEA with all their fancy equipment. Night vision is the best. Use it. Should be able to pinpoint the area close enough to find the camps. Someone know how to use a computer?"

Howie rose to his feet. "Google Earth might be a help, but you realize it ain't always current. Someone could get some cameras planted why then I might could find most of 'em."

Nick came to his feet next to Howie. "I'm your man for that."

Jack swung a hand toward the two men standing. "There you go, a beginning. Let's get that in motion now. Once the camps are located, why then all of you lawmen...." He shouted over the excited chatter, when it quieted he went. "Well, hell, they refuse to surrender and start shooting, why some of you with Uzis, take 'em down. Ought to be able to clean out enough of them that the rest will turn tail and run. These are the hired hands. You don't mess around. Keep it all legal. We got no warrants, but we don't need 'em. Probable cause is enough in these cases. Besides, we got the Feds on our side. And you'll need 'em to chop off the head of this snake."

Again, noisy agreement.

Dal checked out the faces of those thirty or so men finishing breakfast. Most of them appeared eager to get on with it, but how would they feel alone out in the woods in the dark going after a well-armed enemy who didn't give a damn who they killed?

Mac looked around. "Can we hear from the Feds who might need permission to take part?"

J.C., who was in charge of the DEA agents, scratched at a night long beard. "We were sent here to help clean up your county. I might know a few retired special forces fellas tired of sitting around home who could lend a hand. I can swear them back on duty. They're generally up for anything, especially when it's to fight the cartel. Give me a couple of hours to round up some additional equipment. And you're right, we keep it on the up and up. We were sent in here to support the deputies taking on the drug cartel. Well, I say let's get it on. Whatever it takes."

A general cheer went around the room. Some of the waitresses joined the hollering. The cook stuck his head out the door from the kitchen, then he raised his eyebrows. "I have hunted these woods for miles in all directions. Can a former Marine join in? This is my town too. And I got kids I'd like to see grow up safe."

After a lot more conversation, silence filled the room.

Jackson approached J.C. "I need to talk to you about something... in private."

Dal overheard the request, but it wasn't something he needed to know, or the man would share it. Besides, he was tired and needed to get some sleep.

Mac rose and knocked on the table with a knife handle. "Let's all get some sleep and come together in Rocky's gym first thing tomorrow. He just offered the space for our planning. There's lot to think about before then. Write down all your ideas, even guesses where camps might be, and lawmen keep in mind this ain't vigilantism. We have to do this right and keep it legal to put these guys out of business for good. See you tomorrow, eight a.m. promptly. First off, we'll deputize all them that hasn't changed their minds".

Dal remained and followed Mac across the street and into his office. There were some things the two of them had to discuss. This was their town, and they didn't want it burnt to the ground and the streets littered with the dead.

Jessie returned with Beth, Sally, and Lucas and was surprised to find what was going on in town. As soon as she told her story, Tinker volunteered to remain at the jail overnight, since her shift was four to twelve anyway. Howie, who lived at his computer nearly 24/7, offered to remain with her since he'd be busy locating movement in the wilderness anyway. Nick was out there putting up cameras. Jessie left to go to the motel to shower and grab some sleep and met Wendy coming in.

"Howie called, told me what was up, so I'm going to spend the night here, too."

"Okay, you guys be careful. It's doubtful those guys locked up in the back four cells will bother anyone. Someone from the DEA is taking them in to Federal Prison tomorrow. But just be careful. Mac is in his office on the couch, so everyone ought to be safe with three deputies and the sheriff here. See you all in the morning."

She might be going to take a shower, but after that she was putting together the beginnings of a story of a small Ozark town that refused to buckle under to the drug cartel. No telling how it would come out, but what a story it could be. And she would happily have a part in it.

When she pulled into the parking slot for her room, another car slipped into an empty one nearby. A bit fearful, she pulled out her key card before getting out, then hurried to get the door open. Before she closed it, a voice came out of the shadows.

"Jessie, it's me. Dal."

She let out a whoosh of air. "Glad you're back. Sort of getting scary around here, isn't it?"

He moved her inside and shut the door behind them. "Pleased you're being careful." Leaning down he kissed her. "Good to see you."

If he knew where she'd been, he might be upset, but she had to tell him cause the men had to know what she'd found out about the Gold family.

"Sit, I'm thirsty. Want something?" She took out two Pepsis, poured them over ice, and sat beside him on the bed. "You know what we wondered about Sheriff Robert Kimble from Nolton County?"

Dal dragged in a deep breath. He looked worn out, but he turned inquisitive eyes upon her.

"Well, his wife who was supposed to be dead helped Beth Gold let Maizie out so Kimble and Gold could carry out their plans to grab Loren when she went hiking, kill her then move her body down to Parker's."

"No kidding? How'd you find that out?"

She told him about Beth's tale. "But she claims she didn't know anything about the murder plot or the body. She just did as they asked cause they threatened to hurt her kids, but mostly to make them think she was their friend so she could get away. Her husband was looking for her and the kids. And guess who he is? Jason Gold, Kimble's deputy and in on the child trafficking with him. Now turned heroin dealer and running this black tar business. Beth claims she's not to blame, she had to protect her kids. She's over at the jail now to keep her safe till Mac can figure out what to do with her."

He took a long swig of his drink. "Have you considered she might be lying? How did you run into her and where?"

She told him about Jackson and how he'd helped her get away from the cartel, and he stared at her with disbelief. "You went out there again?"

She held up a hand. "Before you go all crazy on me, I know how foolish I was, but I didn't intend to get so involved."

"I'm not going to go all crazy on you. I give up. Just wish you'd be more careful, that's all."

"I was being careful. It happened, and believe me, I don't ever want to be so scared again. I promise to take better care."

"Well, thank God. At last. You were lucky running into Jackson. He showed up at the gym tonight, and he's genuine undercover. Helped us plan a run on the cartel. Swears we can get rid of them. I sure hope he's right."

He kissed her again. "Please be careful, and I promise to do the same."

She picked at a thread on his jeans. "You know how much I love you. And you know how I don't tell you how to do your job."

He sighed. "I'm not trying to tell you how to do your job."

She raised an eyebrow, gazed deep into his eyes. "Okay, what do you think of Beth Gold's story?"

"Good. Changing the subject. I think she's lying."

"Why?"

"Because it's just too convenient, Jackson finding her like that. Good way for her to skinny out of any blame. She was definitely involved with

Jason and the Kimbles in the child trafficking. They're married to sisters. Tighter than drums, the four were. Sure they still are. You think she isn't helping her husband with the drugs, well then you're a reporter. Prove it."

"I don't think so, she's pretty upset, scared the cartel is going to kill her and her kids"

He took a sip of Pepsi. "I repeat, prove it. By the way, when and how did you get involved with this woman and Jackson? I thought you were up at your cabin packing stuff."

"I was, but her daughter was hiding in my closet." She hurried to tell him the story and quickly added she was never in any danger.

"Once you went with them, you were. But never mind, this isn't something we can settle easily."

Swallowing thickly, she pursued the subject. "I'm careful and have never put myself in danger deliberately. Sometimes it just happens. You ought to understand. You're a deputy out there where the action is and in danger a lot. And I never criticize you."

He nearly choked on his drink. Stared at her without speaking. She waited for him to respond, and when he remained speechless rose to face him down. "Well? Say something."

With a sparkle in his eye, he grinned, put an arm around her, and kissed her neck, then her cheek. "What am I going to do with you? Tink suggested I tie you to the bed."

"Not a bad choice, but I wouldn't try it if I were you." She kissed him on the mouth. "You wouldn't even like me if I didn't do the things I do, would you? Besides, how would you like it if I told you not to do what you do? I'll never understand these women who are all besotted about a big tough man so handsome with his gun and uniform, then they marry him and try to turn him into a little milquetoast of a man. Don't they realize that they fell for him because of who and what he is? I don't get it, I just don't." Before he could reply, she went on. "I promise you I will never ask you to be someone you aren't. I love the man you are. And you need to promise me the same or this… we will never work."

He touched the tip of her nose. "Oh, that's a promise, and you want the same from me? Right?"

Though he was trying to be light, she gave him a serious look. "I mean it, I really do. I would never leave you because you are who you are."

He lifted her chin, gazed deep into her eyes, his own green as spring leaves in the sunlight. "Jessie, sometimes love ambushes us, tries to turn and twist us around, even cheats us of all we hold close. Of all emotions, love is the most important, and so it can hurt us the worst. I've nursed my guilt over Leanne's death until I couldn't give you what you deserve. I've cheated you, and I'm sorry."

She nestled her head against his shoulder. "I sure never thought I'd hear you say something like that. Let's leave it at this. No promises we can't keep, and we'll go from there."

Now if only he'd tell her he loved her, but it didn't look like he would. She could wait, because he did love her, and one day, he would figure it out and come right out and say so.

"And so, what's the plan to run these guys out of here for good?"

After he told her, she couldn't speak for a while. It was a dangerous idea, and she wished he wouldn't agree to it. But these monsters wanted to steal their lives, their homes, their children. Someone had to do something, and she'd promised not to tell him what to do.

"Well, please be careful. Will we be bailing you all out of jail?"

He chuckled. "You know how that goes. If it works, we'll be heroes. If it doesn't, yes, you'll be bailing us out." He touched her cheek. "Look into this Beth Gold thing and take what she says with a grain of salt. Don't trust the woman."

"Okay, I will. I mean I won't. And you go out there and make this work. But be careful."

"That's the plan." He rubbed his eyes. "God, I'm tired and sleepy."

She helped him undress, and they went to bed together, too worn out to do anything but curl in each other's arms and go to sleep. When she awoke, a lavender glow fingered its way around the window blinds. He lay asleep, looking so peaceful she let him be for a long while and gazed into his calm features.

He once told her he had a torn spirit. She didn't believe that. Never had. The spirit that lived in him shined as bright as any star. She closed her eyes for just a minute to enjoy lying peacefully in his arms before he left to carry out this dangerous plan.

He awoke a little after seven, and she lay next to him, one arm flung over his chest. For one instant, he memorized the delicate lines that sketched her facial features before preparing to meet the men at the gym in town. Then he crept from under her arm, stepped into jungle camo britches and shirt, grabbed a thermos, and filled it from the pot of coffee already made. Excitement rushed over him. Good God, how could he possibly look forward to this kind of battle? Must be Grandfather's warrior genes. Glancing once more at Jessie, he grinned. What kind of wild-ass kids would the two of them have?

Outside, men streamed from houses all around town. Strangely hushed, they nodded or waved and moved on. Inside the gym, the fragrance of coffee overpowered the scent of men and leather and yesterday's sweat. A gym didn't have an abundance of chairs, and they squatted, leaned, or sat cross legged on the floor. A low rumble of conversation broke the silence.

No time was wasted. The doors were closed at about five past eight, and Mac, Dal, J.C., Ledger, and Jackson stood inside one of the boxing rings, the mic in Mac's hand. He scraped fingernails over it, and what little sound there was stopped as if choked off.

"First, those who are civilians will be deputized. For good reasons, we five you see up here will take turns with that duty. It lays the blame squarely on each of us who are in charge."

A tiny chuckle rumbled through the room.

"Before we do that, one last chance for those of you who have doubts or want out, there's the door, and it isn't locked. This is all being videoed by Howie Duggan, who will leave it on my desk over at the sheriff's office. If you haven't left by now, we presume you are in for the lot.

"Nick isn't here, but that means he's still out there sneaking around climbing bluffs and mountainsides to hang electronic cameras that will help us locate and raid the camps. Thanks to Roy O'Bannon who runs the electronics department at Walmart for supplying an abundance of them."

A great roar and round of applause mixed with the "Oo-*rah!*" of those in the military rattled the windows of the gym.

The ritual of deputizing went quickly when the men numbered off in fives then lined up to solemnly take an oath. Five times, and it was done. Amazed, Dal solemnly took oaths when it came his turn. God, were they doing something entirely stupid? Would they all, or at least the survivors, be in jail within a week or two?

Men accustomed to taking part in team attacks were put in charge of groups. Some would finish raiding the docks, the rest would follow carriers and comb the woods in ever concentric sweeps to take down the camps, destroy heroin and black tar, and officially arrest everyone taking part.

Just before arms were issued and groups sent out, Mac once more took the mic.

"Howie has received camera shots from Nick and will forward locales to our leaders, those of you who know this wilderness should have little trouble with his information. Radios and phones on at all times whether the blamed things are working or not. Take care of yourselves and others with you. God bless you all."

Dal joined the men who filed out group at a time. Standing outside the door, Jessie snapped pictures. He could do nothing but smile and wave at her. He would keep a promise made in his heart that he hadn't yet managed to speak aloud to her.

This had to work. The leaders had spent hours the previous night planning as best they could. It wasn't like they were simply being turned loose to start shooting anything that moved. Most of the men had experience, either in the service or in law enforcement, and they would take care of those who didn't, but he was still dubious. It would be better if they wore uniforms or something red attached to their hats to show whose side they were on. Something no one had thought of.

SUVs, pickups, and a few Jeeps filed away from the square in all directions. He rode with a couple of deputies, two DEA agents, and about ten assorted, armed men.

The battle was about to begin. As Mac had said, God bless them all.

19
CHAPTER

The last of the varied vehicles pulled away from Cedarton hauling a ragtag army headed for victory over the enemy. Jessie raised a hand to wave. Already discussing their attack plans, some of the participants were excited, others nervous. None were looking back. Too bad she couldn't go with them, but that would be pushing her luck with all the men in her life, Dal especially. Mac would just flat tie her up to keep her out of danger.

Yet she had a job to do, and she would follow where her stories led her while hoping to remain safe. Right now, it was time to reconsider Beth Gold's story and draft what she had on the articles up to this point. As the battles raged on, she could only hope no one was hurt, but that was somewhat optimistic. She dare not name those she especially wanted kept safe. That would be placing some people's value above others. So her best wishes went with them all. Better not to think about it. Get on with her work.

While the men fought against the evil of drugs, she sorted through all the clues in an attempt to solve the murders. There were obvious gaps, missing facts to chase down. Tink agreed to help her. They carried notes into the newspaper office and turned on computers that were wired together for writing, editing, and laying out of newspaper articles. That would make it easier to compare what they already knew. Just as they got started, someone tapped on the locked door.

Jessie looked up. "Don't answer. We can't have people coming in and out."

Silence, then the sound of a key, and the door opened with its familiar squeak, followed by a well-known voice. "Sorry ladies, but I need to be here." Wendy waited near her own desk, a hopeful expression on her face.

Tink switched her gaze between the two. "I made us a closed sign and stuck it on the door."

Jessie laughed. "That never did any good before."

Wendy looked stricken. "Do I have to go away?"

Tink and Jessie exchanged glances, spoke together. "No, of course not. You can probably help."

"So, what's up I can help with, even if you did lock me out?"

Jessie tossed a stack of scribbled notes in front of her. "There are some anomalies in the clues of the murders. Things are missing, and we've got suspects who haven't been identified. Let's get these in the computer so we can go over them together."

Wendy grabbed a handful. "I'm the fastest on the keyboard, why don't you two go make some coffee and see if there's anything in the fridge we can gnosh on? I'm starving."

"Hope you can read my scribbles." Jessie laughed and threw the remark over her shoulder.

"Honey, you forget, I read all that handwritten stuff that comes in every week from older folk's community news, who I have to say invented scribbles. And have you ever seen our farm reporter's review? Looks like ducks and chickens climbed out of the barnyard and walked all over his papers. Don't worry, I'll holler if I get stuck."

By the time Tink and Jessie finished in the kitchen and brought out cheese sandwiches, chips and dip, and three slices of leftover cake from a couple of days earlier, Wendy had copied the pile down to three scraps of note paper. While they laid the food out on one of the empty desks and opened pop for everyone, she finished, kicked back, and grabbed a sandwich and a drink. Their discussion avoided worries about the men and concentrated on what Tink liked to call girl talk. Who wore what where. Who went with who where. That sort of thing was good for keeping their minds off the danger out there in the woods. They polished off the sandwiches and cake. Chips and dip would make a good snack later. Time to get serious. With the push of a button Wendy's list came up on three computer screens.

Jessie took charge as was her usual habit. "Okay, ladies, we know what connected these three victims that probably gives us a motive for their murders. They were once confidential informers for the Dallas PD. But why did it become necessary, six years after Leanne's murder to kill Loren and Leslie? Something happened in the interim between murders to make it necessary. They must've found out whatever Leanne knew that threatened someone in the cartel."

Tink raised a hand, almost as if she were in school. "That's all it could be. Whatever Leanne knew probably threatened someone who became involved later. Wait, what if she left something written down and her sister found it? Or what if her sister found out who killed Leanne and went after them?"

Wendy popped up. "Or her best friend found it and shared with the other one."

Jessie nodded. "All good suggestions. As to possible killers, we know that Robert Kimble, his wife whose name we don't have, and Jason Gold were probably only involved in the cartel for the past year or so, since they were trafficking children prior to that, and I don't think they could've handled both at the same time. You know Beth Gold is at the jail with her kids under protection. Dal believes that's a ruse and she is involved too, so we need to look into that. Something or someone else set off the murders. Leanne's death started them."

"Wendy, get this down as we go, could you?"

Wendy giggled that cute laugh she had. "I got so involved it never occurred to me. Give me a minute or two." Silence while the words came up on the screen. "Okay, check if I have it all."

"Yep." Jessie nodded when Wendy spoke up, then looked thoughtful.

"I've had a question for a long time. Remember the picture of the three women taken in front of the boutique here in Cedarton. Had to be over six years ago because Leanne was in it?"

Tink snapped her fingers. "Then she went back to Dallas and was killed. So what were they doing here in Cedarton when none of them would've had a connection to the place?"

Jessie pinched her temples. "Shilo Captree."

"Who?" "What?" from the other two.

"Shilo knew Loren, said she applied for a job or worked for them over in Dallas. And, the DEA suspects the Captrees of involvement according to J.C."

"Don't understand the connection." Tink sounded dubious.

"The Captrees had a pub in Dallas where Loren worked at one time.

They now own what used to be the boutique and is now the Purple Raven. All this happening at the same time as this drug business busted wide open here. Coincidence? Cops don't believe in them."

"You mean like why did the Brits pick Cedarton to buy a pub just when all this drug stuff is happening? And after the dead women had visited." Jessie filled in the silence.

"Exactly what I mean."

"Was Dal's running under that truck hauling stuff to the pub really an accident?" Tink tapped her pen on the desktop.

In the deathly silence that followed, Jessie shook her head. My God, no. Surely not. Yet she could see it fitting into the scheme of things. If the Captrees were involved. She looked at Wendy. "Make a note to talk to J.C. about his suspicions."

"Okay, and I'll interview the Captrees. I can learn a lot by telling them I'm doing a story on their new pub. We need to find out exactly when they decided to buy the boutique and why. We need to learn their prior connection to the women and possible connection to the drug cartel."

"Wait a minute, are we thinking they're involved in the drug cartel, thus the murders?" Tink appeared distressed to think the likeable Captrees were involved.

"What fun. It's like a Sherlock Holmes mystery. We have more than one set of suspects. Now we need to get more clues." Wendy hadn't known the victims, so it was easier for her to have a more critical viewpoint.

"Okay, check to see where the Brits were when both murders were committed. If they have alibis, it still matters why they came here. Murder for hire is very possible. It still might be connected. Here's another of our questions." Jessie wanted to move on. Too much discussion took them in circles with no results. "Why did the killers go to such lengths to see Parker blamed for Loren's murder? They could just as easily have blamed July and saved themselves the trouble of moving the body."

"Maybe they had a reason to want Parker out of the way."

They stared at each other, then said all at once. "Pillow talk." Jessie finished. "Because they thought Loren might have told him something. Or knew she had."

Hooking little fingers, all three nodded confidently. Jessie shook her head. "No, never, never, would he have kept anything like that a secret."

"Unless to reveal it threatened someone he cared about." This from Tink, the more romantic of the trio.

Tears welled in Jessie's eyes. "His fifth wife, he never would say who she was. You don't suppose... it couldn't have been Leanne... no, I'll never believe this. We've gone in the wrong direction."

Tink squeezed her eyes closed. "Why did Dal move here from Dallas? How did he know anything about Cedarton unless at some time maybe Leanne talked about it since she'd been here. We know she was here. We don't know why. And here he comes not long after she dies."

"Stop, stop right now." Jessie kicked out of her chair. "This is ridiculous. We have to back up or stop this amateur detective shit altogether. I won't involve people I love in this unholy mess when none of us knows what we're talking about. I won't. All we're doing is making stuff up." She went into the bathroom and slammed the door.

Pier Eight appeared peaceful, with only one camping trailer parked. Whatever had been used to pull it was gone. Colby nosed the SUV with twelve men crowded inside through a gap in the trees and parked it out of sight of the boat dock assigned the number eight. Dal opened the side door, letting several men tumble out as if they were packed in like sardines. When everyone had unloaded, keeping as quiet as possible, they took up hidden positions in a half circle around their target. Anyone trying to escape would have to jump in the lake. Or take off up the trail that made a *U* around a curve in the shoreline. Horton the Who guarded that curve, well disguised by his woodland BDUs as a bush behind a large boulder.

Dal kept an eye on The Who, as the guys had tagged him, just to make sure he knew his stuff. He came to Grace County after being laid off as a deputy in Nolton County, which made him need watching. But he proved himself in several situations over the summer. Mac had hired him, Eugene Bellamy, and Neal Nelson when the county gained approval for three new deputies. Bellamy and Nelson were right out of training and seemed competent though somewhat untried in the field.

Mac claimed the new hire approval meant the state knew that opening a Walmart and putting through a bypass would bring more crime to Grace County and most especially Cedarton.

Everyone clicked they were in place, but Horton's shoulder was visible through a gap in the bush. Someone clicked an alert, and he adjusted his position. The sound of an engine pulling the curve in low gear alerted the men. An SUV parked in the lot, and three women unloaded and carried plastic Walmart bags through the door of the camper. Might be tourists. Yet they talked among themselves in low voices, not the usual behavior of women having a good time. The door slammed, and it wasn't five minutes till two hikers loped down off the trail, slipped out of their backpacks, and settled in a couple of folding chairs set up nearby.

Dal alerted the men, the sound of their clickers blending with the usual insect noises. Using clickers was a behavior developed by a group of soldiers during World War II when they used the "toys" to message each other during silent advances. A fantastic idea for use in this situation.

In a few minutes, a woman came out with three cans of beer, gave them to the men, and stood there looking around for a while. Then she stooped casually, picked up both backpacks, and went inside.

Colby clicked to move in, but Dal clicked for a hold. Something was amiss here. The men should've wanted to leave directly after the handover, yet they sat where they were enjoying their beer. One surveyed the area closely and tossed his can down. The other two followed with loud clatters from the discarded cans. Two more women exited, handing over a backpack to each man. The way they handled them you could tell they were heavy. Clearly, they had brought in black tar and were returning to camp with raw heroin picked up from the camper.

Dal's beliefs were being proved true. He sure was pleased seeing as how they'd based this operation solely on what he thought. Shouting their identification and loud instructions to drop to their bellies the lawmen closed in. The two men followed the orders, but the women hesitated, just stood and looked around.

"You too, ma'am." Colby was ever the gentleman, but when the women still refused, The Who stepped in and put one then the other down on the dock, their knees knocking loudly against the wood.

That was a little bit harsh. Odd, too. Dal wouldn't have thought of The Who being so rough. Then one of the gals, the smallest, surprised them all and came up kicking and screaming. The Who had a hold of her, but she twisted and ducked under his clasped arms, whirled, and tossed him into the water.

Colby, who had taken charge of another one had this look on his face like he thought "no way" or "holy shit." And Dal couldn't help but laugh when The Who crawled out of the lake looking like a drowned muskrat.

"It's the tiny ones you've got to watch." Dal looked around and couldn't tell who'd said it, but everyone laughed, more at the soaking wet deputy than the remarks. He'd suffer his share of teasing later.

Colby gave up being a gentleman and locked the older, heavy-set one in a choke hold from which she promptly low-balled him with one spike heel. He went to his knees, howling but keeping hold of her around the neck like he'd been glued there. Before the little fighter could do much but dance about out of their reach, The Who tackled her around the knees and went down on top of her. He grabbed her by the arms, yanked her up tight, and locked handcuffs on her. She kicked backward with one heel but caught his boot solidly. Her scream made Dal want to cover his ears, but that would've meant letting his go. He cuffed the next one, and she called him a fucking bastard and went limp, her butt sagging to the ground. He lifted the third easily under one arm while dragging the stout one from Colby's grip to the open Jeep where he fastened all three to the roll bar with another set of handcuffs.

This must've pushed Colby back into battle in Afghanistan, for he leaned down and whispered in her ear. "You know what us Indians do to white women? We take a knife and slice their pretty hair right off their head along with their scalp. Now settle it down."

He gave the woman a wide grin that looked like a vicious growl, turned, and walked away. The wild one calmed down, eyes wide, and scurried behind one of the agents. He had to laugh. These three women were ornerier than any of the men.

The DEA agents opened the backpacks to find large bricks of raw heroin. On the way to cooking more black tar. For the most part these were only hired mules who could make their agreed deliveries, collect their pay, and disappear. What the law wanted most was to shut down the cartels, but it wouldn't happen. So they settled for arresting dealers, scooping up as many of those mules as they could, and making it too hot to do business there. It had become an endless battle.

Dal took his prisoners to the large black prisoner unit the DEA had brought in. It was quickly filling up. He settled on his haunches to talk to the gathering of feds.

"I've got an idea and should've come up with it sooner. These guys are doubling up delivering black tar and picking up heroin to take back to the camp for cooking. Somewhere they're leaving the hiking trail to do their business deep in the wilderness. If we let the next delivery guys go with their heroin, we should be able to follow them to a camp. We'd do better hitting the camps and cutting off the supply of black tar." He shrugged. "Dumb of me not to let these two go and track 'em."

J.C. agreed. "Still, you did come up with how they were getting this stuff flowing, and no one else has."

Dal nodded. "Anyone have a phone with a signal?"

J.C. checked his SAT unit and smiled.

"See if you can relay a message to the other groups about watching for hikers returning to camps and follow them. Tell them to raid the camps."

J.C. went to work.

Dal stood beside him while the prisoners were loaded into the big van and things quieted down some. J.C. reported that he'd reached all but one of the groups.

Determined to make this work, Dal went back to his men once more. "I hate to say so, but this is a pretty smart set-up. Seems to me the best way to put a stop to it is shut down the camps. We stop the deliveries there's no heroin to cook. These guys delivering heroin in RVs are way too hard to identify. There are RVs everywhere. We can't stop all hikers and search them either. And the camps where they're doing the cooking are well hidden in the wilderness. We need to come up with a faster way to locate those doing the cooking. Anyone?"

Nick stepped out of the shadows. "I've planted cameras, but that's really not sufficient. It catches stragglers occasionally, but it's a big world out there."

Colby planted his butt on a nearby rock. "Looks like another load's coming in and going to the camps. I agreed that we need to back off on raids at the boat docks. Instead of arresting them, we get someone to track 'em when they leave for the camp like Dal says. They will lead us to a camp which is what we need to destroy first. Then with the trail and woods filled with agents and deputies destroying their cooking sites we can concentrate on stopping the supply of heroin coming in from Mexico.

Dal studied Colby. "Has to be someone sure-footed and quiet. Let's have them make a move on the next dock. To track not to arrest. Who's gonna be best?"

"Well, Chief, you're pretty light footed and could be you'd get some help." He winked at Dal. Colby was one of the few deputies who understood where his odd investigative technique came from. He went on. "Where did Nick get to? The two of you could get this done."

Maybe Grandfather would show up and lend a hand, though he'd been awfully quiet of late. Hatching a plan maybe. Or giving Dal a chance to come up with something on his own.

Dal asked J.C. to find Nick, who had gone to get some water, and have him join them. "It should happen soon since a new shipment is currently being delivered. I'm going to do the same with dock seven.

And so on. Those hikers pick up the heroin they'll head straight for the camps with it. It's time we ran these buggers out of the county, the state if we can. Soon as we track down the camps, I'm notifying the staties to give us a hand checking RVs out on the highways. Till they're all destroyed. If we can disrupt these camps and shut down at least half a dozen deliveries, we'll be ready to hit more before the word gets out what we're doing. We'll get together at the next dock."

Dal signed off, told the men what was up, prepared his weapons, and they made their way to the next dock where an RV waited. The sun rested on the western mountains when three hikers casually approached the RV, handed over their backpacks, stayed a while, then left with their heroin delivery to some hidden camp.

"We'll signal with those roman candles we brought along," Nick said. "You see them go up, then everyone close in. Okay?"

With a nod, Dal trailed along, taking careful steps through piles of leaves, broken limbs, and nut shells left by squirrels. What few sounds the experienced tracker made could be laid down to those same small animals dropping nut shells from high in the hickory trees. Dal, more adept on the back streets of Dallas, had learned quickly during his experiences following child traffickers during an earlier case.

The hikers led them deeper and deeper into the woods, until the wilderness closed in around them like snatching prickly arms. More than once their prey would stop, settle on boulders, and wait. Perhaps they were meeting others. Once or twice someone moved off in the periphery of Dal's vision, but when he turned his head to look, they were gone. Something crawled between his shoulder blades. What if someone were following them in return? It was all he could do to keep from whirling to catch them at their own game.

Overhead the canopy thickened, blotting out the afternoon sun. At times, shadows appeared to hide something menacing. There were bears and other predatory animals in these woods but none so threatening as what those hikers carried. Soon the aroma of wood smoke and a tang like vinegar tickled his nostrils. Nick touched his arm, and he stopped. Before he could turn, a gun barrel drilled into his back.

Freezing instantly in his tracks, Dal struggled not to react and get shot. No sound from Nick. A scrabbling of leaves underfoot. Too late. No time. None at all. The world tilted, turned black, and someone's voice spoke in hoarse threads that tangled into webs and disappeared.

Dal opened his eyes and took in little. Dried leaves clung to his cheeks. A bug, black with a pointed butt and wavering antenna crawled close to his nose. Something in his mouth. He spat. At least it wasn't a bug that moved off through the dirt and sprigs of grass.

He cleared his mouth with a dry tongue but couldn't move from the position because his hands were behind his back and tied to his ankles. That was as uncomfortable as hell.

"Nick, where are you?" Afraid to speak, he whispered.

No reply.

"You really thought we were that stupid?" A voice hailed from out of the woods.

He strained to see the speaker. Twisted his neck to peer in all directions. Feet scuffled through ground covering. Lots of feet, then after a long while nothing. They were leaving him right here, all trussed up like some kind of—uh well—a tricked lawman. It would be up to him to get out of this, and where the hell was Nick?

Gone, that's where. Either they had him or he—oh, shit—maybe he was with them all along. Nick, a junkie? Stranger things had happened.

He'd been fooled before, but he didn't believe it. They must have Nick, and if they did, he'd get away. He was too damned smart to end up tied hand and foot.

Dal snickered. Too bad he wasn't that smart. Meanwhile, he wouldn't just lay here. Twisting both wrists, he tried to loosen the rope, but it was having none of it, none at all. He was in one hell of a pickle.

Someone hammered on the bathroom door. "Jessie, come on. We need you to get through this. I don't believe Parker had anything to do with this, either, it was just a supposition. We'll clear him, I promise. But someone has to talk to him in case he does know something."

She might as well go out there, they were going to do this with or without her. She washed her face and opened the door.

"Okay, I think we'll have to work in tandem if we're going to find out anything in good time. I'll get the Captrees to agree to an interview. We need someone to talk to Parker, find out what he knows about Leanne. It's a big problem because he was never very curious about his wives' backgrounds, and we'll have to admit what we think. Wendy, you're pretty good on a computer... is there some way wedding licenses can be found online if Parker won't come through? Just knowing if he was married to Leanne would tell us a lot. Maybe he'd fess up to you. If not, Howie's at the sheriff's office. Ask him if you need help on the computer."

Tink stood up. "I can get into the evidence locker at the jail. Let me check what was turned in after both Loren's and Leslie's murders. Maybe there'll be something there to give us some clues."

"Okay, great. Let's get to work. We need to get this done quickly. Stay in touch. Any questions? I'm sure we'll have more to discuss after we get this much done. See you back here soon as possible. Okay?"

Leaving the other two to their assignments, Jessie hurried over to the Purple Raven to interview the Captrees.

Two hours later, she called Tink on her way back to *The Observer* office. "How'd it go?"

"I did find a couple of things. I'm bringing them, but I could be in trouble. I checked out several things. I am a deputy so can do that. Need to be careful is all."

Jessie had to smile at her friend's sense of humor. Sometimes it got a bit out of hand, yet often lawmen faced so much of a hassle they grew weary of stupid hang-ups. "Have you heard from Wendy?"

"No, not a word. You don't suppose Parker tied her up, do you? I doubt he's going to want to talk about his wives, especially Leanne."

"Okay, see you back at the office. I learned some interesting things from the Captrees. Though, I'm honestly not sure they will help us in our investigation."

A while later, everyone gathered back at the newspaper office to share what they'd learned.

Wendy went first, her face flushed as if she were embarrassed. "Parker would only say that he never pestered his wives about tales of their past."

"Not even when they were having sex?"

Wendy blushed even more. "Jessie, I wouldn't ask him that. But he did say that he knew Leanne had been married before or had a long-term relationship with someone. She hinted it was someone high up in law enforcement. That wouldn't have been Dal, so maybe someone else. He didn't know why she visited Cedarton, but that is where he first met her.

He also didn't know she was here with a sister and her friend. He was very little help at all."

"Okay, let's move on for now then." Jessie continued. "Shilo Captree was forthcoming. Guess what? That's not her real name. It's Daphne. She wanted to sound more American, so she changed it. I didn't tell her it was a strange choice that probably wouldn't make her appear more American. She met all three of the CIs when they were here at the same time. They thought it was funny they were all from Dallas and ran into each other in a place like Cedarton. I personally doubt that. They all came together for some reason they wouldn't say.

"Listen to this, though. Shilo said she overheard the ladies discussing something they had learned. Each from a different source, but it was how the cartel had its eye on the Ozarks for eventual drug movement. They'd asked gofers to go to different little towns in the Ozarks and pick the best one to use as a base for cooking black tar. Leanne was terrified because she thought they knew she was undercover for the police department, and she planned on running. Had told the others she would soon disappear and not to worry, she had good plans. With Dal in the hospital, she felt she had no one to go to for protection, though she worked for another cop, but she couldn't do it anymore. Something she'd found out but didn't dare tell Dal. That was all she'd say."

"My God, they *did* kill her, didn't they?" Tink jittered on her feet, like a runner getting set to go. "But we still don't know what she knew. Maybe that's not so important as to know they had a reason to kill her. And all this time Dal thought she committed suicide. He knows different now, doesn't he?"

Jessie nodded.

Wendy kept reading the notes they'd made. "Howie checked marriage licenses. We know Dal married Leanne, but we don't know if she was married to Parker before that. Maybe false ID?"

Jessie snorted. "I don't see what difference it makes if they were. If he doesn't want to talk about it, why then, let it go." Her cell rang, and she picked it up. Parker? She put her finger to her lips, answered.

"I've been going through some of Leanne's stuff." He went silent, as if waiting for praise or something.

Who knew he had anything? No one even knew they'd been married till now. She waited, finally said, "and?" Waited again.

"I think you might want to see something. Where you at?"

"*The Observer.* Can you bring it? We're doing a little clue sniffing right now."

"I'll be there in a few." He was gone without waiting for her to reply.

She turned to face her two cohorts. "Parker. Clues. Leanne." It was about all she could say. How could he have kept this secret from her, from Dal, hell from everyone all these years. Till murder most foul exploded between all them. Maybe she'd just give him a good smack.

"It's more like Agatha Christie than Sherlock Holmes like we thought earlier. Christie is always so convoluted you couldn't guess the killer if he hit you upside of the head and tried to confess. This is getting more and more twisted."

Jessie went to the kitchen for a Pepsi, opened it, returned to face Wendy and Tink once more. "Just wait, I don't even want to try to explain it, but Parker has found something and will be here soon."

Wendy looked up from her computer. "There's a text here from a woman over in Dallas to Dal. Don't ask me why it's on these computers. He may have given her your address or phone number, Jessie. She lived next door to Loren over there and had mentioned to Dal that she'd seen a fellow pick Loren up a few times, like dating. She describes him here in detail. Tall, almost thin, what she calls lanky, eyes a silver-gray. Says he looked a lot like Clint Eastwood in those old cowboy movies."

Jessie snapped to attention. "Jameson? Lone Ranger? In Dallas dating Loren? I told you this was convoluted. Why wouldn't he mention that?"

"Why wouldn't a lot of people mention a lot of things? Anyone else have any secrets they'd like to reveal that might help catch a killer?" Wendy's eyes flashed with anger.

Something in Dal's pocket kept poking him. With his legs folded up over his butt like they were it was no wonder. He squirmed and wiggled, feeling much like a pretzel but finally wrapped his fingers around it. One of those crazy bottle rockets they all carried to use for signaling. Maybe he wasn't so badly lost after all. Course, all he had to do was get it out of the pocket, manage to get back in his pocket and pull out the Bic each one of them decided to carry to light the stupid thing. It was sort of a dumb idea, or so he'd thought at the time. If it worked, maybe it wasn't so stupid. What was he hearing? Voices, conversation, low chuckles. They were coming back. Just as he figured out a way to get out of his predicament, they decided to return and mess up his plans. He'd play dead. No, better yet, he'd roll over there under those bushes. Where in hell was Nick?

Had anyone ever figured out how to roll over and over with their hands tied to their ankles at their back? He was about to set that record. Rocking forward, then backward, he finally got to moving. It was pretty rocky and somewhat painful, but he got out of the clearing before several men hiked into view. He laid there, eyes gritty with dirt and pieces of dried leaves, blinking to clear them up.

It was hikers, three of them, carrying backpacks. Someone hadn't gotten the message through that this camp had been moved. So here they were with loads of heroin, and here he was, the only lawman on site without a gun or his badge. Tied in such a position that it wouldn't do him any good if he were armed.

Well, shit.

Just another day in the life of a deputy in a small town in Arkansas. He ought to write a book, but no one would believe it was even remotely possible. He could always call it fiction.

20
CHAPTER

Parker stepped slowly into the room, not at all like a man who owned the building and everything in it. "I brought these. Maybe they'll help."

Jessie studied the weariness around his eyes. Sad a nice man like him had to suffer such a loss. "What did you find?"

He held out a small bundle tied in a blue ribbon. When he looked back up, tears tracked his cheeks.

For those few moments, Jessie couldn't move. Pain settled like a beating drum in her temples. Why did she fear touching the delicate pale orchid envelopes? As if some message might bring news no one wanted to hear. With trembling fingers, she reached for the letters.

"Take them, Jess." He looked as if they were too hot to hold.

She did, even though she didn't want to. A warmth moved over her skin like the touch of love's acceptance. The room filled with the aroma of flowers, freshly cut and wet from a recent rain, mud squishing between her toes, summer sunlight burning her cheeks, everything about life that she loved. What if it were gone for her and Dal? It could happen just like that. Like it had for Parker. The flow of impressions wouldn't stop. Parker's sadness, Dal's having to deal with Leanne's death all over again and her fear that she was losing him and everything that made life worth living. The impressions hung in the room like fog on a gloomy day.

God, she had to shake this away. Concentrate on all the crap going on right here, right now. *Do* something about it.

A hand touched her shoulder. She flinched. "You okay, Jessie? What is it? What's wrong?"

Hearing Tink's kind voice jarred her to reality. The weird thoughts drifted off as if a summer wind blew through the room and returned her to the present.

"Read them." Holding out the letters, Parker touched her hand. "I'm sorry to have let you wonder about Leanne and me. We were together only a short time, and you know how I am about my women."

"Yes, it's okay. If you're sure you want me to read these." Too many secrets, most no one's business till the murders.

"I do. They'll answer some of the questions about Leanne. Her life, her death. We never married, but she was my wife in every sense of the word, and I loved her as much as I always love. With all my heart. As much as I loved Loren." His glance swept the room, hovered on Jessie and sent her a silent message, a private one. "I'm going back to the house. Call me if you need anything. I'll be here to lay out the paper Monday."

Jessie wanted to say something, anything to ease his pain, but nothing came. After he left, she turned to Wendy and Tink. "I'm not sure he'll be okay. It's like he's in another world. He didn't even ask about everything going on. I'm worried about him. Shit, I'm worried about everyone, everything. This place is coming apart at the seams."

Tink gestured toward the letters. "You going to read those?"

No. Anything but that. She stared at them as if that would make them disappear, but it didn't. A sigh cleared her lungs. "Okay. I think we have to, don't you? To solve some of the puzzle?" She shuffled through the few envelopes. "How about if I read them aloud to the both of you? Save a lot of time."

They nodded, settled huddled around her. She opened the one on top, unfolded the single sheet of fragile paper. Read.

May 1
Dearest Seth,

As soon as I met you, I knew you were the one I would always love. Thank you for being, for caring, for loving me. It's important that I return to Dallas for a while. There are things I must do to cut free from my past. I will be back soon. I promise we will be together forever.

Love,
Lee

Odd for anyone to call him by his first name but deeply personal. "Tink, when we finish can you get on your computer, find out when Leanne was killed?" Her friend nodded.

Jessie folded the fragile sheet and slipped it back into the envelope. Read next.

May 13
I know I promised to return, but I'm afraid things have hap-pened over which I have no control. Often someone in my life asks more of me than I can give. There is a man who lives within and

beyond the law, and he has forced me to do something which I detest. I pray that once it is done, I will be finished with him, and I will be free to return to you. Please know that I love you with all my heart. I know I can trust you to understand. Should anything happen to me I ask you to make it right. Please let my husband know that I'm sorry to have failed him. I'm also so sorry to have hurt you.

Love always,
Lee

She frowned, folded the sheet, and lay it down. Last.

May 21

    Dearest One. I was betrayed by someone I trusted. I fear for my life. My contact in law enforcement has not kept his promise, and my husband has been shot. He may not live. Because of that, I am in custody and plan to give a full written statement of all I've learned about the cartel and their plans while I was a confidential informant. I fear this will be my final contact with you. With anyone. Drugs are the worst curse of mankind. I did what I could. I'm waiting now for the knock on the door. You will receive these letters eventually through a friend also in the dreadful business I've been involved in. I fear they will kill others, as well, but I have done my best to keep those near me a secret. I'm afraid I failed. Always remember our brief time together and how much we loved each other. I will never forget. I regret so much.

Forever yours,
Lee

Jessie glanced up from the note paper. "What a tragic love story is hidden on these pages. Not sure it helps any with our murders, though. She never married Parker. It appears she tried to protect Dal. Things just get more and more complicated. This higher-up lawman, wish she'd said more about him. That she feels she failed to protect those she loved may explain why they targeted Parker and Loren."

She gathered the letters and with great care folded them, took them in Parker's office, and placed them in the center of his desk.

How awful that he loved a woman who had so many problems, was involved in the drug business, and ended getting herself murdered for her own poor choices. Then when he did find someone like Loren to love, it happened again.

At least this was the proof Dal needed that Leanne did not commit suicide. If he learned that she appeared to have sacrificed her own life for his, his reaction might be worse. It was also proof that whoever killed her was involved in the shooting of Dal in that back alley. If Parker had known Dal before he came here to go to work for Mac, he surely would've told him of Leanne's warning. Too damn many secrets. People could be so dense sometimes. Not talking to each other made things so much worse.

She and Dal were guilty of that, as well. She hoped to remedy that—and soon.

Tink cornered her when she returned from Parker's office. "This lawman she was involved with would be who she worked for as a CI. That's the only thing that makes sense. Let me do some digging."

While Tink got on her computer and found information about Leanne's death and the date she died, which she soon announced was May 30, Wendy finished with the information she'd been keeping, saved the work, and hit print to make a copy for each one of them. "Shall I delete it from the computer?"

Holding hers, Jessie studied Wendy, then Tink, then the paper she held in her hand. "Yes, delete it. We can do what we need with our copies, but I'm giving mine to Dal."

"I'll keep looking for her connection to the Dallas PD. He could very well be the head Honcho of the drug ring there. It'll be up to the DEA to prove it, though."

"Leanne must have mailed those letters the day before she was killed, but to who?" Jessie raised her eyebrows and tossed them each a weary glance before turning away to stare out the window. "Note, ask Parker."

Dal's wrists stung and were slick with blood from twisting frantically to get free. If he could reach the Bic and a bottle rocket, he could signal his men. Around him, hikers went about their business of transferring black tar to their backpacks for transporting. While he struggled, they paid him no mind. There were three of the small fireworks stuck down in the cargo pocket of his pants along with the lighter. Finally, his fingers closed around one of the wooden sticks holding the fireworks. Watching their shadows in the tree line, he worked out a rocket.

Meanwhile those idiots wandered around where they were supposed to meet up with other idiots to exchange heroin for black tar. He deeply detested anyone dealing in drugs. The children he'd seen destroyed by heroin and meth... hell all of the stuff mankind managed to produce to bring about horrors, gave him nightmares. The fools hadn't yet noticed his struggles under the bushes, but all bets would be off when he lit the rocket and shot it into the air. If he were lucky, they wouldn't see where it came from. Hopefully his men would. He lost what balance he had attained to shoot off the rocket and fell back onto his belly, still trussed up tight. Twisting his neck, he watched to see if he was successful.

The rocket arced low across the trees, striking a huge branch and falling through the leaves before bursting at ground level.

Shit. He hunched up his shoulders, fearful at least one of them might hear or see the crash under the canopy. No one noticed. Once more he stretched his arms, injuring his already torn wrists to fish around for the pocket and the only thing that might save him. A stick under his touch and his fingers grappled. He had the blamed thing.

Numb hands told him the Bic lighter wouldn't light. Damn things fixed so kids couldn't get them to work. He had a hell of a time. He wasn't going to make it. Maintaining the painful position, his back screamed in pain. He couldn't give up, had to send the message. Gritting his teeth, he held on, clung to the lighter with bloody palms, felt what he hoped were the two buttons that would produce a flame. One hand gripped the stick, his trembling fingers worked the lighter then, neck turned so he could see what he was doing, he managed to apply the flame to the wick of the fireworks fastened to the rocket.

Finally, the damned thing sizzled, and he made a special effort to see it pointed straight into the sky. Just a minute longer. A jag of pain slammed up his spine. He was losing, his body threatening to spasm and dump him to the ground. He let out a whoosh when the sparkling rocket whizzed into the darkness above. Unable to hold out any longer he fell onto his stomach. Didn't see the burst of fire. Closed his eyes and prayed someone saw when it lit the sky in such a brief burst. If they did, they would take it for the message earlier agreed upon and find him. All went quiet, like even the birds and animals didn't care for the disruption. Lying there with his nose in the dirt, his back being hammered by some invisible force, he couldn't help wondering where the hell Nick had gotten to in all this confusion. Surely he wasn't dead.

He could no longer feel his legs, clung to consciousness, and sagged helplessly against the tight ropes.

A noise brought him back from a dark place where Grandfather's soft voice beckoned to him. *"You will not die this night, Grandson. Soon this will pass."*

"Here. Somewhere." Colby's voice nearby, searching, through the brush. They were looking. He could only grunt.

At the same time, men shouted, feet scuffled around every which way. "No, come this way here."

His effort to cry aloud was muffled by the other noises if he made a sound at all. They spotted the men scrabbling for freedom, went after them, leaving him to struggle weakly.

"Down. Get down." Colby's voice. Now they were hiding, prolonging the search. Everything going on at once.

He opened his mouth to yell for help, but nothing would come out. Well, something, but it was so small a call no one heard. They were all making too much noise taking lawbreakers into custody. He'd wait a few moments, till they quieted down.

Finally from his mouth, "Help. Help." If that was as good as he could do, no one would ever hear him.

Once upon a time he could whistle, but he hadn't practiced lately. Moving his lips just so, he attempted the shrill noise Grandfather had once taught him. A hiss of air was all he got. They were rounding the men up to take them to the hiking trail, and soon they'd be out of hearing. Surely they wouldn't leave him here. They had to have seen his signal.

Forming his lips, he sucked in air, and just as he did, a shrill whistle sounded, followed by two or three more. That couldn't have come from him. The air dribbled from between his lips.

"Hear that? Where'd it come from?" Colby. At last. "He should be right here. Dal. Dallas." Shouts. At least someone was paying attention.

Again, the whistle. He could barely twist enough to see the shadow slipping off into the woods. Grandfather. The old man had decided to lend him a hand, after all.

"Here, back over here." Boots approached, and he managed a couple of weak noises. "My God, it's Dal right here under our feet."

"Nick. Did you find Nick?" He croaked the question.

While hands untied him, he managed to repeat the question. A jab of pain drove him into the dark place again, and he didn't remember anything else till he came to, curled up in the middle seat of one of the SUVs. Bandages bound his torn wrists and ankles.

For an instant he couldn't remember… and then he did. "Nick, did he turn up?"

From the passenger side, Colby leaned around the headrest. "Haven't seen him. We looked but no luck. We're getting images of some of the camps with GPS, so he's been planting the cameras."

"I never saw what happened to him. He was just gone. I thought someone grabbed him." He struggled to sit up. Couldn't. "We have to find him."

"He's doing his job. You need to take er easy. We got a lot of the big ones. J.C. and his bunch grabbed Kimble and Gold. Would you believe some of them were in one of the RVs playing cards with a couple of hikers who brought some black tar there from the middle of nowhere? Playing goddamned cards while they waited to make an exchange for a load of heroin. They were making the runs along with some other cartel members." Colby could scarcely hold his disgust.

Mac chimed in. "So, we got 'em in possession of enough to send 'em away for one heck of a long time. At least that's some of 'em. Hoping the others do as well so we can shut this mess down. Not sure what happened to the Gold and Kimble women, but they were both in on it and we'll get 'em."

"No kidding? Both of them? And I missed it all."

Colby chuckled. "Oh, I'm sure you'll still have your chance. The DEA wants us to work with them a while yet until we're sure this business is cleaned up. Not one single cook-fire or camp or RV carrying heroin. Seems their agents have a bit of trouble getting around in these woods. They tend to get lost. J.C. says we may be happy that we're closing it down in our county, but his job isn't near finished. Swears he'll shut down the fences and gates both, whatever that means. He may need some help from us country boys."

The van hit a bump and skittered to one side of the narrow road, and the prisoners in the back complained with grumbles..

"You know what we ought to tell him?" Dal was feeling a bit better and grunted to sit up. "We should tell him that heroin coming into this country is his job security. I for one hope I never see another brick of the stuff."

From a prisoner in the seat behind him came a snort. "You're fools if you think you've stopped it. Fore long, they'll be growing poppies inside your borders. You can't stop it."

Dal stretched to stare into the back. "Shut up, you miserable excuse for a human being. I know your kind. I've dragged your bodies out of your own filth from every alley in Dallas. You'd sell your grandmother or put a gun to her head if it meant more dope. Even the lowest killer is a step above a drug dealer. If I had my way, we'd supply ever one of you with enough heroin to kill you deader than a doornail. You're not worth the powder it would take to blow you all to hell. Now shut up before I throw you off a cliff and tell everyone you jumped."

Colby guffawed. "I was you, bud, I'd listen to this ole boy, he might scalp you first."

The man in back hawked as if to spit, but he shut up.

Bumps in the road jounced them around a bit more. Colby picked up the conversation as if the junkie hadn't spoken.

"Well, we still have some murders to clear up. And it's for sure they're connected to the cartel and this attempted move into the Ozarks with their nasty product. Hey, maybe we can send some more of them off to jail for a few decades. I'm for heading home. We can come back when J.C. needs us to help clean up this mess. I'm sure there's plenty more of these bastards hiding out in the woods."

"I take it Mister Big still roams free."

"Fraid so."

"Sure hope someone's run across Nick." The idea the man might be dead wouldn't leave him be. He'd grown to like him the few times they'd worked together over the years.

It was near dawn when the driver, someone Dal had not met so he must be DEA, pulled into an empty space outside Mac's office. Dal crawled out, staggered a bit, and leaned on the side of the car a moment. "Damn I'm tired and hungry. Those guys don't play nice. I could sure use some sleep and something to eat, I guess in that order."

Colby took his arm. "I'll get someone to take you home, or I can drive you if you'd like."

"You must be as tired as I am."

Colby held the door to the sheriff's station open, then followed Dal in. Behind them, the incessant sound of criminals bitching and moaning while being herded inside to go behind bars until the feds picked them up.

Dal plopped into his chair. "Do you think Kimble and Gold shot Leslie and killed Loren?"

Colby shook his head. "I've asked myself that over and over. Say, did Jameson ever come on back, or did he stay in Dallas?"

"I've had some thoughts about that ole boy." Dal scratched his head, leaned the chair back. "There's plenty of stuff going on that makes him a person of interest. The Big Man in this wing of the cartel. Neither Kimble nor Gold has the wherewithal to run something that big. And their wives, where are they, and what part did they play?"

He'd no more than lowered his tired butt in the chair behind his desk before Tink came back into the room. "A call from Jessie, she's waiting outside."

One more time, he hauled himself to his feet, told Colby to get some rest and with a groan made his way out the back door. A familiar Jeep sat in the parking lot. He headed that way. Everything hurt, but he couldn't wait to crawl in the front seat and lean into a welcome-home hug and kiss.

She whispered in his ear, sending shivers through him. "Hmm, you smell awful."

"Funny. How'd you know we were back?"

"I'm a reporter, don't you remember? Want to go home with me or to your place?"

"With you. Don't think I could climb all those steps."

"As good an excuse as saying how you couldn't wait to crawl in bed with me."

He leaned back, rubbed his forehead, and couldn't help a groan that rolled unbidden from his throat. "Ah, darlin, if you only knew."

Without taking her eyes from the road, she lay one hand across his thigh. "Are you hurt?"

"Battered, but not beat. I just need a hot shower and a comfortable bed... oh, and a pretty lady rubbing my back."

"Just your back?"

"Mmm, tonight? Fraid so."

Silence for a few blocks, then she signaled to turn onto the highway that led to the Interstate and her motel room. "We figured out some stuff about the murders. We think Kimble and Gold hired someone to kill Loren and Leslie for the same reason Leanne was killed. All three women worked for the Dallas PD as CIs and found out too much about the cartel there and those involved. Seems as simple as that."

Eyes still closed, he grumbled. "I think you're right as far as you go. Do we know who the killers are? And what Lee found out?" He sat up with a start. "Hey, wait. Did you know that Beth Gold was in on the murders, too?"

"What? No. Are you sure? She's got two kids. Sally and her brother."

"Well, J.C. said Jason and Beth Gold were in on the entire thing including the murders. And the connection between Kimble and Gold and the law was someone high up in law enforcement in Texas. Who do we know like that?"

"The Texas Ranger? No way. That'll teach me to judge someone by their actions. He played everyone so well, even when I said I suspected him I really didn't. He was more a joker than anything else."

Without saying more, she pulled into the motel parking and nosed the Jeep into the spot marked for her room. She said nothing more about Jameson but hopped out, ran around to his side, and insisted on helping him out, even though he did his best to act as if he didn't need it. Waiting for her to card the lock, he leaned against the building.

Damn, it was good to be home, even if he didn't look forward to what they had to talk about. It was time to clear up his painful feelings about both Leanne and Jess.

Jessie pushed the door closed with her butt and followed Dal's slow limping movement toward the bathroom.

"I still don't believe Jameson arranged the attack in the alley that night in Dallas when I was shot down. Hope it can be proven untrue. We'll see. So long ago, it's best put behind us. Still, I'd like to give him a good punch or two."

Him saying that was a good sign he was ready to let Leanne go as well. At the door, he crooked his arm against the frame, lay his head there, and took a deep breath. Jess moved behind him, slipped both hands under the back of his shirt and pulled it up over his raised arms. Bandages around his wrists snagged on the material.

She fingered the stained fabric. "What's this? What happened?"

"Nothing. Take them off. I'd guess I could use a good washing all over." He made it to the toilet and dropped hard. "Sorry."

"What for? You got no reason to be sorry." His belt buckle gave her a little trouble, but she got it loose and worked the zipper open. "Lift your butt. I'm getting sort of used to this."

He did, and she pulled down his pants and jockey shorts. Unwound the bandages from around his ankles. "Know what this reminds me of?"

He fell back onto the seat and leaned forward to kiss her on top of her bent head. "Yes, I do. That was a long time ago, and you were putting on bandages instead of taking them off."

"And do you remember why?"

"Uh-huh. I thought you were the most beautiful woman I'd ever seen. Wondered why you weren't afraid of a man you barely knew who'd leap from a car to go wrestle with a barbed wire fence rather than have a decent conversation."

And you're still at it metaphorically. She unlaced his boots. Casting her a crooked grin he toed them off and pulled off his socks. Dirt and gravel rattled to the floor.

"I was beautiful? Hmm. I was afraid, but I didn't want you to know it. I had to get in good with such a handsome lawman if I was going to write stories about him and lawbreakers."

"Oh, yeah? And that got interesting real quick."

She bent forward and kissed him on a gritty chest. "What you been doing? Wrestling with a bear?" Without waiting for an answer, she rose and turned on the shower, took his hand. "Come on, get in." In her shorts and t-shirt, she went in with him. Dirty water swirled from his head down through the hairs on his chest and over his legs, like mud when it gurgled down the drain.

Kneeling, she inspected the wounds and glanced up. "Oh my, you were tied. These are nasty. You okay?" He looked pretty beat up. No telling what he'd been through out there in the woods. Ten to one he'd never talk about it, but she was getting used to that.

Soaping a washcloth, she scrubbed his hair, ears, and face, then worked her way down and around. He didn't say anything, just propped himself against the shower wall and allowed her to wash wherever she wanted, even between his legs. Finally finished, she stood in front of him while the water rinsed him clean of soap. He was barely standing on his feet. She looped his arm around her neck and supported him. Tossing a towel on the bed, she let him sit while she dried him head to toe. When she finished with his feet, he curled his legs up onto the mattress, lay down, and closed his eyes.

"Thank you for the wash and rinse." The muffled words were the last she heard from him.

"My hero." Grinning, she retired to the bath to take off her soaked clothes, shower, and clean up the mess they'd made. When she lifted the covers and crawled in beside him, he spooned around her.

Tomorrow they would settle their problems, cause they had them in spades. Maybe he still loved his dead wife and felt guilty for her death. In a strange way she looked forward to it. She wanted to continue a career that he objected to most of the time, and they could hash that out, or maybe they couldn't. She would not go into a committed relationship until they worked things out. Love was easily destroyed by disagreements. And their feelings for each other had to be strong enough to survive the problems their lifestyles created. She desperately hoped they were.

The next morning, he was watching her when she opened her eyes. Dear God, what could she do or say to get this going in the right direction? If she lost him, she might not recover. A knock on the door. Who in the world could that be?

She pawed around beside the bed for something to put on.

"Jessie? You awake?" A familiar voice, but her sleepy brain wouldn't recognize who it was.

"Yeah, but I'm naked and don't know where my clothes are."

Laughter from the other side of the door. Dal shot straight up in bed, grabbed his back, and groaned. "What? Who?"

"It's okay, sweetheart. Lay back down." He did so as if programmed. "Wait just a minute."

"Okay." From the bed. "Okay." From outside the door.

"Good grief. I'm dressing." She hollered it to the door. Another reply with another okay.

Hopping up, she tossed through the drawers of the strange dresser, came up with jeans and a t-shirt, practically all she wore anyway. Slipping into both, she tiptoed to the door and opened it. Wendy, Tinker, Mac, Colby, and J.C. stood like a crowd waiting for kickoff at a football game. She glanced toward the bed where Dal now sat, sheet over his lap, hair tangled around his face, a curious expression aimed at them. She couldn't help but join the laughter coming from the weird crowd.

"Invite them in, Jessie. Hell, why not? They can always crawl in the bed, too. What time is it anyway? Five? Six?"

"No, smartass, it's seven fifteen, time to be up and at 'em." They remained around the door like a huge knot of humanity, looking much too smug.

"Colby, you're the only person in the world can get away with calling me smartass. Get that door shut and give me five. Jessie? Do I have any clothes here?"

"Yeah, I think you changed once here and left the dirty ones. They'd be cleaner than what you wore in here last night." Digging in a pile of clothing waiting to be taken to the laundry, she came up with… she held them up. "What do you think they came for?"

"No idea. You found jeans and a t-shirt. Do we ever wear anything else?"

He pulled the jeans over his feet, stood, and finished the job, then hollered "Come in!" toward the door while sliding the t-shirt over his arms and head.

Everyone found a place to sit, mostly on the floor. Colby carried a tray of steaming coffee, Wendy had a sack of cinnamon rolls from Grandma's. Passing everything around, Jessie then sat cross-legged on the floor at Dal's feet.

"Okay, what's up? We voting on something or what?" As if she hadn't guessed already what was going on. Someone besides her needed to say it.

Mac decided it should be him, chewed, and swallowed a bite of roll with a gulp of coffee, then licked his lips and began. "Parker called me this morning and told me about y'all's layout over to the paper, and we been studying it this morning."

Tink stared at the sheriff. "What time did you get up, anyway?"

"Early enough to figger out if we've got a case or not 'fore we go around arresting folks. Or putting stories in the paper. We need some more information before then, though I figger you've got a good start." He took a big bite and another swallow. "Dang, these are good." He favored the group with one of his bullet-like looks. On the bed, Dal sat calmly drinking coffee. "I believe Dal can help straighten out some of our questions. Ain't that right boy?"

Dal looked down at his roll for a minute. "Well for one thing, these are a bit better than honey buns."

"Don't get smart, we ain't got that sort of time. Those perps are going to the federal building over in Fayetteville today for charges to be brought, and we need some answers." Obviously Mac wasn't in the mood to mess around. Jessie poked Dal on the leg. His expression sent shivers through her. This wasn't going to be good.

He rubbed her shoulder. "Sorry, sweetheart." He cleared his throat. "Leanne was always filled with stories about this place. It was her favorite place to be while she lived with... uh, with Parker." He stared into his coffee cup. "I was pretty much of a mess from the shooting,"

"You knew?" She was right about one thing. This wasn't good.

"When Leanne died, as you all know, I was already torn up bad, emotionally and physically from the shooting. Then after my rehab, they put me on a desk, and I didn't much care what happened to me."

"Get to the subject, boy." Mac's gray eyes were hard as marbles. Clearly, he'd hired Dal without knowing any of this. Trusted him. "How come they targeted Parker and those gals?" Mac's mouth drew a hard line across his wrinkled face. Jessie had never seen him so angry.

"Soon, real soon. I buckled down. I was reduced to digging through old files and learning more about those bastards than they liked. As it turned out, all those we arrested that day in Dallas who weren't in prison were scattered to the wind. Had lost their connections and were forced into hiding. I kept coming down on them hard. No matter where they went, I'd find one or two or three. Pissed them off bad. Hell, I didn't have anything else to do. Every time another one came up before a judge, they vowed to get back at me. Finally, I figured my best bet was to hide out, start a new life.

"Don't look at me that way. Once settled in Cedarton, I didn't think they'd find me. This nowhere town in the middle of the wilderness. Hell, there wasn't but one road even led here then. Lee talked a lot about Parker and Mac and Grace County, but just to me. It was like being read fairy tales. All I could do was lay there and listen. Couldn't hardly move. I swear nobody else knew but the three of them about our connection to this place."

Mac raised a hand, fingers knotted with arthritis. "Stick to what we need, not excuses. Who would they hire as their button men?"

Tink glanced at Wendy, raised her shoulders. "Button men?"

"Hired killers. Now keep going." Even Colby's voice sounded like he felt betrayed.

"My guess would be they'd keep it in the family. Maybe get someone close to do the killing. So Kimble and Gold hired their own wives, huh? Anna Kimble and Beth Gold. Who'd a thought it. I'll be damned."

"Wait a minute." J.C. finally butted in. "How and why did they target the town in the first place? I mean how did they know about Dal or Parker, and those were the only connections to Cedarton they could follow."

Tink held up her hand, took it down when everyone stared. She pulled a notebook from her pocket. "Learned this from the Internet. Names are Beth Harper Gold, who worked for a little while at July's animal compound and Anna Harper Kimble who was always strangely absent. Sisters. This has become a case of the good sisters verses the bad sisters. And by the way, Leanne had no sisters, so the rumor that she and Leslie were sisters is not true. It was something they enjoyed doing, introducing each other as their sister. And they looked so much alike.

"The Harper sisters, the bad ones, both have a record in Austin and Dallas. Nice ladies, they must like to pair up cause their last arrest was in Dallas, looks like before they hooked up with hubbies. The sheriff over in Nolton County arrested them after they started a fight in a bar and shot up the place. Lo and behold, a few months later, they were out of jail and living with their so-called husbands Sheriff Kimble and Deputy Gold. A month or so later, Kimble got involved with child trafficking and was fired. As you all know he escaped before he could be arrested for that episode. For some weird reason, Gold was given the job of sheriff till election time came around, and he was voted out. Folks must've figured out his involvement with Kimble."

J.C. studied the women with a wry grin. "So, who we getting ready to arrest, ladies?"

21
CHAPTER

"Since this is such a confusing case...." Jessie paused to gaze at everyone gathered at the sheriff's office before going on. "...while you were gone, we ladies put together what we know." She curled a teasing grin at them. "Just in case you need assistance."

Tink and Wendy helped her spread out all the information they had so far, uncovered, arranging it on the table normally used to lay out the newspaper. Tink's bagged crime scene evidence, Jessie's draft of the Captree interview, and Wendy's notes from Parker.

Mac and Jessie studied the evidence displayed on the table. They were silent for the longest time.

Jessie let her impatience show. "No matter what we put together, we know what will be brought before a judge is up to you and the DEA. At first, we were just messing around and got to working this puzzle. We hope you'll at least consider our opinion."

Mac picked at a tooth. "Go on girl, you've always had a quick mind, and Lord knows we can use the input. We know most everything. What we need is evidence to convince the Grand Jury, so they have to go to trial, then prison."

"Okay then, here's what we think, but I don't know how to prove it. There were two people in the car that drove by Mac's and shot Leslie. The same people dressed entirely in black shot my cabin to pieces. We're sure Kimble is responsible for putting it all together, but we agree that the people were gunwomen."

Someone laughed.

"It isn't that funny." She eyed the men and waited a moment before going on. "We think the motive for both murders is something Loren and Leslie knew about the one in charge of the cartel and their plans to invade the Ozarks. The murder of Leanne, who was a CI for a higher up in Texas law enforcement, was committed by someone else. This plan to move their production into Grace County was put in place then, and she proved a danger, so they got rid of her and tried to ambush Dal, but that didn't work out the way they hoped. But why am I a target? Because this is like who's connected to who. I'm close to Dal, so maybe I know what he knows.

"I believe it's something Shilo Captree told me that she didn't intend to. She admitted to knowing all three women well and that she inadvertently heard about the heroin plans. Somehow, she managed to get in on this deal, and she mentioned in passing to me how girls in that sort of business had to dress and act certain ways. This was after my cabin got shot up and the conversation made me nervous. She knew way more than she cared to admit and is parked in Cedarton to get her share when the deal goes down. I think she realized her and Marvin said too much to Dal and Colby, so she had the two gunwomen shoot up my cabin while I was in it, afraid I'd put two and two together. If Deputy Marshal Ledger hadn't been with me, I might not have survived. You guys can take it from there for what it's worth.

"By the way, someone needs to find out who sent Parker Leanne's three letters. I would guess they know more than they're telling, too. Probably the man Loren was dating in Dallas. And he's a lawman. Most of us in this room know who he is. Care to put it together? Make sure we're not jumping to conclusions. Anyone know who he is?"

"One of her neighbors saw him a few times and described him to me on the phone as a tall, lanky man in a fancy Stetson," Dal offered.

A chuckle passed through the men. She joined them. "Yeah, lots of Texans look like that, huh? But considering the suspects, it narrows down. Like a man who has gone through all the law enforcement training and service of being a Texas Ranger puts him way up there in rank. Jest saying."

Jessie paused, waited to see if anyone had comments. They just nodded in serious agreement, so she continued.

"Jason Gold's wife worked at the animal compound and admitted to letting Maizie loose. That would have been just at the right time for her and Kimble's wife to kill Loren who hiked in that area frequently and take her to Parker's barn. Hard to place them in Dallas six years ago. Doesn't matter. But we're betting on the two Harper sisters, wives of Kimble and Gold. So, though we can't prove it, it looks like our mysterious lawman, say his name with me gang…."

They all did, unanimously. "Texas Ranger James Jameson."

"Another thing, Beth Gold lied from the beginning about accidentally finding her husband and kids at a Walmart store in Fayetteville. That makes no sense. She's terrified of her husband and supposedly in hiding, so she's going to stand outside Walmart every day openly looking for him and the kids? I don't think so. When you consider Jackson found her living in that ratty old trailer. That was a setup too. Who found her there and took pity on her? Why, an undercover DEA agent Jackson Delray, who by then the cartel suspected cause he helped me get away when they captured me. I want to know why they didn't just kill me and him, that's what I want to know. But I probably never will. Gives me the shivers to think about it."

Tink stuck up her hand, like she always did to lighten tension. Jessie pointed to her.

"He's a real weird guy and the only one involved who has a law enforcement connection in Texas, like she talks about. Let's find out if he really is a Texas Ranger, then go from there."

"Well, he's not the only lawman we know of with a connection to the cartel. But Jackson is the real thing. Mac vouches for him. There might be one we don't know of." Jessie looked up when the door opened to let in Parker.

Her gaze caught a man standing in the shadows of the room, and she knew him immediately. What in the world was Deputy Marshal Ledger doing slinking around? As far as everyone knew, he had mysteriously drifted out of town.

Her attention was drawn to Parker. "Saw you were all here and decided to join you. Say, you know that long drink of water who pretends to be a Ranger?"

"Pretends?" Everyone repeated the word with Jessie.

"He claims to be undercover for them with the cartel, and he's not even a Ranger?" Parker appeared amazed.

"You're always playing around on the computer, Googling all these people. Anyone ever check up on him?"

Jessie shot a glance around the room at the amazed faces and her own flushed.

Parker continued. "Well, I got to thinking about him. Anyone who can fool his enemies can fool his friends. So here's what I found. In 2013, a fella by the name of James Jameson was arrested in Amarillo and charged with assault of a Texas State Policeman, plus armed robbery with his victim's weapon, and he later escaped while in the custody of a Texas Ranger. He's still at large. It's believed he may be posing as a Ranger."

Jessie had found something to laugh about. "Well that ties a tail on this tale, so to speak."

Everyone jabbered to each other, some surprised, others not.

Mac grinned great big. "Looks like we're getting close to proof for the Grand Jury. It's a matter of tying all these folks together, and Howie is working on that. A lot of the faces are either wanted or ex-cons. I got a feeling Dal can play his games with them till one or more turns for a break in their sentence."

Parker shook his head.

Jessie brought up her main concern right away. "Did you know Rangers sometimes come from higher ranks in Texas law enforcement? Say, perhaps a Captain, someone well respected."

Mac looked long at her. "No, I didn't know that. What difference does it make?"

"None, I guess. Unless he was a real Ranger who wanted to keep his pretty star and uniform."

"Well, then, he hadn't ought to break the law."

Colby puffed up. "Well J.C. and I interrogated some of the carriers. A couple of them couldn't take being put in jail for years. So the feds, ole J.C. here, offered immunity if they'd give up the leaders and show proof.

They about liked to run over one another so danged fast we could hardly keep up. Though the two of them claims there's a "big guy" as they call him behind Gold and Kimble. So far those ole boys are afraid to name him. Claim he'll take out their entire families. WITSEC has been called in, and they're still working on whichever one breaks first."

Mac puffed up. "I want this man found and arrested immediately. He's our key. No matter his reasons, if anyone knows the secrets of this cartel, it's him. And he'll talk if I have to water-board him."

Of course he didn't mean that. Mac was prone to unusual threats when he found himself stunned. How they should go about catching Jameson Jessie had no idea, but it wasn't up to her. Even more, if he did know anything, he didn't have to talk. Water-board threat and all. Still she had her doubts they'd ever catch and convict him. He was way too slick.

"Let me handle that." A familiar voice quieted the hubbub, and Deputy Marshal Ledger stepped from the shadows. "He's going on our fugitive list and marshals are good at capturing fugitives. I'll get all the information on him right away."

Now what? Everyone was temporarily stumped. J.C. kept peering around the room as if he'd lost his pet dog. Finally he stood, touched the weapon on his hip as if making sure he was armed, and spoke to the room in general.

"I'll put out an APB on this man as a witness for now and get back to you, but I have to be in Fayetteville in an hour. For now, all of them will be charged with possession of and intent to sell a controlled substance. This'll get them out of your hair. I'll keep in touch on the murder charges and our tall friend."

Jessie leaned back in her chair and eyed Dal. Another case out of their hands, this time they needed to talk.

Dal waited while everyone cleared out of the sheriff's office. Strange how empty he felt about so much. Leanne having an affair with Parker while he was still married to her had hit him hard, but being relieved of his guilt over her death tended to balance the scales, in a weird sort of way. The affair wasn't a surprise considering that he'd been undercover for nearly six months when he was ambushed, shot, and not expected to live. How any wife could take all that without coming apart amazed him.

He took Jessie back to her motel and went in with her. He wasn't about to let this opportunity to settle things go by. Across the room, she sat on the edge of the bed, back to him.

"I'm tired, Dal. Need to think of lots of things. Could we leave this till later?"

Crushed again. He rose from the chair and headed for the door. Opening it, he cleared his throat. "I have to know what happened to Nick. He disappeared when they grabbed me, and I'm worried about him. But when I get back I do want to talk."

"So do I. I'll be waiting."

He paused for a couple of seconds, then left behind the silence of the room.

A setting sun flashed through a slit in lavender clouds, temporarily blinding him. His eyes teared up, but he ignored them. It was just the brightness of the sun.

Back at the empty sheriff's office, he listened to the odd silence for a moment, then went outside. Where the hell had Nick got to? They'd pulled nearly all the dealers and carriers in and stuffed them aboard

SUVs for their trip to the Federal Building in Fayetteville. Maybe they'd left him trussed up somewhere in the wilderness. By God, he'd go looking for him.

His phone dinged, and he dug it out, not really having time for this.

"Dallas Starr?" The caller was blocked, and he almost hung up, but for some reason he didn't.

"Yes, who's this?"

"This is Maggie A'hearn at the Cedarton Clinic. We have a patient here says you need notified. Name's Nick Snow."

"Oh, thank God." He sank on the bench outside the station. "Is he all right?"

"Has a broken ankle but says to tell you he didn't fall climbing." Laughter from the background. *"A fella saw him limping along leaning on a stick down the side of the highway and picked him up.*

"Could I talk to that jarhead?" Relief brought a brightness to his voice.

Nick came on. *"Dal, knew you'd be worried. Twisted the damned thing on flat ground. Gopher hole."*

"Aw shit. I don't believe a word. I'll be right down."

"Naw, I'm staying the night here. If you could pick me up in the morning, I'd be obliged."

"That I can do. But overnight for a twisted ankle?"

"Well, it's sorta broken and will have to be set in the morning. See you then buddy, g'bye."

Dal stared at the phone. *Sorta* broken. Sounded more like a fracture. Well, he'd find out in the morning. He really needed to get things straightened out with Jessie. He drove back up to the motel.

This time he wouldn't give up.

He tapped gently. "It's me, Jess. Can we talk now?"

After a pause, the door opened, and she came out wearing a smile. "I'd love to talk now if you won't go rushing out in the middle."

The sound of her lovely voice gave him the shivers. There was nothing for it, he wanted her too damned bad, yet all he could say sounded hollow and impersonal.

"Nick will be okay?"

"Uh-huh. He's fine. Broken ankle."

"Will you need to go pick him up?"

"Nope, he's in overnight."

"In that case, let's find somewhere quiet."

Exactly what he wanted. "We'll find one of those places where you've always liked to make love and have at it."

"After we talk. There's too much left unsaid between the two of us that sex alone won't heal."

Her words hit him like a raw Texas wind. Swallowing, he reached out to her and she let him have her hand. "Jess, I am so sorry. I know I've not been good on that level for a while now."

She leaned close and cupped his chin in her palm. "Easy there, sweetheart. Let's go see if we can find somewhere quiet. Be together. We'll work this out. Then Parker wants interviews from everyone involved." Before he could answer, she put a finger over his lips. "It'll be fun to combine our jobs. Just like old times." Tilting her head, she smiled. "You know I love you, don't you?" A bit of a tease, a curl to her lips.

Not exactly what he had in mind, but hey. The wind blew a wisp of her hair, and when she reached to finger it back, he thought of the lovely gracefulness of a bird in flight. God, she was gorgeous, beautiful, and brave, and he loved her. Knew he did, but dammit could he handle her insistence on bulling right into the most dangerous of affairs?

Like a balloon deflating, he let go the fear and touched her cheek. "If you can do it, I can do it. I love you so much it hurts when we're not together." He'd never been good at this. Words didn't always mean what he wanted to say.

She tilted her head to gaze into his eyes. "You finally said it."

What had he said now? He stared at her. Laughter filled the room. Hers. Still not comprehending, he took her in his arms. "Hey, you okay? Not going hysterical on me, are you? Said what?"

"You finally told me you love me like you mean it." Her eyes glistened, tears rolled slowly down her cheeks.

"But hell, darlin, I thought you knew that all along."

She collapsed in his arms. All he wanted was to spend their crazy life together. One thing for sure, it would never be boring.

"Hey, let's have a barbecue, invite all our friends, announce that we're gonna do it."

She lay her head on his shoulder, shook with merriment. "Do it? We're gonna do it?"

"You know. Crawl in bed, make love till our bodies quiver, and then—"

"And then? First, let's have that barbecue and announce our marriage plans. Now you've told me you love me, we're gonna wait for sex till we get married."

His eyes grew huge, and he leaned away from her. "You're *what?* After all these years making love like wild beavers?"

"Beavers? Lord, you're gonna keep me entertained the rest of my life."

"I certainly hope so."

That Wednesday, *The Observer* came out with Jessie's article above the fold.

Parker had titled it thusly.

SMALL OZARKS TOWN SKUNKS DRUG CARTEL 20-0

Local sheriff Mac Richards stated that ticks, snakes, brambles, and craggy bluffs along with a large amount of tough law enforcement members were largely responsible for sending the Dallas cartel bunch fleeing. However, most were arrested and are now in the Washington County Jail or the Federal lock-up awaiting charges.

The article went on to tell the tale as she had written it and experienced it. It was picked up by newspapers all over Arkansas, Missouri, and Oklahoma.

As luck would have it, Sunday three weeks later—after charges were brought against the Kimbles, the Golds, James Jameson, and too many mules to count—dawned bright blue and Arkansas fall-warm. All set for the largest barbecue to be held in the history of Cedarton.

Dal and Jessie weren't the only ones with announcements. Wendy and Howie also announced their upcoming marriage. Tink and Burt shouted that they were finally expecting. Forensics specialists Kathy and Dave spoke casually about a year's sabbatical in Egypt to look into the DNA of some of those dead folks. Parker announced firmly that he was never getting married again, so all the beautiful women could stop bringing him cookies unless they were Macadamia nut, and Mac announced he was retiring. He introduced the new sheriff, Dallas Starr, appointed to serve until election year, but he had no doubt that would hold as long as his own service had, and Nick Snow was hired to fill the space left by Dal's appointment.

The barbecue lasted into the night when the town retired to the school gym to dance until way past three in the morning.

The next morning Dal opened his eyes to discover it was ten past ten, and from the lack of activity outside could easily be midnight. He lay curled around Jessie as if to protect her, his heart tucked against hers, the beats matching. He refused to move, just lay as he'd found himself, lips against her temple. For the first time in a very long time, he felt damned good.

After a breakfast of Honey Buns and coffee, he led her to her Jeep. "I'll drive." Brad tried to beat her to the shotgun seat, but she put him in the back. He gave her one of his eye-rolling stares, then stood on hind legs to poke his nose out the opening, tail wagging as if he too hadn't a care in the world.

The road curled around the rim of Devil's Eyebrow, then headed down. Long before they reached it, the sound of white water announced Moonlight Creek. At the low water bridge, he hooked a left and parked. Jessie shifted to get out, but he put a hand on her waist.

"I'll come around. You wait."

Her curious gaze made him laugh. She usually planned these trips. Before she could take things into her own hands, he hurried from his seat and went around to lead her along the shoreline, the noisy rush of water a peaceful backdrop to his thoughts.

An opening in the tree line marked his destination. For a few minutes, they climbed under the canopy, the fall of golden leaves whispering around them. A grotto appeared ahead. A few cubic boulders waited like beds surrounded by perfectly shaped cedar trees.

She stopped, pulling back on his grasp. "It's beautiful. How did you find it?"

"Just one of my Indian tricks."

Pulling his hand to her mouth, she kissed it, lips soft and warm against his skin.

"Come on, we're not there yet." He led her into the darkness of what appeared to be a cave. But toward the back, a glow beckoned, and they soon emerged into a small sunlit meadow. He whirled, one hand gesturing. "Ta-da."

"It's beautiful."

"I know. And I know we've already announced our engagement, but I wanted to do something special so you'd know how much I love you, how much your love means to me."

He raised a hand high above their heads. "A gift for you. The entire world. It's how much I love you."

From out of the endless sky, black wings flashed blue in the sunlight, and a raven settled on a branch nearby. Ebony eyes watched them for a long moment before it called softly in the stillness.

Jessie smiled, and Dal touched her lips with his. The raven cocked its head, uttered the soft sounds once more.

Dal smiled. "What did he say? Nevermore?"

She kissed him, shook her head. "No, she said 'forever more.'"